VIA FOLIOS 58

Baroque

a novel by

Richard Vetere

BORDIGHERA PRESS

Library of Congress Control Number: 2009909308

*The following novel is based on
historical characters and actual events.*

Published by
BORDIGHERA PRESS
John D. Calandra Italian American Institute
25 West 43rd Street, 17th Floor
New York, NY 10036

VIA FOLIOS 58
ISBN 978–1–59954–008–5

"...through the work of Caravaggio, the Renaissance spirit passes into the Baroque..."

Jacques Barzun, *From Dawn to Decadence*

The word *baroque* comes from the Portuguese *barraco,* which designates a pearl of irregular shape.

Webster's Dictionary

"The common characteristic is profusion dignifying a central purpose."

Jacques Barzun, *From Dawn to Decadence*

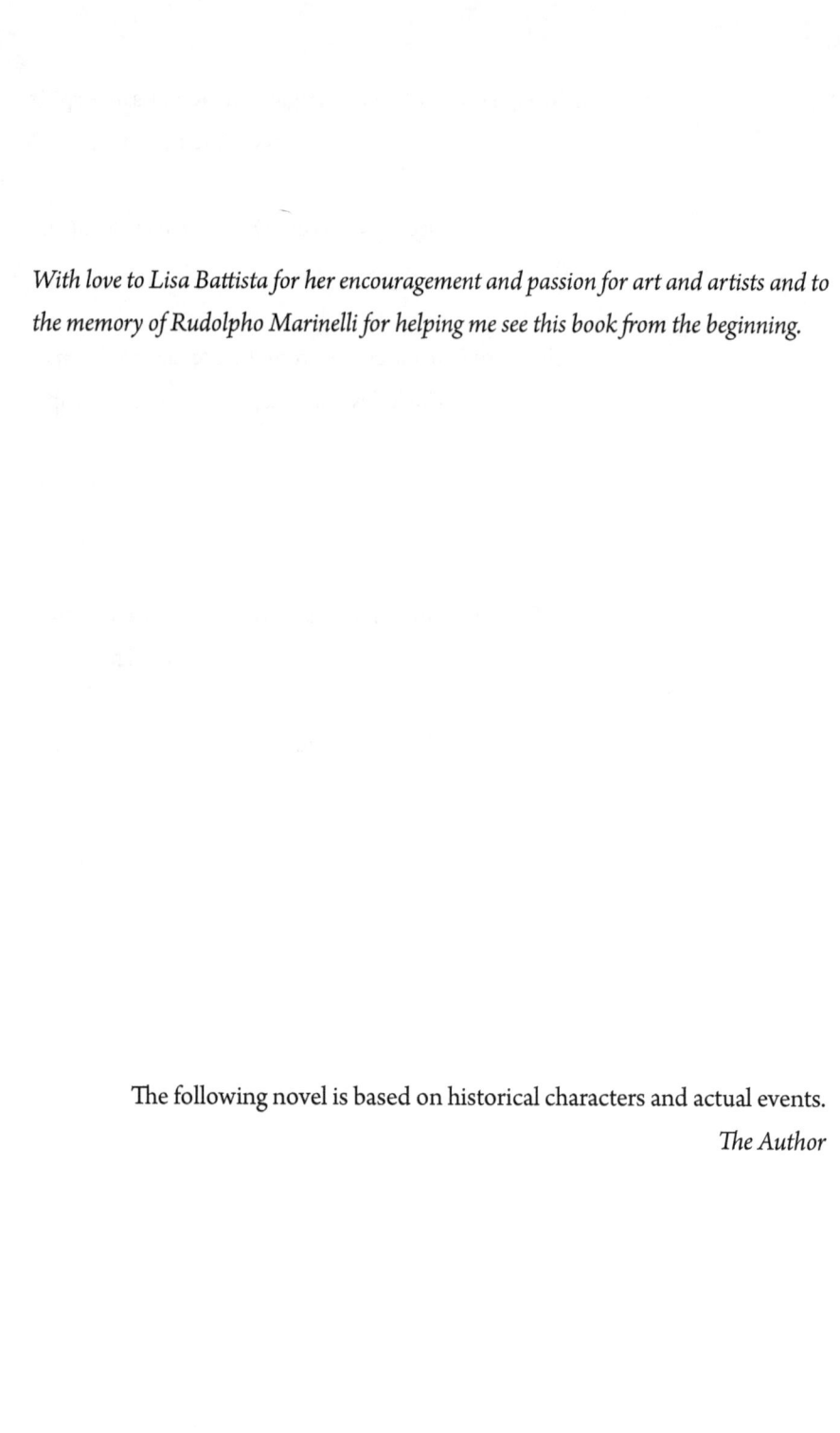

With love to Lisa Battista for her encouragement and passion for art and artists and to the memory of Rudolpho Marinelli for helping me see this book from the beginning.

The following novel is based on historical characters and actual events.

The Author

Contents

Part One

CHAPTER ONE

Rome
1592–1593

The sea was a living breathing force stretching outwardly from the thin aqua colored liquid that caressed the sandy white shoreline to the translucent royal blue heart of its pulsating magic.

He stood on the beach bathed in the glory of the blazing sun. Dazzling bits and pieces of sunlight lit ringlets on his hair as if tiny golden angels were dancing between his curls.

Though he was alone, he knew all the great masters were sitting up in the grandeur of heaven with their eyes on him. Michelangelo, Da Vinci, Titan and Raphael were in awe. They knew what he was and how Rome itself should thank God and the holy saints that he had the courage, the talent and the ambition to travel dangerous miles to claim his right. He held a brush as if it were Michael the Archangel's sword. He designed a canvas with enough passion to launch a crusade that could burn the heretic Martin Luther to ashes with nothing more than the fire of its own fury.

As he saw it, he was the Savior who would rid the Eternal City of all its pretenders to the throne. History would memorize his name. Museums would hang his work for the Ages to come.

He would bear the burden of this destiny with ease as he held the entire grandeur of the remaining years of the Renaissance in his capable hands. Learned men would praise him, women would desire him and other painters announce his greatness. That was the way of his world and he was prepared for it. It was his birthright.

He would create a new art. He was Mario Minniti.

Mario opened his large light brown eyes and stared ahead feeling the effects of too much wine. His face was on its right side in the short grass and his mouth was dry. Only seconds earlier he had been dreaming of a teal blue Mediterranean Sea. In the dream he was standing on a yellow beach facing his easel and painting an enormous orange sun that hung over the horizon. And then he woke up with the same sun burning his face.

He lifted his head. Voices were coming from somewhere behind him as he pushed himself slowly up onto his elbow. His arm stung with pain. His head was throbbing. His clothes were wet from the dew. He shifted to his right realizing that he was on a small slope overlooking the Tiber River. *Just as Taddeo. I awake overlooking the Tiber.*

Looking directly south Mario could see a large metal cross. The cross was on a colossal metal sphere. He knew he was looking at Saint Peter's Church. God has given me a sign, he thought. *I have achieved my destination. Roma.*

He pushed his hands through his thick wavy black hair. He could feel that it was wet from the grass. He rubbed his chin and felt the hairs of a slowly emerging beard.

He lifted himself to his knees and could see off in the distance the scaffolding around Saint Peter's. Back in Syracuse he had heard of the work that was being done on the church and now, seeing it with his own eyes, made him awe struck. It was as astounding as he had imagined.

He then turned all the way around and that's when he saw the body. It was a young man in a dirty dark blouse and black trousers lying only a few feet away directly behind him. Mario immediately recognized him from the night before. He was the young sculptor he had met on the road. The sculptor had curly light brown hair and dark eyes that were open wide and staring up into the sky. He looked closer and saw blood on the man's face. With an even closer look he detected a still raw and ugly bruise on the sculptor's forehead and another cut on his pale cheek.

He could also see how the sculptor's hands were outstretched as if in a struggle when he collapsed. There was also a jagged rock with streaks of blood on it at his feet.

He stood, feeling wobbly. There were several fishermen carrying their nets from their boats at the dock on the river at the bottom of the slope. They weren't paying attention to him. He looked over his clothing. He examined it for blood. He found his right sleeve stained with it. He pushed his face into his own hands. He forced himself to try and remember what had happened the night before. Besides the sculptor he recalled the French soldiers they had met at the river. They were vividly etched in his memory because he wanted to paint their faces. Though young, scars marred their rugged features. They were thin from hunger, months of travel and lack of sleep.

Mario also recalled walking into the city somewhere after midnight and how the young sculptor, who had managed to lurk into Rome previously without proper identification, volunteered to show him how to avoid the guards at the city's gates. He still had vivid images of faces laughing in the torchlight when he walked through a piazza. He also had some vague notion that someone had made an awkward attempt to rob him. Who was it that tried? Was it the young sculptor or one of the desperate soldiers?

That was all he could recollect. So he quickly ripped off his yellow shirt and put on his favorite black one. He then tucked the bloodied yellow shirt in his satchel planning to bury it in the tall grass along the riverbank.

He walked awkwardly down the grassy slope toward Rome. The closer he came to the waking city the louder its clamor. He stepped onto the paved street and looked up at the first street sign he could find. It read "Via Del Corso." He saw a young woman carrying a small child heading his way and stopped her. "Kind woman, in which direction may I find Via Frattina?" he asked as politely as possible.

The young woman, wearing a veil to block out the sun, seemed startled by his dialect. "Do you mean to ask directions to where the artists sell their work?" she questioned.

Mario nodded quickly. "Yes. The market place where the artists sell their paintings," he told her.

The woman tilted her face towards the rising sun. "Follow Via Del Corso and ask directions again when you get to the next piazza," she said and walked briskly away. Mario felt the sting of her trepidation and realized that it was his appearance that must have caused it. He lifted his head and walked into the direction of the rising sun starting the first day of his new life.

Pope Clement VIII dressed in a long flesh-colored gown eyed his breakfast of boiled pigeon and scrambled eggs as he pushed the wooden spoon towards him creating a mound of food. He stopped, reached for a thick jar of black pepper, covered the eggs then leaned his face close to the plate. He lowered his head and filled his mouth.

Ippolito Aldobrandini having been elected Pope Clement VIII in January was fifty-three years old. As he chewed, he felt the sensual pleasure of eating rush through his overweight frame.

He ignored the two young Jesuit monks who were attending to his breakfast, bringing him freshly brewed coffee and a large basket of fresh fruit which consisted of large oranges from Milano and apples from the Vatican orchard. Since it was early autumn the fruit wasn't as sweet as it had been earlier that summer.

The Pontiff ate his breakfast while reading from his leather-bound prayer book pausing every so often to swallow then read aloud a passage in Latin, glancing at a monk who was polishing his chalice, a masterpiece of design consisting of gold and purple jewels.

The Pontiff heard a noise behind him. He was expecting his nephew Pietro Aldobrandini. The Pontiff could hear his nephew's extravagant leather shoes hand-made for him in Florence with the metal taps on the bottoms, clinking on the white marble floor behind him. He could also hear the scurrying of the monks as they quickly prepared his nephew's breakfast.

Pietro, wearing his scarlet cassock and large gold crucifix, signifying his office of cardinal, and holding the morning edition of the Roman newspaper, stepped up to his uncle, kissed him on the cheek then sat down beside him. "Good morning, your Holiness," he said.

The Pope nodded an acknowledgement then lifted the spoon to his mouth.

"I am pleased to witness, dear uncle, that you have completed your fast," Pietro stated.

Clement VIII quickly responded, "Stifle your delight. I'm commencing a new fast this afternoon."

Pietro made a quick observation of his uncle from his mother's side. He was a squat man with an unquestionable air of authority. In all the years he knew his uncle he could never remember him laughing out loud and if he did even allow himself to smile, the jest would have to do with something clever he would read from the parables of the New Testament.

Pietro knew well that Ippolito was from an ancient but undistinguished family of Florentine rulers and took his responsibility of being elected Pontiff with all due seriousness aware of the consequences to the Church if he failed. He had been told many times before by his uncle how Martin Luther had become more than just a thorn in the Church's side. He believed that Satan had inspired the German monk. Luther's Reformation, as he had called it, started a series of religious and political wars that were growing in intensity all across Europe.

It was then that the Pope gestured to the newspaper his nephew had placed on the table. "Horrible! Horrible!" he stated making the monks around him shake.

Pietro frowned. "What is so horrible, dear uncle?"

16

"I do not dare read the newspaper! I fear for the Holy Church every morning," the Pope stated.

Pietro took that as a sign that his uncle wanted to know the current news but he wanted it told to him with less emphasis on the negative aspects. "I will attempt to act as a filter to keep the worse of the news from you if you so request?"

The Pontiff nodded. "I wish you do just that."

Pietro cleared his throat. "France is maintaining her balance despite being devastated and the strife in Poland may, unfortunately, send us even more refugees."

"And that is how you call being a filter protecting me from the calamities that infest our daily world? By telling me that more refugees are coming our way like a swarm of locusts."

Pietro bowed his head then looked up and studied his uncle further knowing that ever since he followed him into the religious life, he would do exactly that, *follow* his uncle. Pietro also knew that their temperaments were in direct contradiction. Or at least, they were developing in that way as of late.

The Pope made the sign of the cross. "Bless our Church," he said then went back to his breakfast.

Pietro was hungry so he ate heartily and watched as his uncle cleaned his plate, then walked to the large window at the far end of the room and knelt facing the Tiber River. Clement bowed his head and prayed quietly. The monks followed his example and knelt where he had stood then bowed their heads and also prayed in silence.

Pietro admired his uncle's determination and his tenacity but wondered if his new found power would change him? Or would his position as Pontiff of the Holy Roman Catholic Church only enhance those qualities that he had already developed over the years?

When he completed his short prayer, Pope Clement VIII stood with the help of one of the monks holding him up at his elbows then walked over to his nephew. Pietro knew what he wanted. He quickly put down his spoon and followed his uncle on a walk to the papal chambers. *My breakfast will have to wait.*

Pietro walked beside his uncle on his right side and that was where his uncle preferred him to be when they had these talks since he was going deaf in his left ear. Pietro knew that his uncle expected him to begin the discussion. The Pontiff liked to listen then decide. "Have you given any thought to what you plan to do about *Rome*?" Pietro asked.

"Have you given any thought on what I should do about Rome?" the Pope asked quickly.

Pietro nodded. "It is a city with an enormous potential for great art, your Holiness," he stated. "I have spent time with many of its noble families. They're willing to invest even more of their wealth to make Rome the center of great art. And as we both know, coming from Florence, that patronizing the arts is a powerful tool for helping with political influence," Pietro said.

"And this is the great notion you have arrived at?" the Pope grimaced.

"It is only what I advise."

"I distrust advice," the Pontiff said.

"Of course you do, your Holiness," Pietro said, reassuringly. He coughed and turned his face. *He asks but he doesn't listen.*

The Pontiff glanced at his nephew and Pietro knew what he saw when he looked at him. He was a small man. Though only in his late twenties, Pietro had the ashen color of a granite statue. His eyes, though bright and clear, were small and dark. He suffered from acne and was already balding. There was nothing youthful about Pietro and nothing pious either. And even though he knew that the Pontiff favored his other nephew, Cinzio Passeri, and allowed him to be known as the *Cardinal di San Giorgio,* Pietro felt his uncle's confidence and how he might possibly invaluable to him and the Church. Though physically graceless, Pietro knew that his uncle was aware how he moved through the elitist halls of Roman nobility with an ease most would be envious.

Pietro noticed that his uncle wanted to smile but stopped himself. "I have made a decision about the art in this city," he said sharply.

Pietro waited to hear more. They walked on a few more steps.

"I find the nudity an insult to the Virgin," Clement VIII announced.

Pietro responded quickly. "Michelangelo painted nudes, your Holiness," he said. *He is the Pontiff now and for this conversation, not my uncle.*

The Pope was unfazed by his statement. "I want to levy a fine of two hundred and fifty scudi for all builders or painters who fail to obtain a license for their works. If they refuse they shall be imprisoned or exiled. I want all painters to submit preliminary drawings for approval before beginning their works," he stated as he stopped at another window facing south. "And as I have said before, I also find the prostitutes an outrage. They strut through these streets without fear of reprisal right outside the windows of the Vatican. I will initiate a dictum to assure that our Church will regain its virtue," he said.

Pietro stopped walking. "And how will you administrate these dictums, your

Holiness?" he asked.

Clement replied, "As the art in this city is concerned, I'll arrange to visit all the churches in this city. I will then have all inappropriate and disturbingly vulgar images removed immediately. I will also make official rules for all sculpture and artifact as well as painting on fresco and canvas as I just told you," he answered sharply.

Pietro winced.

"And as far as the prostitution is concerned, I will gather them up. Every last one of them and put them in the stockade," Clement stated.

Pietro averted his eyes.

"You disagree?" The Pontiff asked, this time looking at his nephew.

"Yes, your Holiness, I *firmly* disagree," Pietro replied. He felt his uncle's eyes studying him.

"Of course you would. You are going to inform me that such a policy would be an insult to many of the Roman nobility, am I correct?" his uncle asked.

Pietro was relieved that his uncle understood that there were some things in Rome you could not change so quickly. Or perhaps not change at all. "Dear uncle, please listen to me. I have had several terse conversations with the Farnese family, especially Cardinal Alessandro, and I must be forthright. We are not favored here in Rome, your Holiness," Pietro answered. "Other than demanding these changes, allow me to advise *another* approach," he said softly.

"As I stated, I distrust advice," the Pontiff quickly shot back.

"Of course you do, your Holiness," Pietro said. "And yet, may you allow me to study the situation in detail and present to you some alternatives to the vulgarity in art here in Rome and the festering of prostitution on our streets?" Pietro asked.

The Pope lowered his chin opening his large hazel colored eyes and focused them on Pietro. Then, without saying a word, he walked down the elegant hallway moving past a full-length mirror without once glancing at his own image. The two Jesuit monks standing behind him quickly followed in silence. One was holding his chalice and the other mumbling prayers with his head bowed.

Pietro heard the Pontiff sneeze. The monks shouted "Bless you!" and Pietro then heard the Pontiff mumbled. "It was the black pepper—"

Now alone, Pietro knew that his uncle's silence was an affirmation of his request. What Pietro made note of was how his uncle walked by the large mirror uninterested in his own image. He didn't even glance to examine his appearance. It not only meant that he wasn't a vain man as many of his predecessors before him but it meant something else entirely to Pietro.

Ippolito Aldobrandini was a man who had no interest in the temporal world. He saw the afterlife as if it was as real as the dawn of another day. There was no question of a debate on the matter. There was no doubt in his mind that heaven and hell existed. They were as real as the external world around him and a belief in an eternity of joy demanded a sacrifice of enormous proportions. That proposed a serious problem for Pietro because his duty was to assure the Church's continued existence in the temporal world.

Pietro returned to his office and closed the door. He glanced around the room surrounded by gifts from Venice that included, among other items, a crimson velvet cloth and heavy clothes of gold that decorated the walls. He gave a fleeting look at his precious belongings of gems and tapestries, rare books and manuscripts as well as his unique collection of cameos which he kept in specially made display trays many of them in gold bearing his Cardinal's coat of arms.

He then looked into the full-length mirror and was disheartened by what he saw. Before him was a little, balding man with beady eyes underlined by dark circles from so many sleepless nights due to his chronic cough and a face of blemished skin with several pock marks on his cheeks.

The physical world mattered to Pietro Aldobrandini. He loved beauty in art and more than that he loved beauty that he perceived in the human form as well. He was a Cardinal and believed in Paradise after death but he also believed whole heartily in the secular world. He enjoyed how having power made him feel. He enjoyed the finer things in life. He enjoyed being cardinal not because the office made him closer to God but because the red scarlet cassock made him one of the most influential men alive in the most dynamic city in the world.

In fact, Cardinal Pietro Aldobrandini could boast that along with the Pontiff, he could be counted among the cadre of nobility and Kings of Europe.

Or so that was what Pietro thought as he forced himself to see an entirely different image in the mirror. He saw a man with physical grace and style of refinement and elegance.

Pietro thought that someday he would hire a great painter to put his likeness on canvas and that artist would paint him the way he would like to be seen and remembered through history.

Prayers may not change the world of the visible but art can and with that change it can accomplish wonders.

Chapter Two

Mario stood assuredly in the sunlight with his silk black shirt trimmed with silver. He wore a gold cross and several rings. One onyx ring was from Persia and the other was an ebony ring from Greece. He wanted to present to the people of Rome a man of style.

Taller than most Italians and with his lanky frame, appealing complexion, and broad shoulders and large expressive eyes, he had the presence of a young man who warranted notice. He believed that all eyes were on him in the street festival in the Piazza Trastevere. Rome will embrace me, Mario thought. I have the physical stature of Caesar, I encompass the originality of a Dante and the masculine beauty of Apollo, he nearly whispered aloud. I will conquer Rome as an artist as Alexander conquered the world as a general, he thought. *I am Mario Minniti!*

Mario wanted to make an impression. He told himself that he would look back at this moment—years from now, telling his children and grandchildren about the time he arrived in Rome and the first day he stood there in the marketplace introducing himself to the gateway of the known world. *My life will be chronicled as the great Da Vinci and Michelangelo's had been before me.*

He walked on through the festival as if an actor on stage. His presence was his soliloquy, his newness is what made him desirable and his silence is what made him a mystery. Reaching the far end of the piazza Mario felt a rush of confidence flow through his body.

He strutted through the festival immediately struck by the smells, the noise, the hustle and energy he had heard about but had never experienced before back home in Syracuse. There were so many people, faces and conversations going on at one time and in one place that he was nearly overwhelmed. The stimulation was immediate and nearly overpowering.

He planted himself and took it all in. There were several small tents lined the streets on both sides and small shops where dealers sold their wares. Booksellers and tradesmen and street vendors populated the piazza. There were tradesmen standing outside their small stores selling rosaries, crosses carved out of wood, medallions of Saint Christopher and small statues of different saints made out of plaster painted in bright colors.

Mario shook his head at the gaudy commercialism of the spectacle but the festival-like atmosphere was contagious making him feel welcomed even though he was a complete stranger to the city.

Mario didn't know a soul in all of Rome yet all of the activity in the piazza made him feel as if he had been in the city all his life. His head turned at every sound and every new odor. Listening to the different accents and dialects made him dizzy. He was also very hungry and since he was penniless he could only stare at the eggs and pork being cooked on large pans frying in the dazzling sunlight.

The lute players also focused his interest with dozens in the quarter. They played for the crowd yet to Mario they seemed oblivious to everything but the small vase at their feet that they hoped would fill up with lira by the days end. They also played tunes Mario had never heard before. He was being swept away by their sounds. This music was unique and alluring. *This is a new world.*

Mario had to step away from the racks of bread and bins of fresh water fighting his impulse to reach out and take the food in reach. So he distanced himself from the large tents concentrating on the paintings. There were dozens of small canvases hanging on rows of small fences with artists and sellers shouting to those who could hear the prices of each canvas. Names of the artists who painted the work were also called out but Mario recognized none of them; and he also felt nothing but contempt for the work itself. He expected quality in the art he would find in Rome.

He was also amazed to see young and middle-aged painters alike hawking their religious artifacts or small canvases on billboards which hung around their shoulders. The artifacts dangled across their chests. The majority of the work was of the believed likeness of the Virgin or Saint Peter and even Christ. The artifacts were painted in bold blues, staggering reds and breathtaking greens and there was gold trim on everything.

He stopped examining the faces around him. They were strangers. He knew no one. A thought occurred to him and he felt a momentary shudder. *Did anyone find the body?*

It was deep into the afternoon when a young man caught Mario's attention. He had noticed the young man following him and it made him feel uneasy. The man, his own age, was dressed entirely in black like he was. He approached Mario munching on a large ripe green apple. "You've been watching me," Mario told him.

The young man handed Mario a sketch. Mario looked at it and was taken aback.

"You *dislike* your likeness?" the young man asked clearly aware of his play on words.

Mario narrowed his eyes. "I'm not insulted by the likeness," he remarked handing the sketch back.

The young man waved his hand. "My gift to you," he said. Mario nodded and just then the young man threw an apple at him. Mario caught the fruit and scowled ready to throw the apple back in the young man's face but realized that the young man threw him the apple not as a weapon but as *nourishment.*

"Eat," he said to Mario.

Mario ate the apple heartily and saw how the young man glanced around the piazza. "The paintings are shit," the young man stated.

"They're not what I expected," Mario replied and took note that this young man *also* had a strong physical presence. Broad shouldered as Mario though not as tall, he was still imposing. What Mario noticed first was his eyes. They were nearly black as coals but luminous with intelligence.

The young man also had dark bushy eyebrows, shoulder-length black curly hair and like Mario he had an olive complexion. His smile was short and his manner curt. His features were nearly feminine. His nose was delicate, his skin was unblemished and his eyelids as gentle as a woman's. Yet there was nothing gentle about his manner. He moved his muscular arms when he spoke with the confidence of a soldier.

Mario edged closer to the young man. *He does not appreciate foolish notions or foolish behavior. Who is he?*

"You're a virgin to Rome's charms, I'm certain," the young man stated firmly. To Mario he sounded educated but not elitist.

"I arrived late last night," Mario answered. "How do you know when I arrived?"

"Two angels are dancing in your eyes, dear citizen. They are named Amazement and Confusion," he answered.

"Yes, I know them well, and you're correct," Mario said, completely devouring the apple then tossing the remaining core to the street. "But I'm capable of resisting their charms," he smiled. *We are the same age. We have the same notions. I can feel it.*

"And last night you slept along the Tiber River just as Zuccaro painted and how he wrote about his starving artist brother Taddeo," the young man said smirking.

Mario felt mocked. He took offence. "It's the artist's journey to come to Rome and struggle and for the final victory, to work with the masters. I will enlighten you with that truth, scum that you are," he shot back. "*The man who disrespects you warrants anger and retribution.*" Mario recalled the text of *Il Cavaliere*.

"Please, don't take offense. I know you have read *Il Cavalieri* but you should also read *Il Cavalieri Compito* a wonderful dialogue composed by Tommaso d'Alessandri," the young man told him, stepping back.

"I shall read it if it speaks of honor," Mario said.

"It does, citizen. It states that a man should thrust his rapier into the heart of his adversary at the very moment of insult. It states that a young man of honor shall never be far from his sword so that he can defend his name and his family's crest," the young man told him.

Mario looked at the young man's belt and saw that he didn't carry a sword. The young man noticed. "The law in Rome is that you cannot carry a rapier without a license to do so," he told him. "And, I should tell you now, that here in Rome, there are *no* masters when it comes to art," the young man said.

"That's blasphemy," Mario said, stunned and still annoyed.

"So, you're a painter, then?" the young man asked Mario without the slightest hint of a reaction.

"I am," Mario answered proudly. He could see that the young man's hands were covered in paint. "And so are you," he said, making it clear that he noticed the young man's dirty hands.

The young man nodded. "I'm a painter. And you're from the south. I can tell by your accent. Sicily?" the young man asked.

"Are you insulting my accent?" Mario asked.

"Not at all. Just making mention of it, citizen," the young man responded.

"I'm from Syracuse. And you?"

"I'm from up north. A small town not far from Milano though I have been living in Florence until I arrived here," the young man answered. Mario could see his eyes darting around the market picking out the artifacts that passed by him perhaps making mental notes of color combination and poses?

"What do they call the small town you're from?" Mario asked him.

"Caravaggio," the young man answered.

"I know of the great Polidoro da Caravaggio. He was murdered in his bed in Messina but he painted a magnificent *Adoration of the Shepherds*," Mario told him.

The young man winced, "I do not speak of him. And one day you will know *my* name. All the world will know it well," the young man shot back. He then looked up at the sun. "I have to get to my work," he stated.

Mario must have looked needy at that moment because the young man stopped. "Are you searching for labor yourself?" he asked, making an expression that he should have known already that he clearly was.

"Yes," Mario told him quickly.

The young man started walking north and Mario followed closely. He gestured to a large palace a few blocks away. "Presently I'm working for Monsignor Pucci at the Palazzo Colonna. It's shit work. We spend all day pulling canvases, cleaning his studio and mixing his paints. It's insulting work but it pays with food and lodgings though the food is nothing more than a salad and the lodgings sparse," the young man said. "But it is better than sleeping along the banks of the Tiber River," the young man said with a mocking tone.

Mario decided to show the young man his bluster and suffering as a badge of honor. "I've hardly slept for two days and nights. There were bandits at every turn of the road. And I left my home without anything more than my brush and some paints," Mario told him.

The young man acted annoyed. "Are we going to talk about our suffering or are we talking about our mutual lack of finances? Citizen, I came to Rome with my inheritance and a letter of recommendation to Monsignor Pucci from the Marchesa de Caravaggio. Today, as we speak I despise the Monsignor and I have ten lira left in my pocket," the young man told him.

"How long have you been here?" Mario asked.

"Three months," the young man grinned.

"And you misspent your entire inheritance in that short time?"

The young man looked more confident than before and even more self-assured. "This is Rome, friend. It will burn up your money, feed desires, enflame your youth but most importantly it will inspire your art. It is worth all that I spent. And, friend, who can ask for more than that in a world filled with mediocrity?" the young man grinned.

Mario could see that the grin was a show of strength. *This young man craves the destiny of the artist as much as I do.*

Mario didn't move. He couldn't. He realized that this young man he was talking to was his *competition*. "Arrogance is a deadly sin."

"I'm beyond arrogance," the young man grinned. "And I relish sin."

Mario decided to take up the challenge. "You mentioned that perhaps the Monsignor has work for me?" Mario nearly shouted. "If so, I can begin work today."

25

"I imagine that today is a good day for you to work. Ha! Follow me," the young man told him.

Mario followed his new friend.

It was then that two policemen from the *sbirri* walked passed them. They were wearing their bright gold cloaks and red vests making them look more like clowns on parade than reliable policemen.

The two *sbirri* strutted by with the palms of their hands on the handles of their swords. Both of them glared at Mario and the young man. Mario could see that they were making a mental note of their descriptions and then walked on disappearing into the crowd.

The young man noticed Mario's intense interest. "They are Rome's police, the *sbirri*. We curse at them in the piazza when we see them at night. They mean nothing," the young man told him. "But the cavalieri are a different matter. They are worth your serious attention."

Mario took in what he said and returned the young man's serious look.

"I noticed how you stiffened when you saw their badges. Are you running away from something back in Syracuse?" he asked Mario boldly

"I'm not on the run from any crime. I'm a good citizen of Syracuse," Mario told him. As Mario said these words he realized that he was not intimidated by the *sbirri* but he did feel himself stiffen as the young man had noticed when he saw the police badges. "I just don't trust the police. Any police either they be the *sbirri* or cavalieri," he answered keeping secret that he was clearly afraid they would trace the dead body on the river back to him.

The young man nodded. "I like your attire. I like black. I prefer its drama to the garish colors of a harlequin. And your rings. Very fine. I approve," the young man said.

Mario wasn't sure how to react to his statements.

"What do they call you?" the young man asked.

"My name is Mario Minniti," he said proudly.

Walking side by side they drifted away from the focal point of the piazza heading south down to Old Rome and the Plazza Colonna. "I am called Caravaggio," the young man told him. "Perhaps together we can do battle with the police, enjoy all the pleasures of Rome and defeat the mediocre talents that have reigned too long in this eternal city," he said with a smile.

CHAPTER THREE

Cavalieri Captain Nunzio Pulzone stood over the body of the dead sculptor on the bank of the Tiber River. At his side was his assistant, Sergeant Carlo Guisto.

Captain Pulzone was slender with wavy brown hair. In his late thirties, his hazel eyes, now focused on the body at his feet, had flecks of green in them. "What can you tell me about the corpse?" the captain asked Guisto.

Guisto knelt down beside the body. "He's no older than I am. His blouse is artistically designed and his trousers stitched by a master. My deduction is that the dead man here was from a merchant class family though he himself was probably an artist." He picked up one of the dead man's hands and looked over the fingers. "No dry paint but I see bits of plaster between the nails. He was a sculptor," Guisto answered with assurance.

"Most young men in Rome have no interest in working for the cavalieri, Guisto," Nunzio stated. "And the cavalieri have no interest in most of the young men in Rome. Why? Because we thrive on discipline and that virtue is sorely lacking among your generation."

"Are you complimenting me, sire?" Guisto asked, with a solemn tone in his voice.

"I certainly am." Nunzio now stepped away from the body and looked around. "Where do you believe he traveled from?"

Guisto shrugged his shoulders.

Nunzio pointed to his face. "The complexion is light. From up north? Perhaps he's Florentine." He stepped over the corpse.

"How do you believe this young man died?"

"He was murdered."

Nunzio pushed his jaw forward in agreement. "Show me how you *know* this."

Guisto leaned down to the body and with his right hand, turned the head revealing the small wound. He quickly examined it. It was on the right side of the dead soldier's head. The wound wasn't deep but it was in an area below the ear where such a forceful blow would cause the most damage.

Nunzio glanced through the tall grass and spotted the bloodied brick. He gestured to Guisto. "The weapon and the wound," he muttered. Then he saw the empty bottle of wine a few feet away. He frowned. *One drunk killing another, the way of homicides in Rome these days.*

Nunzio then turned away from the body and looked out over the Tiber River. He could see the magnificent Saint Peter's Basilica on the other side close enough to touch. He spoke loudly. "My soul is racked with incomprehension. And I ask the Heavens—how could one man murder another in the shadow of our beloved Church? Do men forget that God has eyes?" he asked the heavens.

Guisto quickly rummaged through the man's pockets. "He has no identity papers at all, sir."

"What does that tell you?"

"He managed to avoid our guards posted at our gates."

"Precisely."

"Are there any other clues we should search for, captain?" Guisto asked enthusiastically.

Nunzio smirked. "Are there any *other* clues? What clues do we have now?" he asked.

Guisto turned red. He could see that his captain was mocking him. "I can question witnesses," he stated, trying to recover from his momentary embarrassing question.

Nunzio looked at the faces that were looking down at the hill at body. "This man was killed late last night when they were all probably asleep. His flesh is still warm," Nunzio informed him. He then looked away from the river toward the city itself. "I believe our murderer arrived late last night. He met this dead young man on the road outside the walls of our city. Perhaps there were others with him but I would surmise they were all drunk. There was an argument over absolutely nothing consequential. Perhaps an argument about Martin Luther or the war up north or the *fair beauty* of Rome's prostitutes compared to those in Paris. Then one comment led to another and the argument escalated to violence as all arguments in Rome seem to these days," Nunzio stated.

He then waved his hand toward the now noisy and crowded streets that sprawled up the slope of one of Rome's seven hills. "I can tell you where our murderer is at this very moment," Nunzio said without irony. "He is in our city walking its streets either looking for work or sleeping off his night of drink. He may or may *not* be aware that he killed a man last night," he said.

Guisto glanced in the same direction as Nunzio was. He was looking toward the center of the city. He was searching the multitude, even though he couldn't distinguish one face from another from so far a distance. "The murderer must be brought to justice," Guisto stated.

Nunzio reacted to the words. "Justice will be served, dear Guisto. It is God's will," he told him. Captain Pulzone then walked away from the body and toward the witnesses. "I will give you the opportunity to find a witness. Question the women. Perhaps they trust us enough to help us. They may believe in the sanctity of life more so than their husbands do," Nunzio said.

Guisto followed him up the hill feeling the seriousness of his mission rush through him.

"When you are finished we will go back to headquarters and report what we have found here this morning," Nunzio stated. "And send someone for the body." He watched his assistant step up to the women at the top of the hill. Each of them was looking down at the dead sculptor with trepidation.

Nunzio thought how the handsome Guisto, not as tall as he was, but with a fair complexion, gentle-looking features and soft blue eyes might ease the fears of the young women. They just might have seen something and Nunzio knew that it was easier for them to tell a handsome, sincere young man in uniform what they might have seen or heard then tell someone who had a hardened face with a jaded personality.

Mario Minniti entered the palace walking passed armed security guards placing their hands on their swords as soon as he and Caravaggio were in striking distance. Having recognized him, Caravaggio quickly nodded to them placing his arm on Mario's shoulder. It was clearly a sign that Mario was a friend and he should be allowed to enter the palace.

The palace, which looked nothing like a palace, was actually a medieval palazzo which lay between the church of Santi Apostoli, whose portico fronted the elongated piazza and the dark narrow Via della Pilotta. It was crisscrossed by a bridge that linked it to the formal gardens that were under construction to its south.

"You took the name of your town?" Mario asked as they entered the palace.

"I despise many things but in different degrees. One thing I despise the most is the name my mother gave me," Caravaggio replied.

"And what name was that?" Mario asked as he followed Caravaggio closely. He measured the young man impressed with the way he strutted. He walked with his shoulders forward and his eyes darting around making sure that nothing he needed to see escaped his sight.

"I was named after Michelangelo. He died a decade before I was born. She wanted his spirit to bless me. But I despise his work."

"You chose a giant to despise, my arrogant friend," Mario told him. "What does your mother say about your life here in Rome?"

Caravaggio replied, "My mother is dead. Plague killed her when I was a five."

Mario was silent as Caravaggio directed him to the large four-story structure called Palazzo Colonna. "This way," Caravaggio told him. Mario followed him closely as both men walked through the dust and noise. There were dozens of other shirtless tanned young men working in the warm sun stretching canvases washing down the walls and sweeping the marble floors of dust and wood splinters.

He could see that there were many masons and stonecutters as well as carpenters among the workmen. Mario followed Caravaggio to a large bald man who was standing on a wooden platform directing other workers to move crates to another section of the room. Mario looked up at the sunlight as it blasted through the open spaces in the walls. He could see the dust moving everywhere in the sunlight.

"*He* needs work," Caravaggio told the large bald man.

The large man was attentive. "Is he a carpenter?"

"No, I am a painter," Mario responded.

"A painter? Just what Rome needs more of."

"Yes. Rome needs more painters," Mario grinned.

The large man pointed to a hill of wooden crates.

"Good. Well, bright one, *they* need moving," he said sternly. He then nodded to Caravaggio. "Work with him today so that he understands how we manage our business here," he stated.

Caravaggio led Mario through an array of tables where young men were stretching canvases. He then showed him a large studio away from the flying dust where sunlight poured in from open windows.

When they reached the large room, Mario looked in and counted a half a dozen young men lined up in a row painting at their own easels. He felt a surge of jealousy rush through him. Why are they painting and I am a laborer? Don't they know who I am?

"They were all once doing the work you will soon be doing. But they graduated and now are the Monsignor's *students* though I prefer to call them his assistants," Caravaggio stated as if reading his mind.

"What are they painting?" Mario asked.

"They are all working on *his* commissions. They paint the work and he puts his name on it. He's paid handsomely for the work they create for him. And he pays them only slightly more than what we will earn, and curse the Heavens for that injustice," Caravaggio answered. "And what galls me is that each one of them has more talent than he does," Caravaggio told him. He then turned away and walked toward the large wooden crates that needed to be moved.

Mario stood for a moment starring at the student painters. They were all concentrating as they painstakingly copied a style that was clearly Monsignor's Pucci's style. Mario wondered to himself if he might be so fortunate to one day be that successful? He allowed himself a flight of fancy to be so famous and so well known that he could hire others to copy his method and enjoy the fruits of their labor. "One day I shall have my own studio instructing students. One day I will be famous for those young painters who paint in my style," Mario said as if he could see into the future.

Caravaggio winced, "No great artist cares about or concerns himself with imitators."

Mario threw him a glance. "How wrong you are, my friend. How untruthful to yourself you are just now. All of us want imitators and followers."

Caravaggio shot back. "The most popular do. Not the greatest." He then walked on and Mario followed thinking to himself how wonderful it would be to have his own school, his own studio and his own patrons.

Later in the day, Mario noticed Monsignor Pucci himself visiting the student studio. Mario was drenched in sweat and working shirtless beside the also shirtless Caravaggio. The heat was appalling and yet his own sweat, running down his sides and dampening his chest, his armpits and his neck under his chin, was amazingly refreshing.

They were still hauling the wooden crates which Mario learned were filled with plaster and marble pieces of sculpture the Monsignor had purchased. Mario also heard gossip that the Monsignor was a wealthy man who indulged his senses with fine works of art filling his living quarters with some of the best art he could purchase in Rome.

He glanced over and watched the Monsignor, who was dressed in a brown cassock and white collar, enter the studio. He was a short, squat man with thin, curly gray hair and seemed *not* to sweat in the appalling heat.

Mario could see how he painstakingly examined each canvas berating the student who did not adhere to the strict rule of the pre-ordained design. Mario could hear him shout at one student who gave the commission a touch of his own personal flair. "There are no individuals in this room!" he shouted, hoarsely. "Each canvas must look like the one beside it. Each eyeball you paint, each arm, each set of lips, each sky you color in must look as if the painter next to you painted it!" he told them. The Monsignor then stood patiently in the studio grabbing an offender's brush, dabbing it with paint, showing him exactly how he wanted it.

Mario got Caravaggio's attention. "I would despise myself for allowing myself to be one of them."

Caravaggio made a face of disgust in agreement. "I know those painters. Gino is talented but lacks discipline. Francesco has discipline but he lacks vision," Caravaggio remarked. "But perhaps there is one painter in his palace right now who has the talent, the heart and the soul to be greater than Michelangelo himself!" Caravaggio told Mario with great relish.

Mario looked around. "Where is he?" he asked, needing to know.

"Here, standing before you," Caravaggio answered. He then turned his back on Mario and lifted a crate.

Though he hadn't seen one drawing or painting the young man had made, he talked, acted and thought like one who might one day be a master. *This Caravaggio will dread the day he met me. I will show him what greatness is.*

CHAPTER FOUR

Captain Pulzone left Guisto to question the potential witnesses then walked down Via Del Corso to the cavalieri headquarters at the Piazza Colonna. He quickly filled out the standard forms in the small room where he kept his desk near the window and then handed them to the sergeant at the duty desk.

Sergeant Vincenzo Manzoni was born and raised in Rome and had the face of one of the ancient centurions. He had closely cropped brown hair and a square jaw. His eyes were dark and yet shaped like a hawk's. He had bad teeth but muscular shoulders. When Nunzio handed him the papers giving the location of the corpse Sergeant Manzoni reacted. "This is the fourth corpse in two days. All dead from brawls. Two up north near the Villa Borghese and two near the Colosseum," he stated.

Nunzio was disturbed by the notion that there had been that many. "So many in only four days?" he said more like a statement than a question. "And there were six last week alone."

Sergeant Manzoni gestured to the papers on his desk. "It's all here. Five were soldiers from either the Spanish or French armies. They lay in the backroom still unclaimed and unidentified. The others were young men. Two painters, a poet and two sculptors," he said.

Nunzio sat down on the bench at the duty desk. "Rome has become a city of murder stirred by hands of murderers," he stated.

"I've been at this desk eight and half years, captain, and I've never seen it like this. The barbarian Huns had more respect for human life than the illegal scum who invade us," Sergeant Manzoni said with a voice that sounded like gravel.

It was then that Guisto walked into the room holding up a yellow bloodstained shirt for all to see. Nunzio stood up knowing immediately what it was. "Where did you find this?" he asked. He could feel that the blood was not entirely dry.

"One of the women pointed it out to me. She came upon it a half a meter down along the riverbank near the Ponte Cavour when she was doing her own family wash," Guisto told him.

Without uttering a word, Nunzio rushed out of the headquarters. Guisto looked to the sergeant and shrugged his shoulders. "Where is the captain going?" he asked.

The sergeant sat back in his large wooden chair making it creak loudly. "You're stupid for not knowing. He gets like that when he has a notion. It's an itch he needs to scratch and it appears to me that he has a notion," Manzoni grinned.

Guisto rushed out of the room and into the street.

Captain Pulzone and Guisto reached the Palace Colonna after a few minutes walk. After the guard at the gate waved them in Guisto watched his superior carefully scrutinize the workers from a distance. Nunzio stood in the middle of the open aired palace. "If the man we want is here I want him to see us. Sometimes fear will get the better of a man. He might run so be prepared," Pulzone told Guisto. But after standing in the dust and sunshine, no one reacted.

Pulzone walked up to the wooden platform where the large bald man was standing and watching them from the moment they entered the palace. "I'd like to interview all of your new men. More precisely those who started work for you here today," he told him.

Guisto waited to be alone with his captain. "What gave you the idea to come here?" he asked.

"You found the shirt up river from where we found the body. I conjectured that the murderer was no doubt looking for work."

Mario refused to be intimidated knowing that smart policemen could see through any man's weakness. So, he pushed his shoulders back leaning forward as he waited outside the small studio that had been quickly vacated for Captain Pulzone and Guisto. Three new men had been hired that morning and he was one of them.

Mario had seen the cavalieri captain standing in the center of the palace a short time earlier. He had expected to be called in for questioning but refused to fear the worst. *What evidence could they possibly have?*

He was second on line and waited. When the second man stepped out of the studio after his interrogation, Guisto stepped out and beckoned him in. Mario obeyed.

Once inside the room Mario found himself face to face with the captain. "I'm Captain Pulzone of Rome's cavalieri. Please present your identification papers," the captain told him.

Mario reached into his pocket and handed the captain his identity card doing all he could to remain calm. It was a forgery and that was the reason he wanted to elude the guards at the gates. As he handed over the papers he was expecting that he would be arrested and at that moment he tried to make his mind a blank and accept God's will.

He could see from the captain's demeanor that the man was what Caravaggio had told him the cavalieri were like. He was professional and his attitude one of the utmost seriousness. The captain's eyes revealed the mind of a man who had searched out killers with a dispassionate coolness.

Mario momentarily forgot his predicament being drawn to the face of the investigator. *He would make an interesting model. He could easily pose as an inquisitor or ancient Roman soldier at Christ's crucifixion.*

Mario noticed that the captain didn't move his head once as he glanced over Mario's papers but raised his eyes and quickly studied the face. He then wrote down Mario's name. "I'll check with the authorities in Syracuse and see if there is a warrant for you."

Mario remained calm and said nothing in return.

"Minniti?"

"Yes?"

Nunzio asked, "What profession is your father?"

"He was a trader in spices. But he died several years ago. I had no mother that I know of."

"When did you arrive in Rome?" Nunzio asked him.

"Late last night, captain," Mario replied.

"There is no record of your name at any of the gates."

"I gave my name to a guard when I came into Rome," Mario stated. "Perhaps the guard was drunk?"

"Perhaps. It's known to happen," Nunzio smirked. "Did you travel alone?"

"I met three French soldiers on the highway and we entered Rome together," Mario answered

"And their names?"

"Pierre, Bruno and a short fat one named Claude," Mario said.

"And where are these French soldiers now?"

"With whores I suspect," Mario smiled.

Nunzio forced a smile. "It says here you are a citizen of Syracuse and I see here that you traveled by way of Malta before you reached Rome. Why did you leave Syracuse?" the captain asked him.

"I came to Rome to paint," Mario answered.

"All painters must come to Rome it seems," the captain stated. "Hundreds of young men come to our city each month, don't they, Guisto?"

Guisto quickly replied. "Yes, captain. Hundreds come to our city," he answered.

Pulzone nodded. "These artists come here to search for fame and commissions. They come from all four points of the compass. But when they see how difficult fame is, they search for laborer work during the day and at night they drink and fight in the piazzas. Don't let me catch you fighting with the other painters who come here," Captain Pulzone told him. He then handed Mario back his papers.

"I will be a respectful guest of your city, captain," Mario bowed. He then waited as the Captain Pulzone took one final look at him.

"I will tell you what happened to you last night, citizen," the captain stated. "You met a young sculptor on the highway outside the city. You shared a bottle of wine. You celebrated entering the city and then the both of you decided to sleep at the river bank. However, the sculptor, seeing you were drunk, made an attempt to rob you of what little possessions you had left on your person," the captain stated. He then leaned forward with Mario and Guisto riveted to his every word. "But he underestimated your strength. In the struggle for your life, you picked up a stone and crushed his skull. He fell to the grass and you sat down, your head swimming from the wine. In moments you were fast asleep. You woke up this morning with blood on your shirt and a dead body at your side," the captain told them both. "And then you did what you had planned to do. You came here to find work," he said, then sat back.

Mario didn't move once but he did listen carefully. *He still has no evidence.*

As if reading his thoughts, the captain gestured to Guisto who placed the bloody shirt on the table. "This is your shirt, is it not?" the captain asked.

Mario looked at the shirt. He then looked up at the captain. "It is not mine, captain," he answered.

"I would like you to put it on," the captain stated.

Mario put the shirt on without hesitation. The shirt fit perfectly. Mario did not react but Nunzio stood up and looked at Mario closely.

"It fits you without question," the captain stated.

"It would also fit you without question," Mario shot back with confidence.

Nunzio waved his hand. "Remove it."

Mario took off the shirt. When his chest was bare, the captain eyed his body closely. "You have several scars," he remarked. "No doubt they are wounds from fights."

Mario remained silent.

"You may return to your duties," he then stated.

Mario bowed to show respect then left the room. When he reached the sunlight he sighed in relief but kept his back to where he had come from and walked to where he was last working.

Nunzio didn't move for a long moment as he stared at where Mario had been standing.

"There is one more man to be interviewed," Guisto stated.

Nunzio waved him off. "We don't need to see anyone else," he said.

Walking back through the gates and out of the Palace Colonna, Nunzio knew Guisto was having difficulty enduring his complete silence. He knew that the young man was anxious to hear why they had stopped their investigation. It wasn't until they had their backs to the palace did Nunzio speak up.

"He knew that the truth, half told, is better than a lie told completely," he said. "He also struggled to act calmly in the presence of the police. I sensed his tension and how he struggled not to allow it to overwhelm him. This man did not show weakness. He has been questioned by the police before," he said almost to himself.

"Who are you talking about, sire?"

"I am taking about Mario Minniti. He is our murderer," Nunzio said matter-of-factly.

Guisto stopped walking.

"Don't stop, Guisto, he's probably watching us," the captain stated.

Guisto quickly joined the captain.

"I know what you are thinking, Guisto. We have the bloody shirt. He told us he came to Rome with the soldiers though I believe that to be a lie. In reality he lurked through our gates with that young sculptor who probably showed him the way. He no doubt robbed and killed the young man."

"And the soldiers he spoke about?" Guisto asked.

"They are either a figment of his imagination or perhaps they do exist. And perhaps they committed the murder along with him. I am not sure on that matter. But I'm sure that his papers were a forgery."

"They were?"

"They certainly were."

"Then why don't we charge him for that?" Guisto asked.

"Because if we arrest him and deport him from Rome, we'll never have the opportunity to prosecute him for the more serious crime of murder."

Guisto lowered his head. "And we have no direct evidence to prosecute him with at this time?"

"Exactly. So all we can do is watch him and in time hopefully collect more evidence. We must wait until he tells someone about what he did and then we can arrest him with evidence. His confession," Captain Pulzone stated.

The two Cavarlieri continued on their way back to their headquarters. "What artist do you prefer, Guisto?" Nunzio asked, changing the tone of their conversation.

Guisto shrugged. "I never gave it much thought, captain. Should I?" he asked.

Nunzio raised his eyebrows. "Yes, you should. I could not live without art. Besides my prayers, art helps me transcend this mortal life. I thought it strange that this man said he was a painter. And yet he took a life without a sense of guilt? Where is God in his brush? I can only imagine," Nunzio reflected.

Guisto walked on in silence.

"I prefer Annable Carracci," Nunzio remarked, changing the subject. "After spending most of my life looking into the faces of criminals, I need to look into the eyes of the blessed and Carracci's paintings give me that. They give me hope," he said. "And hope comforts me."

"How are you so sure he is the murderer?" Guisto asked.

Nunzio stopped and looked up into the sun for a moment. It was a warm day and he liked the feeling of God's breath on him. "Because he never asked me why we were questioning him. An innocent man would have needed to know out of fear of being falsely accused. A guilty man already knows why he is being questioned."

"I see," the assistant stated.

"I suspect he left Syracuse to avoid prosecution for another crime. Perhaps even murder. I'll make inquiries though I expect little cooperation from the Sicilians when it comes to sharing such information with us here in Rome," Nunzio sighed.

"What did the Cavalieri want with you?" Caravaggio asked him.

"Someone was murdered last night along the Tiber," Mario replied.

"Every night *someone* is murdered along the Tiber," Caravaggio replied without emotion.

In the cool of that evening Mario and Caravaggio now in short sleeves sat in front of a small fountain in the nearby piazza as Caravaggio strummed his guitar playing a soft ballad that both men had heard a hundreds times before in their youth.

As people walked passed them Mario felt a longing for a life that perhaps would never be attainted. "Sometimes, dear friend, I recall de'Alessandri's words in his *Il Caralieri Compito* when he writes that a "knight should aspire to great thoughts in a grand Roman palazzo," Mario said forlornly.

Caravaggio continued to strum the guitar's strings making a song of the words from the text that he had also memorized and now quoted. "He would be adorned with a magnificent gold chain . . . with enameled rings on his muscular finger . . . with pointed diamonds and horses in his stables . . . and beautiful women dressed in rich clothing of lovely and varied fabrics . . .walking through *palazzo* . . .," Caravaggio sang, with a tender voice.

Mario leaned back on the fountain. "We will achieve that *palazzo* that d'Alessandri writes."

Without missing a string, Caravaggio replied. "I shall! I am not sure about you, Mario, but I know I will."

Mario ignored the insult and allowed himself the luxury of an evening of fantasy and dreams.

CHAPTER FIVE

Pietro wore a red beanie cap, a black cassock lined with red and a black shoulder length cape. Dangling from his neck was a long gold chain with a large gold cross. He sat in a metal chair in the Vatican garden listening to his uncle. The Pope in a long golden robe was sharing his notions on how he planned to stymie the debauchery he believed was eating at the very core of Roman society.

Sitting with Pietro and the Pontiff in the warm afternoon summer air were Pietro's aide and assistant Archbishop Giovanni Romano and Pietro's own first cousin the charismatic Cinzio.

Earlier that morning in the same garden, Pietro had a meeting with Antonio Martelli of the influential and wealthy shipping family. Pietro charmed Martelli, a young and handsome man in his late thirties, quickly and smoothly. "You embody for me, dear Antonio, what I find so alluring about Roman life. You are cultured, generous and most importantly open to new ideas and notions," Pietro said pouring the words into the air around Antonio as if they were musical notes coming from a flute.

"I only want to serve my God, my Pontiff and Roma," Antonio said confidently and then Pietro placed his hand on his shoulder and whispered in his ear. "We will need many lira to continue to keep the Vatican constructions on course and we will need many more lira to keep the heathens from our doors," he stated.

Antonio nodded with understanding. "The Martelli family is at your service." He bowed.

"Excellent," Pietro smiled. "Rome has roads to build and the Vatican many promises to keep."

Now, an hour later but in the same garden and in the same chair, Pietro was listening to the Pope and at the same time eyeing Bishop Romano. Romano was a robust man with a ruddy complexion, a head of thick graying hair and small child-like brown eyes. Pietro chose him as an assistant to his official office for several reasons one of them being was that the Bishop's family, successful merchants in Rome for generations, had strong political ties to some of the wealthiest families in the city especially the Martelli's and Farncese. And what Pietro had learned about Giovanni Romano was that he knew how to use his connections wisely.

There was also another reason Pietro appointed Bishop Romano to the position. Bishop Romano had personal and trusted contacts to very desirable courtesans, which Pietro had yet to request, though the thought of a single rendezvous with Rome's notorious treasures had been on his mind since he left Florence with his appointment as cardinal. He knew it would only be in a matter of time that he would ask for an introduction and he also knew that discretion would rule his behavior in the end. He could trust Romano since he knew Romano to be a man already seduced by the netherworld. The Bishop harbored a shrouded reputation so that not the Pontiff or Cinzio were aware of his deviant activities.

After casting his eyes on Romano, Pietro now turned to his uncle. Pietro was in the garden because his uncle had summoned his trusted advisors so that he might test his ideas of a new papal dictum.

After sipping sweet tea and eating oranges the four men allowed the breezes to flow between the olive trees for a moment in silence and then Clement spoke up.

Clement VIII had a shrill voice when excited and he was, at his moment, filled with melodrama. "We will send carriages of cavalieri into the streets and arrest every single prostitute. I will issue an order that prostitution will be punishable by ten years in Tor di Nona prison and if a woman is found guilty of the vile act more than three times, she will be burned at the stake in the Compo de Fiori," he announced.

Pietro cringed at the pronouncement. He turned his head to the garden pretending to be enthralled not only by his uncle's words but also by the array of daffodils, petunias and the finely trimmed row of hedges that gave him a feeling of seclusion and privilege. Pietro turned to Cinzio to determine his cousin's reaction and could see Cinzio struggle to contain his own displeasure.

Pietro had learned *not* to be jealous of his handsome cousin a long time ago. It took a lot of doing since Pietro was in direct contrast physically to Cinzio. Where Pietro had an awful complexion, Cinzio's skin sparkled with vibrancy. Where Pietro was short, balding and awkward, Cinzio was not only tall and handsome with a thick head of dark wavy hair, sharp blue eyes and a slim physique but he was also graceful and was blessed with beautiful teeth he took every opportunity to flash. It gave him an enormous appeal and compounded his elegance and charm.

However, Pietro thought often, if Cinzio had one weakness it was his physical

41

bearing. His good looks brought everything to him including the Pontiff's loyalty but that, in turn, made Cinzio less ambitious. He was educated but did nothing for art so though he was invited to all the important parties in Rome yet no one sought his counsel or advice. He was a cardinal in the Holy Mother Church but he wasn't pious. In fact, he had no virtues to speak of and no vices other than his own vanity. And his vain nature controlled him. He wore the most expensive clothing he could find and spent hours in front of a mirror before leaving his apartment. Though Cinzio Aldobrandini had the world handed to him he didn't have the foresight, or the ambition, to take hold of it. So, Pietro, aware of how impotent his handsome cousin was, plotted to control everything in arm's length.

The Pontiff continued on. "I have also written an edict—"

Pietro interrupted with a humble bow tinged with slight acerbity. "An edict? How excellent."

"Yes, an edict," the Pope replied. He read his pronouncement from a small script he had prepared and purposely not paying attention to any reaction.

"An edict that will be read by every pastor in every parish in this city stating that nudity in any display, either it be on canvas or fresco and including sculptures, is now condemned. The artist will be punished with a substantial fine of twenty-five scudi. His name will be stricken from the list of artists who can accept commissions from both the city's nobility as well as any members of the Holy Church," he claimed.

"The Vatican will decide who receives commissions?" Pietro asked again interrupting.

The Pope ignored his question. "I will prepare an edict that will make it mandatory that all commissioned art must first pass the scrutiny of a board of censors that I will appoint. I will call that board, the Board of Censors, and no commission will be granted without their approval," he nearly shouted.

Pietro could see that once again his uncle looked agitated and he knew his uncle had to be on another strict fast.

When the Pope was finished announcing his dictum, he looked at the three middle-aged faces sitting around him. Pietro could see that he was quite certain that their reaction would be the one they gave him. Initially it was a reaction of stunned silence. Then secondly, they all had reacted with small murmurs of approval.

"And now I want to hear what you truly believe," he told them when all three quieted down.

Cinzio spoke quickly and without much thought. "The Romans will probably be aghast," he smiled. "And Cardinal Odorado Farnese will not be pleased I'll attest to that. I dined with him just last evening. Did you know, dear uncle, that artist Fabio Albergati dedicated a treatise to him titled *Il Cardinale*? No one has dedicated a treatise to me? That's a crime in itself."

Pietro gazed at his petulant cousin with bewilderment and pity.

Pietro could see how Bishop Romano fretted in confusion knowing that it wasn't his place to speak but since he was a liaison and the only true Roman in their midst the Pontiff wanted him there and wanted his appraisal of the dictum. Though unsure of how to respond, he was about to say *something* when Pietro waved him off.

"I would pause and give serious counsel on such extreme dictates, your Holiness," Pietro remarked.

"We do not criticize God's dictates and everything I pronounce as Pope comes from the mouth of God himself," Clement VIII shot back.

Pietro bowed though he was still sitting. "Of course, your Holiness, but God surely must realize that Romans are unlike others of His creation. They relish their freedoms," he stated.

"God is our only freedom and he is angry at the vices that run rampant in this sewer of a city," Clement said sharply.

Pietro took a deep breath. He needed courage to confront not only this issue and his very powerful uncle. He also knew that if he didn't speak up on the matter, he would bear the brunt of these brutal laws since the Pontiff limited his own interaction with the Romans no matter how significant or how poor.

So, he took his time but made his rebuttal clear and precise which is what he knew his uncle desired from him. "Speaking of sewers, your Holiness, there are rats in ours here in the Vatican and we know that rats breed plague. Perhaps we should address that issue first with a public health dictum and then we can surmise a plan to rid our streets of prostitutes. There is also famine in Rome as well as bandits cowering in the shadows of our city's walls. Perhaps we should address the issue of amassing more cavalieri to make this city safe before our humble followers are all murdered and our collection plates are all but bare," Pietro stated. He felt confident about the points he was making because he had done as his uncle suggested some weeks ago and realized the predictment his uncle found himself in. "Which also brings me to the issue of taxes and famine," Pietro continued. "Neither is good for us or our cause as long as we allow both to fester."

Pope Clement VIII was quiet for so long that Bishop Romano and Cinzio grew worried. Pietro knew that as much as his uncle distrusted advice he knew when good advice was being given. Though he would be reluctant to admit it and would also explore every avenue of destroying that very same valued advice he did occasionally actually follow it. "Are you telling *me*, the figure of Christ in the Church, to ignore the vices that are destroying the fiber of the Eternal City?" the Pontiff asked demanding an answer.

Once again, Pietro took his time. "A simple solution is the best way to solve a colossal problem," he said, knowing that would be intriguing to his listeners.

"Continue," Clement said.

Pietro stood. He wanted to stand in the sun putting his uncle in his shadow so his uncle could see the expression on his face. He knew the Pope judged sincerity as the highest of virtues and Pietro wanted him to see how sincere he truly was. Pietro also wanted to create some drama and he knew by standing in the presence of the Pope, who was sitting, that would give weight to his words. "The Roman census tells us that there are one hundred and ten thousand souls in this city," he began. "Three quarters of them are men. Many are celibate and many are soldiers coming to our city from the wars. These young men are violent with nothing to do all day and night but drink and fight. There are also eighteen prostitutes for every one thousand female souls. That figure includes children and elderly women," he continued. "We don't have enough carriages to carry them to prison if we plan on arresting them all," Pietro added.

Cinzio chuckled. Pietro shot a look his way. Romano stayed silent but the Pontiff did not. "Are you stating that I should not prohibit prostitution in this city?" he inquired with force.

"Prohibit prostitution? Of course, your Holinness, but also *tolerate* it," Pietro exclaimed.

No one knew what to say.

"*Tolerate* it?" Clement spit out.

"Tolerate it. Tolerate it by allowing it to continue in one single quarter of Rome, no more than ten streets long and ten streets wide, where it will be scrutinized, policed and able to function within limits from one hour after sunset to one hour before sunrise," Pietro stated.

Pope Clement VIII was silent. Cinzio spoke up again. "How would you achieve that in an orderly fashion?" he asked.

"A church bell will ring every morning one hour before dawn announcing the

44

immediate departure off of the streets of every prostitute and those who pay for their services," Pietro stated.

Cinzio and Romano were dumbfounded. They looked to Clement who was glaring at Pietro. "That action will sanction the vice!" he exclaimed.

Pietro was unaffected. "On the contrary. It will allow us to contain the vice and in time, eliminate it from our city," he replied.

"And how would that occur, dear cousin?" Cinzio quickly asked again but this time truly interested.

Pietro replied with strength. "All those women who move into this quarter must register their names. We will then have a list of these women of the night and we will keep records on their comings and goings. It will make arrests and prosecution effortless in time," he answered. "And in taking such drastic steps we are showing the faithful that we not only acknowledge the flaws inherent in humanity but that we are also taking strong action to control and condemn such flaws," Pietro replied.

Clement sat back and looked away from Pietro.

Cinzio spoke up as if without control of his thoughts. "It is a spectacular plan but is it feasible?" he inquired.

"And what do you suggest we call this ghetto?" Clement asked with a sarcasm that cut through the summer breeze.

Pietro answered with vigor because he had already thought up a name. "*Ortaccio*," he stated.

"*The Garden of Evil*?" Cizino asked.

"*The Anti-Eden*," Pietro replied.

The Pontiff leaned his face on his hand supporting it on his elbow. "And the disgusting nudity in art? How do you propose we confront that?" he asked keeping his eyes on his garden. A sparrow flew close by and he reacted to it.

"The condemnation of nudity should be strictly enforced only where religious paintings are concerned," Pietro said in a lower tone. He could see the Pontiff shift in his chair.

"And how will this be accomplished?" the Pontiff asked.

"Your Board of Censors will demand a lion cloth or garland strategically placed to conceal the private parts of both male and female representations," Pietro stated.

Clement reacted swiftly. "Put that phrase in writing immediately. That is the basis of my announcement," he told all three men then lifted himself out of his chair.

"Excellent choice, your Holiness," Pietro stated.

The Pope responded. "But I will not waver on taxes. We need lira to run our Church." His two Jesuit assistants then mysteriously appeared and walked him out of the garden.

Bishop Romano spoke first. "Did he decide on how to control the prostitutes?" he asked.

Cinzio shrugged his shoulders as Pietro sat back in his chair. "He hasn't decided as of yet," Pietro replied but he had made his point. "Prostitution is a necessary evil considering that three-quarters of the population of our city is male. Without an outlet for their aggression, this violent city could become even more violent yet," Pietro announced satisfied with himself, for the moment.

"We still have the Farnese family to contend with," Bishop Romano spoke up.

"Enlighten me," Pietro told him.

"Alessandro was cardinal *before you* arrived in Rome. Our Holiness appointed his nephew Odoardo as a gesture of good will *when* you did arrive. Octavio, the Duke of Parma, has amassed his own small army of loyal followers and then there are Dukes of Farnese who own most of the land outside the city walls," Romano replied.

"Yes, I know all this. I also know that they would like a Farnese to be Pontiff someday," Pietro stated.

"To be more succinct dear cardinal, they were disappointed when your uncle was elected Pope and Alessandro was not," Romano replied.

Pietro knew this to be true. "We need them as allies, Bishop Romano, so keep me aware of all of their issues with my family," he told the Bishop then waved him off. He had made a significant impact on his uncle and he didn't want to ruin the momentary victory with more worry. There would be ample time for that.

"I fear that you believe that you can bring change to Roman life and Roman ways," Bishop Romano said.

"Change is possible anywhere," Pietro replied not wanting to think about it.

The Bishop waved his hands. "Change in Rome? Look around, dear cardinal. What you see has been here thousands of years. The Colosseum, the statues, the piazzas, the chapels! Where do you see change?"

Pietro felt the burden of the notion suddenly rest on his chest. He struggled to breathe for a moment. "We represent the Pontiff and he is the Vicar of Christ on earth. If Christ our Lord could rise from the dead, the least we could do, dear bishop, is manage to have Roman citizens consider an enlightened alternative to the past."

Pietro faced the sun hoping to spy God's eyes in the light. He knew he would need all the help he could get to change one single solitary inch of Roman tradition without losing all he had accomplished thus far to the Romans themselves. He looked to Romano, "I have studied my history, dear Bishop Romano. Just a few short twenty years ago Charles V's imperial mercenaries looted this city. That Pope was jailed, the women raped and tens of thousands killed. The Tiber flooded the city and plague nearly crushed it. I imagine you can still smell the incense of death."

Bishop Romano slowly nodded.

Pietro looked up into the sun. "I will work to bring a change to his city and help make it great. I will do that through the power of art and the power of our Church."

Chapter Six

Siena

A barefoot Fillide Melandroni, wearing her clean Sunday smock, was not yet twelve years old but sadness had rushed over her as she watched her older cousin and only true friend Anna Bianchini sitting in the back seat of an old carriage waving goodbye in tears. Accompanying Anna were her older brother Roberto and Fillide's aunt Petra. Petra was Fillide's mother, Cinzia's, older sister.

The rickety wagon holding all the possessions of the Bianchini family was being lead by two donkeys and driven by Roberto. Anna's father had just died of plague the year before and the father-less child looked stricken with panic.

Standing on the side of the road at the very edge of their cow farm and at Fillide's side was her father Enea Melandroni and her own mother.

Cinzia was short and in recent years had grown fragile and pale. She was always ill as far as Fillide could recall. With pale brown eyes, Cinzia's features were round as her body short but her expression never wavered. It was always blank as if the life itself could only be faced head on by showing no reaction to either joy or sorrow. She was always superstitious allowing her Catholicism to become a religion that had less to do with faith than magic. She showed this by attending church but never stepping on the cracks in the pavement on her way to Mass in fear she would bring herself bad luck. She would also dress Fillide in certain colors, which matched certain religious seasons with white in Advent and yellows and blues during Easter.

Fillide decided a long time ago not to look to her mother for guidance and direction but to her father. At that moment of grief, she reached for his large hand and held it but her eyes never left the wagon as it painstakingly moved south in the summer heat down the dirt road Fillide knew as the highway that lead to Rome.

Her father tugged her hand but she refused to move. Her eyes had yet to leave the wagon that was now only a spot on the horizon disappearing under the shadow of the looming mountains that created the landscape of Toscana. "Why! Why did they have to go?" she pleaded with her father.

"Famine drives them away. Starvation is why *they* had to abandon us," her father answered. "There isn't enough food or water for both our families," he continued.

"Anna's mother believes she can support her family in Rome."

Fillide let go of her father's hand and ran in the opposite direction but not in the direction of the modest but sturdy wood farmhouse not far off in the short distance but toward the rolling hills of the fading green pasture.

Enea allowed his daughter to run off a short distance then followed casually after her. "I'll speak with her," he told Cinzia.

Enea found his daughter sitting on a small rock along the running stream crying quietly without sobs or sighs. Fillide disliked showing her father, or anyone for that matter, any sign of weakness.

She looked up at her father as he approached her. Enea was a short man but like the farmhouse *his* father built out of the land decades ago, he was sturdy. In his late thirties his fine brown hair was already turning gray. His dark eyes were nearly opaque and his arms, long and thin, were tightly drawn and powerful like his hands. He wore a short coat and dark work pants and a wool cap that kept out the sun and wind.

Fillide remained quiet as he sat down on the smooth rock beside his daughter and kept silent as he listened to the trickle of the running stream. Only the birds, flying through the olive trees, made any sound. "I'm sad today, father," Fillide told him allowing herself a moment of vulnerability.

Enea patted his daughter's long dark hair. "Then learn from this sadness," he told her.

"What will I learn from sadness?" Fillide asked him.

"You will learn that God has made life harsh for some. There will always be difficult choices to make for all human beings," he told her. His voice was calm and reassuring but urgent as well.

"Why is God so cruel to us?" Fillide asked him, taking his hand. She loved the feel of his hand in hers. Though the skin was hardened the center of the palm was warm and durable. Fillide needed that reassurance and looked to her father for it.

"God is not cruel. But God is forgetful when it comes to his humble creations. That is why He created angels. God made angels to look over us," he told her. "We all need someone to look over us. We all need *protectors*," he smiled.

Fillide looked up at her father then glanced at the rolling hills beyond him and over his shoulders. "Do the wealthy need protectors?" she asked.

Fillide had learned what wealth was by watching the sleek silver and polished wood carriages of the nobility pass by their farm along the highway traveling from

Florence and heading to Rome and when they were heading north from Rome traveling to Florence with their ladies dressed in the finest fashions and the men, handsome and dressed in silks, waving to the little charming poor farm girl on the road.

Enea smiled. "Since the day I first saw your reaction to those caravans, those carriages passing on the road from the big cities, I could see your craving for a world of plenty. You will never be satisfied with being a farmer's wife. You, my dear, are destined for other pursuits though I have no clear notion of what they might be. The opportunities for young women in your social class are limited. You could choose marriage to another poor farmer much like myself or decide on a life dedicated to a religious order and become a nun but I cannot see you accept that fate." He picked up a twig and twirled it as he continued speaking to her. "That is I have tried educating you to the ways of literature and allowed you to daydream of a life away from Siena and the rolling hilly land of cow farms. But child, I do this for you and for myself as well because I've seen in great art and literature an escape from the confines of his own destiny here in these barren hills."

"That is why you took me and Silvio to Florence and Lucca to Pisa!" she said.

"Yes," he answered. "I delighted in showing you all the local artists especially Cimabue, Giotto, Piero della Francesca, Simone Martini as well as the greats, Leonardo and Michelangelo. And that is why I read to you the literature of Dante."

Seeing that Fillide was losing her melancholy he reached into his coat pocket pulling out a small leather book. He opened to a worn page and read her a passage from Dante's *Paradisio* where he described the heavens filled with angels.

He could read the poem because it was written in his vernacular—Italian and not Latin—as many of the great literary works had been written in.

Hearing the poem, Fillide's glum countenance transformed to one of enjoyment and she looked at the dried out banks of the small stream forgetting about the draught and her hunger.

When he was finished reading, he pulled his daughter closer to him and she snuggled in his arms. "You, my dear Fillide, are special and never let any man or woman tell you otherwise," he stated.

Fillide leaned back against her father conjuring the notion as Enea continued.

"What do you mean, dear father?" she asked.

"You must change your life. You must embrace change. You must pray for the strength. You must beg God to give you courage to accept change. You must not follow *my* fate or *my* destiny. You must not live my life. You must throw fortune to the wind!"

Fillide was overwhelmed by the passion in his voice but she remained silent and continued to listen.

"I see that one day you will live in one of the great cities. I see you dress in the finest silks and laces. I see you speaking with great philosophers, artists and poets. I see you as an equal to them," he told her with his dark eyes sparkling in the daylight. "You will dine with powerful men!"

"What powerful men?" she asked. Fillide had no idea who those powerful men could be? The men and boys she knew were all farmers and occasionally at Church her father would point out a man and tell her that he was a *merchant* or another man something other than a farmer.

Enea spun his daughter around cupping her face with his hands. "Use your beauty, my child. Use your mind. Use those beautiful eyes. Use this wonderful hair that men could get lost in. Yet, most of all, use your indestructible spirit to gain a place in our mortal world," Enea said.

He then stood up and Fillide could see a surge of overwhelming melancholy rush through him. "Are you alright, father?"

"I'm not sure what to call this emotion I am feeling. I don't know why I am feeling it. I only know that something about you, my child, has struck me. Perhaps, it is a vision of your future?"

He stood up leaving Fillide perplexed and then faced in the direction of his farm. "Though it is Sunday there is still work to complete. But you stay here and ponder all I have told you. My life knows its course. The end is in sight but your life is sprawled out before you. Live it!" Enea then kissed his daughter on the forehead and walked away.

Fillide watched her father walk down the slope and out of the gully through the olive trees wondering why he showered her with so much attention. She wondered what was it about her that made him call her *special* and spend so much of his time reading to her from his leather book and sharing with her the future he saw for her?

Fillide looked into the stream at her image and saw her dark hair and her large eyes, and smiled. *Am I special?*

She then knelt on the soft earth and said a prayer asking God, the father, to allow her to one day live in Rome and dine with the best families in their opulent villas and never see another farm as long as she lived.

Chapter Seven

Mario and Caravaggio sat on the roof of their dwelling in the palace finishing their meager supper of salad, bread and water. The heat was oppressive for early evening even that late in the summer season but Mario and Caravaggio didn't mind it. Both young men were shirtless and though the sweat dampened their chest and shoulders the slight breeze cooled them. They were happy to be away from their labors and able to enjoy their rest. They were also energized by their decision to leave the palace at first light in search of more appropriate work for their talents.

They had shared a small room with two small cots on the floor for several months and had managed to paint their canvases without getting in one another's way. They also decided to paint the same table with the same basket of fruit sitting on it and both completed their paintings on the same day. They also felt that it was time for them both to share their work with the other.

Caravaggio quickly pulled the cloth from his canvas pushing the lit candle close to his easel so that Mario could view it. Mario inched closer and stopped. He didn't have to study the painting to know instantaneously that Caravaggio had approached the subject entirely differently than he had. Where he had painted the entire table, basket of fruit and chair Caravaggio painted *only* the basket with the fruit.

To the uneducated eye it wouldn't seem like much of a difference but to someone like Mario who knew instinctively that the content of art was about perception, there was an enormous difference in the approach to the paintings. Mario couldn't hide his own disappointment that Caravaggio's approach and execution was far more interesting and more superior to his.

"What?" Caravaggio asked and when Mario didn't respond, he quickly pulled the cloth that was covering Mario's canvas, took a quick look and muttered "oh."

Mario fought to be proud of his work but he *knew* and he was aware that Caravaggio also *knew*. Mario took the candle from Caravaggio easing its light across Caravaggio's canvas. "Excellent," was all he said. The painting was an exercise in the preciseness of detail. It was also stunning in its lack of sentiment. Though the fruit, the leaves and the basket seemed natural, there was something unusual in the sparseness of the content of the canvas and that made the fruit, the basket and the table *real*. It was so simple yet still astounding in its philosophy.

Where as Mario cluttered his canvas with a sprawling display of fruit and leaves he imagined a bottle of wine, a plate of cheese and bread. He romanticized the subject by making it lush and artificial. Caravaggio avoided that temptation and painted exactly what he saw.

Lying on his cot that night, Mario couldn't sleep, distressed by the notion that there he was living with Caravaggio, discussing art nightly and finding himself agreeing with his fellow young painter, yet when it came to executing the work itself, he embellished where Caravaggio defined and this gnawed at him.

Mario allowed himself to sleep when he realized that this exercise was a lesson. Though he refused to accept the one nagging thought—he was now confronting a man as gifted as he considered himself.

The following morning, not long after dawn, Mario and Caravaggio stood inside the artist's studio of Lorenzo Siciliano in Pantani, south of the Forum, in an area of Rome colonized by the Lombard painters. Lorenzo Siciliano was heavy with pudgy cheeks and closely cropped black hair. He had a large piece of bread in his hand as he stood in the doorway. Both Mario and Caravaggio were holding up their canvases of the Flowers and a Basket of Fruit in the sunlight. Both were resisting the impulse to feel desperate, or worse than that, insolent. On their way to Siciliano's studio they discussed his work and decided that he was less than a minor painter, of very little recognizable talent but he was looking for assistants.

Lorenzo Siciliano's studio was the seventh Mario and Caravaggio had visited that morning already and all six previous artists had rejected them. If they weren't offered a position now, they would be sleeping on the street that night.

Siciliano, who seemed nearly blind to Mario, put his face right up against Caravaggio's canvas. "Interesting brush stroke," he said then pulled back. "But the execution it is too cold, too barren for my taste," he stated.

Mario saw Caravaggio cringe. Siciliano then gave Mario's canvas the same scrutiny. This time he leaned back and smiled. "This is my style!" he exclaimed at Mario. "I provide room and board and a weekly wage," he told him.

Mario felt a fire of recognition light up inside him. But he also saw, out of the corner of his eye, Caravaggio walk away. "You must hire my friend also," he told Siciliano.

Siciliano was still for a moment took a bite from his bread then gestured with the same hand. "Fine. But you split your wages," he said.

Caravaggio heard Siciliano and was about to attack him when Mario stepped in front of him and smiled. "We have work!"

Weeks passed as Mario and Caravaggio painted by day in the Lorenzo Sicil-iano's studio copying his style for his commissions and whenever they had time for themselves they painted their own canvases.

Mario's dedication and determination struck Caravaggio and drove him on as both young men ate meager dinners, toiled laboriously over Siciliano's banal cre-ations then at night, painted their own canvases.

Unlike the Palace de Colonna, Siciliano's studio was modest. Mario and Car-avaggio shared a small loft space on the top floor that overlooked the Forum and then had their meals with Siciliano's servants. The servants eyed the two painters with suspicion as if waiting for them to steal whatever wasn't tied down. Both Mario and Caravaggio had the look of criminals about them. They both had dark curly unkempt hair, which was growing longer by the day, and they both had mus-cular arms. Mario was lanky but with his broad shoulders, he looked like a bandit or laborer as his dark eyes shifted around all the time.

Caravaggio had more of a refined manner though he had a temper and the ser-vants who toiled in the school heard it more than once when he was hungry or when one of them misplaced or moved one of his brushes.

Both men relieved themselves in the private lavatories in the basement and then at the end of the day, when it was their turn, they would have to clean them out.

One Sunday afternoon, the men decided to walk to the Via Frattina where many artists were taking up residence. They had heard that week that Annabale Carracci had a new painting commissioned by the influential Cardinal Del Monte and they wanted to view it.

When they reached the small square they found a crowd of artists and citizens standing around the small canvas. The canvas itself was receiving its public display. The public display was mandatory for all commissioned art lasting for two weeks at the very least.

Mario and Caravaggio knew that their young masculine bodies, defined in Mario by muscle and height and defined in Caravaggio with an alluring unique-ness, drew much attention. Their intelligence, beamed from their eyes like beacons in the darkness, also drew looks from many in the crowd. The two young men lurked on the fringe edging towards the painting as if it were prey.

Mario edged closer to the large canvas first. The painting was that of a land-scape rich in the colors of blue, green and brown. There was a boating party rowing toward a thatched house along the bank of a river.

Before Mario could say anything about it, Caravaggio, who was then standing beside him, spoke first. "Masterful," he said. "I see some birds in the dappled rushes and streaked sunlight. And how wonderful the perfectly symmetrical trees make you feel, am I right, Mario?" he stated with a tinge of sarcasm.

"It's probably for some decoration to be placed over the door," Mario replied loudly. "It's pleasing to the eye. It has a sense of the spontaneous and yet there is a certainty about it all. It recalls the influence of Veronese. But it's crap."

Before Caravaggio could agree Mario continued. "Carracci thinks he is giving new life to this conventional formula, but he fails because there is no new life to an old formula!"

He was speaking loud enough for the learned men to hear. He wanted *every-body* to hear. "Carracci is unworthy of this attention," he nearly spit.

Some older men in the crowd moaned but Mario shot an intimidating look at them that made them keep their silence.

Caravaggio was now slowly seething in agreement. He spoke steadily with his eyes trained on the painting and nothing else. "You see Veronese and I see del-l'Abate and the end resolute is exactly as he states. It is not only crap, it is high-minded crap. Carracci tries to infuse *new life* into an old form and I see an unconvincing view of nature. Carracci wants us to imagine ourselves standing be-neath that canopy of leafy branches. I can never see myself standing there. The entire charade is idyllic and a *lie,*" he growled.

Caravaggio then grinned and stepped away walking over to a small fountain and sitting on the marble bench surrounding it.

Mario sat down beside him. He felt Caravaggio's resentment and did all he could to stifle his own. That was when he saw a small man standing away from the crowd. He had short dark hair and large, expressive dark eyes. He was dressed no better than a servant but some quality about him made Mario take notice.

"Carracci," Caravaggio said, raising his head to glare at the man.

Mario was surprised to realize that the man Caravaggio gestured to was the same man who had warranted his own attention. "Are you certain?" he asked.

"I'm certain," Caravaggio answered and then leaned back on the fountain put-ting his feet up to rest but never taking his eyes of off Carracci. "He's wealthy but see how he dresses. He purposely wears the smock of an attendant playing the role of the humble painter," Caravaggio stated. "And the crowd loves him for it."

"He makes it seem like he is one of *them*," Mario said.

"I hear he lives in a villa without furniture. All he has on his walls are his own paintings," Caravaggio spit out.

Mario leaned forward noticing how unpretentious Carracci's demeanor was. It startled him since it wasn't what he expected from a painter so famous. Mario wasn't sure if that modest persona infuriated Caravaggio more than Carracci's actually painting.

It only took a few moments for Carracci to be recognized and the crowd was quickly surrounding him calling out praise and adulation.

"Carracci! Carracci!" some were shouting.

Caravaggio smirked. "He comes here and hides in the crowd wanting to be recognized so that they give him a parade."

"We should throw a brick at him," Mario said.

Caravaggio forced his mouth closed. "We would be coming to the rescue of Roman art if we killed him," he stated.

"That should be *us* the crowd is calling for," Mario said, nearly forlornly.

"They will never call for us," Caravaggio said.

"They will call for me! I know they will," Mario told him. People were now stepping away from the two young men.

"You want to be popular or great?" Caravaggio inquired.

Mario didn't answer. He believed he had been just asked a trick question. "There's a difference?" Mario replied.

Caravaggio smiled then shook his head. "My dear friend, the great are never as popular in life as they are in death," he stated.

Mario felt a chill rush through him. "I'll change that rule. I'll be famous in my lifetime."

Mario wanted to respond some more but it was then that he noticed someone *watching* him. Although the face slightly obscured by the crowd in front of the painting, Mario was sure, the man looking at him was the cavalieri. He could see the captain, whose name he had forgotten, standing with a young boy in his arms.

Mario nearly jumped. "Let's go now," he said without even glancing at Caravaggio who, sensing the urgency in Mario's demand quickly turned and rushed into the crowd.

But something kept Mario from rushing away and heeding his own inner voice.

He couldn't leave without taking one last glance at Carracci.

So he did and Carracci turned to him. Their eyes met. He knew Carracci could have no idea who was standing there dressed in black with the unruly hair. Mario thought that he looked probably more like a soldier than a respectable citizen, and if Carracci figured him to be an artist, he probably imagined that Mario was just another young painter who had come to Rome to find his fortune and fame.

Mario wanted to make his presence known to Carracci and believed that he had, pleased that Carracci took notice. So he left the fountain and headed back with his friend Caravaggio and slept well for the first time in weeks.

Nunzio didn't move for so long a time and was oblivious to his son's crying that his wife, Angelina, stood up and took little, Palo, from him. "What's wrong with you, Nunzio?" she asked.

Nunzio was startled by seeing Mario Minniti in a public arena as he just did. Seeing the painter first gave him enough time to act quickly, take the initiative and make his presence known. He wanted Minniti to think that he had been following the young man. "I'm sorry, Angelina, I thought I saw someone I recognized," he told his wife. Angelina was delicate and as Nunzio remembered, virginal once and he was drawn to that aspect of her. Her oval hazel eyes, much like his, acted as magnets to him at one time. But that was before Palo was born nearly six years ago. But since then, Angelina's once lovely figure all but disappeared and her enchanting presence turned sour and her melodious voice turned harsh.

They hadn't had sex in a year and they both preferred it that way. He was free to work on his cases and she was free to care for the children. The one activity they both enjoyed together was going to Sunday Mass. And that's where their unity ended: bonded by the sacrament but not much else other than routine and habit.

Nunzio Pulzone relished Carracci's artwork as a refuge. Ignoring Angelina's conversation with the children, Nunzio allowed his eyes to breathe in the masterpiece he faced. And he thought it was a masterpiece portraying tranquility and serenity. He longed for both and Carracci always seemed to know what Nunzio needed. He wanted to be in the painting either on the boat, in the hut or lying under a leafy tree. Nature was solace because God had created it. Humanity was where evil dwelled.

"We should go home. The children are tired," Angelina told him without once glancing in his direction.

Nunzio picked up Palo and took his son closer to the canvas. "Beauty is what art is all about, my son," he said, kissing Palo on the cheek. "And that truth will never change," he sighed in relief.

CHAPTER EIGHT

The Tavern of the Tower was noisy from loud drunken conversation. Located on Via dei Greci it was a three-story wooden structure also used as a hotel with several rooms on the top floor.

Mario and Caravaggio were wearing their best clothing and eating in silence. "We *were* famished," Mario said staring at his empty plate.

"I didn't realize how hungry I was." Both men had savored every mouthful of the roasted chicken smothered in butter downing it with two bottles of wine.

"We ate everything," Mario muttered again in disbelief as he glanced around the bar and patted his belly. The two men sat a table on the first level of the tavern. Above them was the second-story of the tavern that could only be reached by wide wooden stairs that were reserved for more desirable patrons—usually merchants coupled with their courtesans. Two big men wearing thick leather belts that held their daggers, clearly visible, blocked the less desirable patrons from mounting the staircase. There were also a half dozen guards posted throughout the tavern, hired by the owner as private police, to make sure that when patrons became too drunk and unruly they could be thrown out immediately.

Earlier, Mario had noticed a less than mediocre painting in the style of Michelangelo hanging on the wall a few tables away and now that he was sedated by his dinner he stood up to get a better view of it.

He quickly returned to Caravaggio. "Terrible."

"We should find the artist and cut his hands off for painting what is a stain on craftsmanship," Caravaggio shouted back.

"Burn him at the stake," Mario agreed. "God will agree with our actions."

"I care little for what God thinks. But it is certain that *that* very canvas insults our senses. It insults our eyes, our emotions and our intellect," Caravaggio ranted even though he could hardly make out the painting through the smoke from candles and tobacco that hovered over everything in the tavern. "Good labor is all about change!" Caravaggio shouted loudly raising his wineglass then devouring its contents.

Mario nodded enthusiastically. "We're here in this city to change the culture! We're here in this city to crush the bland and the foolish that masquerades as art!"

Just then a waiter served them a meat pie they had ordered. Mario sliced the pie in half noticing a man at a table nearby listening intently to their conversation. "We're being watched," he whispered to Caravaggio.

Caravaggio looked up at the table Mario had gestured to. "They suspect us of something," he stated under his breath.

"How can they? They don't know we're penniless," Mario grinned.

Caravaggio ate a large mouthful of the pie and swallowed it with a large glass of what was left of the wine. "We aren't thieves until we walk through the door without paying for our dinner."

"So, then, dear friend, we aren't guilty yet."

"Correct. But I'm sure we won't disappoint our hosts," Caravaggio grinned.

"With our great talent we deserve a free meal despite the truth that we are on hard times. And that will soon pass or I will squash every patron in this hallowed city," Mario said, then longingly eyeing the heavily made-up women who passed his table as they mounted the stairway to the second story dining area.

He breathed in their perfume. There were already nearly a dozen young women on the more exclusive second floor laughing and drinking with their male protectors. The protectors made it possible for them to make their way freely from tavern to tavern as long as they were arm-in-arm with these important and powerful men of Roman society.

Mario struggled with his yearning. He had been in Rome long enough for some recognition but had received nothing. He had yet to be discovered by its high society. He fought off the feelings of failure knowing that he was worthy of accolades. He kept telling himself that he deserved women and privilege unsure of why it was not coming his way. He was also angry and drunk and diapponted with Rome that it was forcing him to run out the backdoor of a tavern because he couldn't pay for his meal. This was the life of the vanquished and not the acclaimed. "I want recognition!" he shouted. "And I place a hex on the heavens until we achieve that very goal," he shouted.

Caravaggio lowered his chin and burped. "I think it is the perfect time for us to jump ship."

Besides the disappointment he was feeling about his lack of fame, Mario also fought the uneasy feelings he was having about leaving without paying for their food. He never told Caravaggio about the dead sculptor he had left at the Tiber and he was still concerned that someone of authority would eventually see that his papers were forged. He knew that forged documents would have him immediately exiled from the city at the very least.

Just as Caravaggio stood and was ready to make a run for the door Mario grabbed his arm. "Wait," Mario said then gestured to the well-dressed man at the table who had been watching them.

Caravaggio asked but stopped then saw the man Mario was alluding to step towards them.

The man had long curly light brown hair and expressive blue eyes. When he reached their table both Mario and Caravaggio stiffened.

Dressed in a fine silk aqua blue cloak and matching vest the stranger made a point of keeping silent. He then pounded their table, stopped abruptly and broke into a hearty laugh. Mario and Caravaggio exchanged looks of bewilderment.

"Are you two leaving without paying your bill?" he demanded to know loudly. "Answer me!"

The man's belligerence annoyed Mario. "What business is that of yours?"

"Go ahead! Leave! The door is open for every man since that is his right," the man said clearly not backing away from Mario's threatening posture.

Though drunk, Mario wasn't oblivious. He examined the man's clothing and quickly assumed that he was wealthy. "You don't work in this establishment so why are you so keen about our behavior?"

Both Mario and Caravaggio stood guard at their chairs. "Answer the gentleman," Caravaggio said.

Mario then slowly leaned toward the man. "If you keep grinning I'll cut your throat, rip out your liver and piss on it," he stated gritting his teeth. "I do *not* tolerate disrespect."

The man absorbed the threat then glared both at Mario and Caravaggio. Mario had seen that *look* before many times in the eyes of swordsmen and painters who moved through Rome. "*Nec spe, nec metu,*" the man stated.

Mario repeated the phrase, "*Without hope or fear.*"

The man's blue eyes lit up with recognition. "Yes indeed, my fair gentleman. Your bill is paid for," he stated then bowed.

Mario and Caravaggio were still confused. "That's impossible. We haven't paid it as of yet," Mario told him.

"*I* shall pay it and I shall pay it with great relish," the man said. "Allow me to introduce myself," he said then handed both men his card. "I am Onorio Longhi. Swordsman, ballplayer, son of the great architects of Milan and a convicted felon and, though at the moment I'm evading outstanding warrants for my arrest, I would enjoy being your host for the remainder of this evening while I am still a free man," he exclaimed. "Ha! What a notion! A free man."

Mario and Caravaggio were now more perplexed than before.

"I'm on the prowl tonight and I noticed how you two slovenly gentlemen were exactly my style. By that I mean I gleamed at first glance the paint on your fingers. I can smell the colors! You are artist and all my friends in Rome are artists," he told them. "I also enjoyed eavesdropping on your conversation about art. I believe I've found compatriots!"

Mario shrugged. "Continue."

"I, too, despise mediocrity and the bland crap that recently passes for art in this city."

"I see," Mario said.

"I suggest we leave this place *post haste* and make our way to a very fine brothel where I'm not only a well-known patron but also a welcomed one," he smiled.

"That is an enticing invitation," Caravaggio rejoined.

"We are penniless but appreciate the dinner and the invitation," Mario said, still suspicious of the man.

Longhi pulled out his wallet. "As I said before, this evening will be paid for by me, gentlemen," he told them.

Mario watched as Longhi pulled a thick handful of lira and scudi and placed it on the table. The man reached his arm up and patted Mario firmly on the back. "*Nec spe, nec metu,*" he stated.

"Without hope or fear," Mario repeated.

Caravaggio asked, "Why are you so enamoured of us?"

Longhi sat back. "Your discussion about art and how you plan to change this city is what I have been discussing about for years, dear citizen. In hearing your conversation it made me realize how we should be friends and confront the mendacity of Rome together," he smiled.

Mario smiled with him and eventually so did Caravaggio.

The brothel was a large two-story brick structure with wood paneling inside. It was situated along the Piazza del Popolo not far from the Tavern of the Turk and just like the tavern it was crowded with men who were drinking wine and beer. Lute players strummed their instruments singing a rough interpretation of "*Voi sapete ch'io v'amo, aniz v'adoro.*"

The men inside the brothel watched the young women seductively parading back and forth from the chamber rooms on the second floor to the wooden bar itself flirting with any man who glanced at them as they swayed exaggeratedly to the music.

The women were nearly nude covering up their breasts with pieces of cloth and wore only thin and flimsy gowns that shifted as they walked. If they bent over, which they often did, their gowns would rise up exposing their naked bottoms and thighs. If they felt bold enough, they would lift the gowns exposing the hair covering their vaginas.

Mario sat with Longhi and Caravaggio at a table in the center of the brothel. "I smell lust!" Longhi shouted.

"You have excellent nostrils," Mario stated.

Again Longhi shouted, "I smell the female! I swoon to her mighty allure!" He turned and gestured to a whore. "Her breasts belong in an Aspertini."

Mario watched as a dark-haired young woman glided by. "I saw her face in a Raphael. Look at her complexion!

I believe it was in *Saint Cecilia*. The altarpiece in Bologna," Longhi said about the same young woman. He was fascinated with the soft blond hair and large nose of another young woman. He pointed to her. "She *could* have been a model for Garofalo," he made note. He turned again to another slender whore walking with a tall man who had deep set eyes. "Correggio had to have painted her," he smiled. "Look at the fierce jaw and the eyes. They look into your soul."

All the while Caravaggio was quiet. Until he leaned back and shook his head. "Not one whore here could ever pose as the Blessed Mother."

"I don't know what you mean exactly, but fine, my friend. If you say so," Mario replied.

Longhi shook his head. "I enjoy lust and I relish in it. I also take exception to that notion, citizen. I believe *every* whore in this room can be the Virgin."

"But then, my new friend, you're not a painter," Caravaggio told him.

Unable to contain his excitement Mario left the table drifting towards several women standing in a corner beckoning him with their smiles. Reaching them, he found them quickly fondling his buttocks and thighs. One was even bold enough to caress his penis through his trousers.

"You have scudi?" one asked in a hoarse voice while the other took his hand planting it on her breast. It was then that one particular prostitute suddenly took Mario's full attention. "Who is she?" he asked the women and they frowned. They made several half-hearted attempts to keep his attention but saw that Mario was infatuated. They walked away from him and he walked back to the table.

"Do you know that one?" Mario asked Longhi.

Longhi glanced at her. "She is called Dominica 'with the auburn hair' so she wouldn't be confused with the Dominica with the 'short brown hair' nor the rather large big breasted and more voluptuous Dominica 'from Naples,'" he answered.

Mario couldn't keep his eyes off of the young woman and spent most of the evening watching her. She'd flirt shyly with him then take another man then another into one of the rooms upstairs.

He was jealous and fought hard not to think about her being with another man even though he knew the notion of jealously when it came to a prostitute was absurd. Yet, it was her innocence that grabbed his attention. Longhi, who frequented the brothel, told Mario that she was a new *face* and she had just come to Rome from up near Florence.

Mario also thought that he was the most handsome in the room and he shouldn't have to pay for the sex. But when he looked around the room he saw many wealthy young men who seemed to have no difficulty paying to make love to the beautiful women who were for sale.

The stories Mario had heard about Rome's prostitutes were all accurate: they were beautiful, luscious and in some instances also exquisite.

It was when Longhi pulled two prostitutes over to sit with him that Mario could no longer control his longings. "May I borrow scudi from you? I want to take her home," he asked Longhi.

"You want to take her home? That would cost more," Longhi told him. "Is that not an indulgence of sorts?"

"I will pay you what I owe you, I swear," Mario stated.

"You're love-struck by this one, aren't you?" Longhi grinned. "Her aura entices you."

Mario didn't respond but he knew Longhi was right. Dominica, the slender young woman seemed vulnerable and created in him a desire to protect her. He also knew that feelings like that for a prostitute were also *absurd*.

Longhi handed him the scudi. "You don't have to pay me back. It is a gift for the first night of our friendship. What I would like for payment instead is a painting," he said.

Mario grabbed his shoulder tightly and squeezed it. "Granted," he said then walked over to Dominica as she sat tired a few tables away with some of the other women.

Mario showed her the scudi. "I believe this is the amount I need to take you home with me," he told her.

Dominica showed little emotion. She glanced to a large bearded man sitting at the last table. Mario knew it was some kind of signal. Dominic took the scudi and walked over to him. Mario couldn't see how much she gave him but she walked back to him. "Where do you reside?" she asked.

Mario raised his hand realizing that he shared his room with Caravaggio so he quickly rushed over to Caravaggio. "I'm taking her home. Give me until noon. I want to be alone with her," he said.

Longhi stepped over to them both. "Caravaggio can stay with me tonight. I have a large apartment not far from here," he stated.

Moments later, Mario and Dominica were walking through the piazza.

CHAPTER NINE

Dominica kept her distance from Mario as he directed her through the small groups of drunken soldiers towards his room in Siciliano's studio.

Mario attempted to make conversation with the young woman but her replies to his small talk were curt. By the time they reached the studio, though tipsy from all the wine he had consumed, he was wondering if his motive for seeing Dominica was less about sex and more about companionship and that was why he was feeling disappointed in her silence.

He unlocked the front door and took her hand showing her the way up to the studio he shared with Caravaggio. Opening the door, he made some room for her to sit then he lit a large candle.

Dominica was still standing when he turned to her. "Please show me to the berth?" she asked.

Her question took Mario off guard but he pointed it out to her where it lay on the floor. She didn't move. Mario stepped over to her looking at her young but sullen face in the candlelight. He smoothed her hair back and patted her head. She didn't respond either way. Mario kissed her on the cheek and felt her shiver. He stepped back.

"I'm sorry," she told him. She kept her eyes glued on his face as he felt her hands grip his arms.

"Why are you sorry?" he asked her. *She's trembling.*

"You're the first man I have gone home with. I have only been working in the brothel this week. Not yet an entire week," she stated. "Before that I worked in my father's studio helping him with the taxes. I'm only in Rome because the famine up north. He believes I came here to work with my cousin. I don't want to disappoint you but I have never been a whole night with a man," she said.

Mario wasn't sure what to do. It wasn't what he wanted to hear. Dominica read the puzzlement on his face. She forced a smile, took his hand and placed it on her breasts. She then nuzzled his ear. "You make me feel comfortable," she sighed.

Mario felt her hand on his thigh. He was immediately aroused. He wanted to see her face so he cupped her head in his hands and before he kissed her, he took one look at her Florentine pale complexion, her soft green eyes and the way her auburn hair fell on her shoulders. "You're like an angel out of Raphael," he told her.

Then he kissed her.

In moments he was pulling her full-length skirt down around her knees and kissed her face, her neck and her breasts. As soon as she was nude from the waist up, he again stepped back so he could see her breasts in the candlelight. "Am I fine enough for you?" she asked.

Mario couldn't respond he was so hungry for the feel of her flesh on his flesh. And despite the efforts of her perfume, he did all he could to ignore the odor of other men on her skin and in her hair and the stale smell of sweat in the room from the warm night. He quickly placed her down on the bed feeling her hands around his member and touching her between her legs finding her moist and waiting.

He also felt her hands on his muscled arms. He felt her smooth fingers across his naked buttocks grabbing and pinching his flesh and sighing.

Mario entered her quickly and thrust into her feeling her arms holding his shoulders tightly. Her nails dug into the sides of his neck and she moaned but he moaned even louder pressing his mouth up against the side of her face as he expelled his semen into her.

The sensation of his orgasm was more of relief than pure pleasure. Mario hadn't had a woman since he was back in Syracuse and now, making love to Dominica as quickly, made him feel that it was companionship he craved more than lascivious pleasure.

The two lay silent together in one another's arms more from shyness. Mario pulled Dominica closer. "What is your true name?" he asked knowing that the whores in the brothel never used their actual names. "God knows me as Lena," she told him. Mario ran his hand down her smooth spine and over the curve of her hips onto her derriere, it felt inviting and he was quickly aroused again.

She giggled when she felt his hard member pressed up against her stomach. She inched back now wanting to see his face in the candle's glow. "You have a strong face," she told him. She then glanced around the room. "You're a painter?" she asked.

Mario nodded.

"So, you're poor, *si*?" she asked.

Mario nodded again. "I'm poor now but someday I will achieve immortality," Mario told her.

"But don't all young painters think that they will one day achieve greatness?" she asked. "I see them starving back in Florence unable to sell a canvas," she told him. "I don't believe *all* of them will achieve immortality."

Mario didn't respond.

"I upset you?" she asked *knowing* that she had. Mario pushed her down beneath him and pushed himself into her. He entered her and thrust back and forth until this time he nearly shouted with ecstasy.

He then fell back in silence as all the wine he had consumed, along with all the physical labor he had done all that day and the release of months of sexual longing, now satisfied, made him sleepy. He pulled a blanket from the floor and covered them both.

"Don't go in the morning," Mario muttered to her. Despite his exhaustion he wanted to get to know this woman and put his arm around her as he gave into sleep. "I would like to have breakfast together in the cafe."

"Wake up!" Longhi and Caravagio both shouted at Mario as they barged into the room carrying two nearly empty bottles of wine. "I smell lust in this room! You fucked with her in every corner! I can smell it!"

Mario groaned. He then leaned on his elbows feeling the warm sun on his face as it came bursting through the window. It took a few seconds for Mario to remember Lena. He also could *smell* her lingering perfume but she was gone.

"She left you, my friend!" Longhi said loudly. Mario could see that both Caravaggio and Longhi were still drunk. He could smell the wine oozing from their pores and now the stench was even stronger coming from their breaths.

"How do you know?" Mario asked.

"We saw her walking back to the brothel. Caravaggio hired her as a model."

Mario leaned against the window looking out on the street below though dizzy and feeling an immense thirst, Mario could still see Lena's face before him. And what was also capturing his interest was that he had felt attached to her. This emotion confused him not because he hadn't felt it before but because had never wanted to paint it before.

He picked up his brush and seeing that it was dry, he quickly grabbed some charcoal and started a sketch.

Caravaggio and Longhi stepped back. "What are you doing? Working now?" Longhi asked. Caravaggio, however, was quiet as Mario worked on the likeness. "It's her," Onorio said in the quiet room.

Once he defined the face in general terms, he began to create an expression. It slowly developed and he had to rub the mistakes away but he continued until he felt it was a true depiction of Dominica. "The expression," Caravaggio stated. "You seized it," he went on.

"Exactly the look on her face when she left the brothel," Longhi grinned. "So?" he said to both painters.

Mario kept quiet and sketched some more. This time he deepened the lines. Lena's expression changed from a distracted and nearly petulant expression to one of sorrow and longing.

Caravaggio turned to Mario. "Was that how she felt? Is that what you're sketching?" he asked.

"No, it is how *I* feel now," Mario replied. He stopped his sketch. He and Caravaggio let the weight of what he had just stated to slowly fill the room.

Onorio was flustered by their silence. He shrugged his shoulders. "So, you already miss the *cortigiana*? So what does that mean?" he asked.

"It means that he misses the strumpet and he is now painting what *he* feels," Caravaggio said.

"Who cares what he feels?" Longhi asked.

"Not the point," Caravaggio shot back.

"I'm expressing what I feel through *her* eyes. I'm important to the painting. The artist's feelings are important. My view of the world is important," Mario exclaimed.

Caravaggio understood instantly. "She's an actress in your production," he said, nearly to himself. "She's a vessel which to pour the elements of your personality. She's a representation of your fears and your hopes," Caravaggio said looking directly at Mario.

Mario nodded in agreement. Caravaggio shared the moment with him. "I've been wondering if that were possible? If it were possible to paint my canvas as a single entity making my painting a personal impression?" he said. Mario sat down. He was lightheaded. "No one who owns a canvas is doing this," he said.

"Yes there is someone doing this very thing somewhere in this city," Caravaggio said. "I imagine there are others doing this very thing. There has to be. But we haven't seen them do it. They aren't being exposed. Their work is in the shadows," Caravaggio said. "*Our* work is in the shadows."

Both painters were in awe of the notion but needed time to digest this thought. Longhi stared at the bed on the floor and frowned. "I have no idea what you two geniuses are discussing but I am now way too fatigued to bother about lust *or* art for that matter," he said and sipped the last of his wine. "I'm going home to bed," he stated then left the room.

Neither Caravaggio nor Mario moved but in their minds the concept that an artist can make his paintings blatantly personal, moved them. Of course all art was personal, they wondered together in silence but the personal philosophy had been kept in the darkness hidden by the use of the symbol. To express an individual belief through words was already a part of Renaissance poetry but what painters dared explore the idea other than in satire.

As if he was reading Mario's mind, Caravaggio spoke up. "Carracci shows us the saints and angels because that is what the people want to see but does Carracci believe in saints and angels? I don't know because he doesn't show me what he believes in!" Caravaggio said.

"I saw the man in that brief moment but I could sense that inside there are inner demons at work but he never reveals them in his paintings," Mario remarked.

"He did once. I saw him do it," Caravaggio said.

"When did you see him do *that*?" Mario asked incredulously.

"When I first came here. There was a painting in a studio near the Colosseum called *The Butcher Shop*. You should have seen it. The way the meat hung on the walls with the blood draining. It was a painting of flesh and raw sensuality," Caravaggio said.

"No, it is not the same," Mario told him. "From this day forward I will paint *my* philosophy," Mario told him. "And damn all the Carracci's who ever lived."

"From this day forward I will do the same," Caravaggio agreed.

"When we are no longer painting miserable portraits for Lorenzo Siciliano," Mario grinned.

"And I'm going to paint this Lena and she will be my Blessed Virgin Mother," Caravaggio told him then fell back on his bed and closed his eyes.

Mario saw that as soon as he closed his eyes he was asleep. Seeing that he now had silence as his servant, he quickly tackled his canvas.

CHAPTER TEN

Though temporarily enthused by their new discovery Mario and Caravaggio were quickly disheartened finding that all of their discussion about a new philosophy for their painting didn't count for much when they were trying to keep the roof over their heads.

Among the many issues they discussed included Pope Clement VIII's dictum about the censorship of nudity in religious paintings and how absurd the notion was since Michelangelo had painted the Sistine Chapel with dozens of nude male bodies and female breasts suspended in the artificial sky. There was talk of actually having someone paint over the limp penises. Other issues they discussed were how to *break through* the mass of mediocre painters who garnished the Vatican commissions.

Longhi made his frequent visits to their studio telling them that if they wanted to sell anything they should paint the *heads* of famous historical and biblical figures. Of course, these paintings were superficial renderings of the *famous* created by desperate artists as well as middling painters who had never managed to break through to achieve major commissions.

Mario saw these very works in the Artists Quarter the first day he arrived in Rome and never thought that he would be painting them. He had to resist his own disappointment and mortification. In the end, his empty stomach made the fight one sided.

Mario and Caravaggio completed a few of these historical heads and found that they both were quite good at doing them. The renderings of Julius Caesar, Attila the Hun, Adam and Eve, Moses painted in lackluster colors of sepia, muted greens and burgundy, were soon filling their small studio. Caravaggio also had the ability to paint them quickly and in a short time both young men were making their way from storefront to studio offering their canvases to any bidder.

Mario paid Longhi back for his night with Lena by giving him one of the heads of Saint Paul. Longhi liked it immensely since Mario painted Longhi's face as Saint Paul and Longhi appreciated the tribute.

Longhi was extremely helpful to them in this undertaking by bringing them to some of his friends who bought the artwork. The only problem was that they didn't sell for many lira. However, it helped both Mario and Caravaggio to save some money to help them execute their plan to leave Lorenzo Siciliano's studio and find separate studios of their own. However, that plan would only work with commissions by powerful patrons and those kinds of commissions didn't come by easily.

One hot afternoon Mario was standing alone in the Piazza del Popolo holding the small canvas of Saint Peter's *head* when a middle-aged man dressed in a Jesuit monk's cloth stepped over to him. Mario tried to catch a glimpse of the man's face but a hood purposely hid it. "What is the price?" the monk asked with an educated inflection in his voice.

Mario was fatigued and expected very little from a monk. "Ten lira," he stated.

"I will pay twenty-five lira if you delivery yourself to my studio, sire," the monk told him. He then handed Mario an address written on a piece of paper and ten lira. "The rest when you bring the painting," he stated. "I will be at that address in one hour," the monk said then walked away.

Mario was confounded as he felt the paper lira in his hand. He knew he could have kept the 'head' and the lira but then again, perhaps if he did deliver the small canvas, he could interest the monk in another? So, he took his time and made his way to a street called Lune right off the Piazza Navona. *I am better than this. I deserve my own assistants who will carry my commissions to my patrons.*

Mario reached the address perplexed since he was facing a more than just modest house on a quiet tree-lined street off of the busy piazza. The house was well taken care of and two-stories tall.

Mario knocked on the front door and was immediately allowed in by a female servant. The servant, a young woman with dark flowing hair and a pretty face, smiled at Mario then led him silently up the stairs to the second floor. Mario thought he recognized her but he couldn't remember where he had seen her before. Once upstairs, the female servant led Mario into a large but empty studio.

Mario waited with the female servant a few moments when a priest entered. He was well groomed and smelled of cologne. His hair was short, streaked with gray and his face pleasant looking. *Was he the monk who bought his canvas?*

The priest placed the remaining fifteen lira on the table and Mario handed him the 'head.' "Would you like to earn fifty lira more?" the priest asked.

"Of course I would," Mario smirked.

With that the priest turned to the female servant. "Undress now," he told her. The servant smiled as she untied one long thin rope that was keeping her garment held to her body and then let her go. The garment fell to her feet and she was immediately nude.

"I will pay for you to be my model. I want you to penetrate her now as if you are Zeus emerging from the heavens to take a young mortal for your appetite," he told Mario.

Mario was astounded and had no idea how to reply.

"I can provide wine if you need some to relax," the priest told him. Mario still didn't know how to retort to that suggestion.

"Undo your garments now," the priest told him.

Mario looked around. "Where are your paints? Your easel?" he asked. He then looked at the female servant. It was then that he recognized her as a pretty wench he had seen in the brothel at the Piazza del Popolo.

The priest stepped closer to Mario then stopped. "I have contacts with the Vatican. I can assure commissions for you if you indulge in my requests," he told Mario.

Mario then realized that the man he was talking to was no ordinary priest. He took a closer look at the man. He could see by the man's physical presence that he pampered himself with ointments and skin creams. Mario was now wary of the man's identity. "You say you can help me? Then tell me your name."

"I am Bishop Romano," the priest responded.

Mario didn't need to hear anymore. He knew the name.

Bishop Romano turned to the female servant. "I paid you well. Entice him," he commanded.

The woman stepped over to Mario pressing her naked body against him. Bishop Romano stepped back, his eyes lighting up with anticipation for what he was sure was to occur. "You are Zeus and you will enslave her with desire," he demanded of Mario.

Mario smirked. *He has no interest in models or art. He just wants to indulge his perversions.*

The woman grabbed Mario's member rubbing it with the palm of her hand through his garments. He felt his penis grow hard. He looked at the woman. She reached up and kissed him. She was then jerking his penis back and forth. Mario wanted to give into the pleasure but then he turned to the Bishop and saw that he was pleasuring himself as he watched. His penis exposed, sticking out from his frock.

Mario pushed the woman away knocking her sideways. She shouted.

He then reached for the bishop grabbing him by the shoulder and then with one powerful heave, he pushed the bishop backward so that he fell against the

73

wall.

Bishop Romano crumbled to the ground but instead of looking afraid, Mario could see a glimmer of delight in his eyes. "Strike me," the bishop demanded. Mario wanted desperately to strike the bishop but instead he stepped over him and rushed out of the house.

That night at the Tavern of the Tower, Mario related the story to both Caravaggio and Longhi. "That fits the description of Bishop Giovanni Romano," Longhi said with a laugh.

"It was way too strange for me," Mario responded.

"Welcome to Rome," Longhi grinned pouring all three men more wine. "This city of smells. This city of lust and blood and death. The Eternal City thrives on the ghostly passions of its inhabitants," Longhi said. "That is a line from my new poem—"

"And this bishop is an important man here in Rome?" Mario interrupted.

"He is the well-respected assistant to Cardinal Aldobrandini who is nephew to the Pontiff himself," Longhi answered.

Caravaggio shook his head. "The Pontiff orders that there be no nudity in our art work and yet, his nephew's respected assistant, a man of the cloth, a bishop nonetheless, wants to see Mario fuck a strumpet while playing Zeus to her virgin mortal," he said in disgust.

Mario was uneasy. He had been that way since the incident. He knew the cavalieri captain considered him the prime suspect in the sculptor's murder and continually feared that he'd be arrested again.

Longhi noticed Mario's trepidation. He suddenly relaxed his tone of voice and sat back. "Our world is complex, Mario, but it's also finite. You must be prudent yet trusting, you must be patient but also ambitious." He grinned. As the great, Machiavelli wrote in his *The Prince,* "Be a lion to your friends but a fox to your enemies."

Mario felt the truth sting him but he was not sure why. He nodded to Longhi. "We need a powerful patron," he stated. "The path to success in Rome is lined with obstacles and dangerous detours." *With one mishap he could find himself in prison.*

"I agree we need a powerful patron. Find us one, dear friend," Caravaggio stated.

"It is possible to find you a powerful patron but I wonder if you are ready to enter Roman society? Is it something you are ready to accomplish?" Longhi asked seriously of both men.

Mario hesitated but Caravaggio didn't. "Give me several more months. Give

74

me time to complete a canvas I'm contemplating," Caravaggio replied.

Longhi sipped his wine. "Time waits for no man, dear friend."

Mario was interested. "What canvas are you speaking of?" he asked.

Caravaggio tilted his wineglass to Mario. "A painting in which you will pose for me but not as Zeus," he grinned. "But as Bacchus," he stated. "When that is complete I will be ready to mark my name in the concrete of this mighty city," he announced. "And since I am too broke to pay a model, you'll be Bacchus."

CHAPTER ELEVEN

1593

Mario was wearing a robe with nothing underneath it. There was frost on the window as well as a stinging draft. "I'm cold. How much longer?" he asked lounging on his elbow with a glass of wine in his hand. He was leaning forward, his large brown opulent eyes bloodshot from a cold. His dark mass of curly hair was messy and grimy. He had dirty fingernails creating a decadent *look*. His muscled arms, shoulders, chest and a nipple were exposed and yet his strong, masculine features were in direct contrast to his brooding, feminine pose: the image of a Bacchus obviously manly but at the same time, petulant.

The image was also strikingly disconcerting while at the very core playful, perverse and for that moment in time, startling. "Why do you have to paint Bacchus again?" Mario asked. This was Caravaggio's *second* Bacchus he had Mario pose for in one week.

Caravaggio sneezed then continued painting. "This time I want to show how seductive you are."

Mario laughed but he knew what he had meant. He had Mario exposed his chest and, nipples. Now, Caravaggio wanted to paint another Bacchus that would hazard even further the accepted norm.

"Almost done," Caravaggio answered.

Mario was the perfect model for Caravaggio's vision. Broad shouldered, bawdy and yet insolent, Mario embodied all Caravaggio had expected and even more.

Light snow blew outside their window while inside a faint fire burned with smoldering embers. Both had fallen ill from head colds. They were also weak from lack of a good diet. Working this closely together their nerves were being tested.

Yet Mario could see that Caravaggio was confident in the work from *before* his first brush stroke and his confidence grew as he painted. Even Longhi, who had visited their small studio earlier that very morning, grinned when he saw what was happening. "You've crossed a line, my friend," he stated with approval.

Lorenzo Siciliano had invited his students to show their own canvases to an invited list of guests for two hours on a Sunday afternoon. He did this once a year to placate his most talented students and used it to seduce new students to work at his studio. Since his studio was small and the competition for talented students was rigorous, he knew he had to allow them some benefits and he reluctantly did so.

There were some rules concerning the little art festival. He himself would have to personally choose those paintings each artist could present. He allowed Mario to show his *Flowers with a Basket of Fruit* as well as a painting that Mario had been working and reworking a self-portrait. The self-portrait was simple in design and dramatic in tone. It showed Mario standing at the studio window looking out forlornly at a cold winter's gloom. He put to detail the spare living quarters and the isolation of the impoverished artist. Mario knew that the romantic tone of the piece was not exceptional but he did relish in his own inclination for the dramatic and the self-aggrandizing.

And when it came to his face, Mario gave the starving artist he was playing, soulful eyes, a lean masculine scowl of self-importance to create what he believed a tragic effect.

He was painting his philosophy and that philosophy was all about *him*. He was painting his agony and humiliation seeing it as a personal crusade. He saw himself as the suffering artist he had read about when Zuccarro wrote about *his* brother.

Caravaggio looked at Mario's paintings but said nothing.

"What?" Mario asked, trying to interrupt the silence.

"We are going in separate directions."

Mario knew his friend well and could see that Caravaggio was probably wondering if Mario would ever accept the glimmerings of the same notions that were percolating in his own imagination?

Mario could actually see his friend's expression change from interest to indifference. He now knew that his friend was, and would always be from that moment on, fighting to keep his own self-preservation. He would do this by keeping his artistic thoughts to himself. Mario knew that he could never seek encouragement from Caravaggio ever again.

The other canvas Siciliano allowed Mario to show was his painting of an angel. He used Lena's face and though he resisted doing it at first, he idealized the moment by giving her an expression of righteousness. Mario could sense that the painting disappointed Caravaggio as much as the self-portrait and yet again both stayed silent on the issue. Mario firmly thought he had done what he had set out to do which was to paint the emotions he was feeling about the whore.

Siciliano beamed. "Good work. I would be proud to show these canvases," he told Mario.

On the other hand, Siciliano glared at Caravaggio's offerings for the show while viewing them in the small studio room. With his puffy cheeks and stomach ailments, which gave his breath a horrible odor, Siciliano was always irritable. "Impossible," he waved his hand. He was examining Caravaggio's *Bacchus*. Caravaggio cringed. "I'm showing this canvas!" he growled.

"I'm not allowing this *mockery* to be shown in my studio," Siciliano growled back. He never liked Caravaggio and only tolerated him because he was the quickest artist he employed. "Show them on the street if you must but you do not have my permission to show them here," Sicilian said and he was adamant on the issue.

Caravaggio then revealed another he had been working on where he again used Mario as a model. It was a painting he called *Gypsy Fortune Teller* and in it Mario played a duped youth. "Excellent but it has no morals," Siciliano stated. "It will not be shown in my gallery either," he said. He then looked at Caravaggio. "You may show that *Flowers with a Basket of Fruit* that you completed despite the fact that it lacks warmth," he retorted then left the room.

Caravaggio flung a brush at the wall but said nothing. He then fell to the floor. Mario could see that though he was pouting he was also plotting. Mario wanted to give him a word of solace but felt foolish because in his heart of hearts he knew Caravaggio to be an extraordinary talent. Mario hid his jealousy in hopes that perhaps he was wrong and Caravaggio was never going to attain the heights of fame he, Mario Minniti, had foreseen for himself. That destiny for Caravaggio as a failure would make Mario happy and he had no trouble admitting that truth to himself.

Several nights before the artist festival Mario, Caravaggio and Onorio Longhi talked deep into the night at the Piazza Navona. Their conversation, helped along by the wine, was fueled by Caravaggio's frustration at being a member of Lorenzos Siciliano's studio.

As they sat in the piazza Mario eyed the small bands of drunken mercenaries, *bravi*, and vagabonds who mulled around the piazza exuding a menacing presence.

"What studio would you choose to be a member if you had the choice?" Longhi asked Caravaggio.

"Cardinal Del Monte's without question," Cararvaggio quickly answered.

Mario had heard very little of this cardinal so he passed the wine satchel to Longhi and turned to Caravaggio. "Why this cardinal's studio over Monsignor Pesce or for the Ambassador Lucciano?" Mario asked.

Caravaggio stood up. "He hires only the elite. But most importantly he garners the most significant commissions for the best of his artists," Caravaggio stated.

"But Cardinal Del Monte has a price," Onorio Longhi said.

"What is that *price* you speak of?" Mario asked.

Longhi, dressed in a sparking gold vest and bright green shirt, had come to wear his yellow reddish hair long as Caravaggio and Mario did. "Del Monte demands a commission for the commissions he finds for his artists," he answered.

"How much of a commission?" Mario asked.

Onorio grinned. "Whatever he has a fancy to ask for. I'd say no less than ten percent for those who are already established but I hear he garners as high as twenty-five percent for beginners in his stable," Onorio told the two men.

Mario waved his arms wildly. "That's criminal!" he shouted.

Caravaggio was oddly silent on the matter especially both Mario and Longhi knew him to have strong opinions on the subject.

"What do you think, Michale?" Mario asked.

Caravaggio spoke softly but to the point. "If a patron as powerful as Cardinal Del Monte would be willing to hire my brush and garner me commissions, I would agree to whatever percentage he demanded," he replied.

Longhi ruffled Caravaggio's hair. Caravaggio pushed him away but Longhi didn't stop there. He now confronted Caravaggio with glee. "You're *ready* for success, my friend. You're ready to embark on the journey you have started the day you entered Rome. You are ready to enter the world you have desired since you took that brush in your hand," he said. "I sense it and I smell the aroma of glory!"

Mario was lost. "What are you talking about, Onorio? You're drunk."

Longhi grinned then put his hand on Mario and Caravaggio's shoulders. "For my services I would like a gift," he said to them.

"What kind of gift?" Mario asked.

"What *services*?" Caravaggio asked.

Longhi turned the three of them away from the fountain as a noisy increasingly growing group of mercenaries were milling around the other side of the same fountain. "The gift will be a painting from the each of you. A painting of my choosing," he told them.

"For what service will you warrant this gift?" Mario asked.

79

Longhi smiled. "Onorio Longhi, friend of Mario Minniti and Caravaggio, will deliver to your studio, on the day of the artist festival, Cardinal Del Monte himself," he stated.

"How is that possible?" Mario asked.

"His family has been a friend of my family for as long as I can remember," Longhi told them.

"You piss drunk bastard of a friend!" Caravaggio cheered.

The three men turned north walking away from the piazza. As they did a wine bottle was thrown in their direction. It crashed at their feet.

All three men broke away from each other turned and glared down at the pack of soldiers who were now laughing at them.

"We're outnumbered," Longhi said under his breath.

"We have no swords," Mario exclaimed.

"*They* have swords," Caravaggio replied.

"*Nec spe, nec metu,*" Mario stated.

Without another word Mario, Longhi and Caravaggio turned and raced toward the shadows of the closest street as they heard the gang of mercenaries pursuing them.

Mario had the longest legs and could run the quickest. He immediately out-distanced both Longhi and Caravaggio rushing towards the river hoping to elude the soldiers at the foot of the Tiber.

He knew certain sections of Rome better than others and fortunately this one was one of those he had walked many times before in the dark.

When he reached the Tiber he could still hear the voices behind him. He recognized them as Spaniards and knew that they couldn't keep up their chase much longer if they were drunk.

He completely forgot about Longhi and Caravaggio knowing that they were clever enough to take care of themselves. So, he found an alley and rushed through it then stopped to catch his breath. He leaned against a small house and saw a lit window. He moved toward it. Inside, he saw a small boy sleeping on a floor and his mother, nude from the waist up, washing herself in a water basin. *Like the Virgin and the Christ Child.*

The scene captivated him and he momentarily forgot why he was in the alley. When the woman walked away from the window, Mario stepped through a small garden and found himself on the street. "*Que!*" a voice shouted.

Stepping out of the shadows, Mario found himself face to face with one of the soldiers. He was a tall man with a beard. He had a deep scar on his right cheek and he was holding a stubby sword at his side.

Before Mario could react, he thrust the blade at Mario but he was drunk and he missed Mario's stomach by almost a foot. But Mario wasn't as drunk. Driven by fear, he grabbed the wrist that held the blade and jerked it down hard. The man groaned in pain and dropped the blade.

Mario picked up the blade and without a second's hesitation, he thrust it into the soldier's rib cage. The soldier let out a moan. Mario stepped back leaving the blade stuck in his side. The soldier grabbed at it then staggered back. In doing so, he stepped into the light and Mario could see his gray eyes pulsating with a quizzical resonance. Mario then raced past the soldier's outstretched arm and disappeared into the shadows of another alley.

While he ran back to the studio he questioned himself on why he had reacted so violently? He was bewildered by his own behavior. He had avoided the drunk soldier's initial thrust and could have easily out run him. He also forced the soldier to drop the blade giving him an opportunity to race away. Then why did he stab him?

At the moment when he picked the blade up from the street, Mario felt an urge to strike out. There was a boiling point of frustration reaching his very core and it lashed out with a force that could only lead to destruction.

Was the wine to blame? Was his frustration at the horror of his life as a struggling artist in Rome the root cause of his violent behavior?

Or did a darker force that had haunted him his entire adult life possess Mario Minniti? He had left Syracuse because he had killed a man in a brawl in a brothel. The man was the ornery son of a wealthy family. As evil as the son's reputation had been, his father wanted revenge. That was why Mario had left his home so quickly.

He reached the studio and waited for Longhi and Caravaggio to appear. In time they did with their own stories of eluding the drunken soldiers.

He lied to them both when it came to the details of his adventure. He said nothing of the soldier he stabbed and listened to both Longhi and Caravaggio discuss another matter.

"We need to carry swords after dark," Caravaggio stated.

"You need a license to do that," Longhi told him.

"I curse the Council of Trent for outlawing dueling!" Mario shouted.

"You have powerful friends. Get us each a license and we will be able to walk the streets with courage and dignity," Caravaggio told Longhi.

Mario leaned against the window and saw lanterns moving along the darkness. He knew that they belonged to the cavalieri as they scoured the streets looking for him. "I don't want a sword," he stated to their confounded reactions.

"Suit yourself," Caravaggio told him.

"Get a powerful patron and you will be allowed to walk Rome armed," Longhi stated.

CHAPTER TWELVE

When Cardinal Del Monte entered the courtyard everyone at the studio focused on him. Lorenzo Siciliano was the first to flutter around the cardinal rushing to him offering all kinds of foods and wines his servants had prepared but since the cardinal's presence at the artist festival was unannounced and Lorenzo was cheap and the offerings were meager.

Mario first glimpsed the cardinal from a small balcony he was leaning on looking down into the small courtyard where prospective buyers glanced at canvases and eager artist waited patiently for their approval. Mario never met Cardinal Del Monte before but knew immediately it had to be him as Del Monte moved into the courtyard swathed in scarlet.

It was an overcast day and the clouds were threatening rain. Neither Caravaggio nor Mario actually expected the cardinal to appear since Longhi didn't attend the festival as he had promised both artists.

Mario watched as the cardinal quickly perused the canvases smiling at some young artist and quickly dispersing after glimpsing the canvases of others. It was when Mario overheard the cardinal asking Siciliano to see both Mario and Caravaggio's work did Mario enjoy a rush of excitement.

Siciliano quickly led the cardinal to Mario's canvas and Mario rushed down the balcony to stand behind his painting as it was customary to do. The cardinal greeted Mario with a nod, took a look at Mario's offerings and then raised his head. "And where is this Caravaggio?" he asked Siciliano.

Mario was devastated. This great art collector glanced at his work and asked for Caravaggio? The slight was so painful and came so quickly Mario couldn't respond. He knew Caravaggio hadn't been feeling well and was sitting upstairs in their studio. And because of Siciliano's warnings he didn't dare exhibit the paintings he knew where of better quality.

Siciliano who pointed out Caravaggio's *Flowers with a Basket of Fruit* and for the first time that morning the cardinal paused. He examined the canvas asking that it be held in the light. Siciliano quickly did as he was told. Cardinal Del Monte examined it even more closely. "I'd like to see more from this artist," the Cardinal Del Monte said.

"This is the only painting of his in the festival," Siciliano stated point blank.

Cardinal Del Monte frowned. "Preposterous," he grinned. "Where can I find this painter?" he demanded.

Recovering from the Cardinal's indifference to his work, Mario stepped forward. "We share a studio on the top floor," Mario told him.

Cardinal Del Monte nodded a "thank you" then climbed the stairs with Siciliano and Mario following behind him.

The cardinal pushed open the door finding Caravaggio, looking pale from his illness. Mario entered the room behind the cardinal surmising that Caravaggio had witnessed the entire event in the courtyard in silence from the window.

Caravaggio said nothing but Mario was not surprised to see *Bacchus* and *The Gypsy Fortune Teller* in plain view. Mario was however surprised to see Del Monte take one look at it, stand in front of the other canvas and then the next, while his eyes sparkling with interest. Without moving, but with his eyes glued to the canvases, he spoke. Mario could hear the lilt of education and a touch of irony in his voice. "You're from up north?" he asked.

Caravaggio coughed. "Yes, I am, cardinal," he answered.

Mario watched as Siciliano stood in the doorway his face blushing with embarrassment. "I refused! And I repeat, refused to show these awful works in my studio," he bellowed to the cardinal making clear he wanted nothing to do with the paintings.

Cardinal Del Monte ignored him placing all of his attention on Caravaggio. "Very unusual," he said. "The naturalism is provocative. The style is northern and reminds me of Brill and Jan Breughel. Do you know these Flemish painters?" he asked.

"I do not, Cardinal Del Monte," Caravaggio replied.

The cardinal now turned his attention on Caravaggio himself. "Do you paint landscapes?"

"I dislike *nature*," Caravaggio shot back.

Mario could see Siciliano cringe. "He did not learn that *here*," he stated.

Mario now watched Caravaggio dance and it was a dance he was doing with Cardinal Del Monte.

"It is conceivable that you do. But you paint people or should I say *characters* very well," Del Monte told him.

Caravaggio bowed.

"I have a fondness for humanity depicted in art as it should be depicted. The way God created us," Del Monte announced.

It was at that moment Mario became aware that Caravaggio knew of the cardinal's tastes. *Did he paint to attract his attention?* Mario wondered if he had conversations with Longhi and learned all this? Or did he study the cardinal's art collection from afar?

Cardinal Del Monte stood in the room and without looking at any one in particular spoke up. "I have an opening for one student at my studio at the Palazzo Madama. I offer it to you, Caravaggio," he indicated without hestitation.

Though feeling frail, Caravaggio bowed.

Mario was stunned. He felt a physical ache as if he had been punched or taken ill from a furious virus.

Cardinal Del Monte then turned to Siciliano whose mouth was wide open. "I will pay you a slight commission for taking this artist from your stable since you have no insight into his vast talent," he said then left the room with Siciliano following.

Mario glared at Caravaggio who walked to the window and looked down in the courtyard. "He choose you," he stated.

"I paint in the style he appreciates," Caravaggio replied, then coughed again.

Mario was dejected and sat on the floor. Caravaggio quickly packed his things. Mario watched him with a rage of envy but stifled his feelings. He sat silently on the floor and after Caravaggio had packed his meager belongings he stopped. "I will find a place for you at the studio," he told Mario.

Mario stood up. "I will find my way on my own," he stated.

"You'll come with me and live in the palazzo. I'll tell the cardinal I need you as a model," Caravaggio told Mario.

"You need me as a model but his studio does not need me as a painter?" Mario shot back.

Caravaggio didn't answer at first and waited until he reached the door. "I need you as a *friend* is what I should have said," he told Mario then left the room.

Mario sat back down on the floor of the studio for the entire day. He listened to the voices in the hallway downstairs and the courtyard outside without moving or uttering a word. He had been more than humbled by the cardinal's indifference to his work. For the first time in his life he wondered if he was as good as he thought he was? For the first time in his life he confronted the truth of failure and it was the bitter pill he had read about in Zuccaro's poetry about his brother Taddeo's plight in Rome but this time the rejection was not just in theory but in reality.

With dusk came the rain and with the rain came the darkness. Mario opened the window with the rain in his face and prayed that his life wouldn't be a failure. He prayed for the strength to continue on his quest of proving to the world that he could paint a great painting. He prayed that he would achieve the respect great artists are due. He mumbled to himself that he would never admit defeat. He mouthed the words of encouragement prodding himself on telling himself that he was worthy of the years of sacrifice that was ahead of him.

When he was exhausted, he shut the window and lay back on the floor. He refused to light a candle and sat in the dark absorbing the night as if it were there to be embraced. He allowed the loneliness of the night to spread through the room and into his own flesh and blood.

Mario Minniti had never felt as alone in his life as he did that moment. He lit a candle. He mixed his paints pulled a new canvas from the closet, placed it on the easel and painted.

It was all he knew how to do.

Several nights later Mario found Caravaggio and Longhi sharing a bottle of wine at a table in the shadows at the Tavern of the Hawk. Mario hadn't heard a word from Caravaggio since the night he left Siciliano's studio and was apprehensive of walking over to the two men. But Onorio waved him over and Mario, feeling lonely, missing his friend and in need of conversation, sat down with the two men.

Caravaggio quickly offered Mario a glass of wine. "I was going to see you to tomorrow," he told Mario. "I have good news," he grinned.

Mario didn't want his friends to see that he was pleased to see them. "And what good news is *that*?" he asked as if it didn't matter.

"Del Monte has agreed that you move in with me at the Palazzo Madama," Caravaggio answered. "Bring over your things in the morning."

Mario was excited. He didn't want to know why Cardinal Del Monte had accepted him into the studio. He wanted to believe it was because the Del Monte saw potential in his work.

"This man is a genius in so many ways," Onorio Longhi announced. "I was afraid to see him because I knew I would have to apologize for my failure in managing to have Cardinal Del Monte attend your festival," Onorio said.

Mario shrugged. "Rubbish. You're drunk. The cardinal *did* attend and we are in your debt," Mario said.

"No, my *pisano,* you don't understand the cardinal had *refused* to see me when I went to visit him at the Palazzo Madama. It seems he has a reputation to protect and since my arrest last year for that ridiculous assault charge, I'm banned from his palace," Longhi answered.

Mario looked to Caravaggio and shrugged his shoulders. "Then why did Del Monte show up? We all know he dislikes Siciliano."

"He was there because of Caravaggio," Longhi replied.

Mario sat back. Caravaggio spoke with a straight-forward tone and Mario noticed a sudden aura about his friend he had never seen before. "I wrote the cardinal. In the letter I stated that I believed I was painting in a *style* he would appreciate and in time, I would complete paintings that would astound. I also told him that I would gratefully pay him a commission on anything of mine he could sell," Caravaggio said.

"You wrote a letter to Cardinal Del Monte?" Mario asked, incredulous.

"Yes, my friend, I wrote it with a pen on parchment and had a messenger deliver it," Caravaggio answered.

"And already Del Monte has buyers for Michale's *Flowers* and both of the *Bacchus* paintings!" Longhi announced. "I smell the scent of success!"

Caravaggio grinned at Mario. "Mario at this very moment, you are hanging in the French Ambassador's Villa on the Via Corso," he crackled. "And tonight, I will pay for our wine," he said.

Mario felt a genuine satisfaction for his friend. They had been struggling and for the moment, Caravaggio was winning the accolades.

Mario raised his glass. "To the master!" he cheered. He then could see Caravaggio blush and then the redness in his face turn to a bright glow in the table's candlelight.

For that moment Mario could only imagine what Caravaggio was feeling and once again Mario felt a rage of envy that only the wine could prevent him from revealing.

He drank one glass then another and listened to Longhi tell Caravaggio that he was already the talk of the city.

Mario forced a large grin, continued to drink his wine, and cursed his friend's success with his silence.

CHAPTER THIRTEEN

"Palazzo Madama"

Mario spent his first night in the Palazzo Madama walking through its vast halls ignoring the inquisitive glances from servants and other guests. He was enthralled with the residence and wanted to savor every moment of living there before the experience was taken from him.

However, after being there for nearly a month, Mario continued to hardly venture out into the evenings, instead he would walk the halls and lounge beside the courtyard fountains pondering a lifestyle he was learning that he relished.

At first he punished himself for believing that this enjoyment for luxury was a weakness in his character and would hinder him as an artist, but that notion slowly disappeared as Mario spent more time in the palazzo.

The Palazzo Madama was modest when compared to other palazzo's most notably the Palazzo Guistiniani which was directly across the road. The Palazzo Madama was austere. Its fifteen-century façade bore a replica of a grand rendering of the Medici coat of arms.

Measuring ninety by sixty meters there were main state rooms and rooms for courtiers on several floors. There were also smaller rooms divided by wooden partitions to make monk's cells. There were various servant quarters, cellars for wine and supplies, a coach house and stables for the horses.

Caravaggio and Mario lived in a small house that was connected to the cardinal's main residence by a walkway. In this cottage that they shared they were next door to the artist's studio.

Del Monte house only six artists in residence and that is what they were—artists in residence. Mario and Caravaggio were paid to paint their own projects. In turn for their room and board, Cardinal Del Monte would have the first right to purchase their paintings at a fair market price. He also had the right to act as their agent and secure commissions for them and *from* them.

Mario had learned quickly that Cardinal Del Monte had a fine taste in all kinds of art but preferred painting above them all. And since he only had room for six artists he choose those he thought would have a future in the Roman art world.

Del Monte had excellent insight into what artist would sell since all of his painters did. All of them were earning commissions and those before them were now famous.

This was the future that the cardinal had foreseen for Mario Minniti. He believed that Mario had a *good eye* for what mainstream art buyers would purchase and, with hard work and an acceptance of this ability; he could become a highly marketable painter. Del Monte saw Caravaggio's career differently. In Caravaggio he saw the seeds of the *unusual* and the revolutionary.

The cardinal offered his artists not only a place to live and paint what they wanted but he also provided a rich and stimulating intellectual arena. He did this by having weekly salons inviting Rome's smartest and brightest and most talented to the palazzo.

One night at one of the salon meetings with wine, trays of cheese and bread being served and conversation flowing, Mario was intoxicated with the atmosphere.

"Do you like the Palazzo Madama?" Cardinal Del Monte asked Mario.

"Being within its walls makes me feel as if heaven came and fell upon me," Mario answered.

Later that evening Bishop Romano entered the large room where Cardinal Del Monte was reading poetry. Mario immediately recognized Romano and he was just as immediately recognized. Both men kept their secret to themselves and at one point Mario noticed Bishop Romano speaking softly to Cardinal Del Monte then both men glanced towards him.

But nothing was said the entire night and in fact, from that day forward, Mario realized that Cardinal Del Monte spent very little time with him. It soon became apparent, or so he believed, that the cardinal was only quasi interested in his progress as an artist and that Mario was only a guest at the palazzo because of Caravaggio.

It was from that night forward that Mario spent more and more time back at the taverns. His favorites were the Tavern of the Wolf, the Tavern of the Blackamoor, the Tavern of the Tower and the Tavern of the Turk which was below the Trinita dei Monte and he spent more and more time at the brothels that clustered around the Mausoleum of Augustus.

Mario found himself painting less but *talking about* painting more with his group of friends including Onorio Longhi and Caravaggio. While at the same time he saw Caravaggio paint more and talk about it less. Mario also found that he had a fondness of beer over wine and whores with dark complexions and dark hair while Caravaggio had a fondness for women with light complexion and auburn hair.

In the crowd that developed around Longhi were many artists, painters and poets, who liked to drink and brawl. They also liked to exchange insults but also sharing their dislike for Roman authority, which included the Pope, and the inability to make a living as artists.

Longhi, though not an artist, was arrested several times a month for starting brawls over art and though Mario was often at his side when these fights occurred, he shyed away from fighting since he knew it'd be wise for him to be prudent. However, Mario was simmering inside with resentment toward the very city he had traveled to to find his fame.

"I have a growing distaste for this city," he told Longhi one night.

"It is possible since this city has not found its taste for you," he said, drunkenly.

Mario was stung by the words and also knew he was fighting his resentment for Caravaggio. He would watch with envy as Caravaggio's reputation as an artist with his reputation on the rise in the Artists Quarter. The Artists Quarter reached from the Piazza del Popolo to the Piazza Colonna and the Pantheon and northward to the Piazza Santa Trinita and included the Villa Medici.

One night coming back home to the small room he shared with Caravaggio Mario, who was drunk, found himself face to face with Cardinal Del Monte.

The cardinal was in his night robes having just left his favorite room on the courtyard. It was a room where he completed his alchemy experiments. Mario saw the light on and was struck dumb when he realized he would have to walk passed the cardinal who was standing outside the alchemy studio.

Mario nodded an acknowledgement but the cardinal would have none of it. "Minniti," he said sharply.

Mario stopped walking. He bowed but his bow was sloppy hindered by his ability to even stand up straight.

"Bishop Romano told me that you assaulted him," Del Monte stated.

Mario felt the blood rush from his face but he refused to accept the accusation with speaking up. He raised his head. "Did he tell you *why* I did, sire?" Mario asked.

Cardinal Del Monte stared at him in the dim light. "I'm quite aware how violence rules Rome's piazzas. I also know how the Medici's used violence to keep their power. But I'm a man who believes in our better nature and I've placed all my hope in the divine inspiration God used to inspire his artists." He then continued. "I see this inspiration in our friend Caravaggio and though I know the young artist will always have a darker side to his nature, I excuse this because I see brilliance in his brush stroke. I do not see this genius in yours, Minniti."

Mario shot back though with respect. "What do you see in me?"

"I see in you one who is capable, ambitious and yet, so far, mediocre. I invited you to the Palazzo Madama only because Caravaggio requested it. Caravaggio made a plea that he needed you as a model. And yet, since you're residency here, Mario, I have not secured a single commission for you. I also have not been stimulated by your new work. Your main contribution to my studio is that Caravaggio prefers you as a model," Del Monte stated. "And now I see you come back to my home and you're drunk."

Mario was humiliated. *All he says is true.*

"I expected more from you," Del Monte told him.

"I expected more from myself," Mario replied.

Del Monte took a moment. He could hear the pride and sincerity in Mario's voice. Mario heard it too. Both men were secretly surprised by it.

"Very well. I will give you one more opportunity to prove your value to the Palazzo Madama," Del Monte told him. "You have the potential to be very successful if you see yourself as a commercial painter. Your work mirrors what buyers want to see. Work hard and you will become a craftsman of note. I'm sure of it."

Mario bowed. "I'm in your debt," he replied. Mario looked up and noticed that Del Monte hadn't moved and his eyes were trained on Mario. *What more does he want?*

"Are you envious of your close friend's success?" Del Monte asked.

Mario couldn't reply. He stood motionless under the large lamp that lit the concrete walkway and the courtyard.

"Envy is one of the Seven Deadly Sins. Satan is aware of your jealousy and he will work to destroy you," Del Monte stated. "Don't allow that, my son. Paint what you can paint and forget what others do. God only cares what *you* are capable of doing," he said.

"Heaven may be indifferent but men *do* compare," Mario told him.

The cardinal forced a smile. "They do and that is the tragedy of life for all of us who love beauty. It is *our* cross to bear," Del Monte stated then walked across the courtyard to his stateroom on the second floor.

Mario was not relieved. He was mortified that someone of Cardinal Del

Monte's influence saw him as less than Caravaggio. He went to bed that night torturing himself with doubt.

Early the next morning he realized that Caravaggio had never gone to sleep in the studio so he decided to find his friend. It didn't take long for him to find Caravaggio in the Piazza Navona talking to several displaced and homeless people who were milling around the fountain. Mario had seen them before and always walked right past them. "What are you doing, Michale?" Mario asked.

"Searching for my Saint Peter," Caravaggio said, momentarily distracted by Mario. He then leaned down inspecting the homeless. Mario knew that though the men may have looked old and worn they were like wounded dogs. They could easily snap and with knives in their belts slice a piece of your flesh in a flash.

Even the women, toothless, gray and with withered skin cursed frequently, had nasty dispositions and would have no difficulty scratching a man's eyes out for a piece of bread.

Mario was stunned as he saw Caravaggio hand two old men and an elderly woman scudi and then direct them back to the studio.

Walking back with Caravaggio he was inquisitive. "Are you bringing them back to the Palazzo Madama?" he asked.

"Yes," Caravaggio answered.

"For what purpose?" Mario asked.

"To paint them," Caravaggio told him.

Mario still wasn't clear about Caravaggio's plan. "Why not sketch them in the street? That way you don't have to bring them back to the studio," he stated.

Caravaggio kept walking and, like the very first day Mario saw him, his eyes scanned the street for faces. "Because I want to paint them *as they are*," he answered. "I want to get every detail exactly as it is."

"Paint them as they are?" Mario asked not sure what Caravaggio meant.

Caravaggio stopped. He looked directly into Mario's eyes. "You are looking at my Saint Peter here," he said grabbing hold of the middle-aged balding man who had the eyes of a convict. "This woman here with her toothless mouth closed like a rat is Judith's attendant as Judith cuts through Holofernes neck," he stated. "And you dear, *pisano*, will be my Holofernes," Caravaggio said pulling at the whiskers on Mario's face. "I need that beard to be longer. Grow it," he said.

He then led the motley crew down the street back to the Palazzo Madama.

Mario watched Caravaggio paint the decrepit and bitter faces of the homeless drinking wine to fight off the stink from the filthy unwashed *models*. Mario couldn't tell who smelled worse, the old men or the old woman but in the end he realized that Caravaggio wanted the smell. It drove him to paint, with accuracy, the grief etched on their faces. Caravaggio needed their wrinkles, sunburned skin, scars and remnants of disease.

Mario realized that Caravaggio was now onto something that was more than just extraordinary, it *was* revolutionary. He ignored the idle chatter between the models and watched as Caravaggio, who always painted quickly, do a sketch of the homeless people leaving in the goiters, blemishes and wounds.

Mario watched as Caravaggio posed his models in various positions but most importantly allowing them to be themselves as they played the saints. *He paints a convict as Saint Peter?*

Mario left the studio and sat outside in the courtyard lifting his face to the sun. He didn't know why it didn't occur to him to do what Caravaggio was doing? He didn't know why the notion of painting people off the street *as* they looked posing them as the great saints of the Church, strike him first? But then again, he thought, no one did that up until then.

Mario knew that Carracci had hired the same models from the street and yet when he painted them he idealized them. In fact, everyone had done that. They paid the homeless and posed them as the great saints but no one up until that morning that Mario was aware of, actually painted the models posing as Saint Peter and Saint Paul and all the great heroes of the bible exactly as the model looked, ragged, exhausted and worn.

Mario spent the rest of the day roaming the Artists Quarter aimlessly hoping to either distract himself from his envy or find inspiration. He was neither distracted nor inspired instead; he witnessed the beginning of something that would change the lives of many Romans for the following decade.

When he reached the Piazza Colonna Mario saw that the *sbirri*, working with the cavalieri, rounding up the homeless refuges which included young women, children and even grown men who did not have the proper papers.

Mario stood back watching the police stopping everyone they came across. Two *sbirri* approached him and asked him for his identity papers and Mario quickly showed them. They then moved on but before they did, they handed Mario a pamphlet. He quickly read it. The pamphlet was a decree by Pope

Clement VIII stating the new laws of Rome. One of which was that all refuges without proper papers as well as the homeless were banned from the city's streets and would be thrown into prison.

There would also be a new section of the city that would house all the prostitutes who had to immediately register with the police. This ghetto would be side by side with the Artists Quarter and would be called the *Ortaccio* from that day on.

As Mario walked through the lines of police and those being arrested, he saw a face in the crowd that he had nearly forgotten about. The face belonged to Captain Nunzio Pulzone.

Both men eyed one another across the piazza as if there were a bond between them, a bond not created from friendship but one of an adversarial nature.

Mario felt an uneasy surge of pride. He said boldly for the captain to hear, "This is *my* city."

The captain replied, "This is my city."

Mario allowed a wave of pride sweep over him. *This is my piazza. This is my Roma. I will kill again to assure my destiny.*

Mario could see that though Captain Pulzone didn't move and remained silent it was as if he could read Mario's proud and tumultuous thoughts.

These two men were caught in a moment of history. One was a police officer encountering violence and chaos with nothing more than primitive tools at his disposal. The Church was his only authority and its power was on the wane. Martin Luther and his *new* Church was encroaching on the Church's domain from the north and the Turks and their Moslem followers from the south.

The other man was an artist who had come to Rome to find his fame and his fortune and in two years all he had discovered about himself was that he was not the most gifted of his generation. Another painter his own age with the same world at his feet and the same element in his veins was the one who was on the precipice of all that he had imagined for himself.

Mario Minniti was facing an uncertain future with only two concrete truths he was sure of. This Captain Pulzone believed he had murdered the sculptor and was obsessed with bringing Mario to justice. And the other truth Mario was sure of was this: despite all his setbacks and all the acclaim that had passed by him and had landed squarely on Caravaggio, he wanted to believe he was a painter of importance.

So, Mario Minniti, new to Rome, stood at the edge of the piazza scared, uncertain and yet, in his heart of hearts, resolute. He took a deep breath and looked one more time up at the morning sun and said a prayer. The prayer was short but concise. "*Omnium Rerum Vicissitudo,*" he said to himself. *In Time, all things change.*

Siena

Fillide was horrified but no sound came out of her mouth when she opened it. She *knew* the moment she saw her father lying in the freshly fallen inch of snow that he was dead. Though the snow barely covered the ground, it gave the winter landscape a semblance of heaven to the otherwise frozen ground.

Fillide knelt at her father's body and crawled underneath it. It was her birthday and she had gone into the fields to find him to bring him home for an early dinner.

Now, she lay on the cold ground listening to the wind and the silence coming from his corpse. She curled up in a fetal position unable to cry. She allowed her father's body to protect her from the elements as he had protected her while he was alive and all Fillide could think of was where was God? And how had he allowed this to happen to her?

It was then that Fillide turned around and looked up at her father's face. His eyes were open and though his stare was lifeless, she felt as if he was still looking at her, lovingly. She knew that as he felt the pull of his heart tearing out of his chest, his last thoughts were probably of his daughter and how much he felt she was unusual and special.

Feeling this warmth even from the dead, gave Fillide the courage to crawl out from her father's body. She faced the ever closing sky and shouted "God be damned!" and then afraid of her own trembling voice, petrified that a bolt of lightening would fly from the sky and burn her alive, she rushed back to her home.

She raced over the gloomy hills in the murk of twilight as if pursued by wolves. She rushed passed dead trees and over the bare landscape pursed by invisible demons. When she saw the light from the hearth burning in the window of her small home, she burst through the open door finding her mother and brother at the dinner table.

Out of breath, she stopped. "Father is dead," she mumbled. Their eyes were suddenly wide open and her mother let out a scream of agony. At that moment Fillide felt instantly older and wiser than ever before. It also made her realize that she, not her frail mother, was now the head of the family.

It wasn't until the burial and the lowering of her father's coffin into the hard earth that Fillide fell to her knees and cried uncontrollably. "God had no right to take him from me!" she shouted at the aging priest who answered the young girl's rage with shock.

"God does not do bad things," the priest told her.

"Yes he does!" Fillide shouted at him trying to catch her breath between screams of grief. Her mother then led her away with little Silvio following behind them.

That night, while lying in bed listening to the echo of the priest's last words that her father was now in heaven, and hoping to find some comfort in them, her mother came to her.

"There's no hope for us here anymore," she said.

Fillide listened closely.

"You will be seeing your cousin Anna again because our only hope is Rome," her mother told her then kissed her goodnight, made the sign of the cross over her and then left her side.

Fillide slept deeply that night but when she did wake up in the dark, she realized that her father's death was the only way she would ever leave the provincial Siena. His death would help her achieve his dream for her.

Rome beckoned.

Part Two

CHAPTER FOURTEEN

Bright orange fires were burning in barrels lining the walls of San Silverstro throwing plumes of smoke into the night air. Fillide Melandroni and her cousin Anna Bianchini walked tentatively through the crowd holding one another's hands tightly. The spectacle amazed and bewildered them both as Fillide carried a can of her aunt's hot soup.

The young girls were delivering the soup to Fillide's mother who was ill in bed with a fever she had developed on the trip from Siena to Rome a short week earlier.

Fillide's mother had used the monies they acquired for their sale of the farm after Fillide's father died and bought a modest apartment in the Artists Quarter. It was the only place they could afford and it was only a few piazzas away from Anna and her family's modest apartment.

The two young girls, seventeen-year-old Anna and thirteen-year-old Fillide, were dressed in long drab shawls, their heads were not covered and both Anna's rich light colored hair and Fillide's black curls fell on their shoulders, highlighted by the fires.

They had planned to take a long but less crowded route to Fillide's home through the Via Del Corso but changed their minds at the last minute. Afraid that the hot soup would be too cold by the time they reached Cinzia, the young girls decided to take a detour down the Via Ripetta and walk past the Mausoleum of Augustus by the Tiber. They had no idea that they had entered the *Ortaccio*.

Since her first days in Rome, Fillide had been hypnotized by the city with its sights and smells as well as its noise and grandeur. She was however, at the very least, intimidated. She had never imagined a place as vast and populated as Rome.

Fillide was also petrified of its danger that seemed to lurk in every doorway and shadow. It was a loud and crass world where women were self-assured and boisterous and men predatory and venal. To her every man eyed her in ways she hadn't *felt* before and women eyed her with a dispassionate glare that mirrored competition that bordered on the extreme.

She spent most of her time indoors with her ill mother and she did visit Anna frequently enough and their walks back and forth from one another's apartments were journeys that soon became learning adventures.

On this night both young girls took a detour that landed them at a *sbirri* check-point. Mistaken to be prostitutes on the prowl when asked to show their identity papers, both Fillide and Anna were confused.

"Excuse?" Fillide said.

The *sbirri* officer toyed with her hair and then stuck his gloved finger in her cheek. Fillide pushed away his hand and he slapped her.

Since ignorance of the law was not proof of innocence both young girls were placed crying into a carriage which took them to the infamous Tor di Nona prison deep in the medieval section of ancient Rome. The concrete fortress stood beside the antique Colosseum.

Fillide and Anna, hugging one another in terror, were placed in a damp, stone cell with two dozen prostitutes of various ages. Though Anna was so upset she did nothing but cry, Fillide actually fought off her fears and gazed at the older women in the cell curious about why they were there. Her aunt had already told both Fillide and Anna that *bad women* lived in the *Garden of Evil* but Fillide didn't know *why* they were called bad women. They all had paint on their faces and wore revealing clothing that mainly exposed their breasts though some women wore shawls that were open in the back revealing their buttocks.

And all of them were fierce. Their eyes were on fire. They cursed the *sbirri* guards, one another and themselves for being *stupido* for being arrested.

None of the women pouted or whined. Fillide took note of this not knowing how to process the notion that these women were stronger than her mother. While Fillide thought this over, Anna knelt down in the cell clutching Fillide, petrified the two girls might be separated.

Fillide eyed one young woman with long dark brown hair that was combed up on her head, black eyebrows and feminine features. Her soft round face painted with light blue liner and whiskers on her upper lip jetting out like a cat. She smiled at Fillide and couldn't have been more than a few years older. Fillide smiled back.

"What are you doing in here?" the Cat Woman asked.

Fillide shrugged her shoulders. It was then that a *sbirri* guard stepped over to the cell, unlocked it and shouted "You" to the Cat Woman. He gestured that she leave the cell. She grabbed her shawl. "Little one. I have to go. My protector has come for me. You should find your own protector," she remarked.

Fillide frowned. *What does she mean?*

The Cat Woman left the cell and for the following few hours Fillide observed that several younger prettier women were allowed out of the cell by the *sbirri*.

Eventually Fillide had the courage to ask one of the younger *sbirri* guards why those particular women were allowed to leave the cell. "They have *patrons*," the guard abruptly told her.

It wasn't until near dawn when Fillide had fallen asleep and Anna was dozing off that a priest, tall, thin and with a scowl on his face, stared at the young girls through the cell bars. "They don't belong in there!" he shouted to everyone.

Moments later, Fillide found herself outside the prison with a tearful Anna facing a priest. "This is a wicked city. Return to Siena. Pray to Our Lord for help and guidance," he told both of them then escorted them both to their respective homes.

That night Fillide thought to herself that she had lost the soup but had gained a valuable lesson. It wasn't something she could share with anyone but it was a conjecture that grew on her. The young pretty women in the cell had protectors. The guard called them patrons. They were *men* who had come to their rescue, men who had kept them out of harm's way, men who came to the prison to rescue them in the middle of the night.

Two questions irked Fillide because she didn't know the answer to either one of them. *Who were these men and why did they rescue those women?*

Several weeks later Fillide returned to the *Ortaccio* this time, however, alone and she went earlier in the evening. She wore the same simple clothing and walked the same streets deeper in the isolated quarter. She also learned to look away from the *sbirri* and to hide her head in a hood making sure no one saw her eyes.

Fillide took walks into the *Garden of Evil* a few nights on her own, each time fear would overcome her, and she would race back to the apartment.

It took her several months of these secret treks into the world of prostitution edging closer to the women who lined the streets before she felt reassured that she wouldn't panic and run home.

Fillide eventually told Anna about her treks into the ghetto. The two young girls were leaving Mass at the San Maria del Popolo one Sunday morning where they had gone alone. Petra, Anna's mother was at Fillide's apartment with her own sister who was still ill and not doing well.

"I watch the men come and give the prettier ladies lira and scudi," Fillide confided to Anna. "In this dirty city people pay the pretty for their beauty, is what I surmise, dear cousin."

Anna was growing into a voluptuous young woman and even though she was older than Fillide her breasts were large for her age and her hips were more than prevalent on her otherwise slim figure. "My mother said we need lira soon or we will be tossed out of our home," Anna responded.

"I have so many questions. I want to know what it is that these women do for the lira?" Fillide asked. She was hoping her older cousin would be able to enlighten her.

Anna was quiet. She herself wasn't sure. "Whatever they do, I know it must be a sin," she replied. "Otherwise they wouldn't be sent away from the rest of the people in the city."

Fillide thought it over. "If it is a sin why are there so many men giving them lira? Are all those men sinners? And they are all laughing and smiling and drinking? If so, is sin such a terrible thing that it makes them all happy?" Fillide asked.

Anna shrugged. "If we can earn money there then I say let's go together," Anna told her. "Show me where you go and we will learn on our own,"

The two girls made a plan to take another trip to the ghetto that Saturday night but that Saturday afternoon Fillide's mother suddenly died.

Fillide stood at her mother's grave in the Santa Maria del Popolo cemetery with one hand clutching her brother's hand and the other clutching Anna's hand but she didn't cry. She didn't cry one tear for her mother. It wasn't because she didn't love her as much as she loved her father but Fillide knew that she was now on her own and all the tears in the world would have no effect on her fate. She had to give the gravedigger all the savings they had left in the world to pay for the burial.

Unlike the gentle and oddly introverted Silvio and even unlike Anna, Fillide didn't pray at the cemetery. Not a single Hail Mary or Our Father left her lips. *God has abandoned me.*

After the burial Petra, overwhelmed by her sister's death, took Fillide and Silvo into their small home over-looking the Piazza del Popolo. Fillide slept in the same bed as Anna and Silvo. Facing poverty and dread, Fillide and Anna talked one night sharing their concerns.

The following night both ladies wore their best smocks, told Petra that they were going to a dance at the Church in the Piazza Novona and instead went directly to the *Ortaccio.*

CHAPTER FIFTEEN

Fillide and Anna studied the prostitutes. They watched as some of them lined the streets while others stood in the windows in the apartments above the streets waving to the men who walked by down below.

Fillide and Anna would watch as the women called out common names like "Giovanni" and "Pietro" pretending to know the men who were strutting through the ghetto. These calls were made to sound as seductive as possible as some of the women would expose their breasts or their thighs making sucking motions with their lips enticing the men to walk over to them in particular before they chose another prostitute.

Fillide and Anna shared perplexed looks concerning this behavior easing their way to the main street where the women lined by the dozens. Fillide was surprised how timid most of the men behaved and surprised by how the women never truly approached the men but preferred to stand a distance away allowing their figures to look more alluring in the shadows from the fires in the barrels that burned along the street.

Besides the calling of names, insults were also being shouted. Some of the women, recognizing some of the men from previous evenings that they clearly did not like, shouted curses at them. The men did the same. They would shout out that the women in question were "ugly" and infected with disease. Mainly all of the curses were wishing the recipient of the verbal deluge a lifetime of boils, sores and syphilis.

Fillide and Anna moved cautiously having no idea what to expect but their interests always peaked when they would watch a single determined man approach a particular woman, hand her lira and the retreat with her to one of the upstairs apartments.

While they watched these events, some of the older women threw stones at Fillide and Anna trying to strike them in their faces shouting for them to "disappear from *my* corner." Fillide and Anna obliged but each time they were told to leave they found themselves further and further away from the main events of the ghetto.

A young woman emerged from one of the apartments on the dead end corner. "You two are pathetic," the young woman, dressed in a lilac smock with black

103

stockings, said sharply to them.

Fillide glanced up at her with no idea how to respond. She could tell that the tone in the woman's voice was more sympathetic than aggressive and certainly experienced in the ways of the *Ortaccio.*

"Little one, I've seen you here before. You have a friend with you tonight, do you? How sweet you both are," the young woman said.

Fillide and Anna watched in silence as the woman, her hair streaked with blond highlights, eyed the two young girls. She walked between them touching their hair, feeling their clothing and then pinching Anna's rump. Anna jumped and swatted away her hand. "Delicious," the young woman purred. "You are like a little devilish angel all ripe and ready for the picking," she said. Then she turned to Fillide. "But you? You have no breasts and no bottom yet that face is priceless. "Have you little ones any notion what you are doing?" she asked.

This time Fillide thought she would respond. "We need to earn lira," she said sharply.

The young woman laughed. She then put her fingers on Fillide's cheek and squeezed it. "Are you both virgins?"

"What concern of yours is that?" Fillide responded. Anna struggled to respond but then just nodded.

"I take that you both are. Good. We will ask extra lira," she said.

Fillide tried to get a clear glimpse of her face but the woman was covered in so much make-up it was as if she were wearing a mask revealing nothing but her eyes, and her eyes were gems. They shined like black coals.

"Follow me," she told them then walked up the stone steps to her apartment.

Fillide and Anna found themselves in a small apartment where women's under garments as well as carnival costumes strewn about the floor, the furniture and on hangers. The young woman quickly cleaned the clothing away. "My name is Prudenza. I used to be an actress in Napoli. Now, I am a whore in Rome. *Cay sera, sera,*" she said with a touch of melancholy in her voice. But she continued on. "You will find every third bitch in the ghetto is named Prudenza."

Fillide recognized Prudenza as the Cat Woman from the cell but she did not tell the woman that she had seen her before and was surprised the woman had not recognized her.

"Now," she said, stopping and focusing on the two young women. "I'll bring men here to you and for that I'll ask for a commission for each man I bring you," she told them both.

Fillide was still confused. "These men will pay us, *si*?" She asked.

"Oh yes, they will pay you," Prudenza stated.

"What do we do with these men that they will pay us?" she asked, suspiciously.

Prudenza stepped over to Fillide pulling up her smock and pulling down her cloth undergarments exposing her vagina where dark hair was just beginning to grow. Fillide pushed her hand away. "Bitch!"

Prudenza ignored her. "The men will stick their penises in your hole and for that you will charge them lira. If they want to stick it in other places, you will charge them even more lira. They will then squirt out their masculinity but don't allow them to do that inside you. Pull out their penises. If you get pregnant you will be at hell's door for the rest of your life," Prudenza told them. "So never work when you are fertile," she said, making it clear that they should be aware of their own bodies.

Anna looked ashen and was speechless.

"If this nonsense it true, explain to us, Prudenza, why do they want to stick their penises in our holes?" Fillide was unnerved by the prospect but wanted to know.

Prudenza faced the mirror and applied more make-up. "It feels good for them that's why. And it will feel good for you to some day," she stated.

"That is ridiculous," Fillide retorted.

"No, little one, it's natural. Even I like to fuck with my boyfriend Louis all the time," she said. She turned quickly around with make-up in hand. With her mask off Fillide could see how striking her features were. Prudenza was just about twenty and was in full bloom as a woman. "Now other things to know are these. They will also lick your breasts and they will want to stick their fingers in your bottoms," she told them.

Anna grimaced. "That's disgusting!"

"Men pay to do disgusting things. So, you should take the time to clean all your holes. Men like them to smell clean and the idea is to make them come back for you. Just you so that you can rely on them to pay to see you," Prudenza preached.

Fillide listened closely. Now she wanted to know *all* the details.

"Little darlings, make them pay for their lust and you will soon be rich," Prudenza told them with a wistful tone. "Now, some other men, mostly the older ones, will want to lick your holes also and I say that as long as it doesn't hurt, do what they want you to do," Prudenza said. "And if they ask you to lick their holes tell them that you will but triple the price."

"And what if *they* smell?" Anna asked.

"Oh, trust me, they will smell. So you tell them that you are not a toilet. If they get annoyed and arrogant you should cut their faces and split their noses!" she said sharply pulling a small knife from her skirt. "And always carry a blade in your belt," she told them. She then took a moment and sighed. "Oh, and always inspect the penis. If it is drooling that is a trait of syphilis so do not touch it! It will kill."

She then rushed to the door. "When I return I'll have two men with me. Little one, you wait in *that* room and you wait in *this* one," she said gleefully.

"We do not get to choose *them*?" Fillide asked.

Prudenza laughed.

It was then that Fillide told her about the night she and Anna spent in prison and how some prostitutes were let free and others were not.

"We'll discuss that another time," Prudenza told her. "But for now, I'm your *protector*," she then took both young women by the hand. "Follow me," she said.

Fillide and Anna followed Prudenza to a small cottage. Once inside, Prudenza lit a candle and quickly made room for the young women. "This used to be a con-vertie. A house for reformed whores," Prudenza told them. "But the reformed whores only stayed reformed for a few months and now they are whoring up at Milano. So, I bought this place cheap and I use it for occasions like this one. To help my own stock of young ladies earn their own living. You can use it to entertain your gentleman callers and I will only charge you a slight fee," she said. "Now wait here," she told them. "I will start you on your way and bring you some men to fuck with and acquire your lira," she told them.

Fillide sat on the rickety bed leaving the door slightly ajar looking at the small candle she had lit on the table. "Lorenzo Nardo tried putting his penis in my hole that one time back in the bar. It tickled when he licked my breasts," Anna confessed to her while standing nervously in the doorway.

"He tried it with me also," Fillide lied. The two young women giggled but then a silence came over them. They knew that their lives would never be the same from this night onward.

Moments later Prudenza re-entered the cottage with two young men.

Fillide didn't want to see his face but did glance at him and saw that he had thin black hair and a mustache. Fillide heard Prudenza shouting for him to hurry up

106

since he was just standing at the bed nervously. Fillide also hadn't moved from her spot near the bed and waited until he walked over to her and pulled his belt loose revealing his limp penis. "You should touch it, no?" he asked. He then jerked it himself caressing his own sack under the penis as he did.

Fillide did what he asked. She felt his penis grow hard and before she knew it, he pushed her down on her back and he was thrusting his penis into her. She heard herself scream but it was a muffled cry and when he was gone, Prudenza came into the room with a rag, cleaned up the splattering of blood and semen. "I have another one for you shortly," she stated.

Fillide fought off tears then sat up. "I curse him," she said to Prudenza.

"I curse all men but what the hell, my little one, we need the lira and they have it, don't they?" she said. She then patted Fillide's hair and knelt down besides her. "I was thinking of a name for you and you know what I decided? I believe Fillide is perfect. It conjures up the Renaissance and all the beloved courtesans of those days," Prudenza told her.

Fillide knew of the Renaissance from her father. She knew it was a golden time of great poets and painters. "Fillide," Prudenza said the name slowly. "Be proud of it."

"What is a courtesan?" Fillide asked.

Prudenza nodded. "A courtesan is a wench like us but one that has reached a great height. She is a live-in mistress to a wealthy man. She can move in and out of the highest of Roman society," Prudenza told her. "A *courtesan* can amass her own wealth. I know some that own their own homes and are invited to the best parties in the city. I know a courtesan who services a powerful cardinal right here in Rome," she said, her eyes lighting up. "I aspire to be just like her one day."

"How does one become of these great whores?" Fillide asked.

Prudenza spoke as if she herself had given it great thought. "One needs great beauty. Great charm. Sophistication. And also a young woman needs to be introduced to the right men who will be her protector," Prudenza answered.

"A woman needs a *protector*," she echoed her own thoughts.

Prudenza shifted her body weight toward the bed and in a moment of childish behavior, she nestled it on Fillide's lap. "I had my own young nobleman. His name was Vinenzo Venturi but he died in a duel last August," she said sadly. "Young men in Rome live only to fuck and fight," she replied.

She then sat up and gave Fillide a motherly kiss on the lips. "I will be your protector for now and we will share what many lira you will earn from your beauty and youth," she said then left the room.

Fillide knew she liked Prudenza but also thought about the idea of sharing her youth with this woman as something she wasn't very happy with. *You're using me but that will end in time.*

All evening one man after another visited Fillide in her room as Prudenza led them inside, took their lira and then left Fillide alone with them. Most of the men were young though older than Fillide. The young men were usually drunk and more physical while the older men were more patient with her and less demanding.

However, Fillide did all she could *not* to think of the men but to only think of the lira she was earning. Even the sex act itself, all new to her and as strange as it was oddly natural at the same time, was something she did not want to dwell on.

It was when the bells from Santa Maria del Popolo Church rang out that Prudenza handed Fillide and Anna their earnings for the night and rushed them out of the apartment directing them through an alley that led out of the ghetto. "You must be out of the ghetto by the time the church bell stops ringing or the *sbirri* will arrest you," she informed them.

By the time they reached home both Fillide and Anna were drained, they ached from thick penises in their vagina's and fingers pushed up their anuses and their make-up had been smeared. "I will never return to that place," Anna told her cousin but Fillide stayed silent. She had already counted the lira she had earned several times and she was delighted despite her physical pains.

When Petra, Anna's mother, was handed the lira from her daughter and niece she took it with a hushed silence. She only needed to glance at the two young girls to realize how they had earned the money. She smacked both girls in the face more to make a point than to cause pain. "Go to Mass and pray for your sins. Confess to the Almighty Father in hopes that He will forgive you," she told them then left the room.

Neither Anna nor Fillide went to Mass but in the following months to follow, they did return to the *Ortaccio.* By the following year, they had earned enough lira to rent their own apartment in the ghetto on the same street that Prudenza lived though they stopped using her to gather up the men. Prudenza wasn't pleased with their decision.

"So you young whores don't need Prudenza anymore, is that it?" she hissed at them watching both Fillide and Anna moving bits of furniture into their apartment on the ground floor of a red and brown two-story structure down the street from Prudenza's *Convertie.*

"We appreciate what you taught us, dear Prudenza," Fillide replied and continued working in the warm sun.

"And we pray for your happiness," Anna shot in.

Eventually Prudenza walked away muttering "I curse you with the evil eye. I pray you sow only boils and fever for all your troubles."

"No, harlot, I pray that boils cover your face and fever takes you to hell," Fillide shot back with venom. She felt relieved knowing that she was now prepared to live in the mean world of Rome's loathsome streets.

In the following weeks to come, Fillide and Anna registered their names as prostitutes with the *sbirri* and earned enough that they could support the apartment, continue to give Petra money every month and also buy the clothing and make-up a lady of the night would need.

The combination of the two young women standing together on the sidewalk in their lacy garments registered much delight in the men who came to the ghetto. Their youth and innocence garnered them much attention with some wealthy clients paying for the pleasure of both Anna and Fillide together.

The ladies charged their clients extra lira for these requests but the cousins refused to kiss or touch one another. The men usually were disappointed at first when their requests denied but they more often than not left the apartment completely satisfied.

Fillide's new life had a routine to it until one day her cousin Anna met and fell in love with a man who she serviced. Fillide was there the night he had come to the ghetto, laid his eyes upon her and was smitten.

Fillide noticed how he returned to see her several times a week and soon invited Anna to dinner with him. All Fillide could tell from looking at him was that he was much older and was loud with a flamboyant style about him.

Fillide also thought that he was probably like many men in Rome at that time, intelligent, violent and a drunk.

Anna never spoke of these qualities when she spoke of him. She would however, tell Fillide how he took her to the Tavern of the Wolf and the Tavern of the Tower showing Anna a part of Roman society she longed to experience. "His name is Onorio Longhi. He comes from a wealthy and well-connected family," Anna said with delight. "And he has introduced me to all of his friends," she continued. She then frowned, "But they are all artists and they are all poor."

"They are artists?" Fillide asked, excitedly.

"All they do is talk about what they are painting. I find it so dull. And he pays for their dinners. I say 'Onorio, they are only your friends because you feed them' and he laughs."

Fillide could see that Anna was truly fond of this man and she surmised that she probably dreamt that he would marry her someday. Fillide, wise beyond her years, surmised that he, much older than Anna, had found in Anna a delightful sexual companion and probably nothing else. Anna also had a bright spark to her personality and strength of character that must have also attracted him to her.

Fillide determined that this Onorio Longhi might one day ask Anna to become his courtesan and when the time came, he would present her with his notion. That would mean that Anna would be educated to the ways of society and Longhi would purchase an apartment for her.

Fillide was jealous of her cousin yet tried not to reveal that emotion. "I have been studying diction at the university," Fillide told her. She had not yet revealed that she spent some of her earnings on sitting in a class at Rome University two days a week.

Anna was confused. "Diction at the university? What on earth for?"

Fillide ignored her cousin's frown. "I want to improve myself. I have been studying poetry and proper speaking. The classes are expensive but I enjoy the books and the intelligent talk I hear in the classrooms," Fillide said, as she held up her head.

"Oh, I see, so soon you will be correcting my diction, is that how it will be?" Anna said without irony.

"Of course not cousin," Fillide chided her as if she would be doing just that.

Several days later Anna told Fillide that, she wanted her to meet Longhi. "I want him to meet the only family that I trust and love," she told her cousin.

So, Longhi invited Fillide along to dinner with them both. They had dinner in a small café not from the Piazza del Popolo.

"You impress me thoroughly, Fillide," Longhi told her. "Your demeanor, your bearing, is exquisite."

"She is taking classes at the university," Anna smirked.

Fillide smiled in her *recently* practiced lady-like manner.

110

"That is admirable," Longhi said.

Anna frowned.

Longhi continued. "I want to introduce you to the son of an ambassador who is a family friend. I smell his lust for you already!"

Fillide quickly interrupted him. "I want to meet an artist," she said sweetly. "I have no interest in a man just for lust's sake."

Longhi shrugged. "So be it. I will introduce you to an artist if that is what you crave. And we'll forgo the lust for the time being."

"But artists are so poor and dull," Anna exclaimed.

"Not at all," Fillide told her cousin.

Longhi took Fillide's hand and kissed it gently. "I have the perfect artist in mind. He is handsome and talented and a good friend."

So, in the early spring of 1595 Fillide Melandroni met the artist Mario Minniti. The supper was in the Tavern of the Wolf only a short distance away from Fillide and Anna Bianchini's apartment in the *Garden of Evil*.

Chapter Sixteen

Mario Minniti had secured his first significant commission of his career when Cardinal Del Monte introduced him to Cardinal Farnese.

The cardinal was in search of an artist to paint his portrait. Aging and yet still healthy he wanted to indulge himself by hiring a painter who he felt would capture his *true nature*. What Mario was told by Del Monte was that the cardinal saw in Mario's work a high romantic exposition and he knew immediately that Mario was the artist he had been seeking. The cardinal saw himself as emboding a true Renaissance soul and Mario was aware that the portrait should be composed of a purely idyllic sentiment.

Cardinal Farnese had a beautiful gallery at his residence near the Piazza Navona. Mario was overwhelmed when he went to meet the cardinal and continued to be elated when the cardinal presented him with a gold chain worth a hundred scudi as a gift.

Mario knew that his career was far from the success Caravaggio's was becoming but he was thrilled to be mentioned in a Roman newspaper in early March of that year along with his friend as well as Carracci.

The article mentioned Mario's commission along with Cardinal Pietro Aldobrandini's commissioning of Carracci to paint a mural in a chapel in the Vatican and of Caravaggio's painting an altarpiece for Monsignor Cerasi.

So, the night Onorio Longhi invited Mario to dinner at the Tavern of the Wolf to meet his whore's cousin was only hours after Mario had allowed the cardinal to view his portrait. The cardinal was more than pleased and Mario was in the best of spirits.

Dressed in a long flowing white shirt and tight fitting black trousers, Mario sat upstairs on the second floor of the tavern with Longhi, Anna and Fillide telling them about his early days in Rome. He told them how he would sit on the second floor smelling the perfume of the courtesans and glaring at their rich patrons with envy. Now he looked down on the first floor gloating at the glances from those men who sat at the table near the bar *looking up* at him. "All life runs in a circle and in time you will occupy every place on the curve of that circle," he said, enjoying the wisdom of the remark.

Mario spent the early part of the evening talking about his new success to the delight of Anna and Longhi. Fillide smiled demurely when she thought it appropriate and this infuriated Mario since he was longing for a night of sexually charged adulation and he couldn't tell if she was interested in him. He was taken with Fillide the moment he saw her at the table in her amber gloves that rested just below her elbows. She wore a flowing scarlet skirt with her bodice tightly laced up revealing her hourglass figure with gold trim surrounding the neckline of her garment exposing her neck, all punctuated by a pair of sparkling emerald earrings. Her hair, sensuous and dark, piled up on her head and yet, she allowed it to fall over her cheeks on the side of her face. It was a style Mario hadn't seen before and it delighted and mystified him at the same time. It was bold but also genuine.

He was also in awe of her bearing despite her youth yet, beyond that, it was Fillide's self-possession that intrigued him the most. She was still a child and yet she was clever enough to be silent around adults and listen. *In listening, is learning and eventually—knowledge.*

Mario was also impressed with how she only sipped her wine and ate gingerly unlike Anna who was drunk and sloppy. Longhi was also drunk and sloppy so he hardly noticed.

Eventually Mario and Fillide huddled closer at the table distancing themselves from the other couple. Longhi and Anna were necking at the table in between bites of their dinner and shared sips from their wine glasses.

"You hail from Siena?" Mario asked.

Fillide hesitated a moment before she answered. She did not like to reveal much about herself. She believed that the more she concealed the less vulnerable she'd be. "I was there, yes, but I prefer it here in Rome," she said making each word sound clear and without inflection. "I disliked dust and cows."

After telling Fillide all about himself leaving out the details of why he left Syracuse and the dead body he found beside him at the Tiber, Mario paid the bill for all four of them to Fillide's delight. He then took her by the hand leaving Anna and Longhi at the table with their lips locked together.

Once outside Fillide attached a dainty black shawl over her shoulders and allowed Mario to gaze into her dark eyes. "Where shall we travel now?" she asked demurely.

Mario felt rambunctious so he swept his arm around her shoulder and pressed her close to his chest. "We will journey to my studio at the Palazza Madama," he told her.

"The Palazza Madama?" she said, exasperated.

"Yes."

"It will cost you more lira if we go to your home instead of mine," Fillide stated directly. She wanted him to know that if this supper included sex he would have to pay for it.

"Of course it will cost me more," he smiled wanting her to know that he didn't care about money.

Once they were alone in his studio, Mario lit several candles allowing the room to be bathed in a soft light. He then opened a bottle of wine offering Fillide a glass but she refused it. He watched her closely realizing that she said very little but she examined *everything* with a keen eye.

He offered her a chair but before she sat in it, she looked over the canvases in the room which included not only his but Caravaggio's. "There are two painters living here, *si*?" she asked. "I notice that there are two distinct styles," she continued.

"You have studied art?" Mario asked with a smile.

Fillide now sat in the chair and shook her head. "Not formally but my father spoke about it to me all his life. He was a farmer and he loved the Renaissance and all the great painters. He read me Dante and described to me the paintings he saw once on his only trip to Rome when he was a boy," Fillide explained.

Mario saw how gently she sat in the chair and how vulnerable she was, like a little girl wearing her shoes with heels to make her taller, wearing her hair up to give her more stature and wearing a particular skirt and blouse with its padded shoulders.

"How old are you?" Mario asked.

"I am nineteen," Fillide lied.

Mario grinned. "You are sixteen winters if you are a day," he said waving her off.

Fillide became seductive. "Are you saying that you don't prefer young ladies?" she asked. He was unnerved by her sudden change in demeanor yet he was also excited by it. He sat in his own chair and eyed her suspiciously with a renewed respect. *She is a cortigiana and I should not forget that. Be on guard.*

Mario watched as Fillide stood up and slowly disrobed for him. She allowed her skirt to fall first and underneath she revealed her silk underthings. They were as white as her skirt and as perfumed. Once she was nude in front of him, she undid the pins in her hair. Her dark mass of brunette hair rolled down her shoulders. She shook her head and it fell in waves.

Though her breasts were petite, the rest of her figure was in perfect proportion. Mario was now more than just smitten he was astonished. It occurred to him that Fillide was a classical mixture of innocence and seduction all in the same young woman's frame and her entire deportment was self-possession. Fillide was something rare. She brought back memories of the classic courtesans of the medieval world.

Mario walked over to her and took her hand. He kissed it. She didn't respond. Instead, she stood motionless but her eyes spoke to him. They were vulnerable and inviting. Mario wasn't sure if it was sincere or a game she knew how to play? *Once again, I am expecting love from a cortigiana.*

And as if reading his mind, Fillide put her hands on his broad shoulders, reached up on her toes and kissed him gently on the lips. "Which bed is yours?" she asked as she pulled away.

Mario had to smile at himself. *This young woman is astonishing.*

Fillide spread the covers over Mario then pressed her naked body against his. She felt his hands rush over her bottom squeezing her closer to him fingering her vagina from the back and licking her breasts.

Fillide closed her eyes. She had yet to enjoy having intimate relations with strange men no matter how attractive they were and Mario Minniti was certainly handsome. She was taken in by his bluster but also his intelligence. When told that Anna was going to introduce her to him Fillide expected that he would be somewhat like Longhi and that disappointed her since she found him an educated but pathetic drunk who was squandering his families fortune and their political connections.

So, when she actually met Mario she could see that he was a man who had struggled. She found him to be a man with the odd combination of street wisdom and education. Fillide was also attracted to his swagger yet the fact that he was an artist thrilled her the most.

Fillide wanted to hide her passionate interest in art since she had no formal education on the matter. Even though she thought of herself as having no artistic talent of her own, she did thrive on the dream that one day she would live in a community of artists and spend days and nights speaking of the importance of great poetry, music and painting.

Fillide did take solitary walks through Rome examining the sculpture and murals that were open to the public. Each time she did, she reflected on her father and his passion for the meaning of art.

Fillide harbored the dream of one-day being a courtesan and moving freely in the world her father had imagined and the *inamorata* Prudenza explained to her that it was possible. However, Fillide didn't know how she would achieve that dream.

Fillide held Mario tightly while on her back with her arms wrapped around his shoulders allowing him to enter her and thrust forward. She reached down and fondled his penis and his sack as he moaned in delight. She had learned that men liked to be touched there and it made it easier for them to eject their semen.

She even allowed him to kiss her on the mouth tasting the remnants of the meal they had shared that lingered on both their lips as she closed her eyes. She buried her face in his neck under the mass of his own curly black hair pushing for him to have an orgasm so she could do what she really desired to do which was to speak of art and the life of the artist in Rome.

Mario made love to the vixen in his arms with relish. He enjoyed her sighs but was distracted by the thoughts that the harlot was pretending pleasure. *I am a painter and she is a love maker.*

When Mario achieved his climax he was immediately disappointed because he knew that she would no longer feign interest in him. This made him realize that he was more than smitten by the vixen. He was intrigued and possibly enamored.

Fillide and Mario lay nude in the bed in the candlelight. Mario had his hands on her waist wishing to be aroused again while Fillide leaned over his chest lifting herself up on her elbow. She played with his hair and both laughed at the joke she had made that they both shared similar physical attributes. They shared long brunette hair, the same complexion and eye color.

"We will be brother and sister," Fillide stated half wishing it were true. She truly *liked* Mario but couldn't see herself becoming passionate about him. He was too familiar to her. He was brotherly in his disposition despite his sexual longing for her.

On the other hand, Mario craved her and knew that she didn't feel that way about him. He could tell from *her* attitude. "You prefer me as your brother?" Mario asked.

"Yes! My older, handsome, keen brother!" Fillide giggled. She then found a basin of water, squatted in it and washed herself in front of him. *Men like to watch me do this and I don't know why?*

Mario was charmed when she behaved like a little girl. He noticed that she did allow herself moments of childishness. "And why am I your older brother?" he asked her.

Fillide twirled his curls with her fingers. "You can protect me and entertain me and educate me to the world of art and Roman society," she told him. She then smiled and looked up. "I cannot believe my senses that I'm in the Palazzo Madama," she exclaimed. "My father told me about seeing this place from the outside when he was a young boy. He marveled at what he called its *eloquence in stone* and here I am," she said proudly. She found a towel and dried herself.

"Your father sounds eloquent for a farmer."

Fillide smiled sadly. "He was."

Mario couldn't resist her lovely, brown eyes and the deer-like gaze she gave him when she allowed the pretense of her hard and dangerous profession to disappear in the candle lit room. "And here you are, my sweet," he told her. He pulled her to him, kissed her on the lips warmly and felt her nubile body respond but when they stopped kissing; she'd giggle and twirl his hair with sisterly playfulness.

It bruised Mario's poise to come to the realization that he and Fillide would not be as Longhi and Fillide's cousin Anna. That was not what Fillide wanted. Mario wasn't sure why that was, but it was instinctively clear to him in those moments in the glow of the candlelight.

Accepting that Fillide was *not* going to cry out her undying love for him, Mario gave in and played the part she wanted him to. He silently agreed to be her sibling and though staying naked in one another's arms, they spent the rest of the evening in his bed with him lecturing his *little sister* on the orb of art in Roman society.

"So what do you think of Giotto?" she asked him.

"I believe he is a respectable painter," he told her.

He then looked at Fillide. "When did *you* ever see a Giotto?"

"In Florence," she said proudly. "My father took me there many times when I was a child," she replied excited to share her experience with him. "We would spend all day walking through the streets looking at Michelangelo and Cimabue and then my father would find a café and we would order steak alla Florentina and drink Chinati wine," she continued. "And then we would discuss Dante!"

Mario was in awe not of her education but of her sincere enthusiasm for all she spoke about. "I have yet to visit Florence or Pisa or any of Toscana," he told her. He then looked up at the ceiling. He then recited a poem. "A thousand flowers, thousand fruits/ Set to weave this cheerful mixture/ This great product of creation/ Into an artistic garland/ Of his own . . ."

"Who composed that?" Fillide asked.

"The poet Comanini wrote those lines regarding Arcimboldo's paintings. I like to think that it also describes my canvases," Mario replied. He then searched Fillide's eyes and saw that she was enjoying everything he told her.

"Let's talk more of art and poems!" she begged.

"What would you like to discuss?" he asked.

Fillide was coy. "I would like some day to be famous."

"And for what skill would you like to be famous for?" he asked her teasingly as he gently squeezed her nipple.

Fillide reacted then just as gently pushed his hand away. "I don't paint nor do I compose poetry," she stated. "But I know that one day I will be famous though I don't know *what* for, as you so wisely ask," she told him. She then cuddled in his arms and closed her eyes. "Let's keep speaking of art," she said.

They continued speaking into the night, and near dawn Mario became aroused again and Fillide took his penis in her tiny fingers and masturbated him with a dispassionate sisterly care. Sleep was quickly overcoming him as she blew a kiss in his direction and said to him, "Did that feel wonderful for you my dear Mario?" And he felt as if she was his sister and watched her dress and in the odd light of early dawn, she left the room with a hushed *goodbye* picked up the lira he had left for her on the table as payment and closed door.

With her hair no longer up in pins and now flowing over her shoulders, Fillide walked passed the sleepy guards of the Palazzo Madama and searched for a carriage. The eastern sky was slowly changing from dark purple to blue and Fillide was pleased with herself. Even though she was invited to the Palazzo Madama as a paramour she had, nonetheless, been *invited*.

She walked along the deserted street proud of her introduction into Rome elite society. She allowed herself to smile and despite the hour; she felt a little fatigue but thought it best to walk to the nearest piazza where she was sure she would find a carriage station.

On the far end of the street, Captain Nunzio Pulzone was on his way alone to the early Mass at Santa Maria del Popolo when he couldn't believe his eyes. Walking towards him but on the other side of the cobbled stone street and the white washed walls was a woman of beauty, Fillide, and she was nothing less than a vision of loveliness.

He paused at first seeing her but then kept up his pace and pushed onward. He focused on her figure and her clothing. Her evening clothing was evidence that she was probably a young courtesan on her way home from a party. He knew he could stop her to check her papers. He knew he had every right to do that. But he didn't.

Captain Pulzone struck by Fillide's presence that morning as if he had seen an angel, a fallen angel in Satan's squadron. With raven hair and a delicate figure more tempting than any he had seen before, she was more than human at that moment.

He kept on moving as she walked towards him and he kept his eyes on her as she averted hers from his and all he could do was mutter—

Temptation never looked so alluring.

So, he didn't stop her and he didn't ask her for her papers because he was afraid. He was afraid that he would then know her address and that would mean he would know where to find her. And that would mean that he could hire her as a harlot and commit the mortal sin of adultery.

Nunzio *stopped* walking as Fillide *continued* walking. The captain watched her until she turned the corner and headed for the carriage stand at the fountain.

He wanted to chase after her. He wanted to rush to her and ask her name but instead he lowered his head and mumbled the prayer the "Our Father" in hopes that he would be forgiven for sinning even if it was just a thought. What he desired from that young woman was sinful and punishable by suffering in hell.

He tore her from his thoughts and rushed to Mass as the Church bells rang and by the time he was kneeling on the hard pew, he had already lowered his head in shame.

Fillide sighed with relief when she realized that the cavalieri captain had not followed her around the bend to the fountain. Though she had papers, that allowed her to work as a prostitute, she should not be seen outdoors at that hour and his harassment would have ruined a perfect evening. In meeting Mario Minniti, Fillide believed she was now introduced to that element of society that could help her achieve her goal of being a true courtesan.

Yet the evening proved successful for even more reasons than that one. Fillide was self-satisfied in that she handled this new excursion into the world of art and nobility with ease and grace.

Fillide was happy in the way she held herself. She knew she had made a conquest and in time, Mario and even Onorio Longhi, would lead her life down a path that could only benefit her.

Just as the sun tilted up and over the taller rooftops of Rome throwing light down on everything below, Fillide reached the carriage station at the fountain and directed the driver to take her home.

CHAPTER SEVENTEEN

In the following months, Fillide and her cousin Anna spent more time on the streets of the *Ortaccio* during the evenings and taking walks through the Artists Quarter during the daytime hours.

Fillide especially enjoyed spending afternoons with her newfound *brother* Mario, her cousin Anna and Longhi. Fillide absorbed everything Mario and Longhi explained to her about art being sold in the market place as well as taking them to private studios where she could watch painters do their work creating *magic* in front of her very eyes.

Anna, on the other hand, would spend all this time with her arms locked around Longhi's telling him how she wanted to marry and have children. Anna irritated Fillide. Fillide was beginning to find her cousin's obsession with Longhi a painful distraction from her own pursuit of the good life in Rome.

And the more time Mario spent with Fillide the more he became enthralled. When she was with him, she was no longer the pragmatic prostitute but the young lady whose excitement for *everything* in Rome including her own life made her more charming than any man or woman he had ever met. Everything interested Fillide. She was curious about every aspect of art and the inner workings of the people who created it. Mario enjoyed this immensely.

More than once Mario playfully announced his growing romantic infatuation with Fillide and every time he did so, she gently put her fingers to his lips and said "hush." She then hugged him affectionately and said. "It can never be."

"Why not?" he would always ask.

"Because you're my brother," she would always softly respond.

"But my heart aches?"

Fillide would then take his hand and kiss it. "If you lust for me that's fine, you know my address. You can come visit me. But I prefer these walks and talks we share. This means more to me than money and love," she announced.

Charmed, and also realizing that there was nothing more he could do to change her mind, he decided to surrender to her will.

On one particular walk, Anna and Longhi had an argument, which had to do with his traveling to Venice where Anna was certain he was involved with another woman. Mario and Fillide left Anna and Longhi and walked on their own.

They were walking along the Via dei Greci when Fillide saw a tall elderly man dressed in a dark green robe tending a garden on the side of his modest home. What made Fillide stop to look was that the garden was filled with oddly shaped and painted stones. The stones were red, blue, orange, yellow and green. There was also a white stone in one corner and a black stone in the other. There were no plants growing in the hard earth and one single olive tree was in the center of the small garden.

Fillide took Mario by the hand and led him to the elderly man. "Kind sir, why do you have only stones in your garden?" she asked him. The elderly man was clearly taken in by Fillide and invited her and Mario into his garden. Mario was also mystified by the rock garden and egarly inquired about it.

"Yes, is it a unique garden?" Fillide stated with her eyes beaming.

The elderly man smiled. "My name is Battista and yes, my garden is unusual. It is a *magic garden*," he replied.

"How long have you owned this garden?" Mario asked.

"I've lived here in this house with my wife for twenty years. She died two summers ago. I'm a poet and I have always seen God's face in nature. I've recognized his voice in language," Battista said.

Fillide responded to his gentleness. "You remind me of my father," she told him.

Battista bowed. "I'm honored," he told her.

In a few short moments Mario and Fillide found themselves standing in his garden listening intently to Battista. "My garden can reveal a soul's future," he said.

Mario smirked. "And how much will it cost to learn this future?" he asked.

Battista shook his head. "I do not charge those who I hold as uncommon souls," he replied as if the question was an indignity.

Mario was impressed with the response. Battista then took Fillide by the hand and placed her down on a marble, armless chair. "Sit here," he told her. Fillide followed his instructions. She found herself facing the garden.

"What do I do now?" she asked him with sincere curiosity.

Mario watched as Battista looked up at the sun, within a few moments Mario saw his head look down at the stones to see how the light fell upon the stones. "It is the sunlight that creates the magic, my dear," he replied. "I'll read the shadows on the stones to interpret your fate."

Mario was now also as intently interested as Fillide was. The stones numbered a dozen of all sizes and shapes, carefully placed in different locations around the garden. Some were in shadow and others were not.

"Make a wish," Battista told Fillide who faced the garden. She took a moment. "The wish is made!" she cheered.

Battista then stood out of the sunlight and read the shadows. Mario could see how the sunlight fell across certain stones and how it missed others entirely.

Battista took his time analyzing the invisible. Fillide watched him and smiled at Mario with anticipation. Battista then turned to Fillide and held out his hand. "Come to the center of the garden," he told her. She took his hand and walked to the center. Her body cast a shadow that reached to the far corner. Battista saw this and smiled. "Your fate is unusual in that you will achieve all you have hoped for," he told her.

Mario smirked. Battista saw but ignored him. Fillide was happy nonetheless. "But there's more," Battista told her. "You'll achieve all you hope for but on one condition," he stated.

"And what is that condition?" Fillide asked.

"The condition is that you must choose ambition over love and then your dreams will be fulfilled. This is true because you don't wish for love, my dear and you know that as well as I," he told her.

Fillide was saddened but not surprise. She looked at the garden. "You can tell this from the stones?"

Battista nodded. Mario handed Battista lira. "For your time and effort. Despite what you said to me before, you must be paid something for your talents. All of us should be paid for our talents," he said.

"You, too, are wise and engaging, kind sir." Battista bowed, picked up a small blue stone and handed it to Mario.

Mario then led Fillide out of the garden. "It's only magic," he told her. Fillide wasn't so sure.

"But he was so sincere, Mario. I have never dreamt of love. I've only dreamt of achieving a place in society," she said with a tinge of regret.

"I know. You desire fame and prestige."

"Yes," she told him.

"As I do and Caravaggio and as does most of Rome," he said. Mario then hugged her tightly handing the small blue stone Battista had handed him to her. "But that's beside the point, my dear, since you are already loved," he said.

Fillide's sadness slowly melted but instead of directing her feelings toward

Mario, she looked back at the garden. "I must remember that place. I'll return as often as I can. Perhaps I can change my fate?" she stated. She placed the stone in her pocket with affection.

Mario walked on with her. "You can change your fate only if you change what you desire," he stated.

Fillide clasped his hand. "You're my wise brother," she told him as they continued on their way.

❖

Fillide kept the promise she had made to herself and visited Battista's magic garden often taking Anna with her when she did. Fillide also made a small necklace with the stone having it ground down to a smooth and perfect surface.

When they were in the garden Battista read Anna's future and found it disturbing. He warned her of being caught in a web of resentment that would have horrible consequences. When pressed to explain Battista could only tell say that Anna was on a crossroads and she had to choose one path or another. If she choose the wrong road, her destiny would be tragic.

Battista apologized for his reading but Fillide took it as gospel warning Anna that her bitterness over Longhi's indifference to her desire for marriage could be what Battista had read in the rocks.

"That is all childish nonsense," Anna told Fillide as the two young women stood on the corner outside of their apartment smiling seductively at the men who were walking through the *Ortaccio*.

Fillide then stopped walking.

"What are you doing?" Anna asked.

Fillide placed the necklace made up of the small blue stone around Anna's neck. "For good luck."

Anna touched the stone. "It's beautiful. It's so smooth."

"Wear this and I will never lose you," Fillide told her then kissed her on the cheek.

Anna was wearing her black laced blouse and long dark blue skirt with a black mask. Her costume made more alluringly dramatic and seductive by her light brown hair and her blue eyes and now the blue stone even heightened the effect of her orbs. Fillide was also dressed in black lace and the two stood side by side when a carriage approached.

Carriages often entered the *Garden of Evil.* Inside were usually diplomats or wealthy merchants who did not want to be recognized. They would stop in front of a particular woman they desired and the door would open. The woman would enter the carriage and the carriage would then return to a discreet location either a tavern or a villa.

This carriage stopped in front of Fillide and Anna. Both of the women acted indifferent to the intrusion but then the drive spoke up. "He wants you," he said gesturing to Anna. Fillide was apprehensive. "Perhaps you should say 'no'?" she whispered to Anna.

Anna shook her head. "I haven't heard from my Longhi for two days now. What does he care who I fuck with?"

Fillide knew that she was upset with Longhi and resented his absences more and more. Fillide remembered what Battista had said about resentment. The driver quickly opened the carriage door and Anna jumped in. Anna didn't even wave goodbye.

Fillide watched the carriage quicken its pace as it left the ghetto.

Anna didn't return that night nor did she return the following morning. Fillide was worried but realized there was nothing she could do. However, the following night the carriage did return and this time the driver scowled at Fillide. "He wants *you.*"

"Where is my cousin Anna?" Fillide asked undeterred by the driver's demeaning tone.

The carriage door opened and the driver told her, "Step in."

Fillide was worried about her cousin so she stepped into the carriage.

When the carriage stopped on the pebble stoned back lawn of a large villa up in the northern section of the city near the villa Borghese Fillide left her seat with trepidation. Her concerns didn't end when a servant led her into the villa through a back entrance. Fillide made a mental note of small, white painted fountain of Cupid perched in the center, aiming his arrow into the air.

She followed the same servant through a candle lit hallway and then into a large room. In the center of the room stood a man wearing a black leather mask bent over a wooden post and beside him was a female servant barefoot and nude who was washing his back with sponges of soap and water. The light in the room was dim and Fillide stared into every shadow until she noticed another woman standing in the corner also barefoot and nude but wearing a black mask. The woman waved. "It's me, Anna," Anna told her.

Anna waved Fillide over to her and Fillide quickly complied. "What's happening here?" she asked.

Anna shook her head. "I don't rightly understand but our host is enjoying this. And so am I. Every time I strike him I think of Longhi!" she told Fillide. "We've been doing it like this since late last night. He's an important bishop at the Vatican but he won't tell me his name," she said. Fillide had immediately noticed that Anna was holding a riding crop in her hand.

Fillide watched as Anna walked over to the man tied and bent over the wooden post and then swung her riding crop at his back slashing flesh. He screamed in pain. Anna hit him again and again Fillide cringed.

She felt terror but also amazement at the medieval spectacle. Anna whipped the bishop on his bare back and buttocks for several minutes and while she did, Fillide watched the naked female servant bend under the wooden post, take the bishop's penis in her hands and ejaculate him.

When he had his orgasm, he shouted in ecstasy and then placed his head back down on the wooden post. Anna stepped over to Fillide and whispered to her. "That was his seventh squirt since last night. The man craves punishment. The harder I hit him the more he screams in joy," she announced then took Fillide by the hand and left the room with her.

As they walked out Fillide confided in Anna, "Be glad it's not you he wants to whip on the post," she said. That said, they were quickly inside the carriage and headed back to their apartment.

Once in the carriage Fillide turned to Anna. "Why did you send for me?" she asked.

"I didn't. *He* did," Anna replied. Anna then handed Fillide a small stack of lira. "What is this for?" Fillide asked.

"The bishop wanted you to witness his pleasure and was willing to pay for it. He's from a wealthy family," Anna told her. "He told me that he has seen me on our corner and has written love poems to me. He handed me one," she said pulling the poem from her pocket.

Fillide refused to look at the poem. "He's a bishop. This is dangerous," she stated.

Anna was resolute. "I'm not concerned whether he'd dangerous or not," she replied. "He told me that he would like to see me again next month," Anna said.

"Don't dare see that perverted man again," Fillide told her cousin but she knew Anna wouldn't listen.

"I'm not a mother nor am I a wife. I'm free to behave as I wish and damn God and all his angels," Anna said staring out the window.

Fillide took her hand and patted it. Anna sniffled then forced a proud smile and held Fillide's hand tightly. "We have come a long way since we were children back in Siena," she told her.

Fillide thought of her father lying dead in the snow. She thought of the rolling hills she used to see out from her window. She thought how they stretched monotonously into the horizon and she remembered how much she feared it would be the only view she would ever observe.

She then turned to the window and saw the Piazza del Popolo. She could hear voices from the young men and their women drinking, strolling and having conversation and agreed with a long silence that *yes* they had come to Rome and it was all for the good.

Several weeks passed and one late evening while she was up in the apartment with a man Fillide stepped to the window and saw the bishop's carriage pull up to Anna who was standing in the usual place along side the street. Fillide knew it was the bishop's carriage because she recognized the driver. Fillide watched Anna step into the carriage and then the carriage pulled away.

Like the last time, Anna did not return that evening nor did she return home the following day. This time what was different was that the carriage did not come for Fillide. And Anna did not return home that day or any of the following days of that week.

Fillide hired a carriage and tried to find the villa she had been to but since it was at night, she wasn't exactly sure where she had been.

She went searching for Longhi and found him in the Tavern of the Blackmore where he was with some men including Mario. Mario jumped up seeing how distraught Fillide was. Fillide quickly explained to both Mario and Longhi how Anna had been missing for nearly a week. She also told them about the bishop.

"This is a matter for the cavalieri only they would not be frightened of a bishop," Longhi told her. Fillide noticed both he and Mario stiffened. Mario took Fillide by the arm and pulled her away from the table.

"I'm sorry, dear Fillide, but I cannot accompany you to the cavalieri and neither can Onorio," he told her. "He has an imposing arrest record and an outstanding warrant," he told her. "No one else here knows this but I'm under suspicion for a murder," he continued.

Fillide was not surprised to hear this information and she was not comforted by it. She left the table and walked out into the street. Mario rushed after her and so did Longhi who had been drunk but the news was quickly sobering him up.

Once outside the noisy tavern Mario and Longhi confronted Fillide who felt suddenly lost and scared. "The cavalieri will not listen to a whore," Fillide said, turning to them. "And they won't care that another *cortigiana* has disappeared," she stated.

Longhi and Mario knew she was correct. "My family does know of a captain. I believe his name is Pulzone," he told her.

Mario stiffened upon hearing the name.

Longhi continued, "I'll have my father contact this Captain Pulzone immediately and see if the can arrange an appointment for you to speak with him," he told her. "The legend is that this captain is not one who can be corrupted nor does he bow so easily to the Vatican and its influence."

Mario held Fillide closely. "I'll go with you to the station house as far as I dare," he told her. *I cannot be seen by this Captain Pulzone.*

"You are wanted for a murder?" Fillide asked. *Is it possible someone so kind to me can be so brutal?*

Mario touched her cheek and smoothed down her hair. He was angry with himself for telling her the truth but he trusted Fillide more than anyone else since he had arrived in Rome. "One day I will tell you all you need to know," he said.

"What happened to Anna?" Fillide asked.

Mario shrugged. "This is Rome," was all he answered.

That evening Fillide went home alone and stood in the middle of the apartment. She and Anna had divided their apartment in two with Anna's possessions on one side and hers on the other believing her cousin would never return.

When done, Fillide knelt and bowed her head. She wanted to pray but nothing came to her. She felt the words she would mouth would fall on deaf ears so she stood up and opened the door once again allowing the flames from the barrels and the cries from whores and their men to fill the air. "Humanity is my God," she told herself.

CHAPTER EIGHTEEN

Dressed in modest clothing of blue silk skirt and a white blouse closed tightly at her neck with a light blue shawl over it, Fillide faced Captain Nunzio Pulzone at the cavalieri station in the Piazza dela Popolo. She eyed the Sergeant-At-Arms with the Roman face and was sure she had seen him roaming the *Ortaccio* sometime earlier in the year. They shared a discreet smile and then he looked away.

Fillide told her story to the captain giving him every aspect. He listened, patiently writing down the details in his notebook. Guisto was also in the room standing behind the captain. Fillide was scared but she did all she could to maintain her composure. She feared the police more than she feared the streets and its violence. The one night she spent in prison made a memorable impression on her.

"And this bishop, you can not recall his name?" Nunzio asked Fillide.

Fillide shook her head. "No, dear Captain, I cannot," she replied.

"Did you participate in this scenario?" Guisto asked.

Fillide again shook her head. "No, I did not. His perversion depended on me just witnessing his humiliation," she replied.

"Your youthful and angelic face combined with the carnal activities that she performed no doubt helped motivate his lechery for her," Nunzio told her.

Fillide thought back to that night in the villa. "Anna did say that he wrote her love poems."

"Love poems?" Nunzio asked.

"Yes. She told me that he would watch her from his carriage and write her love poems," she answered watching Nunzio and Guisto share a look.

Leaving Guisto to compile the formal complaint, Nunzio walked Fillide out of the office and into the blasting sunlight. They advanced down the street in silence for a few moments. Fillide was surprised how comfortable she was in the presence of the restrained police captain. "I do recall a small fountain in the garden. Cupid was perched in the middle," Fillide told him.

Nunzio nodded. "That tiny piece of information and what you stated about the love poems leads me to believe that the culprit is Bishop Romano," he whispered.

Fillide was encouraged.

"I've been to his villa on official business before. I know his garden and that fountain. And he has published a volume of poetry," he told her. "I will do what I can," Nunzio said knowing that there was *nothing* he could do other than make some inquiries.

They began walking again.

"You should mend your ways, my dear woman," he reprimanded her.

Fillide thought it best not to respond with more than the fact that she was already aware of—she had proper papers and worked only in the ghetto.

"I will contact you the moment I learn anything about your cousin. But I'm assuming that she left Rome and will probably reemerge in due time," he told her.

Fillide bowed to the captain. "You have been so kind and I'm grateful the way you have eased my fears about my dear Anna's fate," she told him then continued walking.

Nunzio knew Fillide was the woman he had seen that dawn. He knew the moment she stepped into his office that she was the angel of temptation because he had *yet* to relieve his mind of her image, and then there she was, sitting across from his desk. He could smell her perfume and it intoxicated him. He couldn't wash from his mind what it would feel like to touch the smoothness of her thighs.

Though she was wearing her raven hair up and did everything she could to create the appearance of a noblewoman he knew what she was and the idea of her sexual nature made him shudder. Her delicate features and her magnificent dark eyes demanded too much from him. *I could love this creature.*

That was why Nunzio asked Guisto to be in the room when he interviewed Fillide even though a *missing person* case was the least of their priorities. As Christ's teachings elaborate, this woman is an *occasion of sin,* he thought.

As Nunzio recorded Fillide's statement, her first hand account of the witnessed in the villa made him think of Bishop Romano. The captain had documented several complaints servants had filed in secrecy against the bishop. These complaints were unusual since the servants knew that the police hardly ever investigated any grievances filed toward powerful men in the church.

Nunzio turned to Fillide and couldn't help but smile.

Nunzio didn't move from the spot she parted from allowing himself to enjoy the lingering presence of her perfume.

Just as Fillide was about to turn the corner, Mario Minniti stepped out from a doorway and faced her. Fillide embraced him and then the two walked on away from Nunzio.

He was aghast at what he had seen. The world in Rome was getting smaller and its players seemingly tied together by some invisible string. *What is God's plan for me in this?*

Nunzio walked back into the office thinking that Mario Minniti and Fillide must have been lovers. He was pulled from his thoughts when Guisto handed him Fillide's statement that he had transcribed and now needed Nunzio's signature. "The missing harlot, what do you expect is her fate?" Guisto asked.

Nunzio sat at his desk and signed the statement. "I'm nearly certain that this Anna is dead. She was murdered, probably by accident, in a bizarre sexual ritual. I also suspect Bishop Ramono is our suspect," Nunzio replied. "Her body will wash up at the mouth of the Tiber months from now. Maybe perhaps years from now, if ever, or her body is buried in the hills north of the city and only her bones will emerge long after you and I are dust."

"And this Romano? Can we question him?" Guisto asked.

"The bishop is untouchable. He's in the Pope's inner circle," Nunzio stated.

The following week Fillide visited Battista. He offered her tea and the two of them sat in his magic garden. They spoke of all things Fillide was curious about but the one thing in particular that Battista wanted to discuss was her desire to be a courtesan.

He explained to her what he knew about courtesans and their lives during the Renaissance and how women in those days were cultured, refined and knew the ways of pleasuring and loving a man better than wives did.

This intrigued Fillide because the one thing she did not want for herself, or so she thought then, was to be a wife. She wanted luxury and fame and giggled like a little girl when she would tell this to Battista. "And you shall have all that," he told her. "It is written so in my garden."

Fillide believed him more than she believed the priests and bishops and the God they spoke for. "And what of my cousin Anna?" she would ask every so often.

Battista would only shake his head gravely. "Her soul was clouded by dreams only the fortunate can partake. She is sleeping in a world far from here."

Upon hearing those words, Fillide allowed her tears to swell up and she cried.

131

CHAPTER NINETEEN

Captain Nunzio Pulzone walked through what he called the *Ghetto of Sin* distracted by his anticipation. He could hardly contain himself knowing that he would soon be alone with the luscious Fillide.

He told his wife that he was working late on a kidnapping occurrence, left his home and then purchased a mask from a street artist selling his wares in the Piazza Navona. It was the head of a hawk painted dark green and brown. Once he reached the gates of the ghetto, he put on the mask allowing only his eyes to peer through.

He walked passed the fires as they threw elongated shadows across the whores' faces. He had Fillide's face etched in his memory. He moved among the hundreds of men, some also wearing various masks and harlequin disguises, as they sought out the whores they desired.

When Nunzio reached Fillide's address, he found her escorting a young man from her apartment. Nunzio hid in the shadows as he watched her converse with the young man then bid him a *farewell* and took her place at the curbside.

Seizing his opportunity, Nunzio advanced towards her. They were face to face when she acknowledged him. "Are you looking for companionship, *senor*?" she inquired, eyeing his mask. "You're a hawk looking to play?" she smiled.

Nunzio nodded in silence and Fillide made a sweeping motion toward her apartment. Nunzio waited for her to start and then he followed her up the stairs.

When they reached her room, she closed the door behind her. "Please sit down," she told him. She wearing a long black robe and with her hair flowing down the sides of her face, her eyes gleamed mysteriously in the candle lit room. "You can remove your mask," she told him.

Nunzio was flabbergasted. He was so excited by the notion of his tryst he had overlooked the fact that she would see his face eventually.

Seeing his hesitation, Fillide sat back. "Powerful men and important gentlemen such as yourself have been in this room, *senor*. You have nothing to fear. I am discreet."

"Powerful men have been in this room?" Nunzio asked aware that he was sounding as if he was conducting an interrogation.

"Yes," Fillide answered. "Men of the cloth, police men, magistrates and famous artists have shared their secret desires with me. You have nothing to fear from my lips. You only have pleasure to expect from them," she told him.

Nunzio slowly lifted his mask from his face, lowered it to his waist then bowed his head. Fillide was startled but she kept her composure. She then stood and took his hand in hers. "I never would have expected *you*, Captain Pulzone," she said, flustered. It was now her turn to bow.

Nunzio placed his mask on the night table then his hand on her chin and lifted it. Fillide lifted her head sharing her illuminating smile with him. "I'm flattered," she stated.

Nunzio fought every impulse to pull her towards him. "God sees my sin tonight," he stated.

Fillide led him to her bedroom and gently sat him down. She then disrobed modestly in the faint light. "God expects us to sin. That is why he gave us the sacrament of confession," she retorted.

"You have all the answers for someone so young," Nunzio responded.

Fillide allowed her robe to drop to her ankles. She was nude. Nunzio could see her petite yet firm breast inches away. He salivated yet there was something else that was gnawing at him. It was a realization that he all along assumed it was lust that drove him to Fillide but just then, he realized it was much more than that. *I can love this woman.*

Fillide stared into his eyes, read his thoughts, then lay on her back resting on her elbows. She stretched out on the mattress inviting him to ravish her.

Nunzio let his eyes slide over Fillide from the tips of her toes to her sultry lips. "I haven't stopped thinking about you since one morning, not long ago, when I saw you walking through the piazza from the ghetto," he whispered.

Fillide was taken aback by his sincerity. She tried not to have an interest in the faces of the men she slept with unless like Mario, she felt the need to share more of herself with them. This Captain Pulzone, this cavalieri who could arrest her at that very moment if he so desired to, was another exception to her rule. As much as she despised him for his secular authority she feared him for the same reason and the weakness she caused in him, startled her.

Fillide sat up. "If you sin with me tonight, will you find room in your heart to forgive *me*, captain?" she asked.

Nunzio lowered his head again.

"Then perhaps you should leave before I taint your pure soul," Fillide stated, shocked by the venom in her own voice.

Nunzio didn't move. "My soul is not pure. It's soured by the lust that burns for you. I don't feel this way for my wife and certainly not for any of the other whores who populate this ghetto, but only for you Fillide," he told her.

Fillide wasn't convinced but before she could respond, he held her tight in his arms and kissed her. Fillide was shaken but she didn't resist as Nunzio ran his hands over her hips and then slowly toward her thighs.

Fillide took hold of his right hand. She squeezed it tightly. "I'm not your *lust* angel, captain," she announced. "If you want me as your courtesan, then our business arrangement ends when you leave this room. However, if you so desire to visit me as your mistress, I'd be delighted," she stated.

"You are a gentle-looking woman made of stone and constructed with thunder," he said to her. "And you speak with such poise and pride."

"Pride is all I have, I'm naked," she grinned. Seeing that the veneer of his own revulsion was quickly fading, Fillide took a different tact. She took his hand and placed it around her hips and softly on her derriere. She then pushed her pelvis into his.

Fillide undid his belt. His trousers felt to the floor. She took hold of his hardening penis and then sat back on the bed. She took his penis in her mouth and performed fellatio on him.

Fillide fought her own insight into the police captian but she could sense from his closed eyes and clenched fist that he was fighting the sensations of pleasure with conjured visions of burning in hell.

By the time he was lying on top of Fillide and thrusting into her, she could see the wave of satisfaction rush over him knowing that the visions of hell must have evaporated and all that remained was the sound of his own moans of gratification.

When the sex act was completed, Fillide gave Nunzio more time alone with her than she would any other customer for several obvious reasons. She allowed him to cuddle her since that is what he wanted to do.

They lay in silence until Nunzio made his way out of her bed and dressed. "I must seem like a contemptuous fool to you," he told her.

"Fools are never as wise as you are," she responded as she put on her robe.

They put on their clothes in silence. Standing by the door, he took her in his arms. "My wife will smell your perfume on me and I do not care. God has probably sentenced me to fire and torture for all of eternity and I do not care," Nunzio told her. "I know you have many suitors but I can offer you much," he continued. "I can offer you protection," he stated.

Fillied put her fingers to his lips. "No," he replied. "I want none of that from you," she said.

Nunzio was baffled. "Then what do you want from me?" he asked her.

Fillide fell into his arms. She knew a man with his religious passion could love her body one moment then condemn her just as quickly the next. "I want only your friendship," she said.

Nunzio listened closely.

"And I want to learn what happened to my beloved cousin Anna," Fillide stated.

Nunzio gave her the look he would give anyone who came to him seeking answers.

"When I learn something, I'll tell you immediately," he stated.

Fillide thanked him with her smile. "And if you want my time on a more frequent basis I'll charge you a lower rate than any courtesan charges. I'll hopefully provide *you* a solace away from the harsh duties of your office," she said, hoping her speech didn't sound *too* practiced.

Nunzio fought to leave her. He turned and left and when he did Fillide sighed with relief. Though she found his dignity uplifting and the enormous air of confidence he brought into the room stirring, she also feared him more than any man she ever met.

Fillide knew that Captain Nunzio Pulzone was one of those deeply conflicted men who populated her world. They were men who truly believed in God and His strict laws but had enormous difficulty obeying them. Their faith was such a dynamic in their lives that was so real and present that it occupied the very marrow of their bones.

Men like that perplexed Fillide. There was no path around their faith and its brutal dominion. It was wiser to keep them at a distance and that is where she planned to keep Captain Pulzone.

Throwing his mask in a burning drum, Captain Pulzone walked through the ghetto as if he was walking on thin wisps of cloud. He felt a heated fountain flowing through him. He hadn't felt anything like it since he glanced at his first Carracci painting.

CHAPTER TWENTY

Mario and Caravaggio walked through the garden of the Palazzo Madama. As Mario listened to his friend speak, he couldn't take his eyes off of the yellow roses that bloomed majestically in the sunshine.

"The Vatican has summoned for a commission and I want you to assist me," Caravaggio stated.

Mario stopped walking. He took Caravaggio by the shoulder and griped it tightly. "You have been summoned to the Vatican?" he asked.

"Cardinal Aldobrandini has named me to paint his portrait," Caravaggio told him. "Cardinal Del Monte was made aware of the request this morning. I'm to appear at the Vatican tomorrow at noon with canvas in hand. And you are to assist me," he continued. "My *pisano*," he smiled.

Mario embraced his friend with vigor. "*You* have conquered Rome, my friend." He then made a tepid excuse and left Caravaggio to continue on his way. Mario found a bench in a solitary corner of the garden and sat.

Mario felt the shudder of failure drain his body once more. Despite the commissions he was recently receiving he knew quite well that he had yet to be as formally accepted into Rome's pantheon of intellectuals as Caravaggio had been and wondered if he would ever be accepted with the same fervor as his fellow painter?

The Vatican was everything Mario had expected. The decorations, the paintings on the walls and the monks who serviced his every need since the moment he arrived. As the monks scurried around them, Mario mixed Caravaggio's paints and prepared the canvas.

The two artists arrived at the Vatican early to explore on their own, and astounded by some of what they were able to see. Above the high altar of Saint Peter's Bascilica, Bernini's *baldachino* was a canopy raised on twisted columns toward the dome designed by Michelangelo. The Apostle's grave lay deep below the altar beneath the lighted mosaic of Christ.

The two men viewed everything with a breathless reaction. Caravaggio broke the silence. "We need to find the cardinal's quarters."

The artists walked quietly passed the Sistine Chapel, then passed the Secret Archives, the Vatican Apostolic Library and the Apostolic Palace to the Papal apartments. Finally, they were directed by a Swiss Guard to Cardinal Aldobrandini's private quarters.

Once inside they set up the easel and Mario prepared the paints. He took a moment and sighed in awe at the marble floor that enriched the warm sunlight as it drenched the opened-aired room.

When the cardinal eventually appeared, he was gracious to both men. "I will assume nothing about this process. I'm prepared for you to enlighten me about all you need," he announced. Mario found his demeanor light hearted and yet anything but foolish.

Caravaggio quickly introduced Mario to the cardinal and the cardinal recognized him as the model for *Bacchus*. Caravaggio then promptly instructed the cardinal how and where he wanted him to pose. The cardinal and Mario did exactly as Caravaggio instructed and for the following days and through the following week, Caravaggio sketched the cardinal's form then began the slow process of laying in the paints for the portrait.

Mario watched the cardinal with his balding head, bad complexion and unobtrusive manner and realized that the cardinal, like any other man of God's creation, was tormented by insecurities, doubts and concerns about not only his office but about his personal life. Mario watched realizing that the cardinal never made eye contact directly with him or with Caravaggio. Mario was tall and handsome and Caravaggio had a strong physical presence, but the cardinal, the man who wielded earthly power, had no recognizable physical presence at all.

However, the cardinal's power was obvious since he had to interrupt his sitting many times with spontaneous meetings including one when his uncle walked into the room. Both Caravaggio and Mario were stunned seeing the Pontiff in his shawl and slippers strutting into the room with his entourage of monks following behind him.

Pope Clement VIII, wearing his white beanie cap and white robes, barely acknowledged the two young men shooting them a fleeting glance as he completed a brisk and short conversation with Pietro. When satisfied with the results, he turned and left the room as if Mario and Caravaggio were nothing more than house pets.

During the entire time assisting Caravaggio, Mario never spoke unless he was addressed and when Caravaggio and the cardinal discussed the painting, ideas of art and the world of Rome and its mysterious ways, Mario knew that it wasn't his place to join the conversation. The experience humbled him but he refused to feel slighted. Instead, he would spend the time away from the work itself, walking through the Vatican grounds, examining the sculptures, the fountains and grottos enjoying their splendor.

His walks with Caravaggio back to the Palazzo Madama were invigorating since they enhanced Mario's determination to succeed despite the realistic fears that perhaps fate and the hand of God had passed him over when it came to Rome.

When they returned to the studio one evening, Mario suggested that he'd paint copies of Caravaggio's paintings which were becoming more and more popular. Copies would earn them *both* an income and could be easily sold in the market places for prices less expensive than the originals enabling all citizens of the city to own a "Caravaggio". Mario liked the idea and started painting the copies. Caravaggio also secured him an invitation to a small dinner party Cardinal Aldobrandini was having for him. Mario invited Fillide to accompany him knowing that it would cause a stir.

Cardinal Pietro Aldobrandini's dinner party was held in the section of Rome far from the Vatican in the Artists Quarters on the Piazza Santa Trinita allowing him the freedom to invite anyone he desired and his guest list was kept discreet.

The time he had spent working closely in the Vatican with his uncle had been exhausting. He had managed to secure his position with his uncle as a highly respected political advisor having created a network of powerful Roman businessmen as his allies. The growing merchant class did not want to see prostitution wiped out and Pietro's ability to convince Pope Clement to create a ghetto for whores was quietly applauded in the inner circles of Roman society.

The main task at hand for Pietro was that his uncle wanted to launch a turn of the century Jubilee in Rome. The planning and design of the Jubilee was arduous for Pietro however, all the energy he was applying towards it was slowly gaining results. It was high time for him to indulge his necessities.

This night was significant for Pietro on a personal level. So consequentially, he kept the dinner party a secret from his uncle as well as his cousin Cenzio. His guest list was comprised of twenty men of Rome's elite whom he could trust and their courtesans.

The party was held in a rented suite of rooms in a villa owned by Guilio Mancini who was a doctor, a poet and a playwright as well as a conversationalist, a philosopher and an art collector. He was also an eccentric and a good friend of Onorio Longhi's highly regarded family.

Mancini had auburn hair, a slight beard tinted with gray and blazing blue eyes that seared with astuteness. His animated behavior complimented his fiery temperament. But Mancini also had a hearty laugh, a large round face and a penchant for wearing bright colors and lavishing himself with jewelry, fine satins and multicolored vests. On this particular evening, he wore a royal blue silk vest created from one of the finest merchants in Arabia, Omar.

Mancini was not only a robustly figured man but he also wore his hair long and streaked with silver. His world revolved around Italian theatre and literature which kept him in touch with all the taverns and hence, courtesans. His family was of wealthy Roman stock and he had the dynamic knack of gaining people's trust. He was a politician in the best sense of the word.

Bishop Romano had introduced Pietro to Mancini and this night was the night Pietro would make his first foray into the world of the sensual. Though the celebration was, formally, for Pietro's announcement of having commissioned Caravaggio to paint his portrait, it was truly for Pietro to meet some of Rome's beautiful women, and he was not disappointed.

The bulk of the guests arrived on time and lounged in the garden where servants brought them trays of wine and food. The wines were from the Marche region including Verdicchio dei Casteill di Jesi and Piceno red. Also served were provolone cheese, grapes and thin slices of salami. However, despite the scrumptious food and wine it was Mario's arrival with Fillide on his arm that gained the most attention.

Mario was already drunk when he reached the party knowing full well that he was only invited because Caravaggio lobbied for him. He dressed as if his invitation was *his* debut to Rome's intellectual arena. He wore a striking white cloak with white trousers with midnight black vertical lines of cloth running up and down his sides. With full black hair falling on his shoulders, his tall stature and his broad shoulders, Mario Minniti was the male attraction of the evening despite Caravaggio being the painter they all wanted to meet.

In fact, it was Mario Minniti the model for Caravaggio's *Bacchus* as well as his most recent *Sick Bacchus,* who became the talk of the party. Yet, instead of this circumstance pleasing him, Mario was offended. Though some of the men in the room knew of his recent commissions through Cardinal Del Monte who was also in attendance, it was because Caravaggio had cast him as *Bacchus,* the *Boy with the Basket of Fruit* and *The Card Player* among others that Mario was now famous, and not as a painter.

As Caravaggio was consistently and respectfully questioned by all of those in attendance about his paintings and his newest interests as an artist, those being present would just smile at Mario telling him how wonderful he portrayed Caravaggio's characters.

"Patrons are now calling your painting *Sick Bacchus* more fascinating than your own infamous *Bacchus.* They prefer the *Bacchus* who is ill, dirty and foul," a bishop stated to Caravaggio. "How do you reply to that conviction?"

"Well, Rome herself is ill, dirty and foul, so I can only state the obvious on why it is preferred," he told him.

Those who listened and heard his reply reacted with controlled laughter glancing at Pietro who nodded in agreement.

"What inspired you to paint such a work?" Pietro asked him.

Caravaggio, feeling the wine's effects, waved broadly to Mario. "Mario! What inspired me to paint the *Sick Bacchus*? Can you recall?" he shouted.

Keeping his dignity Mario replied calmly. "I did!"

The room gave in with a collection of chuckles.

Mario continued. "I was ill and foul while posing, that is why that particular Bacchus is sick."

Now laughter filled the room as Mario fought hard not to sulk. One archbishop also flirted with him. The elderly man, with fey mannerisms, waved Mario over to his chair and patted the empty seat beside him for Mario to sit.

"My boy, I'm so pleased to make your acquaintance. In the *Bacchus* I was charmed by the definition in your shoulders and the manly grace of your arms," he said, squeezing Mario's biceps. Mario cringed quickly stood, and made the sign of the cross in the face of the archbishop to mock him. "God bless you," he said then retreated to Fillide leaving the archbishop stunned and embarrassed.

"Ass," Mario said under his breath to Fillide who he joined on the sofa.

After his encounter with the archbishop, during the early part of the evening Mario met the curious eyes of the other guests with a slight grin then looked away. However, one man who did focus on Mario eagerly returned the glare and that man was Bishop Romano.

As soon as Bishop Romano eyed Mario, Mario saw him and smirked. He enjoyed seeing the bishop clearly concerned that Mario, now a personality in Rome, might mention their encounter and not be concerned with the reaction to his own reputation. The bishop could hardly know that Mario had much to fear including Captain Pulzone who was also in attendance at the party and for most of the evening spent shared silent glances with Mario. Mario refused to be intimidated and once, catching the captain looking at him returned the stare. Neither man turned away. It was only Fillide that distracted the captain's attention.

Bishop Ramono spent most of the evening in the outskirts of the party eventually making up an excuse to depart early. Fillide also recognized Bishop Romano and quickly mentioned this to Mario. Seeing the bishop exiting out a backdoor, Mario, fueled by the wine, followed him into the garden.

"Bishop Romano!" Mario shouted when he was sure that both men were alone and out of the light glaring from the villa's open shuttered windows.

The bishop froze in his steps on the lawn. He turned to Mario. "Yes, Senior Minniti?" he asked.

Mario could see the bishop stiffen in the shadows. Edged on by false courage, Mario advanced so close to the bishop he could smell his breath. "Anna Biachini? You are familiar with this whore?" he asked.

"I do not *know* whores," the bishop replied.

Mario inched in closer. "In defiance of your collar you are a liar, *sire,*" he said.

The bishop wanted to respond but counseled himself not to.

"Are you forgetting *our* encounter, Bishop Romano? Because I have not, it's etched in my brain like famine and plague."

The bishop continued to maintain his silence.

Mario continued. "My companion for the evening was in your villa witnessing you cavorting in sinful activities with her beloved cousin Anna. My companion knows you were the last to see her cousin alive. So, again I ask, do you know this whore Anna?" he asked sternly.

The bishop gathered his breath. "Rome is filled with whores named Anna."

Mario grinned.

"And now I ask, how dare you question me?" he said with resolute determination.

Just then, both men heard the timber of a distinctive and authoritarian voice coming from the direction of the lit doorway. "The disappearance of Anna Biachini is *my* investigation, citizen," Nunzio stated.

Mario turned and saw the outline of the captain's face.

"I apologize, captain," he stated. He then bowed and quickly turned to the door but he had an impulse and stopped. He faced the captain. "We meet again, Captain Pulzone," he said knowing that it was better to admit to being a suspect in the captain's investigation of the dead sculptor than ignore it.

"We share a destiny," Nunzio told him.

"Do we, captain?" Mario asked.

"Yes. One that God has designed," Nunzio replied.

"I'm not aware of it? Will God inform me of this destiny?" Mario stated.

"But you *are* aware of it," Nunzio said.

Mario forced a smile. "You are speaking of the dead man at the Tiber?" Mario asked.

"I'm speaking of a homicide, yes," Nunzio replied.

Mario didn't want to tempt fate any longer. He bowed. "Have you found the murderer as of yet?" Mario asked.

"I have *found* him, *si*," Nunzio told him.

"Then Rome is safer this evening," Mario said. "When I can be of service in the future, please call on me. I live at the Palazzo Madama with Cardinal Del Monte," Mario stated wanting Pulzone to be aware of his newly established status.

"I was not aware of your new address," Nunzio stated. But tell me, please, your escort for the evening, how do you know her?" Nunzio asked, pretending ignorance.

"Fillide Melandroni is a *dear* friend," Mario answered. Though they were standing in the shadows, Mario could surmise that Nunzio already knew Fillide and that his inquiry went beyond the mere interest of an investigator.

Nunzio replied, "I thought so. Artists like yourself have many friends in the city. You must know then that I'm investigating her cousin's disappearance," he told Mario.

Mario then shifted the attention to the bishop. "Which leads us to Bishop Romano here?" Mario gestured to the bishop, then turned and quickly left the garden advancing into the light flowing from the shuttered door.

Alone with the bishop, Nunzio squared his shoulders and eyed him. "Again we meet, dear bishop and again I'm searching for a missing whore," Nunzio said sharply.

"I know nothing of this particular whore's disappearance," the bishop shot back.

Nunzio decided that he would have none of it. "Your influence will not protect you from me this time," Nunzio told him. "I will come with shovels and dig up your garden and if I find her body, you will hang," he continued knowingly driven by the thought of avenging Fillide's grief and relishing in her gratitude. He was that smitten.

The bishop could hear in his voice that the captain was being truthfully concerned in his threat. "What can a whore's disappearance mean to you, captain?" Bishop Romano asked.

Nunzio allowed the question to sink in. He was humiliated by even thinking that this bishop knew of his love for Fillide.

Taking the captain's silence as an opportunity to depart, the bishop backed out of the garden and headed for his carriage. Nunzio sighed. He shook his head at his own weakness but was quickly pleased with the visible effects of his authority. Yet he was disheartened by the notion that Mario Minniti was now moving in social circles that would make his desire to confess to the homicide less and less probable.

He returned to the dinning room to lavish his gaze on Fillide as a reward. He had no idea how he would deal with Bishop Romano knowing that it would be impossible to show up at his garden with shovels in hopes of finding a hallow grave. In fact, he knew better than anyone that Anna Bianchini would never be found dead or alive.

As the dinner party progressed, Mario spent most of his night basking in the residue of Caravaggio's glory behaving badly as he sat beside Cardinal Del Monte appreciating the cardinal's mention of his being a part of the contingent of artists at the Palazzo Madama. Again, Mario was quite aware, however, that he was only there because of Caravaggio's insistence that he be his model.

Mario was striking but Caravaggio easily took center stage, dressed in black waist pants with a black cloak over a gold vest. He had now grown a beard that gave him a slightly menacing appearance with his muscular physique, dark complexion and eyes black as coals. Many who met him compared him to a pugnacious Lucifer. His reputation was of a completely sexual man who lived in brothels but was also rumored to also be homosexual, seemed to fascinate the elite. They saw him as an *Infante Terrible* who they could live vicariously through while at the same time, commission to paint religious paintings for them. The irony of the situation did not elude them.

Though they honestly found his work too dark and brutal for their own tastes, they gained gratification by announcing how they had employed the *difficult Caravaggio* and then would place his commissioned paintings in their private chambers.

Despite the aura of having Caravaggio at the party and despite the conversation, which centered on the new wave of art that Caravaggio was creating, there was eager talk about the growing style of the same kind of art coming out of Belgium and the Netherlands.

Caravaggio professed his ignorance of this new wave of art but he did manage to make glib and off hand remarks about the mawkishness of Annable Carracci's *fraudulent work*. This didn't fare well with some people including Cardinal Aldobrandini and Cardinal Del Monte but Caravaggio, as usual, didn't care. The more he drank the more his venom grew.

Pietro soon tired of the talk of art when he was at last able to give his undivided attention to Fillide.

As soon as Fillide had entered the room the cardinal was captivated. Though the other women in the room were stunningly beautiful, dressed in saffron, magenta or cerulean colored shawls and skirts, Fillide wore a dramatic Spanish-style gown of peacock-blue taffeta with the skirt embroidered with threads-of-gold and a coral bracelet mounted in gold. The effect was dramatic but what caught the cardinal off guard was her vivacious smile and the distinct way her lips curled when she smiled.

At one moment before dinner, he took her by the hand escorting her to the small garden where in the dim torch light they stood in a narrow pathway created by tall plants and bushes, the cardinal addressed her in an informal conversation.

Fillide held her breath maintaining her composure despite her being in such close proximity to one of the most powerful men in Rome.

"You have attributes I never expected from a courtesan," she heard Pietro tell her with a sincerity she wasn't expecting. "Though the other women inside are of unquestionable beauty there is something so delightful in your aspect and so enthralling in your person," he said.

Fillide bowed and then studied Pietro. He was exactly as she had been told. Though not attractive, with his bad complexion, small features and nearly bald scalp, his eyes radiated with verve. He was also obviously gentle and though he wore his scarlet red cassock and the gold crucifix around his neck shined brightly in the torchlight distracting Fillide, she knew that despite the severity of his office

144

she immediately knew that she could enjoy his company. "I do not deserve such compliments, dear cardinal," she nearly whispered.

The cardinal was speechless. He was so close to what he had denied himself since his arrival in Rome. He was only inches from the courtesan he had fantasized about for all that time. Though he had made love to women back in Florence, mainly women married to wealthy merchants, that pleasure had been denied him for nearly two years now and he was anxious.

As he eyed Fillide he remembered all the long hours he had spent in his office working on Vatican business. He presided over draining meetings with the Pope and his bishops spending long hours discussing the Church's future in the new and turbulent world and he recalled all the nights in the chapel on his knees praying for his soul's salvation.

All of that sacrifice was only bearable because he would allow himself a reward but only when he felt it was safe to venture into the world of the flesh.

Pietro stepped over to Fillide. "I would like to secure some time alone with you," he said, his voice trembling with excitement.

"I would be delighted to share my hours with the cardinal," Fillide bowed.

Pietro could hardly contain himself. "Excellent! So, inform me, how would we make such an arrangement?" he asked like a little boy.

"You can send for me," she told him.

"As you can well imagine, I would like to keep this conversation and our future tryst circumspect," he told her feeling foolish with the statement but knowing it had to be made.

"It's how I exist," she responded. "All my dealings are circumspect."

"Again, excellent. Then, my dear, *tonight* we will consummate our arrangement," was all he said.

"I'm at your beckoning," she whispered, demurely.

The cardinal was beside himself and quickly, absentmindedly left Fillide in the garden quickly spouting, "I must attend to my other guests."

Alone in the glimmering light from the torches Fillide was also beside herself being quite aware of her accomplishments. She had achieved what all the women in the ghetto were seeking—a powerful patron with direct ties to the Vatican there were none more powerful than Cardinal Aldobrandini.

When she returned to the festive room where the guests were sharing gossip, food and wine, Fillide felt a sense of accomplishment. She was pleased with herself. She helped herself to some olives and savored the smell of tomato sauce and fried veal emanating from down the hallway from the kitchen area.

She searched the crowd scanning the room seeing Mario and Caravaggio immersed in a conversation with Cardinal Del Monte and several well-to-do merchants. She edged over to Mario. "Did you question the bishop about my cousin?" she asked softly. Mario pulled her aside. "Yes, I did. And before I could force my will on him, the dear Captain Pulzone took over the interrogation."

Fillide was well aware of the captain's presence as well as his searching glances. She knew when a man looked upon her with lust and this particular captain was obsessed. Fillide knew the best way to handle such lust was to remain at a distance. "This room is busy with an abundance of powerful men who could easily put me on the rack and torture my *body* to save my *soul* since I'm an *occasion of sin,*" Fillide stated.

Mario demurred. "It is your body that garnishes them attention. You have nothing to fear from these men."

Fillide took his hand. "I can only hope but hope is a disease. These men make me tremble. The cardinal has asked to see me this very evening," she stated then took a long turn around the room savoring the hushed attention she was recieving, delighted in her achievement; and that is when she saw *him* for the first time.

Ranuccio Tomassoni stood in the doorway having just entered the villa alone and unescorted dressed in an emerald cloak over a matching vest tinted with embroidered silver and sapphire trim. He wore a sword on his belt hanging in a silver and leather sheath. He wore his wavy blond curls long allowing it to caress the very tips of his shoulders. It brought an aura of sensuality that enriched his dark green eyes that glittered with gold specs. The combination gave him a mischievous persona.

He strutted into the room in brown leather boots with the bearing of a soldier and by the reception he received, it was clear that he was a favorite of all in attendance.

Fillide could not look at him. She fought not to focus her attention on his physical stature and his lovely face of porcelain skin and manly features. *Why does this man enchant me?*

He was embraced by the host, Mancini, and quickly introduced to Caravaggio and Mario Minniti, who it was clear, knew of him and held him in *low* esteem. Both

Mario and Caravaggio nearly groaned when he entered the room.

Fillide kept her distance allowing herself a glimpse at Rannucio from the other side of the dinning area aware of how the other courtesans in the room reacted to him. Fillide could see that he was their favorite just by the gleam in their eyes when formally introduced. Ranuccio Tomassoni was practiced at the art of discretion.

The guests were summoned into the dining room where Fillide sat with Mario Minniti on one side and Mancini to the other. Cardinal Aldobrandini said grace from his seat at the head of the table and then told his guests to "eat heartily." Fillide, famished, did eat but all through dinner, she and Ranuccio exchanged reticent yet flirtatious glances.

After hours of laughter, food and jovial playful banter, the evening drew to a close and while Fillide mingled with the remaining guests in the vestibule, Ranuccio made his formal introduction.

His boyish grin contradicted his masculine and firm voice. "I know you haven't been able to take your eyes off of me. So, for your pleasure, my carriage waits for us, my beauty," was all he said but it was enough. Fillide had talked and slept with hundreds of men in the few years she had been in Rome but it was the first time in her life she was startled by the likes of a man she had never seen before. It was the first time in her life she felt a pang of emotion that could only be construed as an emotional craving.

Before she could even respond, an emissary from Cardinal Aldobrandini took her hand and escorted her out of the room. Fillide sensed that all eyes were on her. Caravaggio, Mario Minniti, Cardinal Del Monte and most of all, Cardinal Aldobrandini himself were watching her taken to a back room.

The last face she saw was Ranuccio's smile as it faded into a blur mixed with all the other faces that came between them.

CHAPTER TWENTY-ONE

The next months flew by as Fillide was paid handsomely for her dalliances with the upper echelon of Rome. She could now state that her clients included Cardinal Aldobrandini and Cavalieri Captain Pulzano to name a few of the men who sent private carriages to her door.

Fillide was not aware at the time but other men including Mancini and some of his wealthy friends at the dinner party grew interested in her that evening and were requesting her sexual favors.

Fillide divided her earnings into two parts. A majority of it was put away as savings. She took out an account in the local bank and each night before she slept she glanced through the bankbook and it eased her trepidation's of being alone in Rome as she had been since Anna's disappearance. She also put a portion away for clothing noting that she needed to make an impression as a courtesan as wealthy men liked to see women in fine things.

Besides her money and growing reputation in the ranks of the nobility, Fillide was also keeping her eyes on the mirror. She knew that she was not as beautiful as some of her competition and that she didn't possess grand breasts, stature or bulky hips as many men preferred. Her allure was her angelic face, the creamy olive complexion, the soft brown eyes and the raven-colored hair.

Fillide was yet eighteen years of age but she still did all she could to slow down the aging process applying creams daily to her pores. When she took a day off, which was always Sunday, she would spend time in her bath paying careful attention to her body making sure the curves remained curves and not unwieldy angles and that her face, now smooth and without crease or wrinkle, held fast. She did by fasting and not drinking much wine as well as staying out of the sun.

She also taught herself the discipline of banking and since many of her clients were merchants, they easily volunteered what they believed to be prudent investments.

When all this was completed, Fillide would then walk the streets of the ghetto alone searching for a new home. She was saving her money to purchase a house and there were only a handful that attracted her. There was one in particular, which faced the street and had a large porch at the front doorstep looking out onto the street with a modest piazza below not far from the Mausoleum of Augustus.

Fillide had already inquired about the house and learned that the owner was an absentee landlord. She also learned through her investigation that he would sell for the right price but she also knew that as a prostitute she could only purchase property if she had a certificate of exemption from the city council. Fillide hoped one day that she would acquire such a certificate and live on that hill. She made more inquires and found out that the landlord was a local merchant and had many friends in the city including Mancini and Longhi. When the time was right, Fillide would ask those men for a favor and approach the landlord and the city council.

While she walked the streets, shading her face from the sun, she would try to conjure her future but so much was happening so quickly, she couldn't see past the following week. Then the idea of children and a family would creep into her thoughts.

Fillide had no apparent longing for her own family but she always seemed to imagine herself with a child, a husband, how odd she thought. The only fantasy she pursued was the one where she lived a life of influence and independence. She visualized herself as part of the intellectual and insular upper echelon of the great city.

Though she could not recall every structure in Florence, she knew that it would be impossible to compare Rome to *any* city she had ever visited. Though, the sunlight in Florence was spectacular and though the air in Pisa nearly sweet, the very essence of Rome was that of strength and brute force. Its structures beckoned the notions of practicality over meaning and finesse over impartiality. It was a city as impersonal as it was astounding.

Fillide walked studying the faces as she made her way through the city but one face continued to invade her private thoughts even though he wasn't even present to her and that face belonged to Ranuccio Tomassoni.

Fillide saw Cardinal Pietro Aldobrandini several times riding silently in his carriage as it took her to different locations around Rome each time he sent for her. When she was picked up, she always wore a mask to hide her features so that she could maintain her identity. Their interludes were always brief and tempered by heated sex where he straddled her. There was some small talk but the cardinal never divested much about his affairs and Fillide kept the same silences. The cardinal also seemed quite pleased with Fillide and never indulged in religious discussions or moral lectures. He paid her well and he knew he was paying for her discretion. Fillide knew that he was a man who had many things weighing on his mind, more important than the fate of his own spiritual being.

Sometimes she surprised the cardinal. "What do you think of Dante?" she asked him innocently enough one evening as they were both dressing.

"Dante? Excellent choice. He may one day be the *voice* of our Church," he told Fillide. "Though he will never be named one of its saints," he continued. The cardinal then stopped. "What do you know of Dante?" he inquired.

"I've read his *Inferno*. I've read his *Paradiso*," she exclaimed as she applied some lotion to her leg. The cardinal couldn't take his eyes off of her legs nor off of her naked crotch area where her dark pubic hairs sprouted. It would be difficult for him to continue an intellectual conversation with Fillide while eyeing the sensuous line of her leg and foot. "You continue to amaze me, Fillide," he smiled.

Captain Pulzone was an entirely different matter. Fillide knew he was in love with her so she tempered their meetings with small talk and little gifts designed to reveal genuine affection. The captain continued to see Fillide at her apartment in the ghetto always at an appointed hour and most usually during dusk. He stopped wearing a mask but he found an alley that cut behind Fillide's street and entered her apartment through a side entrance.

The captain lingered longer than she preferred but sometimes she wondered to herself how he must be in such conflict believing in an unforgiving God and committing adultery with a whore. He sometimes spoke of his son and when he did, he seemed elated. Fillide continued to be apprehensive in his company but accepted his presence in her life as one of the many dangers her lifestyle had to embrace.

When it came to Ranuccio, Fillide was distressed. Though she had yet to cross paths with him since the dinner party, she realized that she had probably seen him before but had never taken notice. She knew of his family carriage with the family's military crest boldly present on the door.

There was a street fight only months earlier and Fillide recalled the men on the carriage, probably Ranuccio's brothers, and how they were drunk and how they thrust their swords at a small mob of homeless drifters from the Spanish army.

Fillide did not know what to make of the handsome blond, the youngest of the men on the carriage, gleefully thrusting his sword, shouting insults at the men he was stabbing.

One night while she was returning home walking through the crowded streets Fillide heard screams coming from one of the houses. It was a small structure where she knew several young whores lived together cramped in two rooms on the first floor.

Fillide saw a gang of disorderly young men rushing to the door smashing the shutters. They were throwing stones and carrying a torch throwing excrement at the young whores who were running from them in panic.

Filliled had seen this sort of turmoil played out in the ghetto many times before. Young men, who came to the streets only to taunt the whores or, having little or no money and still expecting sexual favors, when turned down, going on a vicious rampage.

"*Deturpatio,*" Fillide muttered to herself knowing the crime had its own name on Rome's mean streets. She turned the corner and headed to the safety of her own home.

Heading up the pathway to her front door, and hearing the screams of the whores under attack and the shouts from the *sbirri* police who were just arriving on the scene, Fillide wanted nothing more than to go inside and lock her own door.

Only a few feet from her own shutters and feeling secure that she was now at her own place of refuge: Fillide saw a shadow rushing towards her from behind her left shoulder. A tall woman with blazing red dyed hair had just hurried out of the shadows from a nearby outhouse.

Fillide lowered her head. She saw the glittering edge of a knife pass by her left eye. Fillide swung her body around. She could see her attacker fall to her knees by the thrust of her own attack gone awry.

Fillide stood her ground watching her attacker who was now on all fours struggling to find some balance after her bungled attack. "Piss on your boils and I pray to God that you die of syphilis," she hissed at Fillide with a horrendous bellow that came from her inner depths.

She was shocked when she recognized her attacker. It was the Cat Woman, Prudenzia from Naples, and she looked as if she was decaying from within. Fillide had seen that look on some of the women in the ghetto before. The same dreaded disease she wished on Fillide caused the swollen glands and boils on her own face. The woman had covered them with layers of bright make-up only to make her look even more hideous.

Fillide had no idea why the woman was attacking her but then again, there was so much that went on in the ghetto that had no rhyme or reason.

She readied herself for another attack reaching into her inner pocket and pulling out a small knife with a blade sharp enough to slice a strand of hair in two. She was once given the advice to carry a blade and she took the advice to heart.

The Cat Woman, now on two feet, not only looked ill but also her face was distorted and she slurred her words. She was drunk as well as feverish resembling a possessed zombie from the netherworld referred to as *the living dead.*

The Cat Woman was holding a knife and rushed across the pathway toward Fillide aiming its pointed tip at Fillide's face. "You owe me scudi and lira!" she screamed.

Again, Fillide dodged the attack but this time as the drunken Cat Woman flew by her Fillide reached out her own blade slicing her face across her cheek from nose to ear. Blood erupted from the wound but the Cat Woman was oblivious to it. She let out another scream as if replenished by the attack. She turned and rushed Fillide again but this time as she pointed her blade at Fillide and could not keep herself on target. She advanced haphazardly with her eyes open in aghast spitting out blood.

The second time Fillide had a slow moving target. She dodged her attacker's advance by keeping her distance but remained in arm's length. As the Cat Woman staggered passed her, she jabbed her neck directly under her chin. The wound was not as deep as it was bloody. It cut through the soft skin freeing streams of blood.

Fillide stepped back preparing for yet another onslaught. She could see that though the loss of blood had weakened the Cat Woman it didn't hinder her resolve. She forced herself forward and rushed Fillide again but this time she tripped on her long skirt and fell to the pavement smashing her face. She groaned for a moment and then was silent lying face down.

Fillide sighed in relief. A crowd had gathered around her made up mostly of other whores and some of their clients. In their drunken state, they were ecstatic about the visceral entertainment.

The crowds cheering on Fillide also caught the attention of several *sbirri.* They summoned more of their officers quickly surrounding Fillide and forcibly grabbing her by her long hair and shoulders.

"Let go of me!" Fillide cried out but to no avail. A police carriage quickly appeared and Fillide was literally tossed into it. She put her arms up to protect herself when she hit the metal bottom of the carriage.

Splattered by the Cat Woman's blood, Fillide struggled to the carriage's only bench and sat up shouting out the barred window professing her innocence. She knew it didn't matter to the *sbirri* who started the fight. She was nothing more than a harlot who was in possession of a knife and though she was defending herself, she could be charged with murder if the Cat Woman died. The penalty for a homicide in Rome committed by someone of her class was death by hanging.

Fillide trembled as she was thrust into a dark cell of the Tor di Nona prison along with a dozen other whores who had been arrested the same evening or previous nights and were waiting for a judge to hear their cases.

The putrid smell of urine and the rotting stink of disease made Fillide vomit more than once. More than these outrageous inflections, she felt a humiliation that went beyond words.

"Hey, bitch, who told you you could vomit in our cell?" a brawny female voice asked. Before Fillide could react, grimy hands were throttling her from all directions. Fillide raised her arms in defense but the women in the cell were bigger and heavier than she was. They forced her head down to the cell's disgusting dirty floor kicking her unmercifully, tearing her clothing, biting her arms and scratching her face.

Fillide felt a rib crack and she screamed in pain. The scream was so deafening it alerted the guards who waited for reinforcements then entered the cell and pulled the battered Fillide to safety.

She was still a lady of the night and her plight garnered little sympathy. Her only consolation was that she was placed in a cell alone and no medical aide was sought for her.

Convinced that if she fell asleep she could be murdered, she fought to stay awake all night. Just before dawn, with the new shift of guards, she managed to crawl out of her rotting bunk and with a broken voice pleaded for the opportunity to send a message to a patron.

A bribe had to be promised and paid in full when the patron appeared so she knew she could only make one request. She dictated an address to the guard who wrote it down and then disappeared.

She crawled back to her bunk. Her cracked rib gave her so much pain that she could hardly breathe and she certainly couldn't stand erect.

She lay in bed refusing to pray, certain that God had abandoned her years ago. To Fillide, hypocrisy was the most despicable sign of weakness so to her, there was no use in praying. On a more realistic level, she knew that if her patron didn't arrive to save her, she would be quickly sent to the main prison outside of Rome where she would be sentenced, and if not hanged, she would rot in a cell for years.

She lay in the bunk with labored breath thinking how far she had come in one sense but still, she was nothing more than a street whore. She only hoped that the man she had sent for would respond to her request and rescue her from her dire predicament.

She closed her eyes concentrating on his face.

CHAPTER TWENTY-TWO

Not aware if it were day or night, Fillide heard masculine voices shouting and they woke her up. She opened her eyes, looked through the bars of her cell and saw a righteous *guardian angel* berating the wicked *sbirri*. "How dare you treat Fillide Melandroni like this! Do you know who you will have to answer to *now*?" He lambasted the guards.

She couldn't move without pain jetting outwardly from her ribs but she still stretched her neck to see Ranuccio Tomassoni's blond hair and blue eyes that were, at that moment, burning with a white heated anger. He was dressed in cobalt blue from head to his brown leather boots and wore a silver necklace with Saint Christopher engraved on it. He stopped yelling at the guards then placed his face up against the bars. "My dear one, my attendants will wrap you in a blanket and take you to my villa," he said to her softly.

She pursed her lips to form a smile. *I am saved.*

Ranuccio kept his word and allowed Fillide to mend in his villa in a spacious room overlooking his tennis court. Fillide didn't bother counting the days to her full recovery but she did count the days she actually *saw* Ranuccio. Immediately after he rescued her from the prison, he left for a long planned trip with his brothers to Milano for business. They were hired to train a small contingent of the city's army. So Fillide had the run of the house including the servants and she stayed just long enough to be able to walk again and in a few weeks she felt healthy enough to return to her apartment.

In her time at Ranuccio's villa she learned that the Cat Woman did not die of her wounds but was so ill from her venereal disease that she was hospitalized and probably would expire sooner than later. Fillide also received a gift of flowers every morning from Ranuccio that the servants placed in her bedroom when they opened the windows to allow in the glorious sunlight.

It took time but she soon recovered and began to pamper herself. She dreaded the thought of returning to the ghetto yet she knew that she had no choice. It was how she made her living.

Then one morning when she awoke, ready to be on her way back home, one of the servants directed her to a storage room and she was amazed to see her personal things neatly wrapped. Before she could react, the servant told her "The master has ordered all of your belongings be brought here to his villa," then they walked away.

The days passed and though the flowers continued to arrive Ranuccio did not. She felt well enough to wander the villa and learned much about the Tomassoni family. Through the artwork that adorned the villa as well as the coat of arms and various plaques that decorated the walls, she surmised that the Tomassoni's boasted a long tradition of military service for Rome and won many honors in the long wars of religion.

There were portraits of Lucantonio, Ranuccio's father who had taken part in the French wars and a great uncle Lodovico who had for many years been in the service of the Farnese family.

Ranuccio had several brothers, all having served in the military. They included Alessandro, Octavio, Giovan and Mario and their faces, painted and framed lined the lobby entrance into the villa. From his portrait, which hung last, Fillide could calculate that Ranuccio was the youngest of the brethren.

She also learned that Ranuccio's villa was only a few streets away from the family's main residence in the Piazza di San Lorenzo in Lucina, which was lengthy yet constricted square overlooking the campanile of San Lorenzo.

One night while she was dining alone by candlelight in the garden, she heard a horse gallop to the back of the villa stopping at the small stable. She then heard boots on gravel as someone made their way toward her.

She was happy to see Ranuccio walk into the garden. She could see his features slowly come to life in candlelight. He walked over to her and bowed then lifted his head and laughed. Feeling oddly timid, she smiled. "I'm filthy from my ride from Milano," he said without excuse. "I'm going to bathe. Wait for me in your boudoir," he told her then turned his back stripping off his clothing with no shame shouting for his servants to quickly ready his bath.

She put down her spoon and pushed aside her soup surprised at herself for being so nervous. She had no idea what had come over her. She obeyed Ranuccio's request making her way to her bedroom sitting in a wicker chair placed at the window facing the door. She asked the servant to bring a bottle of wine to her room for the *master* but she poured generously into her own glass and drank from it.

By the time, Ranuccio entered her bedroom she was feeling the effects of the wine and didn't believe her own eyes. Ranuccio walked into her bedroom completely nude. Though he looked spectacular with his shinning blond hair and well-proportioned physique, the casual act of his walking naked to her made her realize how he saw her. *I am clearly his whore.*

Without a word between them, Ranuccio took her in with his eyes and she did the same. "Will the master, at the very least, close the door and allow this *mistress* some privacy?" she said with an air of pride that made him smile.

Ranuccio bowed, then turned and closed the door. She could see his perfectly formed buttucks. The sight made her sigh. She had seen hundreds of naked men some as handsome as Ranuccio but there was something beyond being merely sensual with him. He was masculine yet playful. He was self-assured yet not entirely arrogant. He had a style that was virile and yet oddly polite despite his sense of freedom.

It might have been that he came from a powerful family and that he came from a long line of war heroes but whatever the reason, Ranuccio didn't seem to be intimidated by anything or anyone. He had an enormous sense of personal autonomy that could be witnessed by body language and his conversation.

This gave him an openness and familiarity that drew Fillide to him. Above all, he was sophistication at its zenith. He was Roman aristocracy and she worshiped at that altar.

She closed her eyes as Ranuccio pressed himself against her. She felt his penis pushing against her thigh. She then felt one of his hands slide down her bottom and the other shoving her hips towards him.

Their mouths locked. She never kissed her clients but didn't think of Ranuccio as a procurer, she thought of him as a lover. In kissing him, she realized she had never been passionate about any man she had ever had sex with before. "Ranuccio," she allowed herself to murmur. She felt his hands on the back of her head as he gently directed her to the bed.

She lay back on the bed allowing Ranuccio to mount her. He entered her wet vagina with a finger and not his penis. She grasped his muscular back pulling him forward.

She lost all control in a way she had never experienced before. Her senses dominated what she saw, felt and thought. It was beyond her comprehension on what was happening to her. Images and thoughts flew into her mind like shattered pieces of glass. It occurred to her how perfectly their bodies fit. A notion of Ranuccio as the last and only lover in her life was another thought that blasted through the sensations she was feeling.

She heard his sighs as his body tensed with his orgasm. She felt her own body heave. She felt the tingling in her vagina slowly build with a sensation she never allowed herself to indulge.

When Ranuccio reached his ecstasy, he shouted out and as Fillide reached hers, her cry was more of a complex response of sheer mystification as if she couldn't believe it had happened at all with a man and not with her own hand.

Ranuccio didn't move for several moments and though she could hardly take the pressure of his weight any longer, she didn't want him to move. When he did, he looked down at her and chuckled. "You wanton, vixen bitch, you make my body ache with lust and I thank the supernatural powers that you have at your fingertips. Ha!" he said then kissed her roughly. He then stood up displaying his nakedness proudly. "You're going to live with me, lady," he demanded.

"Yes, I am," Fillide agreed. "And I must thank you with all of my heart for saving me from that jail cell," she told him.

"I did save you and I had a reason," he told her.

"What was the reason?" she asked. She looked into his eyes as she asked hoping to hear the answer she thought was the correct one.

"I thought to myself what audacity this woman has for sending a messenger to me. I thought how confident she is in my interest in her," he answered.

Fillide listened politely. That was not the answer she wanted to hear.

Ranuccio continued. "I also thought that perhaps, this woman, this vixen, wanton whore, knows something about she and I that I did not know," he proclaimed.

Fillied put her fingers on his lips. "Enough," she told him and then pulled him closer and they kissed again.

CHAPTER TWENTY-THREE

When Mario discovered that Fillide had become Ranuccio Tomassoni's mistress, he was livid. In the passing year Mario and Caravaggio had traded insults with Ranuccio and his brothers Giovan, Octavio, Alessandro and Mario in the Piazza del Popollo.

"His evil ways know no bounds," Mario shouted in the Tavern of the Turk to anyone who would listen.

The Tomassoni brothers were notorious at demanding protection money from any of the whorehouses in their neighborhood and when they were drunk and banded together, they liked nothing more than taunting artists and other drunks they came across as they roamed the streets.

Caravaggio, Mario and Longhi were not the kind of men who would back down from a fight and in only recent days, several bottles were thrown, insults shouted and swords flashed when these two groups of men crossed paths in a dark alley.

Caravaggio also liked to wager money he had earned on his commissions on tennis matches that were held in the Piazza del Popolo on Saturday afternoons and his favorite betting competitor was none other than Ranuccio.

"Who cares that he owns a new whore?" Caravaggio shouted back at Mario. He eyed his close friend. "You are fonder of that whore than I realized. I should have fucked with her so that I could say, "how can you love a whore who slept with your friend, Caravaggio?" he grinned.

Mario resisted responding. He was sitting with Caravaggio and Longhi flanked by three young prostitutes and was beyond amazement when he saw Fillide enter the bar on Ranuccio's arm. Drunk, he pulled a knife off the table and confronted Ranuccio only a few feet from the entrance.

"I pray you sprout boils on your balls," Mario shouted over the clamor of the tavern.

Fillide shocked by Mario's outburst, saw Ranuccio reach for the blade hanging from his belt. She quickly stepped between the two men. "Enough!" she shouted at Mario.

"My balls await your tongue," Ranuccio spit out.

The two men were face to face. Mario, with his long black hair combed back, wearing a black silk shirt with a scarlet scarf hanging over his broad shoulders and

Ranuccio wearing his favorite forest green cloak over a green vest and a dark brown shirt; his clothing adorned with emblems sparkled in the flickering light of the cnadles in the tavern.

The crowd was hushed with the scattering of catcalls as Caravaggio and Longhi raced to Mario's side. Ranuccio saw them coming and clearly fretted that he was outnumbered.

Caravaggio rushed to Mario's side spitting as he lashed out at Ranuccio. "All alone Ranuccio? Where are your bully brothers now to protect you?" he demanded.

Fillide was petrified. Clearly not afraid of violence, she understood too well how these young men thrived on the adrenaline rush they received from physical confrontation. She only had to look in their eyes and she witnessed the presence of Lucifer more than she ever had in the eyes of a man pursuing sexual favors.

"You owe me scudi," Ranuccio spit back at Caravaggio.

"You will collect your payment when you kiss my ass," Caravaggio told him.

"For what I hear you enjoy sodomy more than you enjoy women," Ranuccio taunted Caravaggio.

Caravaggio grinned. "One day my rapier will slice through your chest and cut your heart in two," he said as if reading a prophecy.

Fillide was near panic but fortunately for her, two *sbirri* were sitting in the far corner and though they looked as panicky as she that violence would interrupt, they had to take some kind of action.

When they stood up and advanced toward the group of men at the door, both Ranuccio and Mario backed off. Only Caravaggio stood his ground. He made a fist at Ranuccio. "I'll see you in your grave with your mouth around your father's penis!" he screamed. Longhi shoved him back to his table.

Fillide was relieved when Ranuccio took her hand and with the *sbirri* as escorts, they left the tavern.

Once on the street Ranuccio whispered to her that he would shove his sword in Caravaggio's heart when the time was right. "His insults deserve retribution and I will one day watch his blood stain the piazza."

Later that night Fillide realized that she had been seduced by not only Ranuccio but also by the world Ranuccio inhabited. Living in his villa, she had her own servants who actually tolerated her and actually respected her wishes just because she was his live-in mistress. She also didn't have to shop for clothing or food but she was also afraid of losing Mario as her friend and she was afraid of losing touch with the artists she wanted to be near.

Despite her fears, she stayed mostly in the villa living the life of a kept-woman. Sometimes she did stroll through the piazza staying close to the villa. She longed to visit Battista but was worried that she might come across the path of a client who might not appreciate that she was no longer on the *market.*

One afternoon, while sampling oranges from a vendor along the Tiber River on the Via Tomacelli, she encountered Mario Minniti.

It was a chance meeting and though Fillide smiled warmly at Mario when she first set eyes on him, and he returned the smile just as warmly, their smiles quickly froze.

She watched Mario rush to her side. "How can you throw your life at a malcontent and shallow soul as Ranuccio Tomassoni?" he asked nearly desperately.

Fillide didn't want to hurt Mario's pride but she also had no way to explain what *she* was feeling for Ranuccio. She couldn't tell him how deeply Ranuccio touched her heart.

"Everything you hoped to gain in Rome. Every dream you had of being with artists and poets is slandered by your association with that wealthy fiend," Mario explained.

Fillide knew there was nothing she could say. She gave Mario a cold stare. *This is the only way.*

"You turn your back on your friends. You turn your back on those who love you? Please, don't," Mario pleaded.

Fillide wanted to pull Mario close to her but she knew that a public display of affection would only anger those who were now watching her. She was a courtesan and her emotions needed to be held in check.

"Fillide," Mario said softly.

She turned back to him.

"I know we will never lose our close ties and I'll never lose my heart to another woman as I have to you," he exclaimed more as a tribute than as an announcement of possession.

She was touched more than she ever thought possible. She reached out her hand and he quickly took it though their bodies remained apart. "Do you understand, my dear Mario, that I need Ranuccio's protection?" Fillide said, hoping that this explanation would be enough for him. "In my world there is no survival without a powerful protector," she said.

He let go of her hand. "I can protect you," he quickly responded.

"No, you can not and you know you can not," she retorted. When I was in that prison cell, I was allowed one name to contact. I begged my jailers to contact Ranuccio. Only he had the influence and the daring to come to my aid," she stated.

"I was ready with my sword," Mario said.

"And if Mario Minniti and his minions of heroes came to my aid with their swords we would all be locked in hell's prison cell at this very moment," she stated with authority. This time Mario had no response because he knew that what Fillide was stating was absolute.

"Ranuccio has no fears. He moves through Rome with no care or concern because he *can*," she stated sharply.

Mario lowered his eyes yet she refused to insult him. "My heart is yours for always as a brother and companion in trust and I have every hope that you achieve all that you work for," she told him. She took his hand again, squeezed it.

"He will only break your heart," Mario told her.

"He will marry me," she shot back, realizing that even though she didn't believe that marriage with Ranuccio was possible, she did yearn for it more than she had realized. The realization drove her home. She walked the quickway to Ranuccio's villa. She decided to end her stroll through the street right then and there.

He stood in the dust watching Fillide until she all but disappeared. The sun was as bright as he had ever known it but his heart felt overwhelmed by the wavering gloom of loss and uncertainty. He wondered if he would ever love a woman as much as he loved her.

CHAPTER TWENTY-FOUR

Ranuccio escorted Fillide into the hallway of the Tomassoni villa in the Piazza di Lorenzo. She felt the coolness of the marble walls and the scent of fresh roses adorning the walls as she stepped into the villa leaving behind the blast of red light from the enormous setting sun. *This is the magnificence I yearn for.*

She wore a long white gown with a garnet broach, her birthstone of which Ranuccio placed on her white blouse as a gift for the evening. Her raven hair tied back with a white bow and with her dark eyes flashing as coal as if a bright light had shinned on them. Fillide was the physical embodiment of Roman beauty; or so was the talk of all the men who were present.

She saw the evening as her introduction to Ranuccio's family and the public display of their blossoming romance.

Ranuccio enthusiastically introduced her to his brothers. Fillide found them all broad shouldered with stark dark features and scars on their faces and arms from past battles. They were more reserved than Ranuccio and less talkative. Though Fillied knew they were all married men, their particular favorite mistress accompanied each brother.

She actually recognized one whore in particular from the ghetto. In the *Ortaccio* she was called Prudenzia as many of the other women but she was known to be a woman from Milano named Tita. Tall, big boned and dressed in scarlet that highlighted her auburn colored hair and eyebrows, Tita Scapone was in her early twenties. Fillide had seen her many times in the Tavern of the Turk and Tavern of the Blackmore usually escorted by a rich banker everyone knew was from Venice. On this night, she was with Ranuccio's brother Mario and Fillide had an instant dislike for her. She was patronizing in her glances at Fillide and too flirtatious with Ranuccio.

Fillide was also surprised to see Captain Pulzone and Cardinal Aldobrandini in attendance. The cardinal was not wearing his scarlet cassock but dressed modestly though Fillide knew that he was in disguise since he would be embarrassed to be seen in public in such company in his full regalia. Both men in attendance alone and both men, at separate occasions, threw passing lecherous glances at her.

A large table held several silver pots boiling with hot pasta. Each guest was led to the table by a servant and asked to fill their plates. Fillide took Ranuccio's plate and her own and filled them both with Strozzapreti in Bolognese sauce.

"Strozzapreti means *priest strangler*," Pietro Aldobrandini whispered to her as he stepped to the table.

Sensing Pietro's heart must have skipped a beat, she smiled warmly.

"When your lips curl, my dear vixen, I feel a shudder. I'm taken in by the hard edge that is so arduous to make visible since it is hidden so well by your youth and vibrancy. But there is so much for me to perceive nonetheless and it excites me. My life is plush and luxurious and my attention is on the human condition and you are in the very center of that condition. This truth urges me to inquire more about you. And yet, you already know too much about me," he told her.

Fillide replied. "I feel as if you just created your own oral gospel," she smiled, her lips curling.

"I plan to inquire with Ranuccio when he will share your services again," Pietro told her as his eyes focused on her lips.

Fillide ignored his comment. "I could have filled your plate, dear cardinal, if you had only asked," she told him then bowed, smiled again, aware of its effect on him, then rushed back to Ranuccio who was sitting at the table laughing loudly with his morose brothers.

She placed her hand on his knee grasping it with desperation. She dearly wanted to be treated like a wife and not a whore. She dearly wanted to be loved by Ranuccio and not just desired. Mostly, she dearly wanted to be wedded to this young man who was her ideal in every way.

Though she was hoping that the night would be a special occasion where Ranuccio took her out in public to his family's home for the first time revealing his deep *interest* in her, the dinner party at the Tomassoni villa only filled her with more doubt about her future.

All of Ranuccio's brothers had sent their wives and children away for an extended trip to their seasonal home in Ravenna. Fillide was hoping to meet the wives. She had never met a woman near her own age in Rome who wasn't a prostitute. She had only seen the wives of the wealthy in their carriages looking pale and protected in their own worlds. She was disappointed that she wasn't given the opportunity to meet who she was hoping to be her future sister-in-laws.

She was also disappointed in the party because she found herself fending off an onslaught of unwanted suitors as well as battling female competition reminding her of her corner in hell in the *Ortaccio,* a place she had hoped she would never have to return.

When the dinner party was over, she and Ranuccio headed for the villa's gates when two events occurred that instilled even more worry in Fillide. Captain Pulzone stepped over to her and though he didn't whisper a word to her the entire evening, he said "Your *friend* Mario Minniti will one day suffer the punishment he deserves," as he walked past her in the hallway.

This sent a chill through her but even that threat to a man she held dearly as a friend didn't unnerve her as much as what occurred next.

Ranuccio's brother Giovan approached her drunk from too much beer and wine and smelling of garlic whispered that he was free to "fuck with her" that following evening. He continued to say that he was going to send his carriage for her at dusk.

Fillide was dumbstruck. She turned to Ranuccio but he was busy laughing with his other brothers about some remark one of them made. She then waited for Ranuccio to take her arm and lead her out to the waiting carriage.

She made love to Ranuccio in silence when they returned to his villa that evening. Ranuccio acted as if he had not even notice a change in her demeanor and if he had, he said nothing about it. When he was finished with his lovemaking, he leaned on his elbow facing Fillide. "My brother Giovan fancies you," he said matter-of-factly.

Fillide felt an explosion of rage that erupted from the very pit of her stomach. "I will not fuck with your brother," she spit out.

Her outburst startled Ranuccio. "He will pay the full price," Ranuccio told her as if that would make it a suitable situation for her.

Fillide, lying naked with only the white sheets covering her, shoved Ranuccio away. She felt her teeth clinch and her eyes narrow. She scratched his face then pushed herself out of the bed.

Ranuccio let out a moan and jumped up. "What is wrong with you, woman?" he asked, truly confused.

"I see now what I am to you," Fillide stated.

Ranuccio threw his hand into a pan of water and soaked the cut on his face. "You are *my* courtesan and you do what I say," he told her.

Fillide put her face in his. "You want me to fuck with Giovan?" she asked.

This time Ranuccio didn't respond as quickly. There was something in the tone of her voice that prevented him from being so glib with a response. She revealed an intimacy she clearly felt with him that he had impulses of but never truly defined for himself.

Seeing that she had made an impression, Fillide heaved with a deep breath standing her ground. "If you want me to fuck with Giovan, I will honor your request. As you say, I am your *whore*. But be made certain that if I do share his bed I will shower him with the delight of my most intimate sexual knowledge. He will see me as you have seen me but even more so," she exclaimed then covered herself with her white silk robe and left the room.

Fillide locked herself in the lavatory waiting long enough for Ranuccio to leave her bedroom for his down the hallway.

That night Pietro sat at his desk writing an official letter using the candlelight. He paused, placed the pen down on the table then sat back and allowed himself to think of Fillide. He savored the moment at the food table with her. He savored all the notions and images that came to him about her. He thought of her long black flowing raven hair and her eyes and how, when they looked at him, they looked only at him.

"I'm a man of God," he said aloud but the words were meaningless. There was no one in the room to hear them, or at least, the woman he had hoped to hear them was not there.

Pietro placed his robe around his shoulders and walked to his open window. He looked directly east hoping that through some mystical interaction with the powers-that-be he would be able to see Fillide, nude, in her bath or perhaps sitting at her desk thinking of him.

However, Pietro knew better. She had a young man in her bed and she was infatuated with him. He *knew* that. He also knew that despite the fact that he was so powerful and wealthy and despite the fact that his uncle was the Pope, Fillide cared little for him. She respected him and she had sex with him but she didn't love him.

Pietro turned to the mirror seeing his plump and unattractive image and was repulsed by it. He quickly turned his attention to the canvas Caravaggio had recently completed of him and a warm wave of reassurance washed over him. In the portrait, he was handsome with noble bearing.

"Everything can change," he said to himself but then he thought, *if only Fillide could see me as he as I am in this portrait.*

The following morning Fillide woke and spoke to no one ignoring Ranuccio's attempts at making conversation at the breakfast table. She then spent the rest of the morning and the entire day preparing herself for her evening with Giovan. Ranuccio hovered over her as she took a luxurious bath and adorned herself with her most seductive clothing and perfumes.

That evening when Giovan's carriage arrived for her, Fillide was already in the garden waiting. But as she was escorted to the carriage, Ranuccio appeared at the villa's front door. Holding his sword and swinging it wildly he chased the driver back to his seat behind the horses.

"Return to my brother and tell him that Fillide is not for sale!" he shouted.

Confused *and* scared, the humbled driver quickly whipped the horses and raced down the path leading to the piazza.

She hadn't moved once during Ranuccio's appearance and he was also immobile clearly shocked by his own behavior. The two stood in front of the villa but neither looked at the other.

"You belong to me," Ranuccio finally announced.

She turned and walked back into the villa. That evening, after indulging in wine separately in different rooms, Ranuccio inevitably found her. Without words and indifferent to the servants, they made love on the carpet in her bedroom.

Their sex was ardent and words of affection and desire were generously shared. She fell asleep in his arms that night pleased with her status and the attention of her lover.

Chapter Twenty-five

Months passed as summer turned into autumn followed by a Roman winter hard hit with gusts of winds that came down from the Alps and several inches of snow, that covered the streets and colorful rooftops.

Fillide was used to the chilly air having grown up in Siena and she loved to dress warmly in a small tight fitting fur coat Ranuccio bought her for Christmas. Though she was comfortable with her domestic life with him, he visited her bedroom with less frequency since when they had first met and this behavior concerned her. Not only because she desired Ranuccio more since living with him but because he was spending his nights with his brothers. She didn't believe he was spending those nights with his brothers.

Still Ranuccio continued to lavish her with gifts throwing her a tremendous birthday party on the eigth of January at the Tavern of the Turk. His brothers and their mistresses were in attendance along with some of the most influential and wealthy men of Italy itself.

One of the many men in attendance that night was a small dark man who wore a long dark coat and though his physical presence was that of a man more familiar with shadows and darkness, his smile was warm and his manner more than charming. His eyes were dark brown and his complexion fair. He was Ulisse Masetti who was in the service of the wealthy Cardinal Beneditto Giustiniani.

At first, Fillide, drunk with wine and gifts showered on her by the men and discreetly taunted by sarcastic remarks from their mistresses, thwarted Masetti's attempts at conversation. However, eventually his wit and eccentric grace won her over and she allowed him to speak his mind that he seemed determined to do.

"I'm in the service of the cardinal to provide him with delicious morsels of delight like yourself," he told her.

She gently waved him off. "Since you're a stranger to me, I forgive you for your indiscretion, *Signore Masetti*," she told him. "But I *live* with Ranuccio."

Masetti bowed. "Then, my dear, if you ever find yourself without his protection, I do hope you will seek out mine," he handed her his card. "And my protection does not include sexual favors. I only charge a commission for the work I bring to you," he continued.

"You are a procurer in somber attire," Fillide shot back feeling suddenly sober.

"And you are a ravishing and young harlot holding onto a fantasy that one day Ranuccio Tomassoni will marry you. You may have your nails embedded in his flesh, but the flesh will give away, my dear, and you will find yourself back in the ghetto, I'm sorry to say," he told her. "I've seen it happen before. Not with Ranuccio but others just like him and the sad mistresses who fall in love with them."

She felt flush with anger but she controlled it. With that, Masetti bowed again and edged himself back into the party.

Despite the reverie going on around her, She felt doomed and conjectured that the effects of the curse would strike her soon. She felt this way because of her birthday party. All along, she had hoped that her party would have been held in Ranuccio's villa and this time she once again had hoped that his brothers and their *wives* would have been the guests. Instead, her birthday was held in the Tavern of the Turk and though Ranuccio's brothers were in attendance they brought along with them, not their wives, but their courtesans.

Despite her flights of fancy, that Ranuccio saw her as a wife; it was becoming more evident to her that he continued to see her as his whore and nothing more. "When will I met your brother's wives?" she had the courage to ask him during the party.

Ranuccio replay instantly. "When hell freezes over, my dear," he whispered in her ear.

She then discreetly bit his ear. He wanted to scream but she placed her perfumed hand over his mouth then let go of his ear. While Ranucci was still in shock, she took a napkin and gently dried the wound. "I'm not worthy of your brother's wives?" she asked. "Then you are not worthy of my respect," she told him and left the table.

As the Roman winter wore on and became milder and Ranuccio's evening jaunts from the villa became more frequent, Fillide spent more time with Caravaggio and Mario and also the elusive Longhi. To their credit, her street friends accepted her back into their fold immediately with only slight references to her lover, the despised Ranuccio and his hated family, the Tomassoni's.

One late evening when she was at the tavern discussing her missing cousin Anna with Longhi who Fillide learned when drunk, spoke only of her cousin in loving ways, she thought she saw Ranuccio leaving the tavern's backrooms with a woman.

Mario was aware of her sudden distraction. "You and I can start a new life together," he whispered to her.

No one else saw Ranuccio and Fillide kept it to herself but decided to leave the tavern early. "I will never leave Rome," Fillide told him sharply.

"We both will have to someday for our own survival," he told her.

Fillide was taken in by the seriousness of his tone. "What does that mean?"

"This city will never accept us. I'm not sure how I know that but I can tell you that I say it because I fear it to be true," Mario said, then took another deep drink from his thick wineglass.

Fillide stood, walked away from the table and then quickly left the tavern. By the time Mario reached her, she was already in a carriage making her way back to the villa.

When Fillide returned to the villa, she found a candle burning softly in Ranuccio's room. Fillide could see the flicker of light coming through his shutters.

She stepped cautiously through the garden until she reached the shutters and peeked inside. In the dim light, she saw the whore known as Prudenzia but whose God given name was Tita, straddling Ranuccio. Tita's nude back and buttocks were visible in the candlelight and the moans of sexual pleasure drifted out into the night air.

Fillide wanted to vomit but instead she pushed away from the wall racing head-long toward the front door. Unable to see through the shadows, she tripped over the base of a small fountain cutting her lip against the marble piece as she fell, but she was not deterred instead she continued through the garden edged by the animalistic grunts of her own heaving voice in the dark.

When she reached the entrance to the villa, she rushed past the burning torches down the hallway to Ranuccio's bedroom finding the door to his private chambers open. She pushed it forward and stopped.

Tita, her face, breasts and hips dripping with sweat, threw her head around, saw Fillide and instead of being alarmed, smiled at her. Ranuccio absorbed in the titillation of his own pleasure asked "Would you like to join us?" incredulous that she would have the audacity to interrupt his lovemaking but sincere in his offer of her participating.

She didn't reply to his absurd question and before either Tita or Ranuccio could utter another word Fillide, pulling her blade from inside her skirt, slashed the naked Tita across the face with the knife. Spurts of blood erupted into the air staining the bedspread and falling across Ranuccio's bare chest. She moaned with anger slashing Tita across the face this time narrowly missing slicing her left eye in half.

Tita roared as a lioness, stunned but not shaken. From her position on top of Ranuccio, she grabbed hold of Fillide's hair and pulled her towards the bed violently shaking her. That was when Fillide, freeing the hand holding the knife, sliced Tita across the chest above one of her nipples. This time Tita screamed in pain and flung her body in the opposite direction of her attacker.

Ranuccio, naked and heaving with outrage, stood and with one blow from his clenched fist, he knocked Fillide backward and away from Tita. Feeling the sting of pain on her forehead, she staggered backward. Her legs went out from under her and placing one hand on the wall, she maintained her balance then walked out of the bloodied bedroom.

She walked to her own bedroom, slammed shut the door then locked it. Dizzy from Ranccuio's punch to her head, she threw herself onto her bed and lay there in the darkness.

Before she fell into unconsciousness, she heard the servants shouting for the cavalieri.

Rain pounded on the windows as Fillide and Ranuccio faced the magistrate, their testimonies were given and recorded and the magistrate allowed them to go free on bond. Ranuccio signed a note for the court stating that he would provide the lira as a bond before any trial the following morning.

The bloodied and wounded Tita was being bandaged in the backroom and looked after by a physician who knew only to clean the wounds with soap and water and bandage what he could. If infection occurred, he would place maggots on the wound. Tita was shouting profanities at Fillide, so loudly she could be heard through the closed doors.

Ranuccio and Fillide took the same carriage through the rain back to the villa where Ranuccio starred out one window and Fillide the other.

"In our own home you fuck with this whore?" she asked.

"In *my* home, woman," Ranuccio growled back at her.

It was half way through the journey that she looked to Ranuccio. "I've lost your heart, haven't I?" she asked.

"You never had my heart," he said without looking at her.

"That's impossible. I saw love in your eyes," she said.

Ranuccio was quiet. "You saw lust in my eyes. But no more after what you did.

I want you out of my villa. I want you packed and gone in a fortnight," he stated not once looking in her direction.

She didn't know how to hold onto the man she loved without striking out with her knife and cutting the flesh of those women who were trying to take him from her. It was all she knew how to do, so how could he blame her?

By the time they reached the villa, the servants had cleaned Ranuccio's room and he closed the door on her. She retired to her own boudoir knowing that now, with the court having her name in its file, one more arrest for any infraction and she could be immediately placed in prison.

Yet her fate didn't worry her but losing Ranuccio's love did. It was near dawn and unable to sleep, she went to his room.

Ranuccio was on his stomach with his face deep in his pillow. Fillide stood over him languishing in grief of a broken heart. She sat in a chair at his side hoping he would wake up so that she might explain herself to him.

It was near dawn when he stirred for the first time. He opened his eyes and stared at her before he spoke. "Have you come to kill me?" he asked her.

"How can you ask me that?" she asked.

"I can buy any whore in this city and that is a truth that can never change. What did you expect from me?" he asked her.

She had been waiting all night for him to ask her that question. "I expected your love and I would have been the most loyal and giving soul you would have in your life. That was what I was expecting," she replied with pride and grace.

She could see that Ranuccio was uncomfortable sharing his emotions with her. "I'll be your protector. I'll pay the court bills and provid you with an attorney if it comes to that. I'll order Prudenzia *not* to press charges against you," he told her. "But I want you to vacate my villa. I can not sustain this jealousy. I can not exist with this possessive nature that strangles my very existence," he continued. He then turned over and went back to sleep.

She had her answer. She returned to her room and packed her bags. As soon as the servants stirred, she sent one out with a message to Ulisse Masetti requesting an audience and asking him if he had a room for her to occupy until she found an apartment. A messenger from Masetti arrived by the end of the day extending an enthusiastic invitation to Fillide. He wrote inviting her to join him in the villa he was renting from Cardinal Giustiniani at the intersection of Via Triboniano and Via Crescenzio on the west bank of the Tiber River adjoining the Palazzo di Gius-tizia.

She hired a carriage to take her to Masetti. She waited until dusk hoping Ranuccio would come out of his room to say *goodbye* to her only to find out that he had left the villa hours earlier without asking for her.

She stepped into the carriage and as it pulled away from the villa, her eyes swelled with tears. She took one last look and what she had hoped would be her home. She then pulled up the window and spit.

❖

The rooms Masetti offered Fillide were elegantly decorated with red cushioned sofas and chairs and dark wood paneling lining the marble façade and tall windows with white painted shutters. Masetti told her that he had spent time in Paris and enjoyed the décor there so much he had his home decorated in the French style.

A dinner including porchetta and roasted pig was served on the balcony where Fillide listened closely to Masetti's plans for her near and distant future. Fillide was hungry and ate heartily of the roasted pig. She did all she could to keep her mind off of Ranuccio and as difficult as it was she managed to do just that. She was attentive to Masetti and found that despite his ebony clothing and rather disagreeable physical appearance, he was articulate, mannered and intelligent.

"I see that your situation has changed," he said softly.

"I'm not here to discuss my *previous* situation," she shot back. "I'm here to discuss my future."

Masetti nodded to her. "I provide a service for the wealthy widowers in our city," he said casually. "I match beautiful courtesans with diplomats, merchants, bankers who are either traveling to Rome and need a companion for a night or two or perhaps actually live here but are too shy to be sociable," he said in a voice that was calm and reassuring.

"It must be a lucrative service,"she replied.

"It is. As you can see, I live well and my women do the same. Which brings me to you, fair Fillide," he said. "But let's enjoy our meal and discuss business over desert."

After dinner, Fillide sat in Masetti's small but exquisite den. They drank a bianco di Conegliano wine as Masetti gestured to a gold box on a table. "I wanted you to see this," he told her. He opened the box and held it at an angle so that she could see its contents. "I adore rubies and emeralds and diamonds as well as gold crowns," he exclaimed. He then closed the box and pointed to a calendar on his table. He picked it up and sat back placing the calendar in the light and bowing his head down so he could read it. "This is a calendar of arrivals and departures of the widowers I speak of. If you are interested I believe we can both amass a small fortune with my service," he told her. He leaned back in his chair. "You have a quality that reminds many of these older gentlemen of the Renaissance. You also exude a virtue of innocence as well as an attribute I cannot as of yet describe accurately," he remarked.

Fillide listened closely while sipping her wine.

"But whatever that is, your vivacious charms have already incited men of power and influence," he told her.

"I have no privacy then?" Fillide said with a snap to her tongue.

Masetti quickly responded with a submissive tone. "It's your reputation I speak of. However, I only investigated your past so that I know whom we shall trust and who shall be our allies in our quest," he said. "And that is what I need to know from you, fair lady. I need to know what is it that you want to achieve for the fulfillment of your soul?" he asked her.

She thought hard before she answered. "I've no interest in God's Heaven, dear *Signore* Masetti because I firmly believe God has no interest in me," she replied. "His angels and his saints have ignored me and my prayers since God took my father from me. I have walked the whore's ghetto and lived with the smells and curses and private pleasures of God's men to survive this world and not once has God seen fit to intercede on my behalf," she told him.

Masetti observed Fillide as he listened. "You've been told this before but I need to tell you myself, that you're wise beyond your years," he stated.

She continued. "And when it comes to marriage my interlude with Ranuccio Tomassoni only makes it clearer to me now, this very night, that men have no interest in a woman's loyalty. They have no interest in her love or affection other than the moment's pleasure," she firmly stated.

Masetti frowned but not for her or himself but for Ranuccio. "*Signore* Tomassoni was a fool to let you go, if you ask me for my opinion, *senora*," he stated.

She shuddered at the thought of the man she continued to love so she pushed on with her retort. "Luxury and wealth is what I need for fulfillment," she told him finally.

Masetti gave her a broad smile in return.

"That is the reply you were hoping to hear?" She asked, fully aware that it was.

"Yes," he replied. "It certainly was the response I was praying to hear from your lips."

"What about a protector, dear Ulisse?" Fillide asked.

Masetti understood the value of a protector and already had an answer. "My dear friend Cardinal Benedetto Giustiniani will be our guardian angel," he replied.

Fillide stood. "Excellent. However, it is time I slept. It has been a long day and night for me," she told him.

"I'm pleased with our discussion. May I plan your itinerary?" he asked.

"Yes. And when you do ascertain a price they will pay for my services which you believe is adequate, double it," she said fiercely. She talked across the room as Masetti stood.

"There is one other way I can be of service for you, my lady, with a charge of a slight though added commission," he told her.

Her interest peaked she stopped at the door. "And what could that be?" she asked.

"I can suggest investments in property, bonds and bank notes that will enhance your current and future savings," he told her.

The room was quiet. Fillide allowed the silence to cultivate her own thoughts. She had an epiphany.

Masetti broke the silence. "*Signorina?*"

She didn't even glance at him. "I have achieved what I had sought out to accomplish, that was all I was thinking," she answered.

"Then Rome should celebrate by embracing its fair goddess and you, my dear, should rest for we'll be busy from this day forward," he told her.

That night Fillide rested much easier than she thought she would despite the long and awful day she had lived through. In her deep sleep, she dreamt about her life back in Siena. She watched herself running across the rolling hills with her father. He told her about the greatness of art as her cousin Anna ran laughingly beside her.

When she woke up in the middle of the night, she didn't feel horror or grief about where her life had taken her. Instead, Fillide felt comfort in the fact that she had yet to reach the age of nineteen and all that she had dreamt of achieving was at her fingertips.

She walked to her balcony and looked out on the dark Roman streets. "I curse You, God!" she said vehemently under her breath. "I stand here despite your laws!

I stand here a free woman despite your whore Church and its hypocrisy!" Fillide gripped the railing on the balcony and looked into the stone dark night sky. "I will never pray for your help or ask for your guidance. I condemn You as You disrespect me!" Fillide was exhausted yet she was still hoping to garner some response from the darkness. There was nothing but silence. "I may owe you my creation but I own my own soul," she said then stepped back into her room and drew the curtains close to the balcony.

That same night Mario Minniti sat in his studio in the Palazzo Madama working on his most recent commission. It was the painting of a Madonna and Child celebrating the Ascension of Mary into Heaven for the Pasolini Brothers.

He had already replaced one burning candle with another and took a moment to look out the window at his tiny visage and the image of himself as a young man standing in the Artists Quarter in the market that very first morning shot through his mind.

He had no notion why it had suddenly emerged but the image reminded him how significant the last years of his life had been. He had attained so much on one hand but it was nothing near what he had anticipated he would have accomplished. His friend Caravaggio had been living the success he had imagined for himself and this continued to sadden Mario even though he was securing more commissions. Every time a particular cardinal commissioned him to paint something for his private residence or Sacred Brothers or a bishop for a chapel, another cardinal would hear of it and then pursue Mario in hopes of acquiring Mario to paint a fresco or canvas for *his* residence or chapel. However, critical success still eluded Mario and that was what stung him worse than poverty had.

So that particular night Mario looked out on the rooftops of Rome wondering to himself what kind of artist was he? He had recently overheard someone who he didn't recognize and who hadn't recognized him say to a drinking companion, "Mario Minniti is in the school similar to Annable Carracci." The words infuriated Mario.

And yet, what if it sentiment were true? Was this notion held by all in Rome? And more importantly, Mario wondered, is the degree of success that Carracci attained a curse? Annable Carracci was wealthy and famous though Mario and Caravaggio had despised his work because he followed the beliefs of Michelangelo.

Mario was slowly realizing that he was also envious of Carracci's success. Was it so terrible to be considered as good a craftsman as the well-loved painter?

Mario allowed the night air to wash over him as he pondered these thoughts. He had no answers for himself at that moment yet he knew one thing: he had accomplished something that would only make sense to him years later when he had time to evaluate his life in its entirety: a portion of Roman society *had* accepted him and that, in itself, was a minor miracle.

Despite the precarious nature of his success and the dubious make-up of his lifestyle, he had secured roots amidst the turmoil of the most potent city in western civilization yet he still wondered what would follow next and what path would his life eventually take?

Part Three

Rome
"1599–1602"

CHAPTER TWENTY-SIX

Clement VIII concentrated all of his waking hours on the celebrations he was planning in the Eternal City for the following year for the *Jubilee* of 1600. Cardinal Pietro Aldobrandini worked closely with his uncle for all those months leading up to the New Year.

Since their arrival together in Rome, Pietro had watched his uncle fight off the early gloom of his reign as Pope as well making a masterful acquisition of the Ferrara provinces for the Papal States without shedding an ounce of blood.

Pietro, at his uncle's side, encouraged his uncle but also allowed room enough to conceive a strategy on his own. Pietro observed with pride knowing that Clement's impressive achievement renewed power and authority to the papacy. "We've created an illustrative end to the religious wars and we have brought finality to the Franco-Spanish war," Clement told him at dinner one evening as both men planned a tour of Italian cities in celebration of the achievement. They sat in the library where the Pope preferred to have these discussions. The elegant room was bathed in a golden glow from the reflection of the burning candles off the warmly painted light brown walls and bookshelves.

"The papal court will be preceded by the Holy Sacrament as it visits all of our cities," Clement continued.

Pietro, with pen and paper in hand, jotted down the details. He knew how the minutiae of celebration included a journey taking eight months and an entourage numbering twenty-seven cardinals, fifty priests, musicians, architects and painters. This list Clement was creating that evening included Cardinal Del Monte.

"And you no doubt want his two finest painters Caravaggio and Minniti?" Pietro asked expecting that Clement would want them included.

Clement shook his head. "No. Caravaggio's work is too bold and Minniti's work lacks the vision for the *new* Church," he stated. "I will search out an artist who will bring a fresh eye to the new century," he said.

Pietro could not disagree. "We will invite the Farnese?" he asked expecting an affirmation to his question.

Again, Clement shook his head. "No. We have no need of the Farnese family now. We have succeeded despite them," he replied.

"They will be insulted."

"Then they must learn to live with insults," Clement shot back without looking up from his prayer handbook.

Pietro placed his pen back in its holder. "May I add that we need to appoint a cavalieri official to the new post we have created?" he asked.

This time Clement did look up. "What new official post?"

"You decided that you want a liaison between the Vatican and the Roman cavalieri. We need to make the announcement soon, your Holiness," he answered.

Clement raised his eyebrow. "Oh yes, now I remember the new post. I would like to appoint that Captain Pulzone. I have heard much about his hard work and how he pays attention to details. God is in the details. He is an excellent officer and he will rid the city of the outrageous felonies it is now victim too," he said. "Communicate with him and make the appointment."

Pietro didn't say a word. Clement *knew* that his newphew's silence meant there would be debate. He glanced at his nephew. "We need to appoint someone *else* other than Pulzone?" he stated.

Pietro nodded.

"And why is that?" Clement asked, raising his voice.

"The man is a faultless candidate for the position but we need to make a political appointment for that office. We need to appoint a Farnese or we will suffer the consequences," Pietro told him.

Clement was now the quiet one. He stood up, moaned from gout in his right ankle then hobbeled away from his nephew. "I already discussed this with the captain's superiors," he stated. "I already informed them to make it known to this captain that he *is* my choice."

Pietro shrugged. "You're Pope, dear uncle. You can decide to decide a *second time.*"

The Pontiff thought it over and Pietro said quickly, "I'll announce the appointment when we return from the Jubilee after our triumphant entry into Rome at the beginning of the Holy Year, *Anno Santo.*"

Clement waved his hand in a gesture Pietro was all too familiar. The wave of the hand meant they should move on to another topic. Pietro could not stop there. He *knew* the captain. "I will offer Captain Pulzone exceptional indulgences for his sacrifice."

"Admirable notion," Clement stated. "And remember, in all of your letters to our bishops, make it clear that I want all the churches in all of the cities lavishly decorated. Write to my cardinals and make it clear to them to set a good example and restore the ruined churches here in Rome. We have defeated the forces of darkness, dear nephew, God demands our commemoration," Clement told him then left the library.

Pietro made the notes then sat back and pondered the details of a letter he would write to Captain Pulzone asking to meet him in the Savella Prison in eight months time when the entourage returned directly after the New Year.

Fillide Melandroni was eighteen years old in 1599 and looked up upon the new decade with odd mixture of accomplishment and disappointment. She had achieved so much in a brief five years and yet her life was lived on a tightrope of apprehension. No matter how she tried to transcend her profession she was still a strumpet in the eyes of all who she came across. Though now a courtesan of the elite and though she spent time with the most powerful men in the city, she still dreaded a knock on her door that would send her to prison. Despite the bribes she paid and the alliances she formed, she knew her life still lacked the one component she desired as she worked hard to change and that element was *honor*.

It was early spring and Fillide stood in Battista's garden in a long dark shawl with a necklace of silver and a sapphire tiara in her hair with these very thoughts hoping to see Battista and ask him what the rocks could tell him of her future. She was also holding a dark blue and white parasol to give her shade from the sun. They had become all the rage in Paris that past season and now all the women in Rome were purchasing them.

It had been nearly a year that she had been in this section of Rome and though he was nearly always on her mind, she hadn't had the opportunity to visit. On this trip she took Ulisse Masetti with her since over the previous few months they had grown close because of their business relationship.

Masetti had kept Fillide busy not only with her new clients but they also had traveled together spending time as far north as Milan and as far south as Naples.

Fillide's reputation was growing steadily and her wealthy patrons were demanding more of her time than she ever expected. Masetti was also encouraging her to forget about the villa in the ghetto on the hill that she had dreamt of purchasing. "You must leave the ghetto and purchase property elsewhere," he told her. Fillide then decided to purchase the prestigious Via Palonia in the parish of Santa Maria del Popolo. Though she made the purchase, it was denied at first because of her profession. However, Masetti used his connections and managed to coerce his friends in the city government to grant Fillide a certificate of exemption.

Fillide loved the spacious villa. She oversaw the renovations she had designed. Though she only made small changes to the villa's structure, her most significant wish was to purchase as much art as possible and adorn her villa with framed paintings. She actually spent a few hours a week with Masetti at her side viewing the new artist in the same studios that Mario Minniti and Caravaggio once worked in.

Fillide was also finding Masetti a viable presence in her life and though he was the exact physical opposite to Ranuccio and though he never demanded any sexual activity from her, both spent many hours alone together and eventually, she slept with him.

The sex they experienced was without passion but it did hold a certain amount of affection and tenderness. Masetti was older than Fillide and enjoyed her nubile figure with a vigorous enthusiasm.

Fillide knew that Masetti was earning a good living wage from her but that he also could easily find another young courtesan to promote so she allowed their relationship to go beyond the pale of being solely platonic.

Masetti was always well groomed and though slight and short he was masculine in nature and charmingly witty in bed. He liked conversation and he was educated and refined. Fillide saw him as more or less like an uncle but more than a lover and less than a father figure than a friend.

Their time spent in her boudoir was usually short. It consisted of foreplay working up to Masetti's ejaculation and then both would dress or at least cover themselves and then the discussion quickly turned to clients and investments. They had all the qualities of a business partnership and a sort of marriage whose foundation was built on securing a financial future.

She knew little of Masetti and was surprised to hear that he was actually married. He had a home, a wife and three young daughters living in Venice. He never mentioned them to her but Fillide found out when a banker from a small town outside of Bologna mentioned that he was friendly with Masetti's wife's family.

She had noticed that Masetti did write frequently. He also made trips *up north* as he would say without ever being specific on what his destination was.

However, despite his duplicity in that regard, she trusted him and his advice had garnished her dividends in all of her investments especially with her grand investment being Via Palonia.

Fillide was discouraged that Battista's garden needed attending to and she and Masetti told by a neighbor that Battista had taken ill weeks earlier and was being cared for by Franciscan monks who had a small monastery several miles west of Rome.

She felt a tremendous sadness in hearing this and when she walked past a chapel in the piazza she was nearly moved to pray for Battista but decided not to. Once again, she felt duplicitous in praying to a God she truly believed abandoned her.

Fillide and Masetti rented a carriage and drove out to the monastery in the warm air and quickly founded it buried among rocky hills. They found the pastor of the local church and made a donation to his parish. He then led Fillide to the monastery's infirmary. It was there that she found Battista. He was suffering from a fever but he was alert and his eyes brightened when he saw her. Masetti walked through the monastery's garden giving her time alone with Battista.

"I dreamt of you last night," he told her, his voice quivered. His skin, aged from the sun and years of hard living, was nearly like leather.

She placed flowers in a vase at the table on the edge of the bed and held his hand. "I'm so glad you are not alone and you're being nursed well," she told him.

"How are you my child?" he asked her.

Fillide told him everything that she had experienced in all the time she hadn't seen him. His eyes were watery from the fever and his aging lips dry and cracked but he listened intently.

"You're life is on its path. I pray to God that you remain safe and healthy," he told her.

Battista could not stay alert any longer without falling into moments of sleep and states of unconsciousness. So when a monk came by to bathe him, she headed back to Rome. Looking out from the carriage on the dusty road realizing how lonely her life was and how void of passionate friendship it had become.

When she returned home to her villa and her new rooms, she sat by candlelight and wrote Battista a long letter inviting him to live with her and tend her gardens when he had fully recovered.

Several weeks later looking fit and happy, Battista showed up at her door. Fillide embraced him, showed him to the cottage in her garden and hugged him before he settled in.

"I have a friend now in my midst," she told him.

"And you shall have a special magic garden in your home," he smiled.

The following weeks were uneventful when two tragic events struck Fillide. The first was that Masetti was stricken with a ferocious pain in his stomach. It occurred while he was dinning in the Tavern of the Turk with a young prostitute in his employ. His doctor administrated the best medical attention he could and though the pain subsided, the fever that accompanied it didn't.

"I'm dying," he told her one early morning as he was packing. He had dark circles under his eyes from the sleepless nights he was experiencing.

She was speechless.

"How can you know you are dying?" she asked him more out of an incredulous notion than anything else.

Masetti tenderly took her hand. "I have this pain and a fever that accompanies it before, many times over the years. My father died from it and I know I will also. I need to die with my wife and children," he told her without explaining.

She understood and allowed him that wish despite the fear that she'd be unable to manage the successful business they had created together. Masetti responded to her worried look. "You and I shall open the books and I'll give you a detailed accounting of the men you have entertained. Though my future will be short, together we shall plan a prosperous fate for you."

So, before he left Rome, Masetti answered all Fillide's questions. He also answered one last request for an introduction to Fillide by a Florentine nobleman named Giulio Strozzi. With all his affairs in order Masetti left for Venice on a cool October evening so weak he couldn't even manage a wave *goodbye* to Fillide.

She never heard from him again only being notified by *a friend of a friend*, a merchant from Venice that Masetti died in his wife's arms surrounded by his children.

The other tragedy that struck Fillide occurred soon after Masetti left Rome. It was a sunny and mild day when Fillide went looking for Battista. The servants had told her that he was last seen sitting on the bench in the garden. Fillide had constructed the garden in order that tall hedges lined the villa on all sides creating, not only the privacy she longed for, but also allowing Fillide the atmosphere of refuge.

Walking down the pebbled pathway to the garden, Fillide knew that Battista had passed away before she even saw his face. She found him slumped on the bench his walking cane in one hand and his head slumped forward, clutching his chest with the other hand.

That night Fillide had a dream. She was in the garden Battista had made for her. "The green and yellow rocks are telling me that you must be aware that the path you have chosen will take you to a lonely hill. Get off that path and God will embrace you," Battista whispered to her.

Fillide listened to his advice then shook her head. "God sees everything I do and yet he never helps me," she said and woke up.

She looked into the darkness that were her walls and pondered the future. It included Battista's funeral.

Chapter Twenty-seven

Fillide paid for Battista's burial with her own money and walked alone from the funeral Mass held in the parish of the Church of Maria del Popolo dressed all in black including black gloves, a black shawl and black veil over her head.

She waved off her carriage and walked alone with tears running down the side of her cheeks; and that was the first time she met Giulio Strozzi.

His first words to her were "when you walked by me this evening I believed I was witnessing a beautiful but grief stricken angel coming down to earth to mourn humanity's plight."

Strozzi introduced himself inviting her to a small café. She declined at first but when Strozzi introduced himself, she recognized his name. She had recalled Masetti telling her about the Florentine nobleman who was seeking an audience with her.

They sat in the café sipping their strong black coffee and though she didn't tell him she was grateful for his intrusion into her grief. She was feeling melancholy and knew that it was wrong to indulge her self-pity. She gave into Strozzi's conversation and observed him.

He was of ordinary height and weight with thick brown hair slightly graying on the sides. In his forties, he had warm brown eyes and pleasant features with round cheeks and sensuous lips. He was an attractive man with a nimble sense of humor exclaiming with great confidence that he was a poet, a playwright and philosopher.

He also dressed stylishly as a gentleman with fine tastes from Florence would dress. He wore a green velvet cap with a yellow shirt and collar and dark green vest. His trousers were stripped green and brown and his shoes were clean despite the dirty Roman streets. He had a closely cropped brown beard and a twinkle in his eye that soon delighted her.

He told her he was smitten with her the moment they sat down in the café on the sidewalk overlooking the piazza. "You are more than I imagined," he told her unabashedly. "You are a delight, *signorina*. A sheer delight," he continued.

Strozzi then went on to explain to Fillide how his beloved wife, Concetta, died two years earlier while giving birth to their daughter, Olivia, and how he had been a lonely man ever since. He explained how the Strozzi family had built their wealth by creating one of the first Florentine banks, and now, several generations later they acquired property and other lucrative businesses in Florence as well as in Rome.

He excitedly spoke of his family's history explaining how he was the lone male survivor in the Strozzi family sharing the name with his two sisters, Annette and Rosa, both spinsters and both women who enjoyed their wealth. They disliked the fragile Concetta and now were adamant that he remain a widower. "My sisters love the Church and have remained virgins for Christ. I, on the other hand, believe there is nothing more glorious than the sex shared between a man and a woman," he said, seductively as he leaned in and eyed her lips.

Fillide found Giulio Strozzi's personality compelling and at the same time, she could not take her eyes off of the radiant gold medallion he wore around his neck on just as an impressive gold chain. He also wore several alabaster rings crafted with finesse and taste. "I also appreciate the significance of the sensuality of the union between men and women, *senor*, but as you well know, my income demands that I am selective *and* practical," she purred.

"Your voice inspires me to rush immediately to my hotel and compose a poem for you," Strozzi said, his own voice wilting with sincerity.

She boldly reached across the table placing her hand on his. "I must return to my duties," she stated.

Before she could move, Strozzi took hold of her hand. She felt his delicate fingers and squeezed them gently. He then said, "Your reputation has intrigued me for many months. Though I am, innocencent to the affairs of the heart Masetti enlightened me to some of the particulars. May I entrust you to provide me with the details of how a gentleman makes an arrangement with a courtesan?" he asked.

She nearly chuckled. "You have never had an arrangement with a courtesan?" she asked him.

"Never," he answered.

She sat back in her chair. "You choose the time you would like to visit with the woman. This *time* may include dinner, parties and perhaps travel. A service is provided for and the most significant outcome is the gentleman's satisfaction and his privacy," she told him.

Strozzi also sat back in his chair. "And if I loose my heart to the lady in question?" he asked, playfully.

"There is no surplus charge," she replied, demurely.

She could see that Strozzi delighted in her presence dwelling on the notion that though she was young she had the grace and style of a noblewoman. She could anticipate that he contemplated the absolute exciting notion that perhaps he had discovered a passion that could replace what he felt for Concetta.

"I'm presently in negotiations to acquire an apartment here in Rome within waking distance of your Villa Palonia," he told her.

Before she could say another word, Strozzi spoke, his voice nearly trembling. "Will you dine with me this evening?" he inquired.

Fillide took a moment and realizing that she didn't have any appointments and did not want to spend the evening alone, she smiled. "It would be my pleasure to dine with you."

They dined that evening and in a few short weeks, Strozzi and Fillide became the talk of Roman society. He took her everywhere and she adorned his arm as he supplied her with a vast amount of gifts including gold necklaces and silver earrings. He took her even to Rome's most respectable homes and for the first time Fillide met wives and daughters of the noble class.

To her surprised, she found these overfed, placid and mundane women of aristocrats, merchants, diplomats and bankers disappointing. She was hoping they were educated with refined manners and would talk of nothing but art, literature and philosophy. Instead she found their conversation, the few times she was included, to be beyond the trivial. They discussed their servants, their gardens and their possessions with the contempt Fillide heard their husbands use to discuss *them*.

Though Fillide had inspired to be a wife and a member of this elite society she found wealthy women so defensive and small-minded that she saw little difference between them and the women who populated the *Ortaccio*. Both groups of women were living in distinct ghettos. The wives and daughters may have enjoyed wealthy and plush surroundings but they were submissive and obedient in public to the husbands to such a degree that Fillide remarked on it several times to Strozzi who was impressed with her acute observations.

Yet the meek behavior the women displayed to their husbands and the other men in their circle, was quickly changed to extreme hatred for those not of their race, religion or social class. Fillide knew that they were aware of *what* she was and if they could stone her between the entrée and dessert, each one of them would gladly provide the other a rock.

Though the wives kept their eyes lowered and they never dared flirt with any man at the gathering including their own husbands, they managed to glibly and sarcastically tear apart the other women in their presence. There was one moment when one of the women called Fillide a *harlot* under her breath. She ignored the comment but all during dinner she did all she could to silently seduce the woman's husband.

Fillide's behavior was so outrageous that the women were red with anger and had no idea how to address her aggressive manner. She also marked the woman's thigh with her knife when finding her alone in the villa's private lavatory. The woman, in her thirties and pale with fear, pushed herself up against the marble wall unable to scream. Fillide then put her own face up to her mouth and whispered, "I fucked with your husband in the *Ortaccio* just last week, pig," she said viciously.

When she returned to Strozzi, she demanded that they leave. Once in the carriage, she cried.

"What's this about?" Strozzi asked.

"Despite all I've studied at the university I continue to behave like an animal from the streets. Despite all I have achieved, I continued to resort to what I have done in the past," she said, then turned her head to the window, wiped the tears from her eyes with her hands and sighed.

Captain Nunzio Pulzone had been summoned to Cardinal Pietro Aldobrandini's office in the Vatican on the first morning after the religious celebration of the Feast of the Epiphany. The Epiphany marked the arrival of the three wise men who sought the newborn Jesus and the Twelfth Night that was the end of the official Christmas season.

Nunzio stood in the large waiting room warming his hands at the large fireplace peering at the canvases adorning the walls. He recognized a Laureti, a Galiti and even a Tempesta. He thought for the moment how wonderful it would be to actually own a work of art that could bring ease and contemplation into his conflicted life.

Since he had met Fillide, Nunzio's marriage had become hollow and platonic at best. He hungered after Fillide and thought only of her but since she was no longer available to him his dedication to his police work and his love of paintings was all that held any peace for Nunzio. Whenever he was able, he spent hours enjoying the pleasure painting brought him in the chapels, the public showings and the frescos that adorned the official state buildings.

He knew Fillide was now living with Masetti and that Masetti had procured for her a vast new clientele. Fillide was no longer available to Nunzio in the ghetto. She was now moving among Rome's upper echelon. Her vibrant and youthful beauty and her refined manner made her a favorite among her new list of exclusively wealthy suitors and because of this, she was well on her way to becoming prosperous.

He also knew that her last protector Ranuccio Tomassoni was living a wild and precarious lifestyle carousing the city's streets, the piazzas and the whorehouses with his sword flying and his curses filling the night air.

He had been receiving reports that Ranuccio and his brothers, Octavio and Giovan, had been bullying the neighborhood demanding payments from local merchants for protection. They were harassing the prostitutes and their clients at the most western outskirts of the *Ortaccio* by extorting a protection fee from all those who they encountered. They usually attacked small groups of men flashing their swords and their family emblem as if it were a badge of law. They used the excuse that they were vigilantes battling the violent and lawless behavior running rampant in Rome. Nunzio had learned from his own men that the Tomassoni brothers were so ferocious, particularly in the ghetto, that they intimidated the local *sbirri* as well.

"Nunzio," Pietro Aldobrandini called as he opened the large wooden doors to his office. He walked over to Nunzio, extended his hand and Nunzio kissed his ring. Pietro waved him back over to the fireplace above which hung an enormous but enigmatical Tempesta.

Nunzio realized then that their meeting was to be secret or at least, what was said in their meeting would not be heard by anyone else but the two of them. The crackling fireplace would see to that.

"I asked you to meet me on this day, the Feast Day of the Wise Men, because this morning, dear Nunzio, we need to be judicious," Pietro said.

He listened closely.

"My uncle has made his decision. He wants to appoint you to be the liaison between the Vatican and Rome's respected cavalieri. He wants to name you 'Captain of the Vatican Police,'" Pietro said.

Nunzio was ecstatic but controlled his excitement. "That is a great honor."

"It would be, yes, indeed, it would be," Pietro said pressing his hand firmly but gently on Nunzio's right shoulder. "However, you cannot accept the position," Pietro stated. He stiffened waiting for Nunzio to react.

Nunzio felt his forehead narrow. He shook his head. He was speechless.

"The reason you cannot accept the position, though you deserve it more than any officer in this city, is because Lorenzo Farnese's son, Roberto, needs to be appointed the position," Pietro said.

"Roberto Farnese?" Nunzio said as if the name itself was distasteful to him.

"Yes," Pietro replied.

"He is the most notoriously bribable official in the government."

Pietro confirmed the definition with his silence but his eyes narrowed and he removed his hand from Nunzio's shoulder.

"I deserve that position, cardinal," he affirmed.

"Yes, I agree. You do deserve that appointment," Pietro told him.

"So then why must *he* be appointed?"

Pietro shrugged. "The reason is simple. There are politicial demons at work here, my friend," Pietro informed him. "My uncle doesn't understand how Rome works. The Farnese family needs to be, how shall I say, *invited* to participate in certain Vatican decisions. This appointment is one they insist being a part of."

Nunzio wanted none of it. "Roberto Farnese is not even a police officer."

"Excellent observation, but does it matter?" Pietro asked. Before Nunzio could reply, he gestured toward the window. "Do you see that new building across the garden? Do you see the window on the second floor?" he asked.

Nunzio nodded.

"That will be *your* office. My uncle wants to appoint you Colonel of the Vatican Police subordinate to Roberto Farnese," Pietro said. "With the title comes a substantial raise in your pay and that new office across the garden." He watched the tall lanky man stand and turn his back to him. Though he knew Nunzio socially, he didn't know the *character* of the man. So, he did his own investigation before the meeting. In confidence, other cavalieri told him that Nunzio would be a difficult man to convince to turn a blind eye when it came to the merit of politics.

Nunzio sighed. He realized that the appointment would be a prestigious but hollow one. He was never a man interested in titles. He was annoyed. He faced Pietro.

"You are not pleased?" Pietro asked.

"Honestly?" Nunzio asked.

"Of course. I want your honesty."

"No, I'm not pleased. Rome needs a liaison between the Vatican and the cavalieri. The Pope needs to reign in the violence that runs rampant through our streets. The violence is now reaching proportions equal to the destruction the plague brought us," Nunzio answered, honestly.

Pietro listened closely. "All you say is true."

"Give me the power to show the wealthy that their sons cannot run free through our streets brandishing their weapons. Give me the power to rid the streets of our whores and marauding gangs of lawless soldiers. I can end the violence," Nunzio exclaimed.

Pietro nodded quickly. "No one could do more."

Nunzio was incredulous. "Then why not turn your back on the politics? The Vatican will be free of crime. Rome will be cleansed. I can make sure of it."

Pietro nodded. "Then apply your skills under Roberto Farnese," he said sharply.

Nunzio understood. "That's your reply?"

Pietro was not done with him. Unfortunately, in turning down his offer, Nunzio would have to be silenced. Pietro had to make Nunzio not only agree to the wisdom of the appointment but he also had to make him at ease with his choice and be afraid of sharing what Pietro had just told him. "There is one more reason I must not appoint you," he was stern now.

"There is a reason why you must *not* appoint me?" Nunzio asked.

"Yes. There is a reason why I must not appoint you," he repeated. "My uncle, the Pope, is not aware of your tryst with a very visible and notable courtesan. However, many of the elite here in our society are aware of it."

Nunzio reacted quickly. "You're speaking about Fillide Melandroni."

"There is no reason to mention her name," Pietro said sharply.

"But you know her also, dear cardinal," Nunzio shot back. "You've attended dinner parties in her presence."

"I certainly am aware of that fact, yes, captain," Pietro replied. He now sensed that Nunzio was becoming a police officer in his stance and he would have none of it. He could not allow Nunzio to interrogate *him*.

The two men now had nothing more to say. Nunzio realized this and bowed. It was done. His fate in Rome and his career was now sealed. Though he and the cardinal were both ardent clients of Fillide, Pietro had the power to use it against him and he was clearly doing that now. There was nothing left to say. "I take your leave, dear cardinal and I refuse the appointment you have offered me," he said.

"Are you quite certain, Nunzio? I do wish you would accept the position of Colonel," Pietro lied.

"It would be a hollow title with no teeth and no genuine capacity," Nunzio responded.

"Pity you have such pride. Pride is a vice not a virtue."

"If we're going to quote Church dogma, I should then say quote a line from one of our Savior's gospels— He who is without sin, cast the first stone'," Nunzio said.

Pietro frowned. "I'm disappointed in you. I was praying the Wise Men would inspire you today."

"I see no wisdom in your choice of appointment making me disappointed in the Vatican," Nunzio replied then walked out of the waiting room leaving the crackling and warmth of the fireplace behind.

Pietro waited for him to leave. "A man who loves a whore is a tarnished soul," he remarked aloud knowing he was also speaking of himself. The irony incited him and he made a mental note to inquire into Fillide's schedule.

Nunzio walked the snow covered damp, overcast and chilly Roman streets searching out the nearest chapel. He needed to pray for forgiveness. He knew now that he had lost all of his prestige. He had lost the opportunity to ever make love to Fillide and he had lost the friendship, tenuous as it was, with the second most powerful man in all of Rome.

He knew at that moment that he was never going to achieve more than what he already had. Though an officer with a chance at a tremendous future, he had just stopped his career cold. He would never rise in the ranks higher than he was now.

He found a chapel built in homage to Saint Joseph, entered it, lit a candle, knelt down and faced the altar, bowed his head and prayed to God to forgive him his sins. *I am not worthy of life or love. Forgive me, Lord, and allow me the vestige or your grace and I will do penance.*

Chapter Twenty-eight

Mario was sitting in the Palazzo Madama reading the newspaper when he leaned back on the metal bench, lowered the paper and quickly raced through the garden to Caravaggio's second floor room.

He found Caravaggio packing.

"It says here," he shouted raising the newspaper over Caravaggio's head, "that you are leaving the Palazzo Madama?"

Caravaggio smiled. "I rented a home. I'm moving into the Palazzo Mattei this evening," he answered, then went back to covering his canvases.

Mario was dumbstruck and struggled to find words so that he may learn more. "When was I to know?"

Caravaggio shrugged.

Mario lowered his head.

Caravaggio turned to him and patted him on the back. "My dear friend, I plan on employing my own valet who will carry my sword. I plan on employing my own cook and servants. I can not do that here, now can I? And don't worry, I intend on having a great many parties and you are invited to them all." He punctuated his comments by handing Mario an official Vatican invitation. "Come to the announcement."

"What announcement?" Mario asked.

"I've completed my commission of *The Death of the Virgin* for the Cerasi Chapel. My patron Laezrio Cherubini has entered it in a formal competition with Carracci and Guido Reni. All three of us were commissioned to paint the Virgin and the winner will be commissioned by the Vatican to adorn one of its prized chapels," he told him and Mario could hear the thrill of the rivalry in his voice.

With that he felt as if Caravaggio, with his silence, was dismissing him so he left the room and the Palazzo Madama.

Mario stood quietly facing the Palazzo Mattei and stood in awe at Caravaggio's new rented home. He made himself walk there because he wanted to see it.

The home was in the Artists Quarter but very few artists could rent homes of its like. He could see that it had to have many rooms and a studio in the garden where Caravaggio could paint. It irked him once again that his fellow artist and friend was enjoying a success far beyond his own means.

That evening he returned to his room in the Palazzo Madama only to find a note waiting for him signed by Cardinal Del Monte. The note was an eviction notice stating that Mario was to vacate his room as soon as he found new living arrangements.

He was humiliated and quickly found a modest apartment on the Via della Croce. Though his commissions were not as numerous as he had hoped, he was acquiring a reputation as being a good craftsman and a diligent worker and he was now earning a modest living.

The room was on the second floor overlooking Via della Croce, and was his first time he had his own living space since he had to move to Rome. Standing at his window, he made a promise to himself that one day he would have a villa as impressive as Caravaggio's.

The celebration of the announcement of the winner of the competition was held a week later in the large public viewing room at the Vatican's east wing overlooking the Tiber River and despite his hesitation, Mario attended.

Dressed in white from head to foot, he slapped on his best cologne and wore his long hair pulled back. He entered the main door where a Vatican guard took his invitation then directed him to a row of seats in the back of the room.

He was twenty rows from the front and could catch a glimpse of the thin pouting Guido Reni posing under the sunroof so he could be seen in the glimmering sunlight.

Mario knew Guido's work and was aware of the grace and elegance in his early paintings. He had only met him once at one of the taverns and remembered the slight effeminate pale young man with the curly light brown hair as someone with a sharp tongue and disconcerting manner.

He also knew his canvases to be polished and distinctly *religious* but on that morning, he was surprised to see something new in the artist's work.

It seemed as if the canvas in competition had been painted by someone else entirely. Reni's new work was clearly influenced by the darker colors and somber mood of none other than Caravaggio.

On the other hand, he could see that Carracci hadn't changed his style. His Virgin was once again more otherworldly than human, more divine than flawed.

Mario edged closer to get a glimpse of Caravaggio's *The Death of the Virgin* and was aghast. His friend had painted the Virgin as a corpse with dirty feet and dirty hair. Her fingernails were black and her face ashen with the same pallor of a corpse. This was not the Blessed Mother rising from the dead on Assumption Day. This was a dead woman and Caravaggio presented her as such.

Mario immediately recognized the model as the whore Lena he had met in the brothel a few years earlier. The whispers were flying throughout the room. He could hear voices stating, "He painted a whore as a model to be the Virgin!"

The effect of the painting on those in the room was extraordinary and Caravaggio, who entered the room late and apparently drunk, was not unaware of the criticisms directed at his work. Mario knew that he had heard it all before.

He watched as Caravaggio sat with Carracci and Reni clearly bored by the ordeal as cardinals and businessmen, bishops and Vatican representatives all took their time to examine each canvas. Some of them were judges while others were there to offer commissions from the artists.

Mario saw Cardinal Del Monte lingering in the crowd of wealthy and powerful men knowing full well that he represented all three artists, so he would be the only one to leave a true victor of the event.

Mario wasn't sure if he should acknowledge Caravaggio since his friend had made no attempt to acknowledge him.

At one moment he did catch the cardinal's look, saw a quick wave of recognition cross Del Monte's face, only to be quickly replaced by indifference.

Mario knew there was no reason for him to linger at the event any longer. He had no interest in who the winner of the competition would be figuring all the while it'd be Guido Reni. It was Reni, the Pope recently stated, the Church needed for their battle against the Reformation.

He knew that despite the fact that Caravaggio wouldn't win the competition he would gain an enormous victory. Everyone in that room, and most of the powerful and influential of Rome where in attendance that morning, were well aware that Caravaggio was creating a new and vibrant humanistic style that was nothing less than radical.

Caravaggio had broken through a wall created by apathy, ignorance and sheer arrogance. His dangerous rebellious style, a style that depicted suffering human beings as worthy of God's love was confronting the Vatican's very own dictum on what art should be.

Caravaggio was quietly destroying one culture and creating a new one and he would be rewarded for it while, on the other hand, Mario Minniti was a minor painter who was turning thirty years old.

Mario couldn't contain his disappointment and went to the Tavern of the Turk to alleviate his disappointment. He saw his nightmare become reality as if a storm, brewing off the coast for years, had now directed all of its fury at him.

He was nearly grief-stricken and the emotion made him restless but he wanted to drink alone. For the first time he was becoming homesick missing his family back in Syracuse. He disliked the idea of returning home without the success he was convinced would come his way. Now, all he had were moments of victory spread over several years and just enough lira to finance the long trip home.

He went from the Tavern of the Turk to the Tavern of the Wolf waving away prostitutes and drinking companions. He then walked to the Tavern of the Tower and then from there to the Tavern of the Blackmoor yet it was not until he reached the Tavern of the Wolf that he found someone he did want to speak with.

He saw her sitting at a small, corner table on the second floor. She was petite and wore a cap that covered her face but in front of her on the table was a nearly empty bottle of wine.

He knew her even though he couldn't see her face. He sat down next to her. She didn't even look at him.

"Go away," she said with her mouth half closed.

Mario didn't move.

CHAPTER TWENTY-NINE

Mario sat down next to the woman alone at the table. He leaned forward. "Fillide, are you ill, my dear?"

Fillide looked up from under her massive hair and her cap and shook her head. "I have lost everything and I'm confessing my sins to the bottom of this bottle of wine," she said seriously.

He didn't smile nor did he smirk. He just took the bottle from the table and took a long drink from it. "We're both searching the bottom of our lives for some hint of light," he uttered.

"I studied poise and eloquence," she shot back with a harsh tone. "I studied refinement in manner and dress. I have studied art and I can speak about it with great men. I have fucked with powerful men and listened to them spout their deepest desires and notions to me."

"So, what is wrong?"

She shoved her wineglass to the floor with a simple swaying of her arm. "I behave as an animal would. I'm no better than a wild bore in my heart."

He understood. "You disappoint yourself."

"I do so with great design," she agreed.

He looked away and then back to her. "You have to realize that it's more than you. It's Rome."

For the first time she set her eyes on him. "Explain that enigma."

They walked side by side through the Piazza del Popolo allowing the cool night air to wash over them. "I know I have failed but it is not that I wasn't worthy of my own dream. You say you failed yourself but that is not true. This city failed you. It is fickle and pompous. It allows only the greedy to partake of its rewards," he told her.

She understood. "It teases us. It plays with us as if we were children."

"Precisely. That's why I'm abandoning my dream here."

"What?"

He was forthright. "I'm going to Syracuse and in hopes of a new beginning."

She was stunned. "Why?"

He sat on the ledge to a small fountain. "I came to Rome to paint and line the walls of the chapels in this city with my work but I have had no success. I came to this city to do frescos and canvases that would make the name 'Mario Minniti' one with Michelangelo because I thought that was what God wanted. I presumed the world wanted my talents and now I've learned that it was all only a dream born and breed in my own heart and nowhere else."

Sitting beside him she said, "I cannot return to Siena. There's nothing and no one there for me anymore, except memories."

He took her hand in his. He could feel her resist at first but then she allowed him to hold it tightly. "Come to Sicily with me. We will marry and have children."

"Why would you desire to marry me?"

He could see her dark orbs sparkle in the dim light from the burning torch a few yards away. What struck him was the change in those simple dark brown eyes. "You have changed," he whispered.

She stood and continued to hold his hand. She took it and pressed her lips to his hand. "Don't you know that I still love Ranuccio?"

He felt the air rush from his chest but he refused to show her his frustration. "If I can't live with you I'll leave Rome soon."

He saw a carriage and waved it over. She looked away from the carriage and focused on him. "I didn't say I wanted to leave you."

"If you have no love for me, my sweet, there's no reason for me to remain in your company and I'll not leave you alone on these mean streets," he told her. When the carriage arrived, he opened the door and she stepped up to the carriage. She leaned down and kissed him one more time on the lips. "You are the sweetest man I have met in this ugly city but don't you see that you love yourself far more than you love me or your art?" she told him then sat down, closed the carriage and looked away. "That is why you are so lost, my dear soul."

He watched the carriage rumble into the shadows and silently berated himself for chasing her away.

Fillide didn't leave her villa for days after that evening with Mario and hardly spoke to her servants or Strozzi.

Strozzi sent her flowers, notes of concern and even appeared at her door several times but she told her servants to send him away.

It wasn't until the second week of her self-imposed exile that she allowed Strozzi to see her. "I have a gift for you."

"I don't want gifts," she told him dressed in black looking pale and distracted.

Strozzi was unaffected by her morose attitude. Moments later Caravaggio stepped through her doorway and Fillide was dumbfounded. "Why are you here?"

"*He* is my gift to you," Strozzi said, with a smile that was wider than any she had seen in a long time.

Caravaggio had Fillide pose for her portrait in her own private den. He allowed her to choose her own apparel and she quickly decided to wear an embroidered bodice tied through with golden threads. She wore clustered pearl earrings Strozzi had given her and she simply and exquisitely wore her dark brown curls piled high on her head.

The only direction Caravaggio gave her was to place her right hand at her heart touching gently a small flower at her bosom.

She posed for several days but she was delighted to do so and the cranky and talkative Caravaggio was uncharacteristically hushed during the entire process. Though offered wine and food, he did not indulge. He painted during the day then quietly left.

She wondered if his aloofness had to do with her romance with Ranuccio since she had been hearing through local gossip that Ranuccio and Caravaggio's feud over money was escalating. She allowed no dire thoughts or past regrets to enter her mind as she posed. She had only one aim and that was to allow the great artist to capture her likeness on canvas.

She knew that Strozzi had paid Caravaggio handsomely for the portrait and she could see how he savored every lira he spent. She also knew that it allowed him the opportunity to spend hours in her presence and she could see how delighted he was to do so. She knew he was beyond being smitten with her and his happiness charmed her.

When the portrait was completed Caravaggio left her villa with the same lack of fanfare that he had entered with. She, on the other hand, was revitalized and nearly beyond herself with excitement.

She held Strozzi close as they both stood quietly in her den, facing the portrait in awe. "You're given me a great gift," she murmured.

Stozzi could hardly speak. "My dear, your face will live in eternity," was all he could muster.

She walked around the canvas studying her own eyes as they flew out of the canvas. "Are my eyes so tender?" she asked.

"Look, my lovely! Look how he has captured you. There is such glamour, such elegance in your enchanting features," Strozzi said.

Fillide was not searching for compliments; on the contrary, she was hoping to hear something that would bring her back to earth since she was dangling high on fragile layers of clouds. *A great artist has painted me.*

He sat, as if exhausted by the enormity of what hung before him. Just being in its presence took his breath away.

She placed her hand on his shoulder. "I am overwhelemed. You've brought me *my* happiness."

He searched her eyes. "What do you mean, my dear?"

Fillide could hardly get out the words. "If only my dear father could see what I am seeing. It was his dream that one day I would be a part of the great art of our people. He wasn't sure how I would achieve such an end but he desired it for me and it became my dream."

He stood up and embraced her. "I'm delighted that I have done this for you, my love."

She allowed Strozzi to hold her but then an idea struck her. "I would like to have a public display."

"That is a splendid notion. Where would you like to display the portrait? Tell me and I will have it unveiled immediately."

She thought a moment then answered, "In the garden of the Palazzo Madama."

"I will notify Cardinal Del Monte," Strozzi replied then left.

She sat down and gazed on her own likeness. She soon found that the portrait gave her neither pride nor excitement. What it did give her was even more startling, it gave her a tremendous sense of peace that she had never felt in her life up to that moment.

CHAPTER THIRTY

Cardinal Del Monte was thrilled to have a public display of Fillide's portrait in the garden of the Palazzo Madama for several reasons. The first reason was that the painting, a simple presentation of a young Roman woman, was as realistic a portrait of a human face that had yet to be seen. The humanity etched out in her youthful, sensual face was compelling to all who viewed it. Her sadness, though subtle and hidden, was evocative.

The second reason Del Monte was happy to present the work was that it was painted by his genius protégé Caravaggio. And both of these reasons were why the presentation was an enormous success.

Fillide attended every showing every day of that magical week. Since the canvas was available for viewing to everyone in Roman society from the lowliest laborer to the wealthiest merchant, Cardinal Del Monte had his students at the palazzo work as guards. This was to assure a safe and quick entry and exit as the lines formed early in the morning and didn't disband until darkness.

Caravaggio made his appearance only in the evening of each show looking exhausted from his latest commission— painting the *Crucifixion of Saint Peter*.

He would arrive at the garden and take his bows seemingly more relaxed when among the young painters of the Palazzo Madama who were enthralled by his wit and insights into the world they were slowly entering.

Fillide, on the other hand, graced the event with such poise and refinement that the talk circulating in the garden was that she hailed from an aristocratic family from Milano. With Strozzi at her side through the entire week, she distanced herself from the prying eyes of those who knew her personal history all too well. Though she recognized some of the faces that bid her congratulations on the portrait, she blocked from her mind those who had enjoyed her boudoir and shared intimacies.

One evening Mario decided to appear at the event finding Fillide giddy with her newfound fame and tipsy from the wine Cardinal Del Monte provided for his special guests each evening.

He took her aside and, with glee in his eyes, he whispered in her ear, "you are famous, my lovely."

Fillide smiled and hugged Mario even though Strozzi, a few feet away, was watching. Keenly aware of what she had done, she quickly introduced Mario to Strozzi and in a short time, the two men were discussing art and literature as if they were close friends.

Cardinal Pietro Aldobrandini soon appeared to Fillide's delight and he ushered her over to his side and pressed his lips to her ear. "Excellent likeness, my dear," was all he said to her but Fillide was thrilled beyond words by his approval.

Captain Nunzio Pulzone made an appearance saying nothing to anyone other than a quick and curt nod to Pietro and then stood in front of the canvas speechless. It was an embarrassing display but Nunzio was obviously not in control of his reaction at that moment and because of that, he could not focus his eyes on the physical and *real* Fillide in his presence. He quickly left the garden never to appear there again that week.

Ranuccio also made his arrival, a dramatic and well thought out one, waiting for the very last evening to appear only moments before the canvas was covered up. "I want to purchase this work of art!" he shouted with a booming voice as he stood in the center of the garden.

Strozzi heard him and walked over with a bounce to his step. "My dear, sir, purchasing the portrait is impossible since it is not for sale," he said in the suddenly hushed garden.

Ranuccio swaggered over to Strozzi not once even glancing at Fillide who watched the two men closely. "Why is it not for sale?"

Strozzi answered, "Because it is a gift to the lady who posed for it."

That was when Ranuccio acknowledged Fillide with a twinkle in his eyes. She had been watching him since he first arrived and expected him to say something to her even then, but all he did was grin, bow and then leave the garden with the same dramatic flair that he had entered, only moments earlier.

Mario was in the garden that very evening and stepped over to Fillide once again. He could see she was pale from the encounter with Ranuccio. She still loved him and even Strozzi, who knew nothing of their relationship, as Mario surmised, could see that she was disturbed by his arrival. "He must have his regrets now, my lovely," Mario told her.

Fillide could only whisper. "As do I."

❖

During the week of the showing, Fillide was bombarded with invitations to cultural events, dinner parties, other unveilings as well as fending off several marriage proposals. She was content with Strozzi and was impressed in how he accepted and clearly enjoyed her fame, which was more far reaching than she could have imagined.

Without warning she was recognized everywhere she went in Rome. She couldn't walk the streets without someone waving to her or starring at her in awe. But the invitation she cherished the most was when she received a letter from the Accademia degli Umoristi inviting her to be a member. Strozzi, a poet, was a notable member of the Accademia and lobbied for Fillide to be included in its ranks. Others who were members were Caravaggio, Mario Minniti, Longhi and Mancini along with Giovanni Melesi and Giovanni Zaratini Castellini and the scholar Andrea Ruffeti including the collector of gossip and anecdotes about papal Rome, Giano Nicio Eritreo.

She was well aware that the Accademia only invited artists, poets, sculptors and playwrights to their ranks so when she garnered an invite it was simply beyond anything she had dreamed. She was aware it was her sudden fame and notoriety that garnished the inclusion so she was thrilled all the more.

The Accademia degli Umoristi would meet once a month at the Palazzo Mancini in the Corso in the fashionable center of Rome. Their meetings during the spring and summer months were held outside on the steps of the palazzo in full view of the Roman aristocracy enjoying their evening *passeggiata*. When darkness fell, the members would then retreat indoors where they had a full theatrical stage to themselves.

On her very first night in attendance, Fillide was introduced and invited up on stage. Standing for the outburst of applause was a young poet named Mario Milesi who quickly read a poem aloud, a poem he had written for her. "Only an angel could portray you, the lovely Fillide, creating your lovely face, because you are an angel from Paradise." Fillide's demure smile brought more shouts and applause from the audience.

On another evening, Mario and Fillide performed together a reading of Castellini's discourse on the beard, keeping in with the style of the Accedemia, which was called *spiritiosa*—a display of wit and fancy.

Once they were finished with their presentation, she whispered to Mario that she had now "achieved all her father had hoped for" and whatever followed in her life she would gladly endure. She had just turned nineteen years of age.

What the members of the Accademia enjoyed more than anything was that it afforded them a venue to remove themselves temporarily from the religious passion that the Vatican and specifically Pope Clement VIII demanded from them as artists.

Mario especially enjoyed his evenings in the Palazzo Mancini since it gave him ample opportunity to meet with other young artists on mutually beneficial territory. In their discussions, he discovered that many of these young men held the same belief that he did. They all felt that there was the need for a change in the perception on what art was.

Each evening after the performances were completed the attending members, sometimes a dozen or sometimes over two dozen, would sit in a circle and *cicalata*—talk. The talk included showy displays of sometimes well thought out discussions and sometimes just superficial arguments about everything and anything that had to do with painting and poetry and Roman life.

Despite the relaxed atmosphere, passions ran high and many times painters in competition found themselves being subtlety, and sometimes not so subtlety, insulted and ridiculed.

Several times Mario found himself attacking his old friend and roommate Caravaggio for Caravaggio's relentless *dark visions* of nature *and* society. Though Mario never took the extreme opposite point of view, which was Carracci's school of painting, he did find himself sometimes defending the notion that art should be a comfort and a tool to battle the *immoral* Martin Luther and his Protestant Reformation.

One particular evening their friendly debate grew heated over Caravaggio's recent *Crucifixion of Saint Peter.* "Dear brother," Mario said to Caravaggio with much exaggeration and relish in his speech. "Tempesta paints the world as bleak and cruel but if one placed his paintings along side yours, his vision would be as luxurious as Titan and as innocent and pleasing as Raphel," Mario said. He was standing in the circle with a bottle of wine in his hand facing his friend who was now kneeling as he listened. "You portray poor Saint Peter being executed upside down. Were not the Romans cruel enough to Peter without you reminding us?"

Caravaggio spoke with the same exaggerated and pompous attitude and responded. "I only painted the truth my dear brother. He was executed that particular way. I can only beg your pardon if you believe the vision is too, as you stated, *dark.*"

"But the implication, my dear brother," Mario said with a smile.

"What implication?"

"That life is so painful and the future of mankind is bleak."

"I'm only interested in the truth."

Mario spoke with hands moving and gesturing quickly. "So the truth is that our fates are all bleak and desolate of hope?"

Caravaggio absorbed the thought then lowered his jaw and nodded. "True, cousin. Are you afraid to acknowledge this truth? Or do you prefer to being lied to by the likes of Michelangelo and Carracci?"

Several in the room applauded but Mario waved them off. "If you truly believe this how can you lift a brush to canvas? What is your motivation to pursue the beauty in our souls?"

"Beauty? That is your word, not mine, my sick and perverted Bacchus," Caravaggio shot back. "I don't believe in beauty. I leave *that* for Michelangelo and Carracci. Now, I just ask, my once favorite model, are you joining the ranks of their crowd?"

Now everyone one in the room turned to Mario and he went along with the moment, bowing and then raising his head with a wide grin attached to his face. "Yes, dear sir, I was once your favorite model and now I see you have a *new* favorite," he said, his voice stinging with glee. He then gestured to the young, effeminate—looking boy to Caravaggio's right sitting there with dark curly hair and large, oval eyes.

Caravaggio remained silent knowing full well the accusation was that he was a homosexual. This blunt accusation made everyone uneasy. They all knew that, though their rebellious behavior was in jest and was directed at intellectual targets, if any of them indulged in any rebellious *action,* including homosexuality, they could and would be punished by death.

"And an excellent model he is," Caravaggio said bravely.

"I'm certain he must be," Mario scoffed. "And to answer your question, no, I am not joining the Carracci camp."

Caravaggio stood up. "But I disagree. I believe that you are. I happened to see your most recent work. Your own version of the Virgin's demise now hangs in Cardinal Baronio's chapel. How sad to see her toes so perfectly formed. How sad to see her head tilted toward heaven. How sad to see a corpse not a corpse at all but some vague fantasy forced to paint and pressed on the canvas to pamper the bishops who commissioned you. Because dear friend, I know that you could not believe that painting's theme despite you yourself created it. I know this because I know what you once said about all creativity," Caravaggio lectured and his words stung Mario.

"You question my skill?" Mario shouted. He was now livid.

Caravaggio refused to back down. "I question your motives."

"As I question yours," Mario stated. At that moment, he felt that Caravaggio could see, quite clearly, the sneer in his eyes and the anger heating up in his voice. Mario could recognize that his friend sensed something else in his attack, some other deeper motivation. What had come out after all these years was his resentment for Caravaggio. On this particular night, without any foreshadowing, it had come to the forefront because of this debate.

Later that very night Mario was in the café with Fillide and Strozzi. He was sullen. "I used poor judgement this evening," he told them both.

"I do not know what you mean?" Strozzi stated.

Fillide was silent but Mario knew that she was certainly aware. "You must not compare yourself to him," she said.

"But I do," he meekly admitted.

"Then that is your dilemma, my brother, not his."

Mario was about to reply when a young woman with long light brown hair and tender light blue eyes stepped over to their table escorted by the poet Mancini.

Introductions were quickly made but Mario held back. He could tell by the young woman's olive complexion, similar to his, she was from Sicily. And listening to her speak he immediately knew that she was from Messina. "Your name?" he asked.

"Isabella Parma," she smiled.

Mario could not explain how it happened but he found himself alone at the table with Isabella long after Strozzi and Fillide and Mancini had gone. It was the first time since he had met Fillide that he had been indifferent to his feelings for her. At one point that very evening, he had chided her and said, "You behave like a married woman with Strozzi."

Fillide lowered her eyes as she heard the comment.

Now Mario found himself left alone with the lovely young woman engrossed in a vigorous conversation about painting and Rome among many other topics.

Mario learned that Isabella hailed from a wealthy merchant family in Syracuse, just as he had suspected, and she had come to Rome with her aunt who was visiting another relative. He knew of the Parma family. They had amassed their fortune in almonds and fruits owning several of their ships to transport their good to the mainland as well to Arabia and Africa.

He also quickly learned that Isabella loved painting and was actually hoping to garner an invite to the Accademia as a guest. She was in attendance that very evening and Mario did recall taking notice of her but was locked in the serious debate with Caravaggio so that distracted him from introducing himself. Now, he was pleased that Mancini had brought her to their table.

He mentioned that to Isabella and she quickly told him "I requested to be brought to your table."

"And why was that?" Mario asked.

Isabella lowered her eyes then returned his look. "I wanted to be introduced to you," she answered honestly.

Mario was flattered. "And why was that, may I ask?"

Isabella now was demure. "I must return to my hotel."

Mario and Isabella walked along Via Corso and as they did Mario told an attentive Isabella about his first night in Rome and his early struggles.

Upon reaching the hotel, she bowed and Mario quickly spoke up. "Come home with me."

"I'm not a whore," she replied but without any anger at all.

"I wasn't implying you were," he told her.

"I know how you frequent brothels. I know you were infatuated with Fillide Melandroni and how you roam the piazza's, street fighting and living life to its fullest," she said with a quirky admiration.

Mario raised his eyebrows. "How do you know all *this* about me?"

She touched his hand and looked up into his eyes. "You're famous back home in Syrcause. They speak about your adventures and your work in every cafe. Those who have come to Rome have seen how Caravaggio painted you as Bacchus."

"I'm famous?" he interrupted her.

Isabella reached up and kissed him on the cheek. "Of course, you silly man. Several of your canvases have been purchased and brought back to Syracuse." She then disappeared into the hotel.

Every night of the following week, Mario accompanied Isabella to dinner, to galleries, to unveilings, poetry readings and other artistic events. He also showed her his newest commissions.

He met her aunt who was thrilled to be introduced to him and who also accompanied them both on several of their excursions.

One early evening, when they were actually alone, walking along the Tiber River, Isabella charmingly smiled. "I would like to see the Tavern of the Turk," she said.

"Impossible, it burnt down," Mario lied.

"Then I would like to see the Tavern of the Hawk or the Tavern of the Blackmoor."

Mario turned his head away from her.

"I doubt they all burned down," she chided him.

So that evening Mario took her to the Tavern of the Hawk and then when Isabella asked to see the "inside of a Roman brothel," he grudgingly obliged.

Mario took her to a corner table where Isabella sat in amazement with her mouth aghast as the partially clad women with painted faces reeking of perfume moved back and forth among the tables of men like sleek leopords on the prowl. She eyed how they rubbed their hips and bottoms against the men's penises and laughed heartily as they did.

"This is what you wanted to see?" he asked.

Isabella shook her head. "Yes. I wanted to see what it is like. I don't know if I feel envy or pity for these women."

"Envy?"

"Some are so pretty," she said, looking at him. "I can see how they can steal your heart."

"And your purse if you're not careful."

She took his hand. "Would you offer to purchase me for the evening if I were a harlot?"

He frowned. "Why do you ask such a meaningless question?"

She turned her shoulders to him. "Take me to the ghetto."

"You want to visit the *Ortaccio*?"

"Now, while the wine has given me false courage," she answered.

He saw the impish flicker of delight in her eyes. "You are charmed by sin."

"Yes, I am and I've little opportunity living in my father's house," she told him.

He leaned in and kissed her with an open mouth, then licked her face and playfully pulled her hair. "So, tonight, you are my whore." She didn't answer but seeing the flicker in her eyes was all he needed to encourage him.

He watched her closely as they walked along the curving streets of the sex ghetto. She gripped his arm with both of her hands afraid to let go. He saw her face in the shadow thrown across by the fires and he could see that she was mesmerized by him. She was watching with intense curiosity the scores of women flashing their breasts and buttocks at the dozens of men who walked the streets.

"They're locked in a dance of lust and passion," she told him seemingly stunned by her own reaction.

Mario no longer saw this romantic version of the sight before him. What he saw was pathos and despair. He saw the same thing back in the tavern and the brothel. It was as if some odd metaphysical transference had occurred and he was seeing the ugliness of his life through her eyes as Isabella was seeing the dirt and desperation and mistaking it for excitement and vibrancy.

By the time, they left the ghetto and reached his apartment and the Piazza del Popolo Mario confessed to Isabella, "That Rome had disappointed and tired him."

He was expecting her to be disappointed in his divulgence but on the contrary, she replied, "Of course it has."

"But you seemed so excited by it all?"

"I am. But it is new to me. I see its depth and I also see how trifling a world it is here. There's nothing stable. No part of it seems anchored to anything vital in a man's soul. But then again, you're an artist and an artist must experience it all, do you not believe that?"

He was impressed with what she had said. "Yes. I do believe in that. That is why sometimes I think that I have lost my desire to continue. Not long ago I had decided to leave here and return to Sicily."

"If you did such a thing, they would embrace you with open arms I am sure of it," she told him.

Later that evening he brought her to the apartment he rented in The Artists Quarter for the first time. He thought how it had been the first time in his many years in Rome that the woman he was going to make love to was *not* a whore.

Once they entered his apartment, Isabella walked to the window and looked out on the torches burning in the piazza below. "I wake up every morning still not believing that I'm here," she said. She then walked over to Mario, stopping only inches away. She raised her hands, and touched his long dark hair and then touched his face, "You're a handsome man."

He knew then that it was he who was being seduced. He was the one she had sought out. He took her face in his hands and kissed her strongly on the lips. He saw her eyes close and saw how she breathed in his entire being as they kissed, pulling her up towards his broad shoulders, he felt her shudder in his arms as he held her closely.

Then he felt her tongue in his mouth and her fingers gently touching his leg. "I'm so much like a whore, I know," she whispered keeping her eyes closed.

He pulled her away and shook his head. "You're not a whore."

"But I have never felt this lust before," she said again, this time her eyes wide open.

"Perhaps it was the ghetto? The smell of sin and lechery has enticed you?"

"No, it's not that."

He could see that she was unexpectedly embarrassed by her pronouncements and clearly afraid that he would see her as a proper female. None of this mattered to him since he wanted her and he knew she would allow him that longing. However, he felt oddly restrained. He resisted disrobing her, not sure why, since it was the reason they had gone to his apartment.

He felt Isabella gently shove him back as she lowered her blouse revealing her small but silky-smooth breasts for him. She looked shyly at him for a moment but then raised her nipple towards his mouth. It was dark and wide. He quickly placed his lips on one breasts and then the other sucking and licking them arousing her. He felt his penis grow hard.

She then pulled at her white skirt undoing the aqua sash around her waist and allowed it to fall to the floor. Mario held her hips in both hands pushing her towards him and then, magically, he felt her hands on his penis and heard her whisper, "fuck with me, please, Mario," as she lay back on his mattress lifting her legs in the air.

He entered her and heard her sigh. He rhythmically shoved his hips back and forth feeling her wet inside and as she held him around the shoulders, he felt her mouth on his neck. When he released his sperm into her, he felt her force her hips up against his so bluntly he shuddered with pleasure.

He then saw her open her eyes and smile at him.

They lay together on the bed nude in the soft breeze that blew off the Tiber River, over the piazza and up to his second floor window.

He lit a candle.

"You made my stay in Rome more than I could have imagined," she purred.

Mario kissed her ear lobe.

"I don't expect you to write me when I leave," she said matter-of-factly.

He felt an odd sensation of sudden loss when she said those words. "When are you leaving Rome?"

"Our ship sails in a fortnight."

"You return to Syracuse?"

"Yes. And I return to my father's house. He is looking for a man for me to marry."

Naked, he gently eased himself away from her and stood up, feeling vulnerable and not understanding why.

"What did I say to displease you?" she asked.

"I would be sad if you married."

"I'm not properly engaged as of yet but it seems my father plans an announcement this Christmas," she answered. "This upsets you?"

Mario walked to the window and then looked out on Rome. He felt alone for the first time. He was still unsure why he was experiencing these feelings. "Yes," he told her. He sat on the bed beside her and held her face in his hand.

"I'm confused. You're a famous artist. You live such an adventurous and wonderful life. You have had beautiful and famous courtesans and whores in your bed. I can not touch you in the way these women have?"

He continued to sit in silence.

"I'm pleased beyond my own wishes that I met you and now made love to you. I expected nothing else," she told him then put her arms around his shoulders and hugged him closely. "I don't want you to break my heart."

"I could never break your heart," he told her quickly but gently.

When he returned her to the hotel and her aunt and told her *goodbye*, he walked alone back to his apartment utterly confused about all he had ever imagined about himself and his life.

Several days later, watching her wave *goodbye* from the ship's bow, he found himself unexplainably rubbing tears from his eyes. When the ship left the harbor, he was frozen to the dock feeling a loneliness descend over him the likes he had never known.

Chapter Thirty-one

In the weeks that followed, Mario had an odd parade of disenchanting experiences. The only action he took that pleased him was his letters to Isabella. Though he told none of his friends or companions, he wrote her several times a week and waited for her letters to arrive at his door reading them quickly and several times before allowing himself time to dwell on their content.

In his letters, he wrote that he was planning a visit to Sicily and had every intention of visiting her and her family. She wrote back explaining how excited she was at the prospect of seeing him again and yet her father, adamant about her finding a husband no matter how unattractive, was distressing her. She wrote, *if you plan to visit me at all, plan your trip in haste.*

He considered proposing marriage in his last letter but decided to ask her to marry him in person. He felt that he should damn the consequences. He could paint in Sicily. That evening he went to the Tavern of the Turk to celebrate his decision with Longhi and Caravaggio.

It was the first time in a long time that Mario was in a festive mood and though it was damp and drizzling outside, the tavern was warm from the large fireplace at the far end.

The three men left the tavern drunk and decided to visit the nearest brothel.

As soon as they walked into the brothel and found a table in the center of the room, he saw a whore with long light brown hair and blue eyes. He had to rub his own eyes to make certain that he wasn't looking at Isabella.

He called the young woman over to the table and she sat on his lap. He felt his penis grow hard. He placed the palm of his hand on her bare leg and she leaned over and nibbled on his ear. "I can suck and fuck with you all evening if that is what you came here for," she said in a harsh tone and husky voice.

He looked closely into her eyes and whatever she saw in his, made her reel back. "What do you look at me like *that* for, sire?" she said sharply.

He took hold of her shoulders and saw a rash on her upper lip and a fresh boil under her chin. He lifted her hair, reeking of perfume, and saw a boil above her ear.

He pushed her off her lap and she raced away petrified and humiliated. "syphilis," he said to Longhi. He looked at the young woman now standing in the shadows starring at him. "I wanted her to be Isabella," he said in a near whisper.

He left the brothel without a word to either Caravaggio or Longhi.

He wanted to savor the last morsels of the experience of Rome at night by himself. He walked through the drizzle, north to the Piazza Santa Trinita, with images of his more than a decade in the city. He headed through streets he hardly ever walked, up the Via Felica to the upper boundaries of the Artists Quarter. Drunk, not only from the wine, but with the notion of the hope of a new life away from Rome, he saw a light in the window in an alley and heard a baby crying.

The yellow glow from the torch enchanted him as he walked half way down the dark alley stopping when he was directly under the window. He looked up and smiled. "I have come so far and yet, I never reached my goal," he muttered to himself.

He then turned back to the cobble stone and felt an urge to return home, all the way home. He followed Via Felica south when he noticed how quiet the streets were.

He kept walking staying in the shadows and away from the torches. He was in reach of the Piazza Santa Trinita when three men jumped out of a doorway in single file, planting themselves in front of him. He reached into his boot for his dagger grabbing it just as one of the men came at him to his right and another came at him from his left.

He felt something hard, probably a solid piece of wood, smack him across the forehead. He wanted to fall but he knew that if he fell to the pavement the bandits would kill him. So, despite the blow, he maintained his balance by throwing his shoulder to the building to his right and when the man in the center came at him, he thrust his knife into his throat.

The man moaned with the agony of a stuck boar filling the hot night air with his cry dying instantly. Mario felt his blood stain his shirtsleeve and watched as the companions quickly ran off hearing their boots crackle against the cobblestone.

He staggered away hoping to reach the torches of the piazza. "God give me strength," he heard himself pray, and then fell to one knee. He heard voices and looked up. A hand pulled him by the shoulder and then another hand pulled his bloody dagger from his hand. He looked up into the burning torchlight. He couldn't clearly see the faces of the men looking down at him but he could see from their boots that they were the police.

"You're under arrest in the name of the cavalieri," was the last thing he heard as he went unconscious.

❖

When Mario came to consciousness, he woke up finding himself tied to a large wooden chair. He was dizzy and thirsty but found himself face to face with Captain Nunzio Pulzone.

"You're a heretic," the captain told him. Mario could see that he was in a small room with a small torch burning at the far end. The window had bars on it. It was still dark outside.

"What did you say?" Mario asked.

"You are living in a new age of piety as our Pope tells us. Yet I look around and all I see are devilish machinations of English and German heretics," the captain told him spitting out his words.

Mario shook his head. "I'm no heretic." He now noticed there was now another man in the room with them. The man spoke up. Mario recognized the face. "My name is Guisto. I am your warden here."

"Warden?"

"You are in Campo de' Fiori," Guisto responded.

"Why am I in prison?"

The captain leaned in closer to Mario. "We have an eye-witness that you murdered a soldier."

"I was defending myself," Mario told him. His hands tied around the back of the chair and there was a rope tied tightly around his neck. When he spoke, it pulled him back causing him to loose his breath and making it difficult to speak.

"A young woman up in an open window was feeding her baby when she heard the shouting. She saw you thrust your dagger into his chest," Guisto said.

"She must have seen that I was attacked." Again, the rope burned his neck.

The captain stood up and then leaned back. Mario saw something in his eyes that he had not seen when they had their first encounter many years earlier. He saw a relentless fury and it was directed solely at him. "You are a heretic and you will be treated as such."

Now Guisto led the way with words that spit venom. "The lay brothers of the Archconfraternity of St. John the Beheaded will punish you."

Mario knew what they meant.

"You will be placed on the rack," the captain told him.

Guisto joined in. "And then you will be placed on the *veglia*."

Mario knew that nothing he could say could save him now. He drew a deep breath and shook his head. He lowered his eyes and turned away from both men.

Captain Pulzone then opened the door and two guards untied him from the chair and dragged him out of the room and down the hall.

"This is all because of her!" Mario shouted.

Pulzone could hear his shouts echo down the cement and stone hall.

Guisto closed the door. He looked at Pulzone. "Who does he speak of?" Pulzone shrugged. "The whore Fillide."

Mario woke up early that following morning chained to a wall with just enough leeway on the chain to allow him the ability to reach a plate of bread and a bowl of water near the door. He was also shaking from the damp chilly air that permeated the bleak cell. He heard cries coming from the other side of the cell's thick wooden door and saw a light through the small slit near the top of the door itself. The cries were screams of agony and some were horrible moans of those who had probably lost their minds from being imprisoned.

He knew that Campo de' Fiori was a notoriously brutal dungeon where the most hardened murderers were kept along side heretics. He knew that in the infamous courtyard named after John the Beheaded, public executions were held monthly.

Yet despite his predicament, he refused to accept his fate. He took a deep breath and shouted. "I demand to see the magistrate!" He shouted the demand several times until he fell exhausted.

As the week pressed on, Mario did all he could to count the days and nights that passed by searching for glimmers of sunlight from the tiny window that was cut out of the stone on the very top of wall he was chained to.

Weak, he found meager nourishment by eating the bread and water left for him every morning pushed in through a lid that opened at the bottom of the wooden door.

In the first week, Mario saw no one and heard nothing more than the screams and moans that permeated the prison. He was not officially charged with a crime, never saw an attorney and was never brought before the magistrate. It was the first time that the freewheeling artist came face to face with the power of the Roman State.

During the few days of his time in the cell besides the moans and screams that broke the silence, he heard the banging of hammers and shouts from laborers off in the distance.

It wasn't until somewhere in his second week in his cell that the two guards opened the door, stood him up on his feet, blind folded him and dragged him some distance down the hallway.

Stumbling since his limbs were weak from inactivity and starvation, Mario found himself in the courtyard lined up with a dozen other men who looked to him as mangled and tortured as he must have looked to them.

They were dirty and their faces swollen from beatings and some of them had expressions on their faces revealing that they had lost all sense of reality.

Mario reluctantly asked, "Why are we here?"

A balding man, whose ear had been ripped off but was now healing with puss flowing freely from the wound, gestured to the other side of the cobblestone courtyard.

For the first time Mario noticed a thin dark man dressed in loose fitting black rags tied to a pole on a wooden platform. He then saw a door open and four lay brothers of the Archconfraternity dressed and masked in linen and black cassocks and hoods approach the man.

"God save me!" the man shouted not once taking his eyes off the hooded men who climbed the platform stairs to surround him on all sides. "Repent sinner," they spoke in unison.

"I'm not a sinner!" the man pleaded. "God hears my prayers!"

"Repent or see God's wrath," again they spoke in unison.

The man vomited from fear and exhaustion. Mario watched in horror as one of the lay brothers garnished a silver knife from his cassock, stepped up to the man and with one surgical motion, cut off his nose. Blood spouted all over the platform and the man screamed. Another hooded lay brother than garnished another knife and cut out the man's eyes, the right one then the left.

He looked away but a gloved hand came from behind him forcing his face forward. "You are here to watch the sinner suffer," a guard sternly told him.

He raised his head, feeling his dirty hair stuck to his face crawling down his forehead, watching as the man on the platform was slowly mutilated. As the man continued to breath, the hooded lay brothers lit the straw that Mario hadn't noticed scattered at his feet. They set it afire and in moments, the man was on aflame. By this time, he hardly moaned at all, probably relieved that the flames were at last delivering him from further torment.

As Mario was again blindfolded and led, back to his cell he asked the guard, "Who was that man?"

"The heretic Giordano Bruno," he heard the guard mutter.

Mario then tossed back in his cell and chained to the wall. The same guard who was kind enough to answer his question now glared at him. "Your day will come when you will light the sky with your burning flesh," he said and left the room.

Mario threw himself back against the wall wondering how he could kill himself in his cell to avoid such a horrendous ending to his life.

Chapter Thirty-two

Fillide's newfound fame thrust her into a whirlwind of elite societies with many parties and ceremonies and one evening, she was in attendance at a party given by the Duke Farnese for his brother Cardinal Odoarado at the Palazzo Farnese. Also in attendance were the duke's cousin Cardinal Alessandro Farnese and his other cousin Octavio, the Duke of Parma.

During the party, Strozzi took her aside in the gloriously fashioned gallery room and proposed. "I wanted to propose marriage to you among all this beauty since you, my dear, are so beautiful."

Fillide quickly accepted by taking his hand and squeezing it. "I accept your proposal."

Strozzi bowed then said, "My fear is that you love this Ranuccio Tomassoni," but before she could reply, he placed his finger gently on her lips. "I have asked around and I know what people say. Yet, I accept that I will never own your heart as he does but I know you are fond of me and in time, that fondness will change to love. I'm certain it will," he told her.

The party was celebrating Cardinal Odoarado's birthday and the unveiling of a series of paintings he had commissioned from Annable Carracci to create and tell the story of Polyphemus and Galatea. The body of the cyclops, Polyphemus, had a mammoth magnificence and muscular power. The work seemed as if devoid of personal feeling but filled with the art of character and story telling in the third person.

The cardinal, flanked by Strozzi, Fillide and Carracci himself, eyed the work with pride and exclaimed, "These canvases rival sculpture."

The immediate discussion in the room was about literature and Fillide enjoyed the light-hearted intellectual pursuits carried on by those in attendance who read their poetry as musicians accompanied them with their instruments.

Fillide allowed herself to be swallowed up in the literary *conversazione* but she could never get out of her mind the stench of the streets, the violence she had experienced in the ghetto and the contrary existence she was now living among the wealthy and noble dilettantes.

While the cardinal was eyeing the paintings, Fillide was eyeing Carracci and was awed by the man's humility and humble clothing that consisted of a plain cassock making him easily confused for a monk. She wondered to herself if the artist needed to straddle both worlds as Mario Minniti and Caravaggio?

Cardinal Odoarado whispered to Fillide, "Poor Annable has fallen into a dark despair. Since he completed these works for me over a year ago, he cannot paint a canvas. He has confessed this loss of inspiration to me. I told him that he has lost his inspiration due to the ignorant dictum from the Vatican censoring artists."

Overhearing this, Strozzi then spoke. "I'm amazed, dear Cardinal Odoarado, that this extraordinary display of pagan nudity managed to travel passed the unblinking eye of Pope Clement's board of decency. I, myself, am bored by the dull biblical scenes and personification of the *Virtues*."

Fillide could see how the cardinal's nose opened. A tall man with steel blue eyes and a pure white, closely trimmed beard dressed in his scarlet smock and refined emerald jewels glittering in the candle light, immediately shot back, "I dare that Florentine to come into my house and remove this work of genius," he stated for all to hear with toxin acidity in his voice.

As everyone left the room, Fillide lingered with Strozzi. She smiled at one of the paintings on the ceiling and gestured as she said, '*Omnia vinct amor; et nos cedamus amori.*'

Strozzi agreed. "Virgil was correct."

Fillide then turned and taking his hand, led him out of the gallery. "Yes he was, my dear. 'Love conquers all, let us, too, yield to love.'"

During dinner, the cardinal, fueled by wine began a heated debate about the Aldobrandini's family's incompetence in running the papal state. "All of us here live in opulence but out on those streets not only does violence run rampant but so does hunger and poverty. Famine is our greatest enemy. Who here has been among the people and has *not* seen starvation on their face?" he asked.

Strozzi spoke up, "I've seen this poverty, your excellency."

The cardinal was pleased. "All this current Pope is interested in is his precious Jubilee. I also hear that he has torn his own cassock to acquire a relic. He does this as our people are starving in our streets. I pray to God there are no riots in Rome."

Strozzi wanted Fillide to meet his sisters and a lunch in the Piazza Navona was agreed on by all. Annette and Rosa appeared at the appointed hour both dressed in ruffled blouses and embroidered skirts of dark brown. Though neither woman was older than forty, to Fillide they appeared as aging matrons and when they began to speak, she thought of them as two hyenas filling their bellies on the carcasses of reputations of those not as privileged as they were.

Rosa was, at least on the surface, friendly to Fillide. Though, twenty years older, she had buoyancy in her manner and an occasionally friendly smile formed on her mouth. Annette, however, appeared of bad humor and had the look of someone who had just eaten bad fish. Nothing pleased her, not the weather, not her servants or not even her favorite pet, a dark, bad humored cat who hissed at everyone. Both women did speak of Strozzi's daughter Olivia with some trace of affection.

Fillide had little appetite at the lunch especially after Annette asked her, "How long have you been my brother's courtesan?"

Fillide turned to Strozzi who at once realized he was emasculated and horrified at the same time by his two older sisters. He buried his head in his wine, smelt the air and told Rosa that her "blouse was fetching." This was not the man Fillide thought she knew. He was not the man she had imagined him to be during their brief romance. She was hoping that he would speak up and defend her but that was not what Strozzi was capable of doing when it came to his sisters.

Again, she suddenly craved Ranuccio knowing that despite his brutish ways, he was his own man. *Perhaps the brute in me seeks the brute in him?*

Realizing that she was getting no assistance from Strozzi, Fillide answered Annette's question directly beginning with her life in Siena, her life in the ghetto, the disappearance of her beloved cousin Anna and how, at the age of twenty years, she was an independent woman.

Annette listened closely then turned to Strozzi and asked, "And you want to wed this *whore*?"

Fillide threw a look at Strozzi now curious on how he would respond. Would he say simply, "yes, I want to marry this whore?" Would he condemn his sisters calling Fillide a whore? Or would he continue ignoring his sisters?

Fillide was shocked to see how he completely ignored Annette's question, allowing her inquisition to continue on and off for a large portion of the hour. Strozzi paid the bill and then escorted his two sisters to a carriage. He turned to Fillide and said, "Well, I think that went fairly well, don't you agree?"

Fillide was beside herself but there was something about Strozzi that halted her from ever losing her own temper. He was likable and never wanted to disturb anything despite how uncomfortable something made him.

"They treated me horrendously," she said, without a quiver in her voice.

Strozzi looked hurt. "My sisters mean no harm. It is how they were brought up. I feel sorry for them that no man has ever had the inclination to marry either of them."

"What man *would have* the inclination to marry either of them?"

Hearing those words pour out of her lips, Strozzi now looked offended.

She burst out with, "I cannot marry you. I could not endure those two monsters and their insults again without taking my dagger and slitting their throats," she told him.

She then stood up and left the café. She walked along the street back to her villa needing to concentrate on the one man who still hadn't left her heart, Ranuccio.

To her amazement, Strozzi didn't follow her in his carriage and though she didn't miss him at all, she never did speak to Strozzi again for the rest of her life.

A month later, she received a letter from his attorney stating that he would like ownership of her portrait returned to him. She ignored the letter then engaged her own attorney to dictate a letter to send to Strozzi that she would never return the canvas to him. It was a gift and she was going to keep it in her possession.

A few weeks later, Fillide sent a letter written on parchment with silver embroidery, as any fine lady of Roman society would, via messenger to Ranccuio inviting him to dinner. Ranuccio declined. Fillide, however, was not surprised nor was she disappointed. She instinctively knew that he would be back in her life. Now that she was famous, he would desire her.

However, his entrance was not one she calculated. One evening, late in the winter when the eastern sky was heavy with clouds and the sunset earlier than usual, he sent a carriage for her. In it was a messenger who handed Fillide a letter and with the letter, an exuberant amount of lira. "I send for you," was what the letter stated. She sent the messenger back with an empty carriage and along with the bag filled with lira.

The rest of that evening, she sat by her fireplace and cried. She allowed the tears to flow easily and naturally. Her heart was broken despite her newfound fame and despite her invitation to him as a lady of Roman society; she knew that he continued to view her as his *whore.*

And that perception would never change.

CHAPTER THIRTY-THREE

Pietro Aldobrandini was notified that the artist Mario Minniti was being held prisoner in Campo de' Fiori nearly a month into captivity, and still in all that time, Captain Pulzone had neglected to have Mario appear before a magistrate.

Pietro was more than concerned when he heard that Minniti's incarceration had been made public in a newspaper article. Pietro received the messenger from Cardinal Odoarado Farnese demanding that he, Pietro, *look* into the matter judiciously. Pietro knew that the cardinal's interest in Mario Minniti was not because he was a respected artist since Mario had garnered only a few minor commissions and was not considered at all as one of Rome's elect. However, Pietro realized that Cardinal Odoarado Farnese was looking to capitalize on Mario's imprisonment and turn it into a political affair.

Pietro was aware that Cardinal Farnese was using the arrest as proof that the Aldobrandini family considered art a bastard son of Rome unlike the Farnese who saw art as a significant element of their society. Cardinal Odoarado would point to Mario's arrest as testament to Aldobrandini family's indifference to their artists. Pietro knew that none of this was good news for his uncle, the Pope.

Upon hearing the facts of Mario's arrest, Pietro immediately sent messengers to Captain Pulzone ordering that Mario be brought to a courtroom and given a just hearing.

Nunzio followed Pietro's dictum and yet, when Mario appeared the following afternoon at the magistrate's courtroom, the journalists in attendance took one look at him and wrote, "He had been seriously tortured." The journalist continued in his article that Mario was arrested "…for doing nothing more than defend his life from the unwarranted attack launched at him on the street by three drunken Spanish soldiers."

By the time, Mario appeared in public he was beyond despair expecting his execution any moment. He had spent the previous long hours in his cell famished. He could do nothing more than agonize over his life damning himself for pursuing hollow undertakings. Though, in the darkest of his moments, he never gave up his love for painting and dreamt of some day having a brush in his hand and a canvas to fill.

As he was brought back to languish in his cell, the one thing he could never have expected occurred. The story of his imprisonment, written up in the newspapers, had reached many of Rome's ordinary citizens who were now calling for his immediate release. This fervor reached all the way back to Sicily and one morning Isabella, reading the newspaper on her patio at her father's villa, was aghast when she read about Mario's suffering. She begged her father to use his influence to save a man born and raised on his island home. Andrea Parma took great interest in Mario's arrest since he, Andrea Parma, was a close cousin of the Farnese family.

Andrea Parma sent an emissary of Sicilian merchants, hailing from Syracuse, and when he landed in Rome, he went directly to the prison and spoke with Guisto.

"This prisoner is a murderer and will not be released until he suffers for his crime," Guisto told Parma. Parma refused to listen to a lowly warden and went directly to his own cousin, the Duke of Farnese. The Duke gathered up the entire powerful Farnese family to meet with Andrea Parma and decided on a plan that would release Mario and embarrass the Aldobrandinis.

Mario had no knowledge of any of these events since he was not allowed to write letters or receive them. One evening, he heard voices outside his cell door. The door then opened and his cell was lit by burning red and orange flames.

Men in hoods instantly surrounded him chanting in Latin. He knew them to be the Archconfraternity of Saint John the Beheaded. One of the hooded men knelt beside the frantic Mario and whispered in his ear, "Offer your pain to the souls in purgatory," as another hooded man held before his eyes small panels, *tavolette*, that showed scenes of saintly torture and martyrdom. "Repent your sins and endure your pain," the hooded man demanded.

Mario realized that he was the main focus of a terrible drama, bound together with the hooded men and his execution would be a public display of blood chilling spectacle.

Quickly as the hooded men appeared that night, they disappeared. Mario was certain that the next time they returned, he would be executed in some horrible way and branded a heretic all because of Captain Nunzio Pulzone's obsession for Fillide.

Part Four

Rome
"1603–1609"

CHAPTER THIRTY-FOUR

A letter appeared under Mario's cell door early the following morning.

The short note read, "Be of courage. The Farnese will speak up for you." It wasn't signed.

Seconds later Captain Nunzio Pulzone and the warden Guisto were standing at the door, seemingly aware of the letter; they stepped aside to allow the burly guards to pull Mario out of the cell.

Mario feared they were taking him to another prison making it more difficult to find him. He bit, spit and screamed at the guards as they blindfolded him and carried him out of the stinking hell of the cell he had been living in for over a month.

What Mario didn't see was Nunzio pick up the letter and glance over it quickly. When Mario was out of the cell, he turned to Guisto and said, "This has become a political affair and we are at the center of it."

What Mario was also unaware of was that an emissary from the Farnese family, including Andrea Parma, were at the gates of Campo de' Fiori in Guisto's office demanding an immediate audience with Guisto.

Their appearance had initiated Nunzio's notion to quickly extract Mario from that prison, in secret, and place him in another. Nunzio did this in direct disobedience to an order by Pietro telling him to give the case special attention until there was an official proclamation from the Vatican concerning the situation.

Nunzio secured a carriage having it pull up to the back entrance of the prison and discreetly transport Mario across Rome in secret. Not wanting to attract more attention then he was already receiving, Nunzio had Mario blindfolded, bounded and then quickly dismissed the guards so not to gain attention as the carriage rushed across the cobblestone streets.

Mario listened intently as the wheels crossed over the stone doing all he could to imagine where he was. Nunzio saw what he was doing and pulled the blindfold away from Mario's eyes. "I want you to see your last moments of freedom so that they haunt you all your life."

Upon seeing Nunzio, Mario glared at him. Every inch of his being hated the man he was facing. He could see that Nunzio despised him with the same ferocity. "You are punishing an innocent man—"

"No one in Rome is innocent of sin," Nunzio responded with conviction.

Mario turned to the window. He knew where he was instantly, recognizing the district of Campo Marzio. He then looked back at Nunzio. He saw more anger than when he had seen him during his first interrogation in the prison. He now saw a man whose face was obviously distorted by self-doubt while searching for relief from his responsibilities. "You will not escape your punishment *this* time, citizen," Nunzio spat.

"I've always been free of what burden's men like you. I'm free to love a whore you lust for," he said.

Nunzio looked away placing his hands to his own face and rubbing his eyes. "I hate the politics that suck on the nipples of this city's heart and soul. I despise the venom like you who come here and afflict our streets with your drunken disrespect," he growled.

Without hesitation, Mario saw his moment to act. He lifted his elbow directly at Nunzio's nose, jabbing him with it, causing blood to spout and Nunzio to moan in pain. Even though he was bound with his hands behind his back, he shoved the carriage door with all of his remaining strength as Nunzio reached to stop him.

Mario felt Nunzio's hand on his shirtsleeve but the shirt was so tattered that when Nunzio pulled at it, it disintegrated. Once again, Mario threw all his weight at the carriage door. This time it buckled and Mario flung himself out to the street.

Ignoring the pain from a gash over his right eye caused by the fall, Mario pushed himself up from his knees frantically searching for exactly where he was. He quickly realized he was between Via dei Prefetti and the Piazza della Torretta. He struggled to his feet only to hear the carriage come to a halt. He turned and saw Nunzio leap from the carriage to chase after him.

Mario raced down the narrow Via Vicolo knowing that it was flanked on one side by the vast walls of the Palazzo Farnese. For the first time he felt as if God's hand played a part in his destiny as he raced along the brick walls that were lined with the overhanging branches of olive trees from inside the garden.

With Nunzio in pursuit, he reached the front entrance of the Palazzo only to be stopped by a guard. Mario saw the Farnese chapel a short distance from the gate across the other side of the garden. Out of breath and shouting for his life, Mario barely exclaimed, "Sanctuary!"

The guard was perplexed raising his sword across his chest. Mario pleaded with his eyes hearing Nunzio's hurrying footsteps only yards away.

"Remove yourself from this palazzo," the guard told him.

Mario strained to look into the garden over the guards shoulder and was amazed to see Cardinal Odoarado himself standing with a rosary in his hand and his mouth agape. Mario fell to his knees. "Sanctuary..."he blurted out. He could see that the cardinal was stunned.

"Who are you?" the cardinal asked.

"Mario Minniti, sire," Mario said with deep breaths.

Hearing the name, the cardinal instantly gestured to the guard and just as Nunzio reached the gate, the gate door opened and Mario crawled into the sanctuary of the Palazzo Farnese.

Lying on his side taking deep breaths and feeling exhaustion to the point of going unconscious, the last images Mario could see from his vantage point were Nunzio, also out of breath, facing the tall, imposing figure of Cardinal Odoarado. "Who are you?" the cardinal asked.

"I'm Captain Nunzio Pulzone of the cavarlieri and this man is a violent criminal who has escaped my custody..."

"This man pleads for sanctuary and I grant it, dear captain. With that, the cardinal motioned for his guard. "Bring him to my third floor chambers," he shouted, throwing a stinging glance at Nunzio then went on his way.

The next time Mario was alert he was lying in a plush bed looking out at the evening sky hungry, thirsty and thankful for being a pawn in a much larger game of political chess than he was ever expecting to be involved.

CHAPTER THIRTY-FIVE

Pietro found his uncle in his private chapel, saying his prayers, as he walked passed the entourage of startled monks to interrupt him.

Clement was flabbergasted that he did this but when Pietro quickly explained the Mario Minniti situation, the Pope stood up and retreated from his chapel altar to one of the pews. "Do you know this Mario Minniti personally?"

"Only through an introduction by Caravaggio," he answered. Then he lied. "I do not know him socially, I can assure you."

The Pope eyed his nephew closely. "So, the Farnese intends to exploit this issue?"

"I fear they will exploit it to its fullest, your Holiness," Pietro answered. He had taken notice lately that his uncle had an unhealthy blush to his skin. Pietro usually attributed his uncle's colorless hue to his obsessive fasting but he had noticed that this time his uncle had also seemed more fatigued recently, had lost weight, and also was spending more and more time alone in his chapel.

"What do you suggest?"

Pietro was surprised that his uncle actually asked for advice. *Another sign, perhaps, that he was weakening physically?* Pietro replied quickly. "We must send an emissary to the Farnese and discuss options."

"Discuss what options? This Minniti is a criminal. The magistrate has indicted him, am I correct?"

Pietro nodded in agreement. "Yes, but perhaps that is not the sole issue here. Perhaps it would be better for us to act shrewdly, dear uncle."

Clement then rose from his pew steadying himself on Pietro's shoulder. "In face of this Minniti's violent activity and in lieu of the violence which plagues our city, I condemn the artist to death and announce a *banda capitale* on his very life."

Pietro felt a shiver of dread race through him. "That is *not* wise."

The Pope clenched his teeth. "That is my decision."

"But a *banda capitale* is a death sentence?"

The Pope now struggled down the aisle, his hands on the shoulders of his monks who followed him stride for stride. "That is an accurate assessment."

Pietro followed the entourage raising his voice just enough so that his uncle could hear him. "It is a terrible sentence. It means that anyone, in any place, can carry it out and execute Minniti," he stated.

Clement stopped and faced his nephew. "I appoint you as emissary to the Farnese. I want you to announce to them my sentence and make it clear to them that I expect them to carry it out immediately." With that, he slowly arched his body away from Pietro and the altar, disappearing out of the chapel.

Pietro nearly swooned and plopped himself in the nearest pew. He looked up at the large wooden crucifix on the wall above the altar and made the sign of the cross. "So help me God, I'm in dire straits."

It was nearly three that afternoon that Captain Pulzone arrived in Pietro's private Vatican office. He had a bandage covering his nose and both his eyes were black and blue. Pietro had been waiting patiently since his meeting with the Pope in the chapel. He was now in his office on the ground floor of the Vatican anxious for the cavalieri captain to arrive. He had sent his Vatican carriage for him and when he did enter the office, Pietro noticed a fire in his blackened eyes he hadn't seen before. "I've discussed the Minniti plight with the Pontiff," he quickly said hoping to put out the fire.

"And what action has the Pontiff decided to take?" Nunzio replied sharply.

Face to face with the captain, Pietro made no reference to the bandage or the swollen eyes. "He's decided to pronounce a *banda capitale* on Minniti."

"It was a wise decision."

Pietro winced. He took the captain by the shoulder and moved him closer to the wall. "Can you explain your behavior concerning this man?"

Nunzio stared at Pietro his eyes revealing nothing. "Answer me, captain!" Pietro was now angry.

"I've been hunting him for a murder he committed a decade ago," Nunzio replied.

Pietro sighed. "And this has nothing to do with Fillide Melandroni?" he asked realizing the truth as Nunzio blushed by the mention of her name.

"I'm a cavalieri and the honor due my shield and my duty come before all else," he answered.

Pietro took a moment to reflect. He knew that he had to obey his uncle and would do so until he could conjure up other alternatives. "So, I assign you my Vatican guard. Together we shall proceed to the Palazzo Farnese. Our mission is to re-arrest Mario Minniti and return him to the Vatican for immediate execution. I can use the ruse that he is a fugitive murderer. Wait for me at the entrance to the stable," he said.

Pietro watched as a Nunzio, pleased with the Pope's sentencing, left the office. He then took his rosary from his desk and wound it around his wrist. "Hail Mary full of grace, the Lord is with Thee—"he prayed as he left his office, on what he believed to be the most dangerous of missions.

When Pietro arrived with Captain Pulzone at the Palazzo Farnese, he found the palazzo's entrance guarded by a dozen heavily armed men of the Farnese's private army.

He also saw something else that highly disturbed him. There was a crowd of angry men and women facing the stone walls of the Palazzo Farnese. Their voices rose up in anger when they saw the Vatican seal on Pietro's carriage.

"What is this?" Pietro asked Nunzio.

"It is a *mob*, your excellency," Nunzio replied dryly.

"I know it's a mob. I want to know why they're here," Pietro shot back.

The two men were then quickly escorted to safety to the other side of the wall by Farnese guards.

Pietro and Nunzio were now on the second floor where they were ushered into a vast room with enormous windows and a large balcony. In the far corner of the room, Pietro saw three prestigiously dressed men facing him. In the center was Cardinal Odoarado rooted to the ground in his long white flowing cassock and a red scarlet hat signifying his office. To his left was the short and nearly obese Cardinal Alessandro and to his right was Andrea Parma. There were several personal guards at the doors and at the windows.

Pietro stood facing the three men as the angered shouts coming from the crowd below became louder. He did all he could do to smile warmly and extend his hand to Cardinal Odoarado but the cardinal sniffed the air and gazed *down* on Pietro with an insulting gesture of defiance. He spit out, "What is the reason for your visit?"

Pietro knew that the cardinal *knew* why he was there. He felt the eyes of the Farnese family fall upon him like daggers. He feigned a self-effacing humility. "I'm here on official Vatican duty. Our Pontiff has assigned me the responsibility of taking Mario Minniti back to the custody of our diligent cavalieri—"

Cardinal Odoarado quickly spat out, "Minniti has requested sanctuary and I have granted it to him."

Pietro glanced at Nunzio who quickly saw that it was his opportunity to speak up. "Excellency, with all due respect, you are harboring a criminal who is a fugitive in a murder."

Again, Cardinal Odoarado quickly spat out, "Mario Minniti is a guest of the Farnese. If you want to defy my invitation to him, so be it. Remove him from my home if it pleases you."

"Where is he, sire?" Nunzio asked.

"In the third floor bedroom," the cardinal replied.

Nunzio glanced at Pietro who reluctantly nodded for him to act. Nunzio turned and headed for the door. The six armed Farnese guards encircled him. Nunzio halted his advance. "Your men are preventing a cavalieri to do his official duty, sire."

Cardinal Odoarado nodded. "Yes, captain they are. And they are doing so on my orders."

Pietro felt a lump in his throat. He knew that there was only one way to save the situation and that was to retreat. "Since we are at odds here, dear Odoarado, perhaps the captain and I should refrain from any official duty and allow you the pleasure of your guest."

Cardinal Odoarado smirked, took a few steps toward the balcony and gestured for Pietro to walk over to his side. "I believe the people of Rome would like to greet you."

Pietro felt the sweat on his neck wetting his collar. "I doubt they have any interest in seeing *me*."

"I disagree. I believe they have a lot of interest in seeing you," Cardinal Odoarado said, then gestured to his guard to gently prod Pietro to the balcony. Pietro reached out and grabbed Nunzio's shoulder using him as a buffer against the obvious danger he was now in.

On reaching the balcony, Pietro had no idea what to expect. He didn't think the cardinal would have him physically thrown over the balcony but then again, it was a distinct possibility. What distracted him were the shouts coming up from below. "What are they shouting?" Pietro asked the room.

No one answered but when he reached the balcony, he found himself standing at the railing facing a mob that numbered in the thousands. "Oh my," Pietro uttered.

Nunzio stepped beside him. "Hooligans and rabble," he muttered.

Cardinal Odoarado also stepped closer to Pietro but directly behind him. "I believe they are calling for *you*," he chided.

Pietro listened closely and though the shouting was loud and boisterous he was certain he was hearing the refrain. "Death to the Aldobrandini!" His heart sank before he could react as the balcony door shut behind him and Nunzio.

An apple flung from below struck Pietro under his right eye and then an orange splattered on the wall above. Nunzio was quickly hit in the face with a squash and suddenly both men were deluged with rocks and fruit coming from the mob. The balcony glass shattered and Nunzio bravely shoved Pietro to the balcony platform and threw his body over him. "Endure, cardinal! Endure," he shouted. Pietro was sick with fright.

"Burn the Aldobrandini!" continued to be screamed in his direction along with the flying projectiles.

Fillide heard about Mario's escape from prison and his request for *sanctuary* when one of her servants raced to her as she was enjoying her afternoon lunch on her patio. Fillide quickly dressed and had her carriage take her to the Palazzo Farnese.

She arrived as the crowd was swelling, and though she could have requested entrance to the palazzo knowing that the cardinal would certainly remember her from his birthday party months earlier, Fillide decided to stay with the crowd that was seemingly growing larger as time went on.

Immediately, she was recognized by *many* in the mob, which was made up of day laborers, sailors whose ships were docked in Rome's harbor, recently released soldiers and many merchants who were suffering economically due to the famine.

"Sweet Fillide!" some of the men shouted offering her to sit up on their wagons and one group of young men lifted her so that she could actually sit up on the stone wall and get a clear view of the balcony.

Fillide realized that she was being recognized as one of them. She was of their class despite the rumors that she was from an aristocratic family. "Have I fucked with any of you here?" she gleefully shouted as some older men offered her grapes, bread, provolone cheese and wine.

There were shouts of laughter from the mob but suddenly Pietro and Nunzio appeared on the balcony and Fillide herself felt her throat became dry. She knew both men intimately and here they were, in plain view, threatened by the rabble.

As soon as the two men appeared, an angry voice rang out with chants of, "Kill the Aldobrandini!" From where she sat, Fillide could see Pietro's face take on the mask of complete horror and beside him, the tormented Captain Pulzone, his eyes glaring at the mob as if he was looking deep into his own soul's darkness.

"Hang the Aldobrandini!" shouted the crowd as some of the younger men threw fruit and rocks in their direction. As they did, Fillide saw Pietro and Nunzio take cover on the balcony. Fillide felt a rage erupting in the pit of her own breast. She felt a fury she didn't believe existed in her. "Kill the Aldobrandinis!" Fillide screamed with those around her. "Kill them!" she yelled. The frenzy of utter vehemence she felt for those in power, and at those who held her fate in their hands, overwhelmed her. The depths of her own revulsion astonished her. She disdained those men who she knew tolerated her existence only because they could garnish pleasure from her. Now having the opportunity to literally voice her own opinion, she realized then and there that she wanted to see the mob take both men in their grips and murder them.

Fillide stood up on the wall balanced by two men on either side of her. "Hang them now!" She demanded of the crowd and the mob agreed. "Hang them!" Voices shouted. "Burn them!" Others yelled.

Fillide continued to lead the growing mob into frenzy until at long last several of the younger men actually climbed along the side of the palazzo reaching the balcony unopposed by the Farnese security guards.

Though fatigued and dizzy from his ordeal, the shouting mob woke Mario from his deep slumber. He was alone in the room and though naked under the white linen bed sheets, he found a robe on the chair beside him and managed to put it on, then edged over toward the closed window facing the courtyard.

He pulled the white lace curtains away and was amazed to see what he thought must have been thousands of men thrusting their fists toward the balcony to his right, screaming at the top of their lungs, "Kill the Aldobrandinis!"

At first, he thought that he might be dreaming but the sunlight was so warm on his face that he was sure he was conscious and that he was in the Palazzo Farnese and something extraordinary was occurring because of his imprisonment.

His body was so weak from his recent ordeal he realized that he didn't much care about the outcome of what was occurring outside his window. He needed sleep to heal so he eased himself back into the bed and allowed the shouting crowd to be his symphony as he closed his eyes and slept.

CHAPTER THIRTY-SIX

Two screaming young men reached the balcony with daggers. Nunzio managed to push one over the railing just as he reached him and managed to disarm and jab an elbow to the second before tossing him over the railing into the crowd.

Two more men appeared and then another two, and then another two. As Nunzio wrestled with them, some of the young men grabbed Pietro and pushed him over the railing. Pietro was aghast with shock. His bulky frame hug in the balance swaying to one direction and then another as he was certain to be pushed into the abyss.

Farnese guards appeared pulling Pietro to safety. He was beyond himself when he managed to be pulled into the room with a bloodied Nunzio at his heels.

Once they were in the room, they found themselves once again prisoners of the Farnese. The cardinal faced them. "I order you both off of my property."

Pietro was livid. "They will kill us!"

The cardinal grinned. "Are you asking for *sanctuary*?"

Pietro saw the irony in the situation but he knew that there was no time for negotiation other than asking for mercy. "Yes, we beg for *sanctuary*."

The cardinal frowned. "I shall grant it on the condition that you compose immediately a letter of *safe conduct* for Mario Minniti that allows him to leave Rome when he is healthy enough to travel."

Pietro nodded his head vigorously that he would comply. The cardinal and this entourage left the room but not before he posted several armed sentries on the balcony to calm the mob.

Pietro threw himself across the floor. "Thank you, God, for sparing our lives," he said realizing that his rosary was still wrapped around his wrist. He quickly began muttering the rosary while Nunzio, annoyed and still heated from the fight, stepped over to the window. "Human evil is what they are," he uttered.

Later that afternoon Pietro and Nunzio were escorted to the front gate only to find that all that remained of their carriage was a mass of splinters. Even the wheels were gone. The horses had clearly been taken by the mob and the driver, no doubt, ran for his life.

Once again, Pietro begged Cardinal Odoarado for sanctuary and once again, the cardinal granted it. Pietro then sent a messenger to the Vatican informing his uncle of his predicament but the messenger was attacked outside the gates and badly beaten and had to return to the palazzo.

By the second evening Pietro and Nunzio were thrilled to see seven hundred Corsican soldiers carrying the Vatican banner marching into the piazza directly across from the Palazzo Farnese. Seeing them approach, the mob, which had now slowly disbanded out of boredom, quickly ran off.

The Corsican soldiers escorted Pietro and Nunzio back to the Vatican. By the time he was safely behind Vatican walls, Pietro was hungry, scared and a resolve to question his uncle's political dictates before acting upon them.

He also didn't leave the relative safety of the Vatican walls unless he had to and he also avoided his uncle as much as possible.

Several months later in early March, Pietro was summoned to his uncle's bedside. It was late in the afternoon and the chilly air permeated everywhere in the Pope's residence.

Pietro hadn't seen his uncle for several days and the last few times they did speak in person he found his uncle's demeanor less and less vigorous.

Standing at his bedside, Pietro, listening to his uncle's loyal monks praying in the bedroom, found his uncle lying on his back and his small eyes looking upward. "Uncle? What's wrong?"

Pope Clement VIII swallowed then nodded to the bowl of water on his bedside table. "Water, please, dear nephew," he managed to say.

Pietro reached for the water, poured some in a cup and then turned back to his uncle. By the time he returned his attention back to his uncle, he was dead.

Pietro knew immediately and made the sign of the cross. He then reached over his uncle's face and closed his eyes. "Heaven has a new soul," he said to the monks who were now sobbing louder than before.

Sicily

Immediately after being granted his letter of *safe conduct* Mario was with Andrea Parma and on a ship bound for Syracuse. He healed on the voyage though the ship was under constant threat from the Turks and from the Barbary pirates who beset the perilous waters of the North African coasts.

One of the reasons Mario had left Syracuse was because the intensely nationalist city was tormented by excessive economic difficulties. Calamity, plague, starvation and destitution troubled Sicily itself but as he got nearer the island, he was thrilled to see the rugged, mountainous island rise out of the mist with seagulls flying towards him. He sat out on the deck as the ship entered the large, sheltered harbor anxiously anticipating seeing Isabella standing on the dock waiting for him.

As the ship settled in its mooring he scanned the busy portside for her. Mario!" he heard her shout. Isabella, wearing a long white shawl and a light blue silk skirt, was beaming as she waited for him. He limped over to her, his body still aching from his tribulation. He had never felt so joyous, he thought to himself.

Despite the fact that they were not engaged or betrothed to one another, the couple embraced. Their public display of affection insulted no one. "My love, welcome to Syracuse," Isabella whispered in his ear.

"My new home," he said to her.

They walked along the dock arm in arm. Mario felt an overwhelming burden lifted from his shoulders. He wasn't sure if being away from Rome was the reason for this new found lightness in his chest or the fact that he was back home breathing in the sea's fresh air.

Whatever the reason, as he looked up towards the bright sunlight he said to Isabella, "I'm never going back to Rome."

CHAPTER THIRTY-SEVEN

Rome

After Pope Clemente VIII's death, Alexander de'Medici was elected Pope Leo XI. Being a senior cardinal in the Vatican, Pietro was deeply involved in the debates that transpired in the College of Cardinals and through the incessant diplomacy of the French ambassador, Pietro helped sway the vote to appease the French.

During the coronation ceremony, Leo XI, a small, thin frail man, took ill and died on April twenty-seventh. The city of Rome fell into chaos. With the papal throne empty, the city government was suspended and only the lay officials of each district, the *caporioni*, alone could administer justice. Pietro watched from the safety of his Vatican office as the bell on the capitol tolled for the death of the pope, the city's jails emptied of their inmates, and the last of the prisoners, following the *caporioni*, carried away the *corda*, the rope used in torturing.

Pietro formed two Vatican Sees but had to battle French and Spanish factions. However, no faction could agree on a successor. Pietro knew the dangers of such a fray and saw the makings of a schism.

It was then that Pietro felt the surge of insight that he had always been somewhat hampered by his uncle. The constraints of living in his uncle's shadow had disappeared and Pietro followed his instincts.

He sent an emissary to Cardinal Montalto asking for a private audience with the Duke of Gonzaga. Cardinal Montalto was a loud and boisterous man who delighted in conversation. His family was several generations Roman.

Their clandestine meeting was held at Duke Vincenzo Gonzaga's on the second floor of the Palazzo Mattei. Flanked by reproductions of Titan and Tempesta, Pietro sat face to face alone in the large gallery with the red-haired and heavily bearded and robust Duke.

"I present one name and one name only," Pietro said dressed elegantly in his scarlet cassock.

The Duke dropped all pretence. "And the name of this candidate you're proposing?"

Pietro said the name distinctly. "Camillo *Borghese*."

The Duke smiled upon hearing the name. "Do you know him?"

"I only know *of* him. But I'm certain that he has a following of younger cardinals who have effused our Church with ambition and a desire to triumph over the dark forces at our heels" Pietro replied.

The Duke pointed at Pietro. "Well said."

"Then you agree?"

The Duke sighed. "You know I'm very friendly with the Borghese. I know Camillo very well. We were students together at the university here in Rome," he stated. "I believe your choice is a superb one."

"Excellent," Pietro beamed.

Pietro was facing Camillo Borghese, now known as Pope Paul V, in the same office his uncle once inhabited. There were no feelings of nostalgia for Pietro. He was actually excited knowing that he had brought to power a man who deserved it and by just being in his presence, Pietro knew that this man projected the confidence the Church needed.

Paul V was from a Sienese family who had long-settled in Rome. He was only in his early fifties, near Pietro's age, and he was in good health. Pietro knew that the man was not an intellectual but he was stern and authoritarian and without his uncle's propensity for the dangers of righteousness.

His face was fleshy and he had small but sharp brown eyes with a short pointed beard. He had a melodious voice and though empowered with the most powerful throne in the world, he had a casual sense of conversation allowing Pietro to relax despite the authority he faced was no longer a blood relation. "Trust? Do you understand its power, dear cardinal?" Pope Paul asked.

Pietro opened his eyes wide. "Like faith, it moves mountains."

The new Pointiff spread his arms out across his massive wooden desk laden with papers and paperweights. "In the spirit of our time I intend to lead our Church with the song of piety and charity. I, myself, will be generous in donation. I do not want to see the poor walking Rome any more, my friend," he said allowing his stern nature to be seen.

Pietro spoke. "We need to do our part, your Holiness."

Pope Paul stood and placing his back to Pietro. He then swung around. Pietro was surprised yet glad to see his youthful exuberance. "I'm replacing you with my own newphew, Scipione. I've already summoned him to Rome."

Pietro was stunned. "Replacing *me,* your Pontiff?"

The Pope faced Pietro from across his desk. "I ask you to voluntarily exile yourself to Ravena. This is not a punishment. It is decision based on my own needs. I want my family close and I also need to placate the Farnese."

Pietro remained silent awaiting his fate.

The Pontiff then reached to his desk and handed Pietro an official Vatican proclamation. "I'm appointing you the *new* liaison between the Vatican and the cavalieri."

"How can I manage that from Ravena?"

"That will be your cross to bear. You'll keep your office here in the Vatican and you'll be among my senior cardinal advisors," the Pope said but then added quickly. "Yet only *when* I summon you."

Pietro felt the relief racing through his bones.

Pope Paul sat. "However, there is one thing I demand that you do. I want you to extract these names from your current circle." He handed him an official document. Pietro read the names aloud from the document. "Bishop Romano? And my *own* cousin"? The Pope's tone of voice abruptly changed. "I'm here to reform our Lord's Church. Romano is a deviant and Cinzio a vain leech on our resources. Eliminate them from your public and private circle. Forthwith. I will no longer tolerate sexual activity among my ordained."

Avoiding his direct gaze, Pietro then bowed.

"One other thing, Pietro, whose notion was it to create a ghetto for prostitution?"

Pietro shrugged. "I'm not certain, your Holiness. We had many notions on how to dissuade the whore population from plying its services." Pietro then kissed the pope's ring, quickly turned and headed towards the door to leave the room when he heard the Pontiff call out, "Pietro?"

Pietro stopped, took a deep breath and turned. "Yes, your Holiness?"

"My nephew has written me that he has an artist here in Rome he wants to commission to paint my portrait."

"What artist?"

Pope Paul picked up a letter from his desk and read a name. "Caravaggio?"

"Excellent choice," Pietro bowed and left the room.

Once back in his office he quickly dispatched a messenger to Bishop Romano requesting to see him for dinner in his private chambers. He also sent a messenger to Cinzio requesting an audience that afternoon.

Pietro told Cinzio of the Pope's request and recommended that Cinzio return to Florence. "There's much to do there for a man of your talents and reputation," Pietro told him then left not waiting to hear his cousin's pleas to intervene with the Pope.

During dinner, Pietro told Bishop Romano that he was no longer his assistant and that he needed to vacate his rooms in the Vatican. Pietro knew he needed Romano's loyal discretion. "I'll find a parish in Rome that needs a pastor," he said quickly.

Romano looked close to tears. "Please, don't send me to a parish near the river. The smell can be intolerable in summer."

Pietro then whispered, "My dear friend, our new Pope values chastity, I'll have to obey these *virtues* also. In fact, he's sending me to Ravena."

"How awful."

"Precisely. However—"

Bishop Romano spoke. "However?"

"When Pope Paul settles into his office, I might inquire the residence of Fillide for my own discreet purposes. I'll look to you for guidance and direction when I deem it time."

"I'll remain aware of your address and hers at all times," Romano replied.

Pietro was pleased. "You're an excellent bishop. I'll remain watchful for your career and your wellbeing. That is a promise."

Time moved swiftly in the new Rome and Fillide was meeting with her accountant in her office in her villa one early morning on May twenty-eight which was the first anniversary of the coronation of the new Pope Paul V.

She had made a plan to take a carriage to the Tiber River and attempt to see the festivities occurring in the Vatican from the Ponte Vitt Bridge.

Her accountant, a stout, balding man named Niccolo, who she had met through Strozzi, dressed in a fine linen suit and cap, sat across from her in her elegant room, told her that her investments were doing very well. He nodded as he pointedly gestured to her bank accounts emphasizing how her newly procured properties, especially the properties she had been slowly acquiring over the years in the ghetto surrounding the Mausoleum of Augustus, were rising in worth. That particular neighborhood had been gaining in popularity since the news that Pope Paul V was going to eliminate the *Anti-Eden,* reached the merchant class.

Thanks to information she gained from her contacts, those merchants and other men in high places in Roman society who continued to see her as a courtesan, Fillide was given ample time to buy up the neighborhood piece by piece.

On this particular morning, Fillide told Niccolo to acquire properties east of the Villa Borghese where she was discreetly given inside information that an enormous university was going to be built in the park land beyond the Piazza Fiume.

Niccolo was impressed by the finesse with which Fillide acquired her wealth. "When it comes to money matters, madam, you have the dexterity of a banker, the insight of a merchant and the heart of a politician," he told her.

Fillide was well aware of her growing wealth. Yet she saw money only as a means of gaining privacy and in helping her one day to abandon once and for all the profession she had now been practicing for over a decade.

When Niccolo left, Fillide took her early lunch in her garden and was pleased to see a blue jay dancing among the lower branches of her fruit trees. She sipped her tea and opened the newspaper. When she read the headline it was as if she was reading her own obituary, however, it wasn't her's, it was Ranuccio's. According to the article, the night before there was a brawl in the Piazza di San Lorenzo in Lucina. Ranuccio had a quarrel with Caravaggio and the *painter of some fame these days* delivered a blow with his sword in Ranuccio's stomach. The article mentioned how he was the son of the former Colonel Lucantonio Tomassoni. Ranuccio was mortally wounded and fell to the ground dead.

The article also stated that Caravaggio was slightly injured in the fight and his whereabouts unknown. Fillide read the article twice then lowered her head and swallowed. Looking up, she grabbed hold of the table, lifted herself up, walked to the grass in her garden then sat, fell back and lay prone under the tree.

She felt the same dark hole in her being when her father had died. She curled up in a ball forcing her knees to her breasts unable to answer her servants as they worriedly spoke to her.

Fillide didn't move for an hour. It wasn't until her head maid, Prudenza, helped her to her feet that Fillide allowed her servants to bring her back into the house. She immediately got into bed and lay there until darkness came. Only when she saw the bright full moon sitting high up in the sky did she allow herself the release of tears.

CHAPTER THIRTY-EIGHT

Ranuccio was buried in his family cemetery at the family villa in the Piazza di San Lorenzo in Lucina and though Fillide wanted desperately to attend, she knew that would be impossible. However, on the day of the funeral, a messenger appeared at her door with an invitation to attend an *observance* given by her brothers at Ranuccio's favorite Tavern of the Turk.

Despite her concerns, Fillide appeared at the tavern that evening and though unescorted, she found the Tomassoni brothers on the top floor in a private room mourning their brother. As she had expected they had their courtesans instead of their wives with them.

Fillide had been crying all day and when she arrived the brothers treated her with a fair amount of respect though she was shunned by the courtesans who she knew never liked her. She stayed to herself in the corner at a single table as the brothers made drunken speeches about their dead brother. It was actually, what she needed. She needed to be in a room of people who knew and loved Ranuccio and expressed their grief about his death.

Yet along with the cries of grief were also shouts of vengeance on Caravaggio with an offering of a bounty on his head as well as hexes put on his life and the worst of all, the condemnation of his soul by the *evil eye*.

Fillide understood the loud pronouncements of pain and the need for revenge listening to them all silently. Eventually, Giovan who glided over to her table and though he reeked of beer, she was happy that he came to her. "My brother always spoke fondly of you," he said.

Fillide couldn't even reply, instead, she cried and then buried her head in Giovan's chest. Fillide was heaving softly in his shirt when she heard him whisper, "My sweet, I can console you with more attention if we had some privacy."

Fillide looked up at him wiping the tears from her eyes. "Privacy?"

"There's a room upstairs I can secure."

"Giovan, are you saying you want to fuck with me?" she asked him loudly.

He gently smoothed aside her hair. "Yes, my sweet. I desired you all that time you were my brother's whore."

Fillide swallowed hard. "I curse the Tomassoni family and pray there'd be a plague on your house." She pushed Giovan away and spit at his feet. "Your brother

246

would cut your throat if he knew what you just said to me," she told him then left the tavern.

❖

Syracuse

Mario Minniti was in his new studio painting a landscape for commission for a local merchant when a pregnant Isabella brought him a newspaper from Rome. She handed it to him with her mouth open. "What is it, Isabella? You look ill?"

"I have just read the news. Several days ago, Caravaggio murdered Ranuccio Tomassoni in a brawl. Pope Paul has issued a *banda capitale* on him," she whispered.

Mario sat down and quickly spread the newspaper open reading the article, desiring to know every detail. When he completed reading it twice, he sat back and sighed, "It says Longhi was with them when it happened."

"You could have been with them," she stated.

"Yes, I might have murdered Ranuccio myself. Or I might have been killed in the brawl."

Hearing the words, Isabella knelt by him and hugged his shoulders. "I pray every night how thankful I am that you left that city," she said.

"You saved my life," he told her.

She then gently eased away from him. "Where will Caravaggio flee?"

Mario shrugged. "I can only surmise that Cardinal Del Monte will protect him as best he can if that is possible under the circumstances. Ranuccio Tomassoni was a ruthless man but he did come from a well-respected family. Only time will dictate Caravaggio's fate."

Later that afternoon, sitting on the dark green grass alone on a hill above his modest home, a gift from Isabella's father, Mario gazed north toward Rome. He felt himself tremble at the thought of all he had experienced there, most of it was a dark and vicious experience that never seemed so bleak and vile when they were occurring, however, now, they haunted him. Images cut through his dreams, dim images in the half-light of brothels and taverns.

When he walked back to his studio, he found a young man waiting for him. He was a journalist for the Syracuse newspaper who wanted a quote from Mario for an article he was writing on Caravaggio. The young man was aware how close

Mario and the painter were at one time.

Mario told the young man, "Caravaggio's eccentricities and stormy escapes were distasteful and that is why I have now settled my life here in Sicily."

Pleased with the quote, the young man left him alone. Mario looked around the studio, then outside the window viewing the lush pasture with ripe olives dangling from the trees and smooth rolling hills; still he wondered on how magically he arrived there. He took a closer look at the clear blue sky, and the evidence of peace and quiet without another home in view, gave him a sense of serenity.

He listened to the noises of the environment and remembered how Caravaggio used to state how much he disliked nature. He shuddered and realized that for the grace of God and good fortune, Mario had found a semblance of peace and only God knew what was now in store for Caravaggio.

That evening sitting by the fireplace with Isabella in his arms, Mario heard a knock at the door accompanied by harsh male voices outside the window. He glanced through the drapes and saw the emblem of Syracuse police on the saddle of one of the horses.

He threw on his coat and grabbed Isabella by the shoulders. "They've come for me," he said to her.

The second knock on the door, this time accompanied by men shouting, alarmed Isabella. "Who *are* they?"

"The police."

"What do they want with you?"

Mario looked deeply into her eyes. "Before I went to Rome I killed a man here in Syracuse in a tavern near the docks. I was drunk and so was he. His name was Favio Guilliano. He and his family were nothing more than thieves and cut-throats but I murdered him just the same," he told her. He could see Isabella was petrified. "I need to take refuge. You must ask your father to speak to their family. Offer them anything or I'll be sentenced and hung," he told her.

He then rushed to the door with Isabella following. "Where will you go?" she asked.

"I have no destination."

"Ride to the Carmelite monastery. Sussino Parma, is my father's first cousin, and is extremely influential there. Do you know how to reach it?" She said, handing him his cap and cape.

Mario nodded. "I'll take the high road along the hill. The moon is bright. It will

248

light my way."

"Stay north of the city's walls," she whispered with intensity.

He kissed her and then stood back. "You are my refuge." He quietly opened the back door that was hidden by a tree in the backyard, found his horse in the barn, then took a moment to listen to the police continue to shout for Isabella to open the door.

Once mounted he kicked his horse and took off down the gully behind his home heading straight into the darkness holding onto the reins, racing through the woods with only the nearly full moon to guide him. He then thought of a passage from an old Jewish proverb he had read in the Talmud many years earlier. "If a man walks through the desert with a full moon above, he does not travel alone."

Mario rode along the high cliff somewhat relieved that the police didn't follow him. He could see the white stretch of moonlight to his left throwing a white line down and over the dark sea. To his right, he saw the rugged mountains narrow toward the darkness behind him as he passed over the rocky terrain.

He also saw the Spanish garrison and their fires burning brightly where the ruins of the ancient city still stood.

Riding for an hour, he reached the three-story monastery and knocked long and hard on the wooded and iron bolted door. A face appeared at a window and Mario could see a monk's hooded head peering silently down at him. He shouted, "I'm Mario Minniti. Son-in-law of Andrea Parma!"

The tall wooden door opened immediately and a hooded monk said to him, "Follow me."

The monk led him to a top floor room, which reminded him of the room he inhabited in Tor di Nona prison except this room was clean; it had a basin, a mattress and a window that looked up at the night sky.

The monk closed the door and Mario sat back on the bed and prayed to God not to destroy the happiness he had at last found for himself.

CHAPTER THIRTY-NINE

Rome

Nunzio Pulzone was now Cavalieri Colonel Pulzone having been offered the position of liaison between the police and the Vatican. Pope Paul V made the appointment based on the counsel of Cardinal Pietro Aldobrandini.

His new office was the same room he had been offered years earlier by Pietro Aldobrandini and worked diligently on ridding Rome of the druken brawls and street fights occurring nightly.

Pope Paul V kept his word and closed down the *Ortaccio* driving prostitution once again underground where it was to become vibrant and busy commerce inside the brothels as it was once outdoors.

Nunzio had also taken on the case of the murderer of Ranuccio and on June twenty-eight, an official in charge of inquiries, a man named Angelo Turco named Caravaggio, Onorio Longhi, Giovan Tomassoni in contempt of court.

With an armed guard at his side, Nunzio rushed into the Tomassoni villa arresting Giovan and placing him in his custody.

A few days later, while in his office, Nunzio sat back at his desk aware of how satisfied he was that Ranuccio was now dead. He daydreamed that Ranuccio's death would allow the love of his life, Fillide, to openly love him.

This glee in Ranuccio's demise made him rush to the confessional where he offered a penance to Christ for feeling such joy but it didn't stop him from lusting for Fillide. He had to struggle to stop himself from visiting her villa until one day that week one of his assistants came into his office to tell him that the cavalieri were in the process of digging up Bishop Romano's garden.

"Why are they doing that?" he asked.

"It seems that one of his dogs had dug up a bone."

Nunzio smirked. "So?"

"The bone in question was the remains of a leg, colonel. The dog had in its teeth *human* remains."

Nunzio felt a sudden surge of memory. He had known this all along. "And when we dug up the garden what did we find?"

The assistant told him. "We discovered six skeletons, colonel."

Nunzio immediately thought of Anna Bianchini.

❖

Upon reaching the bishop's villa, Nunzio found that Bishop Romano already banned from his garden was now under house arrest. He quickly walked to the garden finding the skeletons lined up one beside the other. Just from their petite size, Nunzio surmised that the skeletons belonged to female whores. He stepped over each carefully but then stopped.

Seeing something shining from one of the shallow graves, he leaned over and noticed a small blue stone attached to a rusted metal necklace. He picked it up and placed it in his pocket. He then directed his carriage to take him to Fillide's villa. When he reached her home, Nunzio was escorted into a small enclave where Fillide, dressed in her long silk white robe with a white blue and yellow tiara in her hair, greeted him. "It's been years, captain," she bowed.

"I'm a colonel now, Fillide, and yes, it has been *years*," he told her clearly, as he felt an ease in saying her name. Fillide, seeing herself in the large mirror behind him, saw herself in a different light and expected that Nunzio would be disappointed. "The few years we speak of have taken their toll on me, dear Nunzio."

"They have not, dear woman," he responded but she expected that he was lying. Even though she felt healthy, she knew that she no longer wore the face or carried the bearing of a nineteen-year-old woman— the Fillide he had lusted for.

Nunzio then handed her the blue stone and rusted chain it was attached to. Fillide immediately recognized it and clutched it to her bosom. Their eyes met and he nodded severely. "This was found near a skeleton, one of six, found in Bishop Romano's back garden."

"Anna?" Fillide muttered.

"I only wish I had the capacity to dig up that wretched cemetery years ago," he stated.

"You were right in thinking he was the culprit."

"But his office protected him."

Fillide frowned. "And will it continue to protect him?"

Nunzio shrugged. "Perhaps all that has changed now. The time for such things in Rome is on the wane."

"We can only hope," Fillide said. "Anna was like a sister to me. I have hoped all these years that she was missing she had married well and moved up north."

Nunzio said without irony. "She is in heaven with God. All is well with her, I assure you."

Fillide was speechless in reacting to his solemn but sincere announcement. She hesitated then opened her arms. "Would you like a refreshment?" She tried not sounding as if she was seducing him since that was *not* her intention.

"How do you exist now that the *Ortaccio* has been condemned and closed?" he told her.

"I have not frequented the ghetto in years," Fillide stated proudly. "And any service I do perform I do as a courtesan in the privacy of the gentleman's home."

Nunzio listened in silence.

"But I was offering nourishment, colonel, nothing more."

Again, Nunzio was silent.

She could see that he was still interested in her. "My benefactors are now older gentlemen and my list of such is short but they are of the affluent as you must well know," she said.

Nunzio continued to perplex her with his stillness.

"There is something on your mind, Nunzio?"

He was staring at something in the distance, in the far corner of the room. He took a step towards it. Fillide noticed and took his hand directing him to her portrait. She gazed at it for a moment. "Though less than a decade ago, I was a mere child. Look what the genius Caravaggio made of me! A wild but demure whore."

Nunzio stammered, "So many of us lusted after *her*." He gestured to the canvas as if the portrait of Fillide was *not* the Fillide standing at his side. Now it was Fillide's time to remain silent. "I was there," he whispered.

"I know you were," she told him.

"I was so in *love* with you I couldn't control myself. I left immediately without saying a word to you or anyone else."

"Love does that to our hearts," she replied. She then took his hand and squeezed it. "And your marriage?"

"Angelina and the children are healthy," he told her.

Fillide smiled, "That's good to hear."

Nunzio turned to her. She saw in his eyes the same look she had seen the night he alluded to, the night he came to see her portrait in the Palazzo Madama garden. With his head lowered, he turned and walked to the entrance.

Fillide called after him. "Please send my cousin's remains. I would like a ceremony to bury her."

Nunzio turned back to her. "She was a whore, Fillide, she can not be buried in sacred ground."

Fillide felt flush with anger. She knew the church law but was outraged that he had to remind her. "No one knows she was a whore."

"*I know* she was a whore," he told her and then left her villa.

Fillide rushed to the door and slammed it shut. She then felt her blood run through her as if it was driven by demons of regret. "How righteous of you to remind me that I will never be buried in hallowed ground, dear Nunzio," she said to herself.

Nunzio immediately took his carriage to Pietro's office finding the cardinal just completing an engagement with several other Vatican cardinals of the Holy See. Nunzio waited to be announced and then was immediately allowed to enter Pietro's office. There were also crates some opened and some nailed shut in the office. Pietro noticed Nunzio observing. "I have been spending time in Ravena, due to the whims of the Farnese. However, I'm very pleased that you are now the official liaison as I had always hoped you to be," he said.

Nunzio spit out, "Six human remains have been found in Bishop Romano's garden. I believe they are whores he had gathered up in the ghetto and murdered over the years."

Pietro nearly collapsed. He managed to reach his desk where he sat quickly and steadied himself. He then looked up at Nunzio doing all he could to keep Nunzio from reading the panic etched on his face. "Have you questioned him as of yet?"

"I intend to do that very duty immediately but since this is a delicate situation I thought it best to discuss it with you first," he told the cardinal.

"Very wise of you," Pietro stated. He then thought over what he should say very carefully. "Since you are the Vatican liaison for the cavalieri and since Pope Paul will not tolerate such behavior and will, no doubt, punish the bishop forthwith, I instruct you arrest Bishop Romano immediately and bring him blindfolded and in shackles to Tor di Nona dungeon. Once there you must immediately hand him over to the Archconfraternity of St. John the Beheaded."

"But the bishop is not a heretic," Nunzio stated. "This is a crime against our state."

"A crime against our state *is* a crime against our Holy Mother Church," Pietro said sharply.

"If I'm to hand the bishop over to the Inquisition I would like that directive in writing from you," Nunzio requested.

Pietro nodded then quickly wrote an official letter ordering Nunzio to do exactly as he had stated. "Do you disagree with this punishment?" he asked as he handed the letter to Nunzio.

"Not at all, cardinal." He bowed and left the room on his way to arrest Bishop Romano.

Pietro then called upon his aide to deliver another letter to Father Fria. Fria was his contact in the Archconfraternity at the prison. In the letter, Pietro asked for Romano's immediate execution by hanging, but before that, he implored that Romano's tongue removed.

Pietro continued in the letter that he would gladly take full responsibility of the directive since Bishop Romano was just found to be a murderer of women and children and part of a satanic cult formed by the heretic Martin Luther.

After sending the letters, he ordered his aide to pack.

"But dear cardinal, we just arrived?"

"I have urgent business in Ravena," Pietro quickly snapped.

After a sleepless night, Pietro woke up finding a letter posted on his door. It was from the monk Fria and the letter stated that Bishop Romano had been tortured, his tongue removed, and he was hung as requested the night before. He repented during the inquisition and his remains buried in the hallowed ground at Saint Luke's Church.

Relieved to hear the news and now knowing that the veiled truth of his own sexual liaisons with the whores of Rome would be kept secret, Pietro went about his Vatican duties. Finding his aide standing in the lobby with his belongings all packed, Pietro waved him off and said, "Change is the virtue of the humble. We are staying in Rome. You may unpack my things."

CHAPTER FORTY

Syracuse

The second day of Mario's refuge in the monastery, Andrea Parma appeared with an escort of men from his private security force. During his stay Mario had done exactly as he had been told by the monks. He stayed in his room and monks continued to feed him and act profoundly generous with their salutations and prayers.

Now, as Andrea stood in the doorway to the cell, Mario waited anxiously. Mario knew the moment he met Andrea in Rome where Isabella had inherited her blue eyes. Andrea Parma had striking blue eyes, a small clean-shaven face with chiseled features and thin lips. He hardly ever smiled since there was a serious nature that ran deep in his being.

Mario watched as Andrea scanned the room examining its cleanliness and comforts. "I have met with the Guilliano family. They refuse to forgive you for your act of murdering their only son," he stated sternly.

Mario felt wobbly.

"However, I'm in negotiations now with city's authorities. The mayor, Musco and the merchant, Scatturo, are very close friends of mine. I'm working to have them intervene on your behalf."

Mario took Andrea's hand and kissed it. Andrea waved him off. "It is common knowledge that the man you killed was a petty thief, a bully and a criminal beyond question. However, the fact that you ran from the authorities instead of confronting the consequence of your deed puts you in a negative light for the time being."

"I understand."

"I spoke with the magistrate and in his words, you are under house arrest here in the monastery for a *homicide casually committed*. However, he agreed to your taking refuge here in the monastery until we can sort all this out. And my cousin, Sussino, writes me that you are being well taken care of."

"I am."

"I expected as much."

Mario nodded in gratitude and then asked, "How is Isabella?"

255

Andrea spoke up. "My daughter is the rock on which I place my heart. She prays for you daily. She loves you beyond any comprehension."

Mario knew he needed to speak up. "I'm grateful that she does."

Andrea nodded, "Is there anything I can bring you?"

Mario answered quickly, "Yes. I require paints, a brush and a canvas. The monks have charitably offered me a room on the second floor which contains enormous windows. The light is glorious from dawn to dusk."

Andrea actually smiled. "That is a superior notion, son-in-law. Paint to your hearts content. I'll keep you in paints for as long as you are condemned to inhabit this place."

A tedious month dragged by and in all that time Mario was not allowed a single visit from Isabella. It was Andrea's thought that Mario needed to show that he was doing penance in the monastery and in time he believed the Guillianos, ignorant and poor, could be placated for their grief by a small sum of lira. The noble families who were allies and friends of the Parma's would offer this lira and then ask the magistrate to drop all charges. In effect, it was a bribe and bribes were a way of life in Sicily.

On his subsequent visit several weeks later, Andrea Parma was astounded to see that Mario had nearly completed a painting of the *Assumption of the Virgin*. Not exactly a man of culture, he was awe struck by the large canvas and from that moment on looked at Mario in an altered way.

He even spoke to Mario differently making it clear that he respected Mario's gift and what he felt was Mario's genius. Mario was happy with the painting and created it from an earnest sense of penance he was feeling, not for the murder of the treacherous man who tried to kill him, but for putting Isabella through the humiliation of what she had to endure in her own home city.

"*When* will it be completed?" Andrea Parma asked Mario.

"In two weeks time," he replied.

Two weeks later Andrea Parma arrived at the monastery with the mayor, Musco and the banker, Scatturo, who comprised the authority on the city's Senate.

The moment the men eyed the canvas, they were awe struck. Mario knew then and there that his talents, perhaps taken for granted in Rome, were not the usual for a provincial city like Syracuse.

Before any of the men could speak, Mario told them, "This is my gift to the Senate of the great city of Syracuse. You may place it whereever you prefer."

Andrea Parma faced him. "I speak for all of us here today. We are honored that an artist as great as you, Mario Minniti, has considered to live among *us*. And I believe our own court building has a wonderful room to hang this canvas."

Musco, the mayor, spoke up. "I'll speak to the Guilliano family on your behalf and I can *assure* you that you will no longer have anything to fear from them or the magistrate, *citizen*," he proclaimed.

Andrea then spoke, "Return to Isabella immediately."

Before Mario could thank the men, Scatturo approached him. "I have a piece of property on the hill above the city. It has plenty of room for a studio and a school. My son is a painter. Though he is young, I would appreciate if you took him in as a mentor?"

"Of course I would," Mario answered.

The Syracuse Senate was excited to be a patron of Mario's school on the hill. They eagerly donated generous sums of lira to his school. He was able to transform his home, once a two-story brick farmhouse, into a villa. Soon he combined the property Isabella's father gave her as a gift with the remaining land surrounding it. He then proceeded to build two large studios side by side twenty yards from the house each containing huge windows, a high ceiling and enough room to accommodate a dozen students. One studio was for Mario's private use, and the second was for his students.

Mario's villa also had enough rooms to hold his growing family that quickly included two sons and a recently born daughter. Though, Mario felt comfortable around the children and the home Isabella had created, his longing was always for the canvas and he spent many of his hours, days and evenings, a few short yards away in his studio.

His art school slowly grew to embody twelve students and his reputation as a painter who had lived in Rome and painted with Caravaggio, rushed across the island like fire. Students came to him from Messina, Palermo and even some traveled down from Naples to study with the great Mario Minniti who had once lived and painted in Rome.

When Mario completed his largest canvas to date, a *Raising of the Widow of Naim*, for the Capuchin monastery of Santa Maria Concezione, he found himself inundated with more commissions than he had ever imagined. It was then that he took a lesson learned from Lorenzo Siciliano all those years earlier. Though his memories of those days were painful, Mario took a different approach to his students by turning them into devoted assistants.

The best of his students were enthusiastic to work with such a master, as Mario had become. He had the best sketch in his compositions allowing them to often bring the work to finalization; then he himself would add the last touches. He did all this without the nasty comments and audacious bullying he had experienced with Lorenzo. He also allowed them to discover their own styles on their own canvases. Yet, when they painted his work, like Lorenzo, they painted what he had demanded of them and in *his* style.

Mario told everyone who would listen that he was fortunate to be crowned with success and was attracted to his native country by a desire to display his "happy, pleasurable and soft style of painting."

One night while Isabella was breast feeding their baby girl, his sons were asleep and they sat by the fire before they retired for the evening, he told her that he realized that he was a *student of Carracci* without ever understanding how it happened.

"I always admired Carracci," Isabella said glancing at her swollen nipple as her baby fed from it.

Mario saw her profile aglow from the fireplace. "But I once despised his work! I can still recall a night Caravaggio and I were in a piazza somewhere in the Artists Quarter and a new Carracci was being displayed. We insulted the canvas loudly and at that one moment, I was sure Carracci, who in attendance, locked eyes with me. I wanted to destroy him and his reputation that night and here I am, all these years later, having taken his mantel from the altar, holding it up and rushing into the future with it firmly in my hands," he said.

"And that confuses you?" she asked.

"Beyond words," he replied.

Mario also liked to spend the summers in Messina where, through introductions from the Syracuse City Council, he was presented to merchants and politicians who commissioned him to paint for the city government buildings. Soon he was so busy in Messina, he took an apartment. Leaving Isabella with her father on his estate and having one of his trusted assistants oversee his school, Mario would spends weeks at a time in the city. As time went by Mario experienced that there wasn't a small town on the entire island of Sicily where Mario Minniti wasn't esteemed and loved by all Sicilians.

It was at a time in the early autumn of 1609 when he was returning from one of his trips to Messina that Mario was shocked by a surprise visit. He had only been home a few days and was happy to see his wife and children as well as the students and assistants he had employed and was teaching.

It was early in the afternoon as he was in his studio that his assistant Luigi appeared at his door with a message from a man who said he was a good friend of Mario's. "Did he tell you his name, Luigi?" Mario asked busily directing one of his students who was sketching a female model, a daughter of one of the local farmers. "He said his name is Caravaggio and that you would know him," Luigi said.

The entire room was hushed as each student passed along the name to the other in whispers. Mario dropped his brush and quickly left the studio.

He found Caravaggio sitting slouched on the metal bench in the front garden. Seeing him sitting there dressed in a dusty black cloak with worn brown muddied boots from a recent rain and his silver dagger with his gold handle dangling from his brown belt, he looked more like a swordsman to Mario than the famous painter he had become. He was wearing a close-fitting dark blue shirt and dark green trousers both made of silk. "Look at you," Caravaggio remarked. "You're respectable. You dress with elegance and you have a beautiful home," he told Mario with a hoarse inflection.

Mario took one close look at his friend and he saw that he was exhausted, drained and doubtlessly hungry. He rushed to hug Caravaggio but heard, as Caravaggio slowly rose from the chair, the painter moan.

Though they did manage to hug one another, Caravaggio said, "I have been on the rack in Malta."

Mario shouted to his servants to prepare a meal. "You have to eat and rest," he said not wanting to press his friend for anymore information. Caravaggio stood and removed his shirt, as if showing a proud emblem of his tenacity. Mario could see the still deep lacerations from the whip on the painter's back.

Caravaggio put his shirt back on, rubbed his hair, and put his face in his hands then without raising his head he raised his eyebrows and said, "Yet I survived, huh? I'm here and I bring with me my great talent and my appetite."

Mario watched Caravaggio devour the pasta *con le sarde* and swallow the Marsala wine as they sat together in his studio allowing the ocean breeze from miles away to blow through the open windows. He could see that despite his hunger his friend's health was severely tested. "I hear that Laezrio Cherubini placed my *Death of the Virgin* on the market. He's attempting to recoup his investment by taking advantage of my celebrity," Caravaggio muttered.

Sitting at his side and nibbling on some bread, Mario questioned him, "Did Ranuccio come at you with his sword?"

Caravaggio shot a glance at him. "Yes, he came at me with his dagger and I lifted mine up for protection. In doing so, I pierced his stomach. He bled to death."

"He was a savage and a patrician without nobility or refinement."

"And yet Pope Paul sentences me to certain death," Caravaggio said, hauntingly. Mario saw in his eyes the inner terror of a hunted man. Caravaggio gestured to the sunshine outside the window. "It is like Eden here."

"I could no longer live as I lived in Rome."

"I miss Rome," Caravaggio interrupted. He pushed away his plate. "No one can paint great work in a paradise."

Mario felt humbled by the comment but disregarded it. "Let's walk, friend," was how he responded.

The two men spent the rest of the afternoon together, Mario showing Caravaggio his land and the stretches of rolling green hills that danced east toward the sea. "I saw your eldest son's face. He has your features."

"I believe he does. My daughter favors Isabella."

"How does it feel to preside over a brood?"

Mario shrugged. "It is not something I spend much time reflecting on. The family is my wife's duty."

Caravaggio quickly changed the subject. Mario could see that he was irritated. "Cardinal Del Monte is lobbying the Pope to pardon me."

Mario noticed how his voice was sullen despite the fact that he was struggling to be optimistic. "The cardinal has great influence but something of that nature will take time," Mario replied.

"Yes. And in that time I need to eat and that demands that I paint and earn scudi. I need to stay one step ahead of the Tomassoni."

"Have they placed a bounty on your head?"

Caravaggio cringed. "They have. I also need to stay one step ahead of the

Knights of Malta."

"The Knights of Malta?"

Caravaggio found a large smooth rock and sat with Mario hovering closely. "I sought refuge in Valletta so I aquired a commission to paint the portrait of the Grand Master of the Knights of Malta, Alof de Wingacourt. So, after traveling to Naples where I painted *The Seven Acts of Mercy* for the high altar of the new Pio Monte della Misericordia, I sailed to Malta."

"That is a prestigious commission you garnered in Naples," Mario replied.

"Yes, it was. They paid me two hundred ducats. And dear Mario, it is my most favored of all my work, I say to you now. I was sad to leave Naples. Between us, at first, I enjoyed Malta just as much. The knights were anxious to commission me for several paintings," he said. "Including the portrait of the Grand Master, I saw this as a wonderful opportunity. I explicitly negotiated in my contract to be named an honorary knight. The Grand Master agreed. Being an honorary knight would afford me the right to gain a license to carry my sword in Rome."

"It's what you talked about back in Rome. But how did you come to be placed on the rack?" Mario asked.

"I insulted someone of prestige. I'm not certain who I insulted."

"That is one of your eccentricities," Mario remarked.

Caravaggio hung his head. "I did all I could to remain in good reputation while there. I did paint what the Grand Master asked. Yet, there were these arrogant noblemen, other knights, who were vile and repulsive. Most were French. I drank and argued with them. They accused me of all kinds of vicious crimes." He stopped. "They punished me for who I am."

"And who might that be?"

Caravaggio waved him off. "It matters not."

Mario thought about Caravaggio's secrets even those he knew nothing about. He hesitated a moment then said, "Malta is *not* Rome."

Caravaggio looked up at Mario. "Yes, my friend. Malta is not Rome."

When evening fell, Mario and Caravaggio continued to speak spending their time together in the studio allowing the large candles to throw shadows across the room. Outside the studio, a wolf howled and an owl flew across the crescent moon. Mario noticed but he said nothing to his friend who stared into the fireplace with his coal black eyes radiant from the flames.

"I'm between two worlds," he said. "I'm a bandit, condemned to death and I'm a citizen of a great city in exile."

Mario shrugged. "It was how we lived back in the ghetto and the brothels and taverns, my friend."

Caravaggio agreed with his silence. "But there's more contradiction. I'm a painter who must paint. I absorb the world I inhabit, Mario. That is what God demands of me. The wealthy of Naples appreciated my charm and distinction. The Neapolitan nobility is uncultivated and they posses none of the refinement of what we have seen first hand in Rome. The Neapolitans are devoted to the novelties and latest fashions of Rome. And I am not all that," he said slowly.

"A novelty and fashion?" Mario said then stopped. "I understand since I'm that very same thing *here*."

"I supposed you are. In Naples, they are brutal. They are a violent lot." He looked up at Mario. "And I believe I responded to what I saw there. In my work in that city, I discovered a new, harsh darkness. My models are all brown with weather-beaten skins, goitrous throats and their suffering is fatalistic, Mario. I painted with the same feverish urgency and I felt it surge through me from the bowels of that swarming city."

Mario contemplated what he heard. "Perhaps. *Or* you painted the turbulence of your own life."

Caravaggio took a long deep breath. "That's what we spoke of when we were struggling to earn a living wage as painters. I remember having that conversation with Longhi and you. How we spoke all night of finding a way to express what we were *feeling*," he stated.

Mario missed conversations about art with his peers. Like, Caravaggio had experienced in Naples, Mario knew, as he had stated, that life on Sicily was the same, *he* was the emblem and standard of great art. It was a lonely position to inhabit.

"Yes, my friend, as we spoke about," he stopped, noticing that Caravaggio was breathing heavily. He walked over to his friend and found that he was asleep.

Mario covered him with a blanket then left the studio and returned to his villa a few yards away.

He found Isabella reading by candlelight while sitting up on her bed. She glanced at him and then closed her book. "I was reading my prayers," she told him. "How is your friend's frame of mind?"

"He is being hunted by the Knights of Malta and by the Tomassoni's," he answered. "In many ways, he's already a dead man. However, in another more profound way, he is the greatest painter of our time."

Isabella frowned. "What are *we* to do? How did he become your responsibility?"

Mario shot back quickly, "He's my friend."

"He's a murderer."

"As I am."

Isabella looked away then muttered. "I don't know why he's your concern?"

He sat down on the bed beside her and removed his boots. "My first day in Rome in the Artists Quarter, I was alone and I knew no one. It was on that very day he befriended me. In many ways, my life changed from that moment on."

"And you believe you own him a debt?" Isabella inquired, turning to him.

"Yes, that is so."

She shook her head. "That was a *lifetime ago*. Its secrets and its mysterious as well as its actions have no meaning here. I know I was interested in them once but I'm no longer. I wasn't your wife in Rome but I am your wife here. I implore you to send him on his way before we're visited by these Knights of Malta. Allow him some time to rest but send him on his way. I cannot live with the police showing up at our door demanding your arrest, *again*," she demanded of him.

Mario lay back on his pillow. He remembered waking up his first morning in Rome along the banks of the Tiber River with his face in the grass and his mouth dry and the dead sculptor at his side. He leaned forward and blew out the candle putting Isabella in darkness without replying to her demands.

He then closed his eyes and fell asleep with a sense of comfort knowing he'd never again awake along the grassy banks of the Tiber River with the dead at his side.

Mario wore long flowing white robes in sharp contrast to darker clothing Caravaggio wore as Mario introduced him to the city senators. He did it with a flair that made him think he was presenting the Michelangelo. Mario was very aware that this introduction also enhanced his own reputation.

Mario addressed the Senate by saying how he would be greatly appreciative of them if the city could employ Caravaggio allowing him some time to be able to evaluate the greatness of "our new Michelangelo." Though Mario saw his friend cringe at the comparison, they both knew that such a comparison would weigh heavily in their favor.

Mario knew that the Church of Santa Lucia, just outside the city walls, was being restored at this very time. Mario told the Senate, "It would be in the great interest of our city to commission Caravaggio to paint the altarpiece."

Musco, the mayor, spoke up, "Caravaggio would you accept our offer to paint our beloved patron saint Santa Lucia?"

Caravaggio stepped forward and faced the Senate. "I would be honored to paint your beloved patron. I also would prefer to paint Saint Lucy's burial rather than her martyrdom," he replied.

All eyes on the Senate slowly turned to Mario. "Brilliant," he grinned at them. "It is a *rare* subject to paint her burial. We would like to have one of the few such subjects."

Caravaggio immediately asked to *see* the models he could use to *pose* for Saint Lucy in his painting. Though she was a corpse in the painting, he took excruciating painstaking planning to make sure he hired a model that had the attributes he was searching for; attributes he kept solely to himself.

Young women from across Syracuse, including daughters from the Senate members, appeared at Mario's studio in hopes of being *cast* as Saint Lucy. It was a great honor to portray her in a painting and nearly two dozen young women appeared at Mario's studio to pose.

Isabella was beside herself with distaste for what was happening to her quiet home. Mario learned from this experience that the uninhibited woman he had seduced, or had been seduced *by* when he first met her back in Rome, was actually an extremely conventional mother and matron. Though she kept her fair beauty through the years, she did age with her hips expanding after each child and her time in front of the mirror grooming occurring with less frequency. He could see that she believed, and rightly so, that these young women parading in her house were a threat to her.

Though Mario invited her to attend the *casting sessions* Isabella declined. Mario, however, did attended them all including those held for casting the middle-aged cemetery workers, a bishop and a military man, all needed in Caravaggio's conception of Lucy's burial.

When it came to casting Lucy, Mario implied that it "would be politically expedient" for Caravaggio to choose one of the daughters from the senate. Caravaggio disregarded this notion, casting a lovely poor farm girl named, oddly enough, Lucia.

Mario knew what was in the future for the painter and his model and eventually he was correct. Caravaggio seduced her. Painter and model shared a bed, under the stars, outside of the Santa Lucia Church in the courtyard or under a tall elm.

Isabella was appalled when she heard the gossip and Mario was forced to speak to Caravaggio about his blatant display of hedonistic behavior. "You're no longer in a brothel in the Piazza del Popolo," he sternly told his friend but Caravaggio ignored him spending from dawn to evening with the greened eyed slim young lady. "To see you sleep in nature's bedding, you must be fond of this one," he told him on one particular afternoon when they were alone.

Caravaggio let out a hearty laugh. Mario had not heard him laugh with that much vigor since their early days together. "I'm fond of her and so are *you,* my respectable friend," Caravaggio snickered. Mario knew he was correct. He *was* fond of her. It was hard not to be. She was young and nubile and he was smitten with her innocence and feminine demeanor from the moment he first saw her. She had the same olive complexion as his wife and the same regional inflection when she giggled. Even the way her light eyes sparkled when she spoke, made him think of what Isabella must have been like when she was a mere seventeen year old.

Mario found himself avoiding his own work and spending more and more time in the Saint Lucia Church watching Lucia pose. He fought himself from talking to her directly and found excuses to tell Isabella why he was spending his nights sleeping in the small town instead of traveling back over the dark roads to his own home. More than any other time, he looked forward to seeing Lucia in the morning. He found himself spying on her as she washed herself in the stream, not far from the church, hiding in the bushes hoping to catch a glance of her smooth nude skin.

"You never left Rome," Caravaggio once said catching him in the act. "When I leave here you should come with me," he told Mario. "I thought I could hear the piazza's cry out your name deep in your soul. I was wrong. Now I realize it is *you* crying out *for* them. Your misery is not buried very deeply, my friend."

Mario shuddered at the thought of such an observation because of two reasons. He did long for Rome and at the same time, he feared it.

"Afraid of the loneliness?" Caravaggio asked, seeing the struggle in Mario's face. "Or do you fear the fame you truly crave and are afraid to pay the price it demands?" He walked away rushing to the nude Lucia throwing himself into the stream. "I love nature," he shouted sarcastically as Lucia laughed.

Mario bowed his head walked back to his horse and rode home.

It was when he arrived at his house that Isabella confronted him in his studio.

Your Caravaggio is the subject of gossip."

"Slander is a sin," Mario rebuked her.

Isabella continued, "He has been seen with one of his models in Syracuse late at night in the bars there."

Mario pretended ignorance. "Who has he been seen with?"

Isabella replied, "He is the one who is the military man in the painting."

"What did you say?"

"The young man, I'm told his name is Leonardo. They have been seen together in a sinful way. His presence here will only be a determent to your career."

Mario was perplexed as Isabella left the room.

The legend of Saint Lucy was that when her mother was miraculously healed of a terminal disease by praying to Christ at the shrine of the martyr Saint Agatha in A.D. 304, Lucy gave her wealth to the poor and offered her chastity to Christ. Her husband denounced her as a Christian to the local Roman authorities. In a fury, the magistrate ordered her to be dragged off to a brothel but when nothing moved her, not oxen or men, she was stabbed in the throat and died. The legend placed piety and innocence against brute force. When the painting was unveiled at a Sunday morning ceremony in the church, Mario saw how Caravaggio was portraying not only the legend of Saint Lucy but he was dramatizing his own struggle against the brute forces working towards his demise.

All in attendance were not only moved by the work but also grateful to Caravaggio as well as Mario for the chance to have such a masterful work created for them in their own humble church. From that moment on, Mario's reputation was more than solidified despite what Isabella feared. The great master Mario Minniti could do no wrong in the eyes of his fellow Sicilians.

Several evenings after the unveiling of the altarpiece, Mario and Caravaggio celebrated quietly in a tavern in Syracuse. They ate fish, fruit and wine in a city where luxurious displays of wealth hid the mask of misery caused by slum conditions and periodic hunger riots by the angry poor. Mario knew he was one of the prosperous privileged few as they ate their hearty dinner.

Mario and Caravaggio were not alone during dinner. They invited Lucia along with them to share their meal and she clearly enjoyed the masculine attention of her two admirers. Once outside the three walked the streets passing Capuchin monks helping the homeless sitting in the shadows of the alleys at their feet, collecting them, and bringing them to the city shelter.

During their walk, Mario sensed someone was following them. He turned and thought he saw the young man Leonardo standing in the piazza.

Mario also sensed that Caravaggio was restless and told him so, "You seem anxious."

"I'm leaving for Messina," he told Mario. Mario could see Lucia didn't flinch with the news so he expected that she already knew. "I received an invitation from Giovanni Battista de' Lazzari. He is offering me a commission to paint the *Resurrection of Lazarus* for a high-altar chapel in the church of Padri Crociferi."

"A Lazarus for Lazzari," Mario kidded.

"My notion, actually. A play on the name," Caravaggio replied. "He offered me two thousand scudi. I intend to live lavishly in Messina. I also intend to visit the hospital there to view a corpse," he said.

Mario and Lucia paused in their steps. "It sounds gruesome," Lucia stated.

"It will be a battle of light and dark. Night and day. Good and evil. Life and death. My life, my death," Caravaggio said sounding prophetic.

The three then rode horses out of town with Lucia holding onto Caravaggio with her arms wrapped around his waist. They rode the hills over the backroad towards Mario's villa. A newly formed full moon that nearly jumped at them like a beacon lighted their way. It was a magical night, Mario thought, and he knew much of what he was feeling was because he was so close to Lucia.

When the three riders reached the fork in the road that led east to Mario's villa, Caravaggio dismounted, handing the reigns to Lucia. "I will see you at this place at dawn, my sweet," he said then rushed over to Mario and jumped up on the saddle behind him. "Ride my friend!" Mario looked back at Lucia until she and her horse disappeared in the gathering mist, then he kicked his horse and headed home.

When they reached his studio, Mario told Caravaggio that he would like his friend to wake him when he left. "I offer you my horse to take you to Messina."

"I'll walk. I prefer it," Caravaggio told him abruptly, icy in his speech and manner.

"Stay here with me in Syracuse. You'll be protected from the world here. The Senate adores you. My wife and I want you to stay."

"It's a meager offer. I'm sorry to turn it down."

"A meager offer?"

Caravaggio patted him on the shoulder. "In time, I'll become familiar to the senate and they will soon grow tired of my behavior. In time, your wife will curse me, if she hasn't already. And most importantly, I'll grow stale as an artist if I stay one more hour."

Mario could see Caravaggio's dark accusing eyes in the glimmering candlelight yet he was undeterred. "At least stay until Cardinal Del Monte procures your pardon. Stay at least until the Pontiff sends you a letter of safe conduct."

Caravaggio packed his one small bag. "My plan is to travel to Messina and work. From there I'll sail to Naples where my uncle, the great Marhesa di Caravaggio, will allow me to reside in his magnificent Riviera di Chiaia. I'll then wait there for this *letter of safe conduct* and return to Rome. It has been nearly three years now and I long for my adopted city."

Mario understood. "Then fill your bags with food and water for the journey. Messina will take a day or two along the main road."

"I cannot travel the main roads, my friend. I've enemies everywhere."

Mario understood that truth also. "I'll draw you a map to show you how to find Lucia at the place you left her."

"I'm not taking her with me."

"She believes you are? I surmised that from what you told her."

"She is my gift to you, Mario," Caravaggio smiled.

Mario contemplated his friend's unruly black hair, how it seemed mangled and disorderly in the shadow. "Messina has wide straight streets and elegant buildings. I will write you a letter of introduction to the senate. I summer in Messina and I know all of the important civic commissioners."

"Did you hear me?"

"Yes, I heard you."

Caravaggio could see that Mario was ignoring him. "You have become another Cardinal Del Monte," Caravaggio grinned.

Mario again ignored what he believed to be an off-handed insult. "It has a population of nearly one hundred thousand. On its southern edge is the Castle of Gonsaga and it also has a garrison of Spaniards in the Citadel to the west."

"I appreciate all you have done for me," Caravaggio then replied.

Mario and Caravaggio then shared a hug with Mario realizing that Caravaggio, being a man of the night, would not wait until morning but probably leave immediately using the moon as his guide.

Mario walked to the studio door. He stopped. He looked at his friend a long time then asked, "What do you think of my work?" He watched Caravaggio glance at the canvases in the dark knowing that Caravaggio had probably assessed their artistic value when he first entered the studio.

"You would make Carracci proud," Caravaggio told him without the slightest hint of irony or unkindness.

Mario knew this to be true so he couldn't understand why the words felt as if they were daggers cutting sharply into his heart.

"I'm a respected painter here. They know me to be great."

"And what do they think of you in Rome?" Caravaggio asked.

Mario was livid. He lowered his head and then venom flew from his mouth as if secretly concealed inside his inner organs for years. "Have a safe journey and remember, here in Sicily, just this year, our chief hangman, who had executed homosexuals, was executed for the same offense."

Caravaggio didn't wavier from where he stood.

"I have holy water near the door. Take some when you leave and bless yourself. You're a sinner who is unable to repent," Mario told him. He then opened the door and heard his friend call out. "I do not need the holy water," he replied. "As you well know as my friend and confidant, all my sins are *mortal*." With that Caravaggio rushed to Mario and hugged him in a way Mario had never experienced Caravaggio to do before. Mario was taller feeling Caravaggio's curly hair at his chin. Caravaggio then stepped back and said, "All these years we have been friends and I have felt so much for you." He then gazed so deeply into Mario's eyes that Mario had to look away and leave the room.

Mario returned to his villa a few yards away, climbing the stairs to his bedroom where Isabella slept soundly. As he undressed, he glanced out the window and just as he had surmised, he could see Caravaggio slip out of the studio. Caravaggio carried his traveling pack on his back as he walked down the hill toward the main road. He then stopped and stood in the quiet road for a long moment. That was when Leonardo stepped out of the tree line.

Mario saw the two men face one another, embrace, and then vanish into the mist of the soft blue light tossed casually from the sky by the bright glowing full moon. In the moments following their encounter only the tops of the trees were visible and only the night owls could be heard in the murky distance.

The following week while attending a ceremony held by the Syracuse Senate, Mario was told that there was disturbing news from Rome. The beloved painter,

Annable Carracci, had hanged himself in his studio. He had not yet reached the aged of fifty and he hadn't completed a canvas in several years.

Mario left the ceremony and walked into the first chapel he came upon, entered it and knelt in a pew. He lowered his head and mumbled a prayer for an artist he once despised.

Part Five

"1610–1640"

CHAPTER FORTY-ONE

Mario heard very little of Caravaggio other than a newspaper report that he had beaten a man nearly to death outside of Messina.

The report stated that a local schoolteacher had found Caravaggio, in his words, *sketching his pupils, all male, while they were playing soccer in an open field.* The teacher made a remark about Caravaggio's behavior insinuating that the painter was a *pervert.* Caravaggio immediately beat the man with a rock crushing his skull though not killing him. He quickly boarded a boat and landed in Naples.

Mario shared that news with his wife who was clearly joyful to be rid of what she called, "a dangerous man".

After that, Mario heard nothing. He knew Caravaggio disliked writing letters so he expected none and the information he did hear about Caravaggio were mainly newspaper reports. One that concerned Mario was about how the painter was badly disfigured in a notorious tavern on the dangerous Naples docks. The place was named Osteria del Cerriglio. Though it was frequented by poets, writers and artists, it was where four men, so the newspaper reported, attacked Caravaggio disfiguring his face. Reading this, Mario shuddered remembering the awful wounds from Malta his friend had shown him.

"Enough of this man!" he once shouted to himself while hiking in the woods to find some relief from his own conscience and forgiveness for the last words he spoke to Caravaggio.

Mario also found it impossible to paint and stayed away from taking trips to Lucia's farm, where he would hide in the woods and watch her work. He was beginning to believe his life was a lie and this disturbed him.

Isabella noticed and mentioned his sulking many times to him and his students also noticed since he seemed unable to concentrate on his commissions. The truth was clear— he was profoundly affected by Caravaggio's comparison of his work to Carracci's. The comment was a dagger in his side. The cut forced him to bleed memories of his dreams of greatness that had never been fulfilled, at least, in his mind. Caravaggio's off-handed comment forced him to question his very talent, the proposition of his very existence and the honesty of the driving ambitions that drove him to Rome. Compounded by his lustful thoughts of Lucia made him realize another truth he was in denial about, his fidelity to Isabella had been a ruse and untested until Caravaggio appeared back in his life.

One afternoon he coincidentally came across Lucia on the road to Syracuse while she was traveling to the market. He offered her a ride into the city and she accepted. A few miles out of the town, they stopped by a stream to refresh Mario's horse.

Sitting in the quiet warm meadow, Lucia said to him, "I see you watching me while I work the farm."

Mario couldn't help himself. "I haven't been able to release you from my mind," he told her.

"You're married," she told him.

"I am."

"And yet you stop me from my happiness," she said.

He was confused. "How did I do that?"

"You prevented Caravaggio from taking me to Messina."

He shook his head. "I didn't stop him from taking you, Lucia." He could see her eyes narrow and he could see her distrust and more painfully, her dislike.

"You lust after me like an old man. You're a famous painter and you want to play with me in the fields and then go home to your villa. I'm not an educated woman. I'm not even yet a woman, but I know you're a hypocrite and I despise you. Caravaggio was cruel, yes. He was a braggart and a heathen but he was honest. Are you?"

He saw a flash of Fillide in Lucia. He saw it in her fiery temperament and how physical she became when she spoke up. Her body swayed to an inner rhythm as if all of her youthful energy needed to express itself.

"I will not be your whore," she told him. She then picked up her empty basket and walked toward the road. She then turned on him like a snake and struck with venom. "I only accept your invitation so I could tell you what was inside me all these months. I never want to speak to you again, master Minniti."

Mario watched her slim, sensual figure move away from him as quickly as Lucia could walk. He then mounted his horse, and headed back to his villa and never again rode by her farm. Years later, he learned she had married a young farmer from Catania. They had a child but Lucia died while giving birth.

On July eighteenth of the following year, Mario was in his studio with his students when a messenger appeared on the horizon on horseback. There was something about the morning that gave Mario an odd stirring that he couldn't explain. The weather was nearly perfect and the seemingly ever present sunlight pouring its warmth everywhere.

When the messenger arrived, he handed Mario a letter that was addressed to him from Onorio Longhi. "Dear friend," it read. "Caravaggio is dead."

Mario read the words then lowered the letter and walked out of the studio. Ignoring his students, he walked down into the gully behind his home finding the rotting remains of a dead tree trunk and leaned against it while covered in shade from the canopy of a large, leafy living standing timber. He continued to read. "He died in the small fortress town of Port'Ercole while traveling from Naples to Rome. He had been granted a letter of safe conduct from his Holiness but to no avail. I hear rumors that agents of the Knights of Malta imprisoned him while others say that the Spanish garrison imprisoned him. However, all is rumor and nothing is certain. I hear that he paid a king's ransom as a bribe to be released. Once free, he attempted to journey to Rome on foot destitute and alone through a desolate, marshy terrain infested with mosquitoes. His last days on earth were spent in a lawless land with bandits and evil lurking everywhere. I can smell the putrid stink of such a world. Caravaggio contracted the dreaded disease malaria while on this journey. I have friends who tell me that they have heard that he found refuge and comfort with the Confraternity of San Sebastiano and died in the local infirmary. I hear that those who attended him were unaware of his great reputation. It is a dreadful act of God for the great Caravaggio to die unknown. I write you now from my refuge in Milan. My family in Rome informs me that his Holiness will grant me a pardon this autumn and if so, I shall return to the Eternal City immediately. We both know our dear friend had lived and experienced so much life in such a short time."

Mario was not saddened by the news of Caravaggio's death. What he felt was much worse for him to bear. He felt jealousy. He believed that such a death would bring to his long time friend a regard that he could never equal. He felt, at that moment with the letter in hand and the shade from the canopy as shelter, that Caravaggio had certainly, with such an awful tragic end to his life, gained an instant immortality that would haunt Mario until his own dying day.

Though news of his friend's demise became the topic of conversation everywhere he found himself for several months to come, he did not speak of his friend for nearly two years. Instead, to the delight of Isabella, he issued a self-imposed exile on the topic spending his time painting in his studio, playing with his children and leaving his brooding when he was alone staring into the fireplace.

CHAPTER FORTY-TWO

Caravaggio's death was the talk of Rome in every influential household. Its noblest of families had been working to have his safe return to the eternal city. These families included the Colonna, the Doria, the Gonzaga and the Borghese.

Pietro, who had secured a portrait of Pope Paul V as a commission for Caravaggio, was summoned by Cardinal Del Monte to meet him in the garden in the Palazzo Madama. Pietro arrived finding Del Monte sipping a compari. Pietro noticed how badly Del Monte had aged. His face was pale and his frame seemed to have shrunk. Whatever hair remained on his head and face was an odd hue of gray.

"I'm taking for fact that I'll never be named Pontiff now," Del Monte said as if the words were rehearsed. "It's a disappointment beyond comprehension. And what makes matters worse is that I have no influence with his new Pope," Del Monte told Pietro as he sat and was immediately brought a compari by one of the male students attending the Palazzo. "I tried to get Caravaggio pardoned last year but I found very little interest from his Holiness."

"Our new Pope has his own inner circle," Pietro agreed.

"Caravaggio died like a dog."

"So I hear."

"God treats animals with more kindness than he did that young man," Del Monte spit out.

Pietro felt his forehead crease. "But he was pardoned?"

"The *letter of safe conduct* had been issued, yes. That was managed, I dare say."

"Then why was he imprisoned?"

Del Monte shrugged. "No one seems to know. Perhaps it all has to do with what whatever happened when he was in attendance at Valletta."

"This Grand Master issued an order to have Caravaggio arrested."

"Alof de Wingacourt."

"Yes. He was running his own Inquisition on Malta. But why Caravaggio died I have no idea. I'm in the dark as the rest of Rome."

Pietro sipped the compari enjoying its tangy taste. "And what has become of his paintings?"

"His recent work was on the felucca and traveled to Naples without him. I have instructed Deodate Gentile, the Bishop of Caserta, to inform me of an accurate account of what truly happened as well as an accounting of the missing paintings."

"And what have you learned?" Pietro asked.

Del Monte replied, "I learned that three paintings were still at Chiaia, two *Saint Johns* and a *Magdalene*. I have informed Gentile to guard them well and not let anyone see them for they are already paid and spoken for by Scipione Borghese."

Pietro sat back. He felt the bulk of his weight fall against the metal chair. He knew he had gained considerable weight in recent years and it made him feel clumsy. "There will be problems concerning the painter's heirs as well as his creditors."

Del Monte coughed.

"Are you feeling well?"

Del Monte looked to Pietro. "No. I have not felt well in a year now. I dare say, dear friend, we are both aging before our very eyes."

Pietro looked up toward the sun that was now behind a cloud but he could see its outline glowing like a white-hot memory of something vague and long past. "It's only a matter of time."

Del Monte waved the student over for another compari. The student poured him one and then quickly left. Del Monte eyed him as he walked away. "I had my pleasures on this earth. I can only hope God forgives me for indulging in them."

Pietro forced a slight smile. "Of course he will."

"Ironically, it seems that the Fra Vincenzo Carafa, the Prior of Capua, has sequestered some of Caravaggio's canvases. He believes that they belong to the Knights of Malta."

"Is that true?"

"No. It seems the Prior is unaware that Caravaggio was defrocked," Del Monte smirked. "I believe the claim is a foolish notion meant only to take possession of what is valuable. Trust me that I'll use all my influence to demand that those canvases are returned here to Rome."

"*Your* influence?"

Del Monte turned to Pietro. "That's the reason I asked to see you. You have more influence with this new Pontiff than I do. I ask you to have him demand the return of the canvases. You see, you *are* my influence."

Pietro's face went blank. "I've been exiled to Ravena. What influence do I have?" The lack of expression on his face was not wasted on Del Monte.

"You may tell the Pontiff that if the paintings are returned I will ensure that they hang in the Villa Borghese," Del Monte told him.

Pietro stood keeping his balance by putting his hand on Del Monte's soft shoulder. "Excellent. And what do you get for this?"

"A slight commission," Del Monte replied. "You are going?"

Pietro stood. "I have an audience with the Pope in an hour."

Del Monte also stood and wobbled as he started to take his leave.

Pietro eyed him. "The legend is that *you* discovered Caravaggio. Is that true?"

"If you asked, did I bring him here to the Palazzo Madama? The answer would be *yes*. But I didn't discover him. He discovered himself as all great artists do." Del Monte took Pietro by the arm and the two men walked toward through the garden. Pietro relished the yellow and red flowers and how the sunlight made the garden seem otherworldly.

Del Monte spoke, "It's a sin for someone as brilliant to die so young."

"Unless it's God's will," Pietro reminded.

Del Monte frowned. "Now you sound like your uncle." He then walked away in the other direction.

Pietro felt the impulse to call out to him. "Be safe, Francesco and my God be with you."

A month later, while swatting flies on his patio in the modest yet neglected villa, Pietro's aide brought him the news that Del Monte had died in his sleep. "In such a violent world as this, I pray to God that when it is my time, he sees that I leave this earth in the same manner," he said to his aide.

CHAPTER FORTY-THREE

Rome
1612

It was a cool and crisp early December morning when Fillide received an official notice from the local magistrate summoning Fillide to appear in court. The summons stated that a third party had accused her of solicitation and prostitution. That third party was Annette Strossi.

If the accusation hadn't been so ridiculous, Fillide would have been concerned. She had recently bowed out of her profession since her investments were bringing her tidy sums of income and she actually didn't have to work at all.

However, occasionally, she was asked to *escort* wealthy ambassadors and certain city officials to secret parties that she knew would be nothing more or less than sex orgies held in discreet locations around the city. The majority of these sex orgies were held in villas as in the old days but the guest list was formed differently than it was then.

Since Pope Paul closed the ghetto, sex was no longer openly for sale in Rome; those who had a craving for it had to form private clubs. These clubs had members who were very wealthy, mostly middle-aged men, merchants and men of the clergy who still had a compulsion for such pleasures.

Strossi had died and that was why his sisters had made the accusation. Fillide learned of Strossi's death several weeks earlier. His demise was sudden and his death allowed his sisters to do all they could to retain what they felt was theirs now that he was gone; and what they saw as theirs was Fillide's portrait.

Comfortable in her villa on Via dei Greci, Fillidee knew that if she was prosecuted and found guilty of prostitution she could be exiled from Rome for life. So, the following day she decided to rescind her statement. She realized that Strossi, despite his monstrous sisters, had been a good man to her. She could also surmise that the two monsters had been torturing him, while he was alive, with the fact that the painting, now worth a small fortune, was in Fillide's possession and should be in theirs and his daugther's.

Fillide contacted her attorney, a young man with a pleasant disposition named Camillo Paladino, about the threat of indictment. They met at her villa where she presented an idea to him. She would write to the Strossi sisters that it would be stated in her will that upon her death, they would inherit the canvas. "I have no heirs to leave it to. Let the man's family own it after my passing," she said to all who had asked about it.

The letter was sent but the sisters refused to drop their claim. Camillo recommended her to 'leave Rome' voluntarily instead of facing a public trial that she could possibly loose. He explained a strategy where during her *self-imposed exile* he would work with the Strossi family attorney on details of a settlement. Fillied made it clear to him in their final meeting that she would not forfeit the portrait under any means. "It's my one prized possession," she told him.

She then made plans to take a long excursion she could clearly afford. She booked passage to sail to Naples and then on to Sicily where she hoped to see Mario in Syracuse.

The night before she left, Fillide wasn't sure why a recent memory flashed before her. It was the evening, only two short years earlier, when she stood up on the small stage facing the large crowd at the Accademia degli Umoristi at the Palazzo Mancini on the Via Del Corso. She held the epitaph the poet Marzio Milesi had written for Caravaggio and read it aloud.

Since the day, she was asked to appear she felt it odd how she was paying tribute to a man who had murdered the one man she had ever loved. What was also odd was that Caravaggio, the man who murdered her lover, Ranuccio, was the man whose portrait changed her life for the good.

Fillide left the following morning taking her small entourage of a cook, a hairstylist and a dresser along with her. She left her villa in the care of her most trusted servant, Maria, and left Rome for the first time since she had arrived nearly eighteen years earlier.

Syracuse

Mario received Fillide's letter that she would be visiting Sicily in the early spring and he made arrangements to be in Messina to greet her. Once again, like Caravaggio, when he told Isabella he had heard from Fillide she again responded in a way that surprised him. She was immediately jealous of Fillide though she had never

281

met her and even though the two women were close to the same age, Isabella grew stiff when Mario mentioned her name.

"How else do you expect me to feel when you tell me that you have heard from Rome's most famous whore?" Isabella replied.

Mario was watching her feed their daughter who was growing to be as beautiful as her mother once was. Mario's sons were already spending more and more time away. His eldest son, Andrea, was an apprentice to a craftsman who lived in Catania. Andrea enjoyed working with wood and metal and Mario wondered if someday his eldest son might not be a sculptor? An irony not lost on him.

His second son, Mario, was considering the religious life and Mario found this also ironic. He wondered at his young son's reverential and pious behavior. He marveled at how he spent his leisure time at the church in Syracuse as an altar boy and walking the hills around the family villa praying. He also would sit alone and gaze at Mario's religious paintings hanging in the studio. One night he actually told Mario that he wanted to be a priest and perhaps a martyr. Isabella was appalled and cried all night while Mario asked her, "Why are you so unhappy?"

"I have lost him to God," she answered.

"I thought you loved God?"

"I love my son more," she shouted back.

Mario found contentment in his home and was continuing to make money from his constantly religious paintings. So when he received Fillide's letter he never made mention that she was visiting Messina and he certainly didn't tell her that he had scheduled one of his many trips to that city to coincide when she would be there.

Mountains hemmed in Messina and yet its harbor made it a key city in the Mediterranean. Its city offered a respected school for painting and Mario was consistently paid very well to appear for sessions with the more advanced students.

It was also a city of connoisseurs and collectors. One of these men who owned a cottage high at the footsteps of the mountains with a splendid view of the harbor that Mario rented for what he was hoping to be a tryst with Fillide.

The former lovers decided to meet in front of the church of the Madonna Del Pilero. Mario was dressed in a black shirt and dark blue trousers attempting to present a figure much the one he portrayed all those years ago back in Rome.

Fillide, on the other hand, wore a long dark red and black wrap from the finest linen thread that was manufactured. The borders of her skirt were lined by silver and gold thread. She was wearing black velvet summer gloves. She wanted him to see a *new* and more reserved but auspicious Fillide.

Mario saw her walking toward him from the direction of the Messina Hotel where she was staying. She was walking into the blazing sunlight and he could see how she wore her hair long and over her shoulders. Though he couldn't see her features, he knew she was smiling.

The café was nearly empty as Fillide and Mario shared a lunch. Mario knew that to any bystander they had to look like two lovers on holiday. After the waiter took their order of cuscusu, he told them that the owner wanted to buy them a bottle of Malvasia di Lipari wine. "He says you make such a lovely couple," and then left bringing them the bottle.

Mario chose that café to meet Fillide because he didn't know the owner personally and wanted to make certain he wasn't noticed. He looked at Fillide's smile. "You're a lovely *woman* now. More beautiful than I expected," he told her. He had always a weakness for her long dark hair and how it cascaded down toward her shoulders, in waves. Her hair was just as thick and rich and her eyes, always playful and sturdy, seemed now more relaxed but even more appealing.

"I *have* lived, Mario," she told him.

Mario recalled these qualities of Fillide that were so evident when they first met that evening at the Tavern of the Hawk, but he could see now what had altered by the passage of time.

The impish quality that he delighted in was now long gone and replaced by a sturdy fortitude and he told her so. "I needed to find other qualities to survive," she explained.

"You have replaced your street bravado with a fragile elegance," he continued.

She explained, "I aged and that street attitude that fits well on a young woman, looks more like folly on one at my stage of life," she said without regret and with wisdom.

Mario touched her hand and gently turned her palm to his and caressed it. "There was a burning curiosity in your eyes for everything and now I see a woman who *has* seen everything."

"I have."

"And it has changed you."

Fillide now took his hand with both hers and held it. "What you see is a woman who has lost everything dear to her. I lost Anna and Ranuccio. I lost my father and

283

the man Battista. I lost my mother and my God a long time ago. I'm close to no one, Mario. Not a soul on this earth can I truly call a friend."

Mario sensed a steadiness in her voice that contradicted the sadness the words were telling him. "I see all that in your eyes."

Fillide glanced out the open door to the street. He could see how she was suddenly bedazzled how the sunlight danced along the very tip of the edge of the rooftops facing them. "The light does that here in Sicily. It is everywhere at once," he smiled. She allowed him to take her in and he did again. He knew that she was a woman who he would never grow tired of looking at. He wasn't sure if it was an aesthetic element, an emotional one or just because he was in love with her? "And what about me? How have I changed?"

Fillide chuckled placing her hand to her mouth to stop herself. "I would never have recognized you! You're a man of taste and bearing now. You walk differently. Back in Rome, dear Mario, you sauntered and here I notice you glide. Back in Rome, you were insecure and that made you reckless. Here, you are so cautious I can smell your fear that someone will notice us holding hands," she told him bluntly.

He leaned back and pretended not to be offended. Fillide, always knowing what a man wanted to hear, leaned forward. "In a physical sense you are just as attractive and even more so. You wear your hair shorter now but it is still as thick and well groomed. Your eyes are now oddly more confident despite some fire of lament I see at their very depths," she said describing him. "You're a father."

"Yes, I am."

"And you're a husband," she told him.

He didn't answer her. It was something he knew she was aware of but oddly he wanted to hide it from her and he didn't know why he did. "It's silly but I don't want to discuss that with you."

"I have no interest in discussing it with you. But it is a fact that you are married. I meant nothing more than that."

Mario then felt another overwhelming sense of loss. "Yes, it's a fact."

"Do you regret leaving Rome when you did?"

He answered quickly, "No."

"Then why do I see such pain in your eyes?" she asked.

"Do you not know at all?" he replied.

Fillide again put her hand to her mouth as if to stifle a laugh. "Mario, you and I could never have been."

He felt humiliated. "You never cared for me?"

"Of course I did. But I was a whore. You would never have married me."

"How can you say that? Strossi proposed to you?"

"Yes, he did, but that was he *not* you."

He still didn't understand.

"If you and I married we would be dirt poor and living in some hovel in the ghetto waiting for our landlord to evict us. I'd be ill from syphilis and you would be dying from drink. Instead, today I *own* much of the ghetto property where we used to have our walks, some consider me an heiress and you, my sweet, are a wealthy painter. We have wonderful lives, do you not think so?" He could see that she was pleading with her eyes for him to agree.

"I have rented a cottage on top of the hill above us."

"For what purpose have you done this?"

He felt trapped by his own proposal. He wanted to hide under the table, rush away from the café and lose himself in the streets of Messina.

"You are expecting us to indulge in a rendezvous?"

Mario noticed how she used the French word with such refinement and yet with an accent he knew she would never loose. "Yes," he answered.

"How clever," she told him.

The two of them walked Messina that afternoon visiting the galleries and making the point to see Mario's *Raising of the Widow of Naim* which she wanted to see. They traveled by buggy to the Capuchin Monastery of Santa Maria Concezione. Along the way, Mario told her of his adventures in Sicily beginning with his meeting Isabella in Rome and how he married her in a ceremony back in Syracuse on her father's extensive and lush villa which was now, for all intent, his property.

They spoke of Caravaggio. She told him how desperate she was when she had learned he had killed Ranuccio. "I thought I would take my own life back then. I was stunned by God's treacherous will that he would have the man who changed my life murder the man I loved. It was cruel and vicious an event and it only feeds my disgust for my own creator," she told him.

In hearing her speak about God that way, Mario knew that he was wrong. Many qualities of Fillide had changed but in her soul, she was the same intractable woman she was when they had met all those years ago.

That night, he brought her to the front door of her hotel and walked her to the entrance. The two friends stood there in the torch light listening to the sounds of the busy city slowly fading in the background of their conversation.

They were face to face when Fillide spoke first. "So you are staying in Messina?"

Mario knew that she already *knew* the answer to that question since he had mentioned the cottage he had rented. "Yes. Would you like to have breakfast?"

He could see Fillide hesitate. "I would prefer lunch. So I can sleep late."

"Then I shall meet you here and take you to lunch."

She smiled. He bowed and then took her gloved hand and kissed it. She quickly removed the glove. "Please kiss it again."

He did.

"Mario," she told him with a tone of voice he could sense was being sensitive and yet always evocative to him. "It's a false notion to believe that people as ourselves, people who have lived so much, could ever return to those days of innocence."

Mario shrugged. "But my sweet Fillide, were we ever innocent?"

She pursed her lips knowingly. "You were. I was. Who was not?"

"Caravaggio?"

"No, he was as innocent as we were. Perhaps he was less gullible? Perhaps this and perhaps that but I can only say for certain that we had hoped to change the world we inhabited and I believe we did. We brought realism to it. We stared in the face of the charlatans in the Vatican and we showed them what life was all about. And what it was for us back then was grime, and violence and suffering," she said. "And we made life from all that."

Mario touched her face. "I can see it all by listening to you now. I hear the sounds from the piazza in your voice and I see all of the city's confusion in your eyes."

"But I'm no longer confused," she told him not afraid again to be blunt.

"Goodnight," Mario told her.

She now curtsied turned and entered the hotel.

Mario immediately mounted the buggy he had rented and instead of heading up to the mountains to the cottage where he had hoped to spend the night with Fillide, he decided to head south along the lonely dark road back to his home in Syracuse.

There was no full moon this night and the ride would take him until noon before he'd arrive. He wanted that much distance between himself and the memory of what he would never again experience with Fillide.

He also knew that despite their plan on meeting for lunch she had no intention of seeing him again. Though he wasn't there to see what he already surmised Fillide did check out of the hotel a little after dawn just as Mario had left the city of Catania, to his back, and could see the sun rising out of the Mediterranean to his left.

It was about then that Fillide was already in her rented carriage and with her entourage in tow she was half way to Palermo. By the time Mario had reached Syracuse, Fillide was already buying a ticket for a sea passage the following day that would take her across the sea to Naples where she planned to rent a villa and wait for word from her lawyer.

That evening, while Mario found himself spending more time than usual with Isabella in their main living room and not in his studio, Fillide was accompanying an ambassador from Florence she had known from Rome. While Mario sat alone facing the fireplace nibbling on a dinner Isabella had had prepared, Fillide was dazzling a small dinner party. She did this by telling stories of her wild nights back in Rome at the Tavern of the Turk and the Hawk and her affair with Ranuccio and her being painted by Caravaggio.

While Mario was giving into his desire for sleep while his wife sat across from him cuddled up with their daughter in her arms, Fillide was lying back alone on her bed looking up at the ceiling.

For a brief moment both, at the same time perhaps, thought of the other, not in terms of their kinship, but more in terms of the jagged lines their lives had etched upon one another.

As both Mario and Fillide slept they came to realize that what they shared was somehow original and what they had now was what they had needed and desired all along.

They also both knew that they would never see one another again and both, oddly enough, found solace and even comfort in that conclusion.

CHAPTER FORTY-FOUR

Rome
1618

Fillide celebrate her thirty-seventh birthday at an exclusive restaurant, La Dole on Via Corso with Camillo, her attorney. As she had told Mario, she no longer had any close friends. There were no romantic ties to any men in her life and it had been that way for several years. She had no close female friends since her reputation as a courtesan eliminated the possibility of any married or respectable women befriending her. Those remaining courtesans in Rome her age disliked her with the same ferocity with which she disliked them.

She had returned to Rome two years after her *self-imposed* exile when Camillo summoned her with the news that he had bridged a bargain with the Strossi sisters. The women had eventually agreed to withdraw their complaint if Fillide agreed to forfeit her rights to the portrait upon her death.

That was two years previous and for those two years she had lived an uneventful existence in Rome spending her days in the luxury of her villa and her nights in the same manner. Occasionally, she was asked to attend certain dinner gatherings but her days as a well sought-after courtesan were long over. Many of her former clients were either too old or dead and the new wave of clientele desired young female flesh. So, Fillide accepted her fate knowing every day how fortunate she was to be wise enough to have invested the many lira and scudi she had earned over the years. Money was a great solace to loneliness she told herself and her servants often.

"It is well worth it to be rid of the two hags," she said as they sipped a precious Castelli wine while dinning on artichokes, lamb and spaghetti alla cardonara.

"But how did you managed to change their minds? I offered them the portrait after my death and they ignored me?" She asked. She allowed herself to gaze on the young man sitting across from her. He was in his late twenties, she suspected and had thin light brown hair neatly combed to the side of his head, as it was now the fashion. He had hazel eyes that she found elusive when it came to revealing anything personal. They had a way of flattening when she discussed his personal life but when they were speaking of finances the hazel eyes, rimmed with flecks of green and gold, brightened. She noticed that in reply to her question, they brightened even more so.

"They are represented by a very prestigious law firm but one of their young attorney's is a friend of mine from Tivolli. My friend needed time since the primary attorney representing the Strossi family was retiring. This senior attorney retired and my friend took the Strossi family account. He explained to the family that they had no recourse but to accept your offer since if you died and the painting was still in your possession, you could presumably will it to anyone including a museum or gallery. If you did so and they still desired the painting, they would then have to purchase the portrait from the gallery assuming the gallery would even sell it to them. And that asking price would be an enormous sum," he grinned. "They would be better off allowing you to will the portrait to them."

Fillide touched her lips with her napkin. "You are a clever young man, Camillo."

"Thank you, Madam, but we must not forget that the Strossi women are childless and they have no heirs themselves and they will be long dead before you pass," he told her.

"So, here we are, three spinsters fighting over a painting of me! When I was a young and sexy whore! Ha!" Fillide chuckled.

Camillo lowered his eyes and raised his eyebrows.

"So what made them change their minds, do you think, besides the chance that they may loose the painting?" she asked.

Camillo shrugged. "I believe time did. As the months passed their dislike for you faded. I hear from my friend that Annette is suffering from an intestinal disease and Rosa, when not caring for her sister, is herself losing her eyesight."

Fillide again chuckled. "Ha! What a pair they make. Annette, the cranky witch is dying of flatulence and the silly one, is loosing her eyesight. Well, one thing we learn from all this is that God has no pity on the wretched fools that we humans are no matter how wealthy, how kind or how cruel," she philosophized. She then sat back in her chair and felt flirtatious. She wasn't quite certain if a woman her age would be attractive to a young man like Camillo though she knew he wasn't married.

Dressed in her finest silk and black lace dress and with her dark hair up in a swirl with a deep purple tiara holding it together, she wasn't sure if she had put on too much face make up or if she had made her eyebrows too dark?

On the other hand, she was uneasy with the truth of her life at this moment in time. It didn't hurt her or even offend her that she had no one but Camillo to celebrate her birthday with but it did disappoint her. She knew he was accompanying her only because he was her solicitor.

When dinner was completed, they rode her carriage back to her villa on Via Paolina.

Camillo accompanied her into the villa where Fillide invited him to share some coffee and sweet liquor with her. As Camillo walked through the marble halls, Fillide could see how he was noticing the pristine hand painted artifacts and the works of art she had collected over the years. She could see how he was amazed by the sculptured pieces of bronze, which decorated the carefully carved wooden reading desk, and the shelves of well-taken care leather bound books lining the walls.

The servants served them in Fillide's favorite room. It was small but it had a large window that faced her garden. There was a table in the far corner, draped in a green velvet cloth with the edges embroidered in gold and there were tasseled cushions stacked in another corner.

The floor was made of black and white marble tile and the doorway flanked by antique-style pilasters.

Though Camillo has been in her villa, a few times, they had always adjourned in her office. This was the first time she allowed him to witness, first hand, her opulence and property.

"I'm awestruck by your home, Madam."

"Please call me Fillide, Camillo. I'm not an ancient female goddess, or am I?"

Again, he lowered his eyes and raised his eyebrows showing her a slight smile. Fillide sipped her coffee and her lips curled in a way she once remembered Cardinal Aldobandini told her *excited* him. She wondered if it would have the same effect on her young lawyer? "You must think of me as an aging spinster?"

Camillo looked offended. "Excuse me?"

"I am not unattractive at thirty-seven, yet, am I?"

Camillo now looked confused.

"It is the life of a courtesan. One either ends up as a homeless woman begging for bread in the Piazza del Popolo or one ends up a lonely wealthy lady as I have. I'm fortunate to be of the latter." She can see that Camillo was anxious. "You have something on your mind?" she inquired, expecting that it was sex he had on his mind. She had been thinking of that possibility all evening and was still not sure how to bridge the subject if it came up.

She wasn't certain that it was wise to have this young man see her body, though to her it was still firm and sensual but mainly because they did much business together. He was the one person in her life she had to trust with her money and that meant she was entrusting him with her future.

When it came to sex, however, she felt that Camillo was asexual. "I need to speak you about someone," Camillo blathered.

"You need to speak to me about *someone*? Who is this someone?" she asked.

Camillo sat forward. "Her name is Menica Calvi."

Fillide sat back. "What about this Menica?"

Camillo was now whispering, "I come to you with this since I know you have experience and perhaps, you can guide her."

"Guide her?"

"She is my courtesan," he spat out.

Fillide nearly fell forward upon hearing the news. "You have a courtesan?" *Now he looks insulted.*

"Yes. I do. I met her at a dinner party for my firm. She was hired by the senior partner, but whatever the case, she is living with me and yet, she brings me all kinds of worries."

"Of course she does. How old is this Menica?"

"Nineteen."

Fillide frowned.

"So she says. She may be eighteen? Maybe seventeen?"

Fillide chuckled again. "You have been very entertaining tonight, Camillo. I have not chuckled with suprise like this in a few years, I believe." Fillide stood up and felt her legs tighten. "And what is it you expect me to teach this whore of yours?"

She knew the word *whore* would sting him and that was why she used it.

"I don't really know. I thought if she saw how successful you are she would see no reason to be so wild."

"Oh, she is wild, then?"

Camillo nodded.

Fillide took a moment. "Send her to me. I will do this as a favor for you and for no other reason."

Camillo stood. "I'm eternally thankful."

"Of course you are. Now, go home and fuck with this Menica and tell her that

I will speak to her."

Camillo bowed several times and when Fillide called her servant, he followed her to the front door and was about to leave the villa when Fillide called to him. "Camillo?"

He stopped and turned to Fillide. "Yes?"

"Did you ever see it?" she asked walking toward him.

Camillo shrugged. "See what, Madam?"

Fillide waved for him to follow her. He walked towards her and then opened a door to her private study. Her servant quickly lit a large candle and then another and another.

Fillide watched as the light crossed the portrait and lit the canvas hanging at eye level on the wall. Camillo, hesitant to enter the room at first, quickly stepped beside her.

They both gazed for a long moment before Fillide spoke up, "Charming, isn't she?"

Camillo replied, "She is and has been for many years now."

Still side by side, Fillide reached for his hand and grasped it. "Thank you for sharing my birthday with me."

Camillo bowed again then made his way back to the front door and left the villa.

Fillide sat down on a chair she had set up purposely so she could gaze for hours at the canvas. She rubbed her leg. She was finding that her muscles were tightening up more often and was annoyed that they were. She then made a face and nearly laughed. "He wants me to speak to his whore and advise her and here I was wondering if he was going to try and fuck with me," she told no one in particular other than herself since she was the only one in the room.

"Ah, but if I looked like *that* he would be paying me at this very moment to be with me," she whispered.

Menica arrived one afternoon several days later. Fillide greeted her in her library. When Menica was escorted into the room Fillide was immediately put off. The young woman was clearly from the street and forced herself to be polite in Fillide's presence. Fillide knew that behavior well.

She was also disturbed to see that Menica's hair had been dyed an ebony color that was clearly not her natural one. Her eyebrows were darkened and her outfit seemed somewhat similar to what Fillide had worn in her portrait, from the style of her clothing to the style of her hair to the kind of jewelry she was wearing.

Menica bowed and pretended graciousness but her energy was that of a restless cat with one eye on the master and another on the window of which could lead her to the street.

"So, tell me about yourself, Menica?" Fillide asked as she sat back in her chair. She wore a modest blue shawl over her lounging skirt and allowed her hair to fall over her shoulders.

Fillide noticed how Menica couldn't take her eyes off of her hair. "You have such lovely hair, Madam," she expressed sincerely.

"How lovely of you to notice. So, where are you from?"

"Siena," Menica said.

Fillide frowned. "Is that so?"

"Truly, Madam."

"So you are a poor farm girl from Siena who has come to Rome to be a courtesan," Fillide said curtly. She wondered what Camillo saw in her since other than her youth and light blue eyes there was nothing singularly interesting about the girl, Fillide thought.

Menica nodded quickly to her question.

"And I am your ideal?"

"Yes, Madam."

"And what do you know about me, Menica?"

Menica hesitated. "You're from Siena. You're famous. You're wealthy."

"And you know all this from?"

"Camillo!" she said nearly with glee.

Fillide jutted her chin forward. "And how do you feel about Camillo?"

"He's a gentleman alright. I live with him now. He wants me to learn the ways of a courtesan."

"And is this the profession you are interested in pursuing?"

"Yes, Madam. I see how lovely your life has been and I know it is something I can manage. I can only hope you would take me under your wing and show me the path to all this success you have acquired."

"Did you memorize that speech, dear?" Fillide asked.

Menica was startled.

Fillide waved her servant over. "Wine?"

"Yes!" Menica replied.

Fillide realized that Camillo had sent Menica over with a plan. In his dastardly heart, he had planned this meeting in an attempt to test the waters and see if he could move Fillide to sympathy for the young woman, in seeing herself in the girl, and perhaps take her under her wing where the both of them would then work to separate Fillide from her fortune.

During the next hour as Fillide showed Menica her villa and told her stories of her jaded past with both women laughing through the conversation, Fillide did begin to feel something for Menica and it wasn't sympathy. It was more like empathy.

Eventually, while sharing a light dinner in the garden, Fillide told Menica, "I was you, once, my dear. And you were who I was. If you can understand that." She could see that Menica did not have the intellectual or the emotional depth to understand the weight of such a remark.

Menica seemed pleased with Fillide's comment as if it was something Camillo told her he'd hope she'd hear. Fillide then said, "We *are* alike in many ways. You are where I was once. But unlike me you *will* end up dead in the gutter, dear girl."

Menica stopped chewing. "Huh?"

"Did you hear me?"

"I heard you," Menica said with a chill in her voice.

"I cannot see you living beyond twenty winters. You'll end up with syphilis or gonorrhea or murdered by some other whore or some man you think loves you. And he'll be a drunk with a sword and either you will cut out his liver or he will slice your face in pieces," she hissed. "I'm certain of it. You don't have the wit or the distinct beauty to end up any other way. You don't have the intelligence to fend for yourself nor do you have the insight to manage any success that comes your way. I was younger than you when I started my days in the ghetto and was so much more alert and gifted."

Menica dropped her salad fork. "I didn't come here for insults."

"Of course you didn't. You came here for my money. It wasn't your notion to do so. I imagine it was Camillo's." Fillide leaned forward. "Do not entrust your future with him. He will grow tired of fucking with you and find another younger version of yourself. He will introduce you to an older man probably married or someone in the clergy and you will end up like my dear, beloved cousin Anna, buried in a shallow grave."

Menica pushed away her chair and just as Fillide had expected, she saw her true nature emmerge for the first time. "You are an old whore and a bitch," Menica shouted. "I only pray that you die in your bed alone with boils and fevers!"

"We are born alone and we all die alone, dear Menica."

Fillide saw her raise her fork and made a move to come at her. Fillide shook her head. "Child, I made more whores bleed in my day than the Roman army hung Christian martyr's from the rafters of the Colosseum."

Menica took a stance at her end of the table and with a thrust of her arm, knocked over the porcelain plates and delicate glasses to the garden tiles and then rushed towards a servant. "Which is the way out of this hell?"

The servant actually looked to Fillide for guidance. "Escort her to the door before I cut her face and ruin her whoring career."

Menica turned and shouted at Fillide. "Your wealth will do you no good when you are old and decrepit."

Fillide knew than only a street urchin not yet eighteen could even conjure such a notion. She also knew that unless this young whore had a miraculous transformation, her life would end as bleakly as Fillide had foretold.

The following morning Fillide sent a letter she had written the evening before to Camillo stating that she would no longer need his services as a friend, companion or attorney.

Camillo sent her several letters in response but she didn't answer them. He sent emissaries begging Fillide for a reason why she no longer wanted to see him. He even appeared at her door one Sunday afternoon but to no avail. Fillide had decided never would she ever allow him to see her face to face again.

Fillide survived by never trusting strangers, never letting her guard down and never making the mistake of believing in anyone's better nature. They had all disappointed and left her in the end. Her father was the only one she had forgiven for dying so young and leaving her alone but there were nights she cursed him for abandoning her to a life where she had to fend for herself. She learned to survive without lasting friendship and love because God had showed her how, she thought. God had never once lifted his hand to help her. God had never once brought someone into her life that hadn't caused her disappointment or pain.

Ranuccio and his family disrespected her and Caravaggio who gave her what she desired more than anything, killed the man she loved.

Fillide felt there was no justice in life. One survived on their wits and that was all. She shuddered when she would hear some people say, "If only for the grace of God, go I."

Then she would ask, "What grace? What God?"

Through a suggestion of her banker, she found a new and more reputable attorney from a family who had lived in Rome for generations.

Zaratini Castellini, a remarkably unassuming man who was married, loved literature and enjoyed Fillide's company especially when she felt comfortable enough to tell him some of her stories of the ghetto and the wild parties Pietro Aldobrandini used to throw with his secret guest list. "The cardinal paid the price for such a dedication to sin. The new Pontiff exiled him to Ravena," she said.

"I hear he's still active in Vatican politics," Zaratini told her.

Fillide could see that in his early sixties, he could have retired from practice but he told her many times how he looked forward to going to his office not far from Fillide's villa. "You are a wealthy woman, Fillide Melandroni," he liked to say to her.

"Yes, I am."

"I'm probably correct when I say that you may be the wealthiest woman in all of Rome."

"It would give me great pleasure to believe that to be so," she smiled.

Fillide could pinpoint the exact day and nearly the exact time when she knew she had an aliment that was going to eventually take her life.

She was cutting roses alone in her garden. It was early morning and the air was still cool enough for her to work without becoming too uncomfortable. She felt a pain in her chest and though for a moment she thought it might be her heart, a moment later she coughed up blood. She was bent over a rose and spit the blood across the stem. She leaned back and saw more stains on her white apron.

She knelt for a few moments, took a deep breath and then felt a pain in her chest that was severe enough for her to call her servant and, in turn, a doctor.

The doctor, Vinenzo Lauria, examined her and told her that she had tuberculosis. He had many patients terminally ill from a potent strain that many feared had made its way to Rome from ships from the British Isles.

Fillide was not stunned when he told her that from what he had learned from his examination the tuberculosis had spread through her lungs and was festering in several places. "My dear, your breathing is erratic and you have a fever. Your lungs are infected beyond repair. It is time you make your peace with God," he said.

Hearing this, Fillide sent letters to Colonel Nunzio Palzone and Zaratini her attorney.

Zaratini was the first to reply and when he came to visit her Fillide was in bed as she told him to expect her to be.

Before he could utter a word, she pleaded with him, "My money? My property? Who will take possession of it when I die?" she asked him.

"Since you have no heirs the City of Rome will acquire your estate."

"I don't want the Church to get a single lira."

"But the city of Rome is the Vatican."

"I feared that," she said cutting him off.

Zaratini stood solemn in his dark jacket. "Would you consider donating a portion to charity?"

"No. The Church will *keep* what I give." Fillide then handed him a small envelope. "I have another alternative."

"Alternative?"

"I want you to please read this document carefully."

Zaratini read the document. He then lifted his head. "Are you certain *this* is what you want to do?"

Fillide was having trouble breathing as she sat up with several pillows at her head. "Yes. I'm certain. I want you to take that amount and do with it exactly as I ask." She then handed him another small document. "I have known you only a short time, my friend, but I trust you and I have trusted very few people in my life. When you have concluded this mission for me, this is your payment."

He read the document. "This is too much."

"You have children and they will have grandchildren. It can help them." She lifted her hand and took his. "Please take the time to act upon my wishes. I want to hear that you were successful. I'll wait for you to return."

"As you wish, Fillide," he said then left the room.

When Nunzio Pulzone received Fillide's letter he was more than stunned by it. In her letter, she stated simply, "I'm dying. Please come see me one last time. I have a request of you."

Nunzio stood at Fillide's beside unable to grasp, that the young woman he had loved for so long, had aged beyond her years.

Fillide read his mind and forced a grin but she was weak from fever and couldn't maintain her impish nature for long. "I know the room smells of ointments and medical liquids. I'm sorry," she told him.

Nunzio was taken aback by her candor. "I have never understood you, Fillide."

"That is probably why you desired me so much all those years ago. I was a mystery to you," she said without irony.

She had never given him such a long look as she did just then. She saw that his haggard face long and brooding had changed little and she saw that his shoulders were still solid. "I was there at the Palazzo Farnese when I saw you on the terrace," she told him.

He was startled by the revelation.

"I was calling for your death," she said.

Again, he was startled by her candor.

"I asked you here today to ask for your forgiveness."

Nunzio was lost in a whirlpool of emotion. He never expected that in his lifetime he would be at her deathbed. "I forgive you," he said gently and quickly.

"I'm not a courageous woman. I tell you the truth because I know you can not punish me."

"I would never have attempted to punish you."

"I made you sin."

"But the Church preaches to *forgive the sinner but hate the sin.*"

She was quiet but then coughed and then was still again.

"Is there anything else I can do?"

She nodded. "Please protect my property until it is all taken care of. I have left lira for my servants and I have taken steps with my attorney to have my art donated to particular galleries," she told him in a voice that was quickly loosing its timber and range.

"I'll assign a cavalieri posted to your front door until all is taken care of," Nunzio told her.

"You are so kind," she said. She felt Nunzio take her hand but she was too weak to hold it so he pressed it as tightly as he could without hurting her and then turned to leave.

"Nunzio?"

"Yes?" he asked.

"I cannot bear the sunlight anymore. Please ask my servants to cover my windows completely."

Nunzio replied. "Of course." He then reached down and kissed her cheek but she had already closed her eyes.

Zaratini sat in the carriage feeling dirty and covered in dust. The young driver leaned into the carriage and shouted, "This is it, sire," with a harsh tone to his voice.

Zaratini pushed open the door, stepped down from the carriage and took a few steps away from the carriage. "Are you sure that was Siena back there?"

"You read the signs the same as I did, sire."

Zaratini nodded. "Of course, of course," he muttered. He looked up and saw that the clouds had massed above him and the air was heavy.

As if reading his mind the driver shouted, "It will rain soon."

"Of course, of course," he muttered again.

"What is it you're looking for, sire?" the driver asked.

Zaratini felt odd announcing his mission aloud. "I need to find a poor family along this road where there is a young daughter."

The driver made a face. "Odd thing to search for."

"Of course it is," Zaratini opened Fillide's letter again making sure that he was close to the road she had written about, the farmhouse she once lived in. "This must be it," he said then placed his hand to his eyes to help see further along the horizon since despite the clouds there was still a glare.

He saw several farmhouses in the distance when suddenly as if she was an angel; a young girl appeared, seemingly from nowhere. She cautiously approached the wagon and Zaratini could see immediately that not only was she poor but she was hungry and the ravaging effects of famine had taken their toll on her young frame.

She had mass of brown hair that was as dirty as her face. Her fingernails were black, her clothing nothing but rags but her dark eyes, like most youth, Zaratini thought, were wishful and full of hope.

"Are you from the city?" she asked sounding like a miniature adult who was nonchalant and yet inquisitive.

Zaratini bent down to her. "I am. And what is your name?"

"Costanza," she said with vim and vigor and a lighthearted grin.

"And where do you live?"

She pointed off to a farmhouse off in the distance at the foot of the nearby ancient hills. "There!"

Zaratini stepped up onto the carriage and slide in. "Would you like to ride with us?" He could see that she had never ridden in a carriage before and was afraid. "Take me to your mother and father."

Without saying a word, she ran off toward the farmhouse and the carriage followed.

Zaratini was again at Fillide's bedside but this time her doctor was also there. "Can she hear me?" he inquired. The doctor took a moment. "I believe she can. But keep your voice low."

Zaratini placed his mouth to Fillide's ear and whispered. "I found the perfect little girl. She appeared along the road just as if out of nowhere. Her name is Constanza. She is delightful and so innocent."

Fillide could hear Zaratini though she was so fatigued she could only raise her hand in response.

He continued. "She lives in a farmhouse not far from where you grew up. But honestly, it is more a shack than a farmhouse. I met with her parents. They are destitute and yet they seemed like good people."

"Their home?" Fillide asked in a hoarse voice. "Did you feel love?"

Zaratini nodded, "Yes."

Fillide felt herself fade. "What did they say when you told them?"

Zaratini pursued his lips and arched his eyebrows. "They did not believe me at first. But when they saw that I was not on a mission of folly but a task of truth they knelt and prayed, hugged me and told me that they would pray for you."

Fillide shook her head. "No prayers."

Zaratini stepped back and heard the doctor say, "Let her rest."

Fillide heard the door close and again she was in darkness but though she had no strength left in any molecule of her body, she felt a surge of happiness.

300

Outside the bedroom, Zaratini explained what he had been describing to Fillide. "She requested that I leave a small fortune in a trust fund that I would oversee to a poor girl who had grown up where she had in Siena. I just returned from finding a perfect candidate."

"She seemed pleased," the doctor said as he packed his medical bag.

"Yes, yes, of course she was pleased," Zaratini stated. "I'll call on her tomorrow and answer any other questions she might have."

The doctor spoke up, "She will not be asking you any more questions tomorrow."

Zaratini asked, "And why is that?"

"She will not live out the night," the doctor said then closed up his medical bag.

Fillide Melandroni died in the early evening on June twelfth in the warm womb and splendor of her villa. She was unconscious and immobile devoid of memory and physical longing. She was thirty-seven years of age.

Rome was its usual busy self with café windows lit with candlelight and conversation. Young men and women roamed the piazzas as the Vatican went about its business battling Martin Luther's followers.

Upon hearing of her death, Nunzio did as she had asked. He posted a twenty-four hour a day guard at her front door until all of her belongings were sent to their rightful owners. He left the guard in place as her home was sold by Zaratini, her servants paid in full with a pension she had arranged and her portrait was carefully packed and sent to the two Strossi sisters in Florence. Oddly enough, both Annette and Rose, though thoroughly incapacitated, had outlived her. Rosa was blind and couldn't see the canvas. And the hearsay was that Annette, upon seeing Fillide's face was so upset, she had a massive stroke and lived as an invalid for another six weeks with the portrait hanging in her bedroom and was unable to communicate with her servants that she wanted it removed.

Nunzio met with the pastor of the church of Santa Maria Del Popolo requesting that the infamous Fillide be buried in hallowed ground but his written request, which journeyed all the way to the Vatican, landed on Pietro's desk where he quickly had it denied. He did so with great regret but though feeble and aged, he still was worried about official Vatican fingers pointing at him if he made allowances for the condemned courtesan to be buried along side the virtuous and the saved.

Undeterred Nunzio took Fillide's body up north along the Tiber River by wagon searching for a place where the river and the shore met.

In late afternoon, he found a place he thought was appropriate and was what Fillide might have chosen herself if she was able. It was a grassy knoll near the river's edge where a large oak had been standing for nearly half a century. There was something oddly serene about the spot.

It was here that Nunzio dug a hole and placed Fillide down to rest. He lingered a long time in silence allowing his mind to wander over the sensuous nights he made love to her back in the *Ortaccio*. He then respectfully made the sign of the cross.

When he felt it was time, he shoved dirt and leaves over her body and left the unmarked grave.

CHAPTER FORTY-FIVE

Rome
1620

One night in November two years after Fillide's death, Nunzio was walking along the same streets he had many years earlier, reaching a new market on Via Corso and crossed the Pointe Mazzini on his way home to his wife and son.

Nunzio had prayed that his son would become a painter but it seemed the boy wanted only to be like his father, to wear the cavalieri emblem and carry the police sword.

He was now old enough to join the cavalieri ranks and in a few short weeks, he would graduate from a new school which was formed to train Rome's young men for the task.

It was on this particular cold night, as Nunzio walked with a cape covering his shoulders that he came across three young men who were standing on the bridge tossing debris into the Tiber. He could hear that they were drunk and they were French as they hurled insults to everyone who walked by them. Nunzio was off duty and preferred to ignore the act of vandalism but something inside of him flashed to the violent Tomassoni clan. His mind quickly conjured up others including the painters Mario Minniti and Caravaggio and their friend in arms Onorio Longhi. These memories forced Nunzio to confront the young Frenchmen. He felt it was his duty to protect Rome. He harbored resentment that there had been so many years where the gangs came close to destroying Rome with their ruthless violence and nihilistic comportment.

Driven by this deep resentment he crept up to them. There was no one on the bridge. So, he stood his ground and demanded in Italian, "What are you doing?"

The three faces blended into one another and though Nunzio had just turned fifty a few months earlier, his eyesight was still better than average so he couldn't understand why when he looked into their faces he saw Ranuccio, Minniti and Caravaggio.

"Kiss my ass!" one of the young men called out in broken Italian and before Nunzio could react, the three young men quickly surrounded him.

"I am cavalieri," he told them while drawing his sword but instead of showing him respect, all three pulled daggers from their belts and thrust them at him.

Nunzio stepped back to his right making the young man to his left miss him completely but he wasn't as fortunate with the other two. The young man to his right thrust his knife into his side and Nunzio could actually feel the steel rip through his cloak, slide through his flesh, crushing a rib. When the young man pulled the dagger back, Nunzio lost his breath and stumbled forward.

The young man directly facing him planted his right foot and thrust his dagger into Nunzio's chest for the kill. Nunzio could see this young man's face grimace with anger, his yellow eyes focused on Nunzio.

The torch burning on the bridge directly beside them threw a flash of light across the young man's face and Nunzio could see the stubble on his chin. "Why?" he asked as he felt an explosion in his chest as if a wall had been breached and a hot liquid poured through the crumbling remains.

He fell to his knees feeling all his stamina escape his being. He put a hand on the bridge's cold wall grasping with his fingers desperately, doing all he could to hold on to its damp and slippery stone.

Just then, one of the young men kicked him to the pavement, and like hyenas, they all pounced on their prey. However, instead of ripping Nunzio apart with their teeth, they pulled open his cloak stealing everything they could find in his pockets. Nunzio reached up to the young man with the yellow eyes and grabbed his lapel pulling a red military ribbon from his cloak then wrapping his own fingers around it.

The young man saw what Nunzio had done and desperately attempted to pry open his hands but couldn't. The fingers had been clenched in death.

Seconds later the three young men raced across the bridge to the opposite direction heading south towards the Piazza Venezia.

Nunzio died while on his back. His eyes were open to the last second *feeling* the darkness gradually covering him from within and at the same time, he felt the same darkness invading his being from without.

Off in the distance the golden lights from Saint Peter's Basilica were the brightest creation in that blackness. Nunzio said "God forgive me" and stared once more at the worldly existence that had brought him so much confusion.

The last thing Nunzio saw before he died were the warm lights glowing from fireplaces and candles from within the Vatican.

❖

Two men in Rome reacted quickly to the news of Colonel Nunzio Palzone's death. One was Guisto and the other was Pope Paul V.

Nunzio's widow and her children grieved and cried out for justice, however, the Pontiff wanted more than justice, he wanted retribution. Calling in Pietro Aldobrandini from Ravena, he asked him to suggest a man worthy of Nunzio's office and Pietro immediately recommend Guisto. The Pope appointed Guisto the new liaison between the Vatican and the cavalieri and for his first case he was ordered to find Nunzio's killers.

Outraged at the blatant murder of not only a high ranking cavalieri officer but his own mentor, Guisto worked day and night using all he had learned from Nunzio to find and arrest the culprits. His most significant clue was held in Nunzio death grip. Nunzio had ripped a military ribbon from the young man's lapel. Guisto knew it to be the ribbon of a French soldier who had fought the Spanish in the Balkan campaign.

Armed with the *banda capitale* issued on the murderers by Pope Paul it took Guisto less than a week to capture the three young men as they drank and cowered in a brothel in the Piazza del Popolo.

Upon being told that the men had been captured, the Pope immediately ordered their public execution. It was to take place the morning of the coming Sunday directly after the celebration of the twelve-o'clock Mass. He also wanted all three men hung from scaffolding on the same bridge where they killed Nunzio. Guisto quickly ordered the scaffolding built. Pope Paul then ordered Pietro to oversee the execution.

"Our Pontiff does not want to involve the Farnese in this execution," Pietro told his aide. "I have the lovely fortune of having blood on my hands."

On that particular Sunday morning, a huge crowd appeared on either side of the Tiber River to witness the death sentence. Guisto stood beside Pietro as Pietro read his official announcement to the onlookers. When Pietro lowered the announcement, Guisto ordered the hangman to place a noose around each of the young men's necks.

The three young men had been placed on the scaffolding in the same manner in which they stood when they murdered Nunzio. Guisto placed them that way after forcing their confessions. The young man who delivered the final blow was in the center and his two compatriots were to either side. Pietro listened as the two men flanking the middle one prayed in French. His superb knowledge of

French made him aware that they were asking God's forgiveness but the young man in the center glared at the crowd. Pietro felt a shudder as he sensed that the young murderer was starring at him in particular.

With his wavy dirty blond hair falling to the sides of his face and his brown collar up against his neck and his hands tied behind his back he was the epitome of the angry youth Pietro had seen first hand and had feared all his life.

"We have failed to bring love and charity to the world," he muttered from some deep place in his consciousness loud enough for Guisto to hear.

"They are nothing more than craven animals and less than human," Guisto whispered back in a harsh voice.

The floor opened and both men turned to the scaffolding just in time to watch the three young men fall. Their necks snapped as they lingered somewhere between agony and death for a few horrible minutes; and then one after another they quietly died.

Pietro made the sign of the cross as Guisto quickly ordered the bodies cut down and thrown head long into the river.

Several months after the executions, Pietro was struck by a painful bout of gout in both his ankles that disabled him so severely he was bedridden. Unable to attend any social or Vatican related function and certainly unable to return to Ravena, a place he was slowly finding a comfort, despite its lack of luxury, he fell into a malaise so profound nothing helped him alleviate it.

The wave of young bishops who had come to Rome in the previous decade infused the Vatican with such force and intellect it gave him hope for his beloved Church. Even though Pope Paul had been of ill health as of late, his example of charitable works and a force of personality gave Rome an infusion of a much-needed verve.

However, other events in the world worried Pietro. The Thirty Years War pivoting Catholic against Protestant continued to rage in the northern forests of Europe and it was causing famine and poverty across the continent.

To combat his spiritual fatigue Pietro made daily acts of confession and contrition. In his prayers, he begged God to forgive him for his constant forays into the sexual world.

The more he prayed for forgiveness the more he found himself craving one final tryst. His connections to that world were no longer in existence and he spent his nights in bed in the dark with fantasies of his enjoying the flesh of the young whores of his past.

These sins of fantasy, instead of comforting him, only made him acutely aware of his human weakness. What was even more damaging to him was that he firmly believed his health was failing and there was no changing his destiny.

One morning, while in his bath and being attended to by a young seminarian, Pietro saw his image in the mirror and was appalled. He had grown fat and old, seemingly overnight. Never a handsome man, his appearance took on that of an over-fed child who was approaching the decrepet age of seventy. His eyes darted about in his head like a hungry chicken, and his bald skull dotted with fleshly dark markings and freckles repelled him.

His bloated belly was constantly aching and his arms were recently always tight and inflexible. "Our earthly presence is short and coarse," he told the young seminarian who was drying his back. "And we forget the true purpose of why our God created us."

"Which is?" the aide asked.

"As Augustine writes, *to freely love Him,*" Pietro said sincerely.

Not long after that bath, Cardinal Pietro Aldobrandini, nephew to Pope Clement VIII died peacefully on a mild spring evening in his sleep. The aide who found his body stated that the cardinal had dined on a supper of lentil soup. The aide also told an ailing Pope Paul who was sitting up in his bed in his Vatican apartment that, "We said our nightly prayers together and the cardinal asked to be alone to read from his daily Missal, as he had done every evening most recently."

The aide also told the Pontiff, "The cardinal must have passed into heaven before he actually closed his eyes to sleep since his candle was still burning and his prayer book was still in his hand when I went in to look after him sometime before midnight."

With a large basin of hot water on the bed in front of him and a warm towel covering his forehead and feeling a massive fatigue brought on by chronic bronchitis, the Pope struggled to listen to the aide. "The cardinal has sold off all of his art work in the last few months, your Holiness, except one last painting in his sitting room. It is the portrait Caravaggio did of him. What should I do with it?"

The Pope coughed and then fidgeted with his bed cloth. "Caravaggio painted it, you say? Send it to *me.*"

That afternoon Pope Paul V ordered all the church bells in Rome to ring for ten minutes the following noon in honor of one of their beloved who had served the Church and Rome.

CHAPTER FORTY-SIX

Syracuse
1640

The last day of Mario Minniti's life had begun no differently than the decade of mornings that had preceded it. He woke up in his studio where he preferred to sleep since his wife Isabella had died eight years previous.

Her death was premature as Mario used to tell neighbors, since she passed long before her once lovely light colored hair had yet to have a strand of gray. While she was dying, her doctor told Mario that due to the hardship of childbirth and the toil of raising children women died much earlier than men did. "These activities take their toll on the body," he stated.

Through the years that they were married, Mario had noticed how Isabellla kept these pains to herself keeping secret her illness and infections with all the stoicism of ancient Roman nobility, she was always proud to compare herself. She borrowed her father's assessment that the Parma's were from Roman stock right down to their ability to speak Latin and the proof was the strain of self-possessed verve in their blood.

"There is nothing medieval about the Parmas. We are Roman from our profile to our livers," she would tell their children and Mario would often chide her with, "Then you are a pagan as well?"

Isabella would frown and end her discourse with him. Mario would feel superior to her for a few moments afterward but then search her out in the house and do his best to console her. She would have none of it. "Pity is for whores and you know much about *them*," she'd said and when he would ask her to elaborate, she would again leave him for another room in the house.

The last years of her life had been that way between them. As the years progressed, he found that she was so far distant from the woman he had met in Rome that he went about calling her *the stranger* to himself and occasionally to her face. She never replied telling him that he was "precisely the knave and the disappointing man she had known him to be *then* as now." However, while in bed together, she would pull him to her and though they would not make love, she would cry in his arms. "How much I've loved you all these years and you see nothing but folly

309

in our marriage," she would whisper.

The day she died, she asked to see her father but Andrea Parma had been dead for nearly a year. Mario thought her to be delirious with fever. With her two sons and her growing daughter at her side, she slipped away during the early evening and Mario held her hand as he felt her breathing stop. He allowed the children to cry and each in their and own way pay their respects with poems and songs at her funeral.

He didn't cry at her funeral or at her burial. Yet one day, six months after her death, he was traveling back from a meeting with the Syracuse City Council where he was now a member. He saw his villa on the horizon and Isabella's smiling face, the one he had known in Rome, appeared to him. It was then, realizing that she wouldn't be waiting for him when he unsaddled his horse and entered the house as she had been all those years, he felt as if a mountain of regret fell from the sky and onto his shoulders.

He threw himself from his horse burying his hands in his face shedding tears in the middle of the road. It was nearly dark by the time he walked the horse home reaching the villa and finding his daughter. "You have your mother's spirit," he told her.

Two years later Isabella, named after her mother, married a banker's son from Catania and moved to that city. Mario's eldest son followed his dream and was a parish priest in Bari and his second son became a sculptor and moved to Naples.

For several years, Mario lived alone on the large estate with his servants and yet he was never alone since he was constantly inundated with students and assistants.

He soon came to realize that he didn't need a villa. He didn't need a stable of horses or a prestigious position in government. He was fulfilled working in his studio. He took his meals there, he directed his students there, he gave lectures there and he slept on a bed in the corner near the window. He wanted to live this way until the end.

On the last day of his life, he did exactly what he always did every morning. He washed his face, then looked in the mirror, then dried himself with a clean towel and remarked to himself that despite being sixty-five years old, he still had the bearing of a model and then chuckled at his own reference to those many years ago when he actually was one for Caravaggio.

There was nothing left of his once long black, thick hair. He was now nearly bald on the crown of his head but he did allow his hair on the back of his head to grow thick, long and and white. It cascaded over his shoulder presenting the image of a prophet. He perpetuated this image by wearing a long white gown trimmed with black, punctuated by placing on his neck a gold medallion given to him by the Sicilian business community for being an "Upstanding Citizen of High Moral Bearing."

The vision in his right eye was growing cloudy and he was losing the hearing in his left ear. His left hand shook sometimes when he was working but it didn't matter since he painted with his right. In the last few months, he was feeling odd sensations throbbing in that very right arm and blamed his long walks over the hills and his long hours in the studio.

On the last morning of his life he took his routine walk to the family plot where he knelt at Isabella's grave and spoke to her about what had happened the day before and what he was expecting to occur that day. He found himself speaking to her more since her death than while she was alive.

He would then make his appearance in his second studio, the one called *The School*, and on a typical day he would push open its large wooden doors finding a dozen young men busily painting religious canvases following Mario's specific directions from previous meetings. He would check over their work, call them all by their first names then proceed to a small enclave and meet with the young Giacomo, his school's accountant.

Mario's school had a tremendous output of religious paintings and the orders were always backlogged waiting to be filled. Giacomo would remind Mario of incoming orders and Mario would then make notations for his own reasons. On this particular day, orders had already come in for a Saint Peter's Crucifixion from a bishop in Reggio di Cal, an order for a Madonna and Child came from the Order of the Sacred Heart in Salerno and an order for Michael the Archangel came from a merchant who resided in Syracuse. Mario would always sketch the paintings first and in a few days time handpick certain students he felt would do the work justice, to actually create the painting.

When he was done with Giacomo, Mario pushed open another door where another fifteen or twenty students were waiting for him to begin the morning lecture.

The students were mainly from wealthy Sicilian families who either lived in a new dormitory-like structure Mario had built for the very purpose or lived in hotels in the city and would travel to the school every morning.

On this particular morning, Mario allowed the students to ask him general questions that varied in subject matter. Some beckoned him to give them a discourse on his own opinion of art, to his personal experiences in Rome to a general musing on art history.

On this particular day, Mario felt an odd inclination to sit on his wooden chair in front of the class and muse about his own personal experiences. He started by telling the class that he had met Pope Clement VIII and that he had outlived Popes Leo XI, Paul V, Gregory XV and heard that Pope Urban VIII was of ill health. He then discussed his life in Rome with them. "Was it exciting to be there at the turn of the century?" one of his students asked.

Mario leaned forward knowing he had their full attention. He decided on this day to hold nothing back. "We lived in squalor, Caravaggio and I. We bathed when we could. We caught colds but could not afford the remedies. We met a man named Onorio Longhi who paid our bills when we dined in the Tavern of the Turk or the Tavern of the Hawk. When we were fortunate, we would spend other nights in the brothels where we would fuck with some of the whores and hire others as models. It was how I met Lena."

"You knew Lena?" one of the students asked abruptly.

"Knew her? I fucked with her," Mario replied.

Since his death, Caravaggio's reputation fell off considerably. He was actually called *the anti-artist* by living artists and critics alike because of his realism. Carracci was considered the great master. Yet to Mario, there was no other great artist but Caravaggio and in his school, what he believed was gospel. However, every student in that room supposed that Mario was great because he was a follower of Carracci and *not* Caravaggio.

Mario had no idea of this assumption since he never really spoke with the students on a one to one basis and there were no else in Sicily he could talk to art about. He was the authority. They came to *him*. "Another student asked brazenly, "Did you love any of the whores, master?"

Though some of the other students snickered at his question, Mario smiled to himself and answered sincerely. "Yes. Fillide. I was infatuated the very night I met her. We dined at the Tavern of the Hawk I believe or was it the Tavern of the Blackmoore? And spoke of art. She was beautiful and young. I was beautiful and young. It was at time when I was beginning to garner commissions."

"Why did you leave Rome?" another student in the back shouted.

Mario shrugged. "It was a difficult city unless you were wealthy. It was competitive, wild, eccentric, violent and impersonal," he told them. He then hesitated, "Yet I'm profoundly glad I lived there when I did."

There was a silence in the room and Mario, suddenly and without warning, become somber. He shook his head and lifted it eyes back to the students. "Let's continue. Any other questions?"

"Yes! An eager student shouted. "Was Caravaggio a great painter in your opinion?"

Mario felt stung by the question and felt his jaw slacken and his eyes go glossy. He impulsively turned his head and put both hands on his knees. "Yes, he was great! He has his followers doesn't he? Orazio Gentileschi, Carlo Saraceni, Bartolomeo Manfredi and Orazio Borgianni are all smart men who follow in his style though most are dead now. I think I'm the eldest of the lot."

"But, master, *why* do you admire Caravaggio? You don't paint in his style." Another student stated, "You paint like the great Carracci!"

Mario sunk back in his chair for a long moment, rubbed his chin, and then jumped up. He walked over to the wall where he had a small closet that held some of his older canvases. He opened it and two canvases fell past him. Several students came to his aid. He took one canvas from their grasp and held it up for all to see. "Look at this! This can certainly be considered to be painted in Caravaggio's style."

None of the students reacted in agreement with his statement. Mario felt slighted as he scanned their faces. They seemed confused. He looked at the canvases again. "No, not this one," he said and then walked on to another closet.

A student shouted out. "My father says that there's a great Dutch painter… "

Mario stopped him. "He speaks of Rubens. Yes, I have heard of his *Descent from the Cross*. I havn't seen it but I hear that it has been inspired by Caravaggio and our style."

"Your style and Caravaggio's are so different," someone stated.

"Who said that?" Mario demanded to know.

The room was quiet. He took a deep breath feeling his heart pumping faster. "Caravaggio and I created our own style back in Rome." His voice was growing adamant in tone. "It was a notion we both had one night. We were discussing the subject like two young lions forcing a vision of the future. *Our* future. The future of art," he explained. "The conversation was magical and the style was realism. We stared Carracci in the face and said, 'You're a liar! You're a fake!' We stared

313

Michelangelo directly in the eyes and said, 'No! Nature is not like this at all! Human beings suffer. They are dirty and foul. Their bodies are awkward and lumpy. They're missing eyes and they have goiters and wounds!"

When he was done with his lecture, he searched the room and nearly every student was looking back at him with the same quizzical look on their faces as if a plea to know, *what realism of yours are you speaking of? The people in your canvas don't suffer. You paint like Carracci. How can you condemn him?*

After a long, awkward silence, someone was wise enough to change the subject and asked, "Do you have any regrets, master?"

By the later afternoon when the class was adjourned, Mario found himself in the studio with several remaining students and asked them to carry his wooden chair outside so he could enjoy the remainder of the day sitting on the grass looking out toward the setting sun.

Though the air was warm, an earlier rain shower had brought freshness to the air and though it dampened the grass, Mario enjoyed how it felt on his feet with his open sandals.

Onorio Longhi's face came to mind and Mario recalled the letter he had received from Longhi's wife that Onorio had died of syphilis ten years previous. He allowed his memory to open the door to the tavern where he and Caravaggio first met him. Oddly, Mario smiled to himself realizing how little any of that mattered now.

It was then that the dead began their parade through the narrow hall of his memory. He could see their faint images marching through his mind then out across the rolling grassy hills surrounding him. He first saw Cardinal Del Monte and Pietro Aldobrandini. Cavalieri Nunzio Palzone's face followed and he recalled how someone told him that hoodlums had killed Palzone leaving him to die on a chilly night like a refuge on the bridge across from the Vatican. Mario had no resentment towards him and found no irony in the man's death, only apathy.

The dead sculptor's face flew into his mind and Mario shook his head. Had he killed the man? He was never certain what had happened. Was that why he needed to leave Rome?

There were too many ghosts already for Mario to confront but more wanted to show their faces. There was the wonderful Fillide. Fillide, when she was young, devastated his heart. He knew, even back then when they made love the very first night in his small apartment in the Artists Quarter, he would have never craved another woman with the desire he had for her, despite that she had no interest in being possessed by him.

The losses mounted and his mind wandered to Caravaggio. Had he been close to greatness with nothing to show for it other than memories? He, Mario Minniti, was rich and owned his own school and Caravaggio died in a swamp with a burning fever and terrible anguish? How could their lives compare?

He, Mario Minniti, was loved and highly respected in Sicily yet it pained Mario to know that Caravaggio wasn't around to hear the great accolades heaped on his paintings.

Mario wondered if these accolades would be permanent. What would the decades to come decide when it came to who was worthy and who was forgettable? Mario knew that Caravaggio's realism had already fallen by the wayside. People didn't want to see the truth they wanted to see loveliness, splendor and prettiness. Wasn't that always the way? And that would make Caravaggio a footnote to art history and followers of Michelangelo, like Carracci, would be seen as one of those who touched greatness.

Ironically, none of this soothed Mario's doubts and he continued to ask himself, "Am I a Caravaggio or a Carracci?" There was no one around to tell him. He was perplexed and frustrated and though he tried denying that he cared, it was fruitless to fool himself because he did care, very much so.

He found himself on his feet starring at his studio off in the distance. The sun, which he had ignored since he sat down, was sinking, pouring a heavy spray of orange light over everything.

He walked towards the studio through the thick grass seeing his shadow following. He was thinking of a painting, the one he searched for in his studio that would show the world how he had created a canvas that had that realism he and Caravaggio discussed that night. It was there, and he was sure it was, since he had seen it so many times. He had placed it back in storage since there was no demand for it. "A Carracci or a Caravaggio?" he thought. "I gave them what they wanted," he told himself. The public wanted Carracci and Mario had to survive and prosper so he painted what they wanted. Yet he painted that special painting just as Carracci had painted his painfully real, authentic *The Butcher Shop*.

Mario walked on feeling the weight of his own body as if gravity was pulling him lower to the earth. *I have a painting I created that is a Caravaggio. I know it's there in my studio. In a special place. Perhaps I was both a Caravaggio and a Carracci? Is that possible?"*

"Regrets?" he heard himself say as if the question had been lurking in his mind all that time since the student had asked in the studio. *"Regrets?"*

His studio seemed miles away as he walked towards it feeling wings spourting out from the back of his shoulders. Neither the sun nor moon mattered now and all he could see, sense or feel was the grass at his feet and the smell from the lilac trees off in the woods. The hills were a living, breathing force stretching outwardly towards the halo of the setting sun.

They were all waiting for him in his studio. He could see them standing facing him, Michelangelo, DaVinci, Titan and Raphel. He knew their eyes were on him watching as he crossed the pasture. They were waiting for him to show them the canvas, the one that would prove his worth to all the centuries to come. It was there and he was sure of it. He had painted it. He had made it. He would no longer hide it and he would no longer deny it. He had made his fortune and now he could be the artist he always thought he was. That canvas came from the depths of his heart and soul and from his blood and bones. It only existed because he had willed it to be.

"Regrets?" he heard asked. "Regrets?" he asked from somewhere along his journey.

He would answer that question as soon as he reached the studio. He would tell them all what he believed had been accomplished; and perhaps, he thought, they could enlighten him and the few questions he had.

He would meet them all in moments. It had been a long journey. It was time he returned to the studio since it was his home and it was the only world he ever truly knew.

Fine